Dorothy Taylor

COME, FILL THE CUP

Come, fill the Cup, and in the fire of Spring

Your Winter-garment of Repentance fling:

The Bird of Time has but a little way

To flutter—and the Bird is on the Wing.

—*The Rubaiyat of Omar Khayyám*

COME,
FILL THE CUP

BY HARLAN WARE

RANDOM HOUSE · NEW YORK

To James H. Richardson,

"The Last of the Terrible Men,"

with gratitude and admiration.

COME, FILL THE CUP

1 Lew Marsh came up through the obsession of the day's work, tossed a last sheet of copy into the wire basket and rolled down his sleeves. Here it was now: time for a drink.

On the low-roofed building across the way an electric beer sign flashed its colors against a patch of evening sky. Seven green dwarfs with kegs on their shoulders climbed a sketchy mountain trail, disappearing into a cave. Running red letters twinkled:

MADE WITH PURE SPRING WATER. NON-FATTENING.
IT'S GOOD FOR YOU.

But not for me, he thought.

Seven years, now. Seven years, three months. In other days he'd have taken the stairs and the alley short cut to Abe Rouch's bar, to slouch with one foot on the rail, erasing the day. A good, stiff, biting slug of rye. Make it a double, Abe, I'm tired tonight. There would have been good talk and laughter. That's what he missed nowadays: the laughs.

I don't drink, he always said. It was easy. Sometimes on the way home, as a test, he would visit a North Side bar, sniff, recollect his disasters, study the minor idiocies, and walk out. You were an observer when you'd quit. You were benched.

"Mr. Marsh?"

Lew pushed one finger against the edge of his desk and swung around in his chair.

"Yes?"

Bobby Ferrig, a copy boy, always stood too close. He was a hard breather. Eventually, when he became a reporter, he would produce stodgy, unreadable, heavy-handed stuff. You got so you knew your types.

"There's a Greek in the reception room," Bobby was saying. "His name is Achilles, but everybody calls him Kelly. He wants to see the city editor."

"What for?"

"Well, somebody beat him up. His face is a mess."

"Who did it?"

"He didn't tell me."

"Did you ask him?"

"Yes, sir. But he wants to talk to you."

'Yes, sir.' They called him "sir" now. He was getting old.

"Okay, Bobby. On my way out."

4:47. Lew listened glumly to the shuffling sounds of the change-over. Prompt departures were nipping off dayside overtime. Here, drifting in, were the twilight commuters and their freshly shaved faces; the night staff always looked aggressively neat and clean. They were suburbanites who spent their afternoons outdoors, raking leaves, or clearing away their gardens, or shopping meekly with their chubby wives. These were not the reporters of song and story, not any more. They were dutiful Guild members, who made regular dates for golf or canasta, and belonged to the Parent-Teachers' Association. But the departing dayside staff boasted colorful remnants of another era, including five ex-drunks on the rewrite battery who embraced their work, ignored the clock, and lingered in the halls to talk. Newspaper people.

As he shrugged into his coat, Lew saw Ike Bashaw making a final, nervous trip from the rewrite desks to the water cooler. Ike had had a birthday yesterday. Hangover today.

"Did you give your usual rendition of the *Rubaiyat* last night, Bashaw?" Lew asked. "Somehow you look more than one day older."

Ike nodded glumly. John J. Remorse was on his shoulder.

Lew snapped, "Remember the spot you were in when I gave you a job?"

"Yeah. Sure."

"Keep saying it to yourself."

Lew waved him on.

Then, as he locked his own drawer in the desk, he sensed the sidling approach of Travis Ashbourne III, an "apprentice reporter." There were no "cubs" in the Guild's fancy language.

"Mr. Marsh?"

Travis couldn't control an impulse to remind the city desk of his existence. He had originally turned up bearing a note from Mrs. John Ives, wife of the publisher. Irene Ives had known his mother in college;

she never lost track of old friends, nor the deadwood sons of old friends. Travis was top-drawer deadwood.

"Well?" Lew studied him from head to toe. A journalism graduate—the hardest to teach and the slowest to learn. "What is it this time?" he asked, wearily.

And now, having brought himself to his city editor's attention, Travis suddenly felt inadequate—and was.

"I'm assigned to that Button Collectors' banquet at the Hotel Sherman," he said, "but your assistant didn't tell me just what to do. What'll I do?"

"Show 'em your zipper," Lew suggested.

Frightened and red-faced, Travis backed away.

Damn. They were manufactured in cloistered halls nowadays, stamped out at public expense on the GI bill, delivered with diplomas in their hot little hands, and not worth the powder.

Five o'clock. And sure enough, Sam Prisk, the night city editor, came in on the dot. Sam was never late. He was pressed and polished. And reliable. And uninspired. And bald. Lew watched him at the lockers, unwinding, unbuttoning, stowing things away. Sam wore a new felt hat tonight—and a muffler. Last to relinquish his felt in the spring, first to put it on again. It was three o'clock in the morning when he went home, remember. Sam caught colds.

"'Evening, Lewis," he said, with his taut smile. "Nippy tonight."

Lew gave him the chair. Checking the schedule of tomorrow's news always took longer than necessary; Sam had to be dead sure. When the neat mind had folded everything away, Sam asked, laying out eight cigarettes, one for each hour, "Did Mr. Ives phone in about this morning's paper?"

"Not that I know of."

"I hope he liked that armadillo story. He sometimes comments favorably on animal stories."

Lew thought: starved for love—that's Sam trouble. He sniffed in any corner for a crumb of reassurance.

Lew slapped on his battered panama and walked away from Sam's bright good night. I let 'em get me today, he thought. The low gate swung violently behind him. Let's quiet down. Let's get out of here.

Sixteen elevators, all on other floors. He had pressed the button for the third time when he saw the Greek sitting patiently in the wide reception room. A Greek in a polo coat. There was a raw bruise on his right cheek, near his eyes, and his lips were cut and swollen.

"Do something for you, Mr. Achilles?"

The man moved too quickly.

5

"You the head city editor, mister?"

"That's right."

"I don't want a juke box!" Achilles launched into his story midway somewhere. "I don't need a new juke box, see, mister? I got a old juke box, works fine. These guys they come in, four-five times, and say what I need is a new one. No, no, I says to them, thanks just the same, boys. Why do customers want a juke box, anyway? Loud music until you can't even think. So I tell them no, they can take out the one I got and I don't *want* a new one. Skip it, I say, and pretty soon—polite—I mention they should leave. And then I am in a hospital and I got a new juke box, louder than the old one."

"Who was it?"

"It was Lenni Garr. It was Lenni Garr in person, I think. I wouldn't be surprised."

"You know him?"

"No, but I'm sure, practically. Lenni Garr."

Lenni Garr. A second-generation hoodlum who'd had a year in college and owned a coin-machine business as a front for other rackets; his father, who had served fifteen years in Leavenworth, had been a henchman of Al Capone's. They did things better nowadays—the same old things, but they did them better. Lenni delegated the rough stuff to his muscle boys. The Greek was mistaken. It couldn't have been Lenni Garr.

"It says Garr Music Corporation on the box," he was saying. "Every month it's serviced. It don't need it, but I pay anyhow. That's to some union. At the hospital this morning, I get flowers. I got no friends would send me flowers, mister. Down inside is a card from the Electrical Workers' Federation, Juke Box Division, and how do they know I'm in a hospital? It's a joke, my wife thinks. Lenni Garr beats me up and then tells the union to send me flowers, a high-class joke . . ."

"All right, all right," Lew said. "You can tell it to a reporter."

From the doorway, he surveyed the local room. The day staff was clearing out. All the lights were on, most of the typewriters busy. But the ex-drunks were still cluttered around the water cooler with Ike Bashaw. Hated to go home, maybe. Stretching out the day. Lew pointed a finger at Don Bell's clever, saturnine face. Don was thirty-nine, graying and sober, and when facts permitted, wrote acidly, tongue-in-cheek.

"Want this one?"

"Sure," Don said as he came up. "I'm off at five, though."

Overtime, Lew thought.

Don caught the look in his eyes. "Oh, hell, I'll take it on my own." But Lew hesitated. The Guild had spoken to him about this, twice

6

now. Not that they minded the men doing an occasional favor. Not at all, Lew. Not really. But it wasn't good practice. See?

"Never mind," he said. "Let the nightside do it. Take this man to Sam, will you?"

Tomorrow's paper would now carry it written straightaway by one of the nightside commuters, with his mind on a rose garden. The writing would lack Don Bell's deft awareness. But the city desk would have saved a few dollars' overtime. And the Guild wouldn't be annoyed. All would be quiet, all would be snug and proper. The brave new regulated world.

And to hell with it, he thought.

The sixteen elevators were again on other floors. He held a savage thumb on the button. He was an executive, dammit, a guardian of severance pay, an overtime watchdog. But for three years, now—almost from the day they'd made him city editor—he'd been reminding everybody that he was, after all, a reporter, only temporarily shackled to a swivel chair with golden chains. Hadn't he done enough penance for his sins? Sam Prisk yearned for the day desk. Sam could have it.

Heavy-footed Bobby Ferrig raced down the hall.

"Say!" He was bug-eyed with earnestness. "Mr. Cuscaden wants to see you before you go. Mr. Ives is on the phone!"

"Oh, fine," Lew said, rattling the golden chains.

Julian Cuscaden, the managing editor, held the phone tight against his good ear, agreeing to something he didn't approve of. He was a lean man with chronic acidosis, a mink-coated wife, a Cadillac, and a home in Highland Park; he was fifty-six years old, wise, tired and without illusions.

"Yes, Mr. Ives," Julian was saying with all the bodily vigor he could muster. "Yes, indeed, Mr. Ives."

Lew waited at the high window. The green dwarfs jerked upward with their beer kegs, disappearing into the cave. The cheerful red letters ran steadily around and around. Below him, on Randolph Street, a rolling river of felt hats moved stationward in the fading sunlight. September, everybody! All together now: felt hats!

"Yes, Mr. Ives," Julian said.

Yes, yes, yes, Mr. Ives.

Lew studied the escaping crowds. They were jerking homeward like the seven green dwarfs. They, too, had caves into which they disappeared at night only to emerge, running again, in the morning. He himself often talked to Charley Donahue, the tall Negro, his friend and servant, about living in a cave or going to Tahiti. Maybe the commuters were running toward Tahiti. That was it. Tahiti had other names—Barrington, Wil-

7

mette, Winnetka, Glencoe, Highland Park, Lake Forest; and television, bridge, four pre-dinner cocktails, a sleeping pill, or the little woman. They were marching away, under their bobbing hats, bound for their caves. They would be marching tomorrow night, too, and the next night, and Saturday noon, and every day but Sunday. Everybody was going somewhere. Usually away.

"Well, certainly, if necessary, Mr. Ives." Julian's voice was soothing now. "He's right here. I know Lew will be delighted!"

And what would he be delighted to do for Mr. Ives this evening? The Old Man had once said, "Let Mr. Marsh do it—he'll do it right!" thus making it a matter of policy to let Mr. Marsh handle piddling chores. Tonight, perhaps, Mr. Ives would ask his city editor to comb Chicago for an old-fashioned croup kettle because his old-fashioned chauffeur's old-fashioned child had virus-X; or possibly the gentle Mrs. Ives had read about the little boy who lost his pet armadillo and would Mr. Marsh find another like it, or the original armadillo, if possible at all? The special orders that came to Mr. Lewis Marsh through Mr. Julian Cuscaden were sometimes enough to drive a man to—well, not quite.

"Going shopping, am I?" Lew asked, spinning his hat.

Julian hung up, dropped an effervescent bromide into a glass, splashed water from the carafe and watched the tablet bubble and dissolve.

"Lew," he complained, "your passion for resuscitating drunks has finally caught up with us."

Finally, he had said. More compliment than rebuke. Through the years, Julian had sourly predicted disaster when, one by one, Lew recruited the men who now composed the dayside rewrite battery, the five legendary alcoholics. Give me a reformed lush any time, Lew had often told him. Your solid citizen watched his time chart and wrote the facts for you, but the reformed dipsomaniac could let himself go and give you emotion; they were sensitive, alert and eager, and they took to work as if it were whisky. Time and pressure had sifted out five talented men, abstemious, of sterling character. Dedicated men. He wasn't too sure of Ike, but the others had made it, and were the best in town.

"And now what?" he asked, bristling, ready once more to come to their defense.

Julian downed the fizzing water and mopped his lips with a clean, folded handkerchief.

"Mr. Ives wants to know if I can spare you for a while."

"What for?" Then with a brief, forlorn hope, Lew said, "If it's Europe, I'm packed."

That's what he'd been asking for: London. Johnny Richards, his best friend, managed a news bureau in London. Johnny had begged him to

8

come over. You were cut down to a queer kind of loneliness when you were an executive and had quit drinking, Johnny had written. And that was a fact. Sobriety narrowed the field. Lew had been trying, through channels, to wangle a spot in John Ives's London office. The paper countered with raises. He couldn't be spared.

"I'm afraid it's a croup kettle," Julian said, smiling bleakly. "Mr. Ives wants you to sober up Harvey Copeland's little boy. He thinks you can cure Boyd."

"What?"

"Now, don't take off!" Julian warned. "The Old Man's got one of those fixations. I've talked to him twice today. He thinks a lot of Harvey. They're very close."

Julian cleared his throat. It wasn't unusual to be told to rustle up a croup kettle for a friend of Ives; but this one went further: young Boyd Copeland had played football at Princeton, marched with the infantry, made a single successful appearance with the Chicago Symphony Orchestra—and married Paula Arnold, the best girl reporter who ever walked into the local room. In recent years he had disappeared from sight. He was said to be a covert drunk—the worst kind.

"What is this, Julian—whimsy?"

"Mr. Ives is dead serious." Julian's glance slid away. "He told me Boyd's in bad shape."

"But this is nonsense, palsy. I can't cure anybody. I don't know how it's done."

"He says you're a practical psychologist and he needs you. Right now. Tonight."

Lew stared in disbelief.

"You mean—leave the desk?"

"Sam Prisk stumbled through during your vacation. We'll move Sam up."

"God damn it," Lew shouted, "what in hell makes him think I can sober anybody up? Julian, I'll give it to you straight, I'll tell you the secret of the Old Man's success: his limitations. His goddam obtuseness. That's how he appeals to the mass mind. I'm always amazed by the fools who somehow get rich. Nothing succeeds like stupidity!"

He felt a dry flash in his throat and a torturing flood of saliva. Tasted like liquor, damned if it didn't. His own glands could taunt him by manufacturing a synthetic shot of rye. No spreading warmth, though. No lift. The hot, dry flash and the flood of saliva and you knew you were still a drunk. All these years and still a drunk. He heard himself shouting, "He's soaring off into one of his cockeyed conclusions . . ."

9

"That'll do," Julian said, sharply. "I took a chance on you once. Have you forgotten?"

He hadn't forgotten. But whom did he owe? Julian had fired him, back there, for what had been the last time. "You're only days from the gutter," he'd said, a harassed city editor reaching the end of his patience. "You're broke, and overdrawn—you've lost your wife and your friends. You can't drink. But you won't find it out this side of the gutter. You'll be panhandling in front of this building before the week is out." It had been a shrewd prediction. Lew had gone down until he heard angel feathers in the county hospital, and he'd inched his way back through a fresh air period with lunch pail and shovel. His health regained, he had clawed into an advertising agency where he had written copy for luxury hotels and popping breakfast foods, going slowly mad because no newspaper anywhere would take a chance on him. And then the break had come, in a curious fashion. One noon he had found Don Bell selling suits in the basement of Marshall Field's; no paper would take a chance on Don Bell, either, and Don was a brilliant reporter who had been sober for years. That night, in his office at the advertising agency, Lew had written a stinging letter to John Ives, then, as usual, wintering in Santa Barbara. Not about himself, about Don. A few days later he had received a surprising telegram: QUITE A LETTER SPEAK FOR YOURSELF SEE JULIAN CUSCADEN. JOHN COWPER IVES. Fearing a gag, Lew had taken the wire to Julian, who, in the meanwhile, had been upped to managing editor. Reluctantly, Julian had made a long-distance phone call which had ended in the customary defeat: Yes, Mr. Ives. If you insist, Mr. Ives. And that was that. He worked his way to choice assignments, and to his by-line; and then he had gone beyond, to the city desk and the golden chains. But he didn't owe Julian. He owed John Ives. You pay and pay.

"No," he said, "I haven't forgotten."

By then, of course, he felt like a heel.

Glancing through the glass partition, he saw Don Bell and Ike Bashaw still hanging around. Classic drunks, sure, but they'd been sober when he hired them. That was the point. He knew a good risk when he saw one: if a man was living soberly with the same problems that once had driven him to drink then you might reasonably assume he'd given up the solace of the jug. A few had failed him. He was no psychologist. He had built a staff with the best men he could find. Had Julian made that clear, or hadn't he?

"Now wait a minute, Lew," Julian said, irritably, "I even gave him an argument. Some day you tangle with the Old Man and find out what it's like. I did all I could."

All he could. He had said, "Let-me-think-it-over-yes-Mr. Ives." Now he murmured craftily, "He paid you a high compliment on the phone just now."

"Uh-huh."

"He said this was a situation nobody else in the world could handle."

"I'll bet."

"No, that's a fact. He spoke highly of your work—of you, personally."

"Good, good."

"Look here," Julian said, as if the thought had just occurred to him, a nimble passing of the buck, "why don't you discuss a foreign assignment with him yourself? Go ahead—it's okay with me." He swung around in his chair. "Let's see," he mused, "when does your contract come up for renewal?"

"January third," Lew said promptly.

"You'll be in a good spot to talk to him."

"Oh, sure."

"Well, anyhow, you've got the green light—do what you can for yourself. You're leaving at nine."

"Leaving for where?"

"Minocqua. They're still at the Lodge. Boyd's parents are up there—and Boyd. That is, if he hasn't run off again. They had him locked in a guest room this morning."

Lew waited. There was more, apparently. Julian approached it obliquely. "Mr. Ives sent the plane down."

"For whom?"

"For you and Paula Copeland." Julian busied himself drying the water glass. "She's been sweating it out in their Lake Shore Drive apartment, right here in town. Boyd's been missing for weeks, I gather. He turned up at the Lodge yesterday in pretty bad shape. They're very concerned."

"They shouldn't worry about a little thing like that," Lew said, harshly. "All drunks eventually turn up in bad shape. Want to see where I broke my elbow?"

Julian was stretching now, reaching as high as he could.

"It'll be nice to see Paula again, anyhow, won't it?" he suggested, falsely, revealing how much he knew. "I often think of the day she first walked in here, right out of high school. I've never seen a prettier young girl. Were you here then?"

"Panting out in the hall," Lew said, so they wouldn't have to kid each other.

"That was way back when I was city editor," Julian said, conversationally. "She wore something crisp and white with a yellow belt, and flowers. It was a hot day, but she looked—oh, I dunno—kind of—well,

11

touching. There's a period when they're so darned fresh and beautiful—eighteen, nineteen, along in there. And so earnest, Lew. She was scared and she stuttered a little." His voice took on a paternal tone. "She said all the right things but her knees knocked together. I knew from the way her white skirt quivered. Awful nice girl. Shy but brave. I guess that's why I hired her."

"Uh-huh," Lew said.

"Hell of a reporter," Julian looked up. "I hated to lose her."

"Oh, sure. We all did."

Everybody had lost Paula. By the time she had proved herself the whole staff was in love with her. They called her Butch because they admired her courage and because it was an incongruous name for such a pretty girl. She could have stayed on the paper forever. But out in Santa Barbara, California, one winter, Mrs. John Ives had been made chairman of the table-decoration section of a flower and garden show. The show needed publicity. John Ives sent for Paula Arnold—a long-distance croup kettle—and she had met young Copeland and had never come back. You saw her now across theatre lobbies on opening nights, or at a window table at the Tavern Club or—a glimpse, maybe—riding down Michigan Avenue in an open convertible. If she noticed you she always waved with shy friendliness. Also, she was always seen with people you didn't know. Well-dressed people. Mink. Dinner jackets.

"Anything else?" Lew asked, coldly.

"Unh? No, I guess not." Julian pulled up a sheet of copy. "Municipal Airport. Nine o'clock." He added, "Maybe you can have a little fun at the Lodge, Lew. The lake's full of muskies."

Naturally, John Ives's lake was full of muskies. Who should know better? Lew himself had put the pressure on the Wisconsin game commission through a pal on a Madison paper. It had been stocked with muskies and walleyed pike and bass. Fish would be fin-to-fin up there. They'd leap into your boat.

The managing editor turned to his work with pretended absorption and Lew thought grimly: Julian hadn't spoken to John Ives on his behalf at all. London? The publisher had never heard it mentioned. They would leave him on the city desk until they pensioned him off. They'd raise him and praise him and age him there, and every few days they'd send him on a silly errand. He had almost reached the door when Julian said, "How's Bashaw doing?"

Lew looked back with honest admiration.

"All right. Why?"

"Just wondered," Julian said.

Smart, wasn't he? Couldn't fool Julian. He'd stroll through the local room chewing a cold cigar, hands behind his back, eyes shuttered. But he didn't miss a thing. Sees all, knows all—that was Cuscaden.

Ike Bashaw was ready, at last, to go home. Lew stopped at the lockers.

"Ike, they're worried downstairs about the water bill. What happened to you last night?"

"Why? He say anything?"

Lew ducked the question.

"Think the *Tribune* would take you back?"

"No."

"The *News?*"

"No."

"Any of 'em? *Herald? Sun-Times?*"

"No."

"Keep saying it, Ike. Let me down and I'll make it a personal matter, understand? I'm going away for a few days and if I find you've let me down—firing you won't be the end of it. You'll never get another newspaper job."

"I believe it."

"Yesterday was your birthday, wasn't it?"

"But I didn't drink anything today," Ike said, quickly. "It hit me pretty hard, being off it so long."

"You won't know what hit you if it happens again."

Lew paused at the cooler, flipped the paper cup over his shoulder, watched it land in the basket, and went on out. Don Bell was in the elevator lobby. They didn't speak going down.

"Tired tonight," Don said and dropped behind him in the busy street.

Lew knew about that. This was the hour you had to get through by yourself. The battle of the bottle—Don had once called it—when, with conscious effort, you shook off the irritations of the day and tried to make yourself intact for the long evening.

In the parking lot, Sid Cohen, one of the legendary five, was matching coins with the attendant for the day's parking fee.

"I hear you've got a new car," Sid said. "So have I."

They compared cars.

"Not like the old days," Sid mused, proudly. "Imagine me with a new car and a kid in private school!"

You kept convincing yourself that everything was better now. And it was, too. A hell of a lot. It sure as hell was. Lew sat at the wheel of his maroon convertible, stretching the tension out of his neck and arms. He had driven a second-hand jalopy in the days of the week-end riots. Once, a little more than mellow, he had taken Paula Arnold for a rattling ride in it, out through Lincoln Park, along the North Shore to her father's home in Ravinia. He'd always had the bad luck to be more plastered than usual when he ran into Paula outside the office. That day he had literally bumped into her at a students' art exhibit. And that evening she had sobered him up with hot coffee in her kitchen and introduced him to an older friend who lived on a big estate next door—a girl named Alice. Alice Pryor. Lew had married Alice. He never quite knew why. He had married Alice Pryor and her mother, Mrs. Elsie Pryor, and her Uncle Edward. He had married the whole family. It hadn't worked out.

Now, he drove east on Wacker and north on Michigan, and made himself the evening speech: *the only drink you don't take is the first one. It's not for you, boy. It's not for you. Want it all to blow up?*

Not me, he said, not me.

He had a roomy apartment on Scott Street, with paneled, book-lined walls and a practical fireplace, and furniture that spelled good taste, and money in the bank. Thinking about it brought a sense of well-being on a bad evening. And thinking about the mornings, too—that helped. These days, he woke up with a clear head; no grotesque abstract horrors in his dreams, no half-remembered violence, no hangover breakfasts.

Sober, now, from day to day, from year to year.

He unlocked the door to 721, his own particular cave. And there was the typewriter stand in the living room, with paper neatly stacked on the refectory table. A hint from Charley Donahue—days had passed with nothing done on the book. A fire crackled on the hearth, the curtains were drawn, the world shut out. All this because he'd once looked up from his typing to make Charley a promise: they'd spend a year on a freighter in the South Seas if the novel made any money. They'd see some of the places Charley had read about in the prison library at Joliet.

"'Evening, Mr. Lew."

The tall Negro had come from the kitchen wearing the handsome chef's bonnet Johnny Richards had sent him, as a gag, from London. He was a light-skinned colored man, with a pencil scar from a knife-cut on his right cheek, remnant of a bloody argument with a lifer in the exercise yard at Joliet. Tonight he also wore his serving jacket, Lew's old linen evening coat. Proud of himself. Felt good.

"I got the house slicked up," Charley said, beguilingly, as Lew stopped to sort the day's mail. "I've been thinking maybe it's about time to have a few folks in?"

Two hints. Let there be gaiety—or work.

"I'm going out of town," Lew said, shuffling the letters.

"Oh." Charley looked around unhappily. "And not work on the book, either, hm?"

14

"No, Charley."

"Oh. I thought maybe you'd better *do* something because lately you been kind of edgy."

"That so?"

"It's the truth."

And so it was. Cracking down too hard at the office. Unreasonable here at home. At such times it was wise to fill his rooms with chattering people and put Charley back of a makeshift bar in the sunporch. Charley's face always glowed with pride when he served Lew's guests. It helped, sometimes, just to *pour* it, he said. Charley, too, had had his troubles with the jug. Indeed, it had clouded his past and sent him to prison. His name wasn't Charley Donahue at all.

"Out of town, where?" he asked, following down the hall.

"The Lodge."

Charley leaned morosely in the doorway, studying the fingernails of both hands, managing to contain his curiosity for all of thirty seconds.

"Business, or what?"

Lew said, brusquely, "Later. What's for dinner?"

"You wait." Charley's spirits lifted. "It's something special I got outa *Gourmet.*"

He had once had a cellmate, a French chef, one M. Camille Didot, a bigamist, and in the course of that enforced association he had acquired an astonishing knowledge of sauces and salads, of odd regional dishes with French names which he could almost pronounce. Lew, as a young reporter, had lived on hot roast-beef sandwiches, preferring cheap restaurants to all others and stools to chairs; but he had gone along with Charley's culinary enthusiasms in the beginning, sensing that an absorbing new interest was a prerequisite in the battle of the bottle. Sometimes, after a rough day, he helped around the kitchen to get safely through the pre-dinner hour when time hung heavy and his nerves were a raw tangle under his skin. Now, coming from the shower, he grabbed a towel, and called, "I'll make the salad, Charley!"

Then, as he gave his hair a vigorous brushing, he studied himself critically in the bathroom mirror. Not a gray hair in his head. No sag under the eyes. No double chin. Pretty fair shape, in spite of everything. His own drinking had begun mighty early—in high school, as a matter of fact. His parents had died in a hotel fire when he was ten, and he had grown up in Winnetka with his grandparents, a scholarly old couple who vaguely resented his intrusion and imposed restraints unmixed with affection. Grandfather Marsh had been a professor of sociology at Northwestern, a correct, busy little man, in love with the masses but indifferent to his grandson, and Grandmother Marsh read weighty tomes all day and opened cans for dinner. Lew had had a bewildering and restless boyhood, dominated by a single, fierce desire. Looking back, it always seemed that a dull ache in his heart had been eased for the first time by a furtive swig of muscatel back of the high-school cafeteria, during the junior prom. Quite a discovery: brightened the stars in the sky and made him a dashing fellow—witty, carefree, a card. Heigh-ho! Seven years now without the jug. He was forty-two. He'd given his body quite a beating so he must be made of durable stuff, tough, peasant material. Resilient.

"Here we go again!"

Charley appeared with a zombie glass of tomato juice on a serving tray. Olives on toothpicks. Cocktail napkins which some girl had sent for Christmas, reading "Lew Marsh" in green.

"If this should taste a little flat," Charlie grinned, "just think about our room on Clark Street."

It was an almost nightly joke, a ritual. Not that they'd forget, though the room on Clark Street was years behind them. Back there, in Lew's drinking days, a last glimmer of pride had kept him from panhandling in front of the Ives Building as Julian had predicted. But he'd sheepishly borrowed a quarter from a tall Negro on Clark Street, a man he'd seen somewhere, a vaguely familiar face. "Two bits, boss?" the man had said. "Why, yes, sir. I'm kinda high, myself."

Charley Donahue had taken him in and nursed him, sent him to the county hospital—and only Charley had come to see him there. Charley had been full of racial prejudice—he hadn't liked white people—but he'd been friendless, also, and there had been a salvaging of pride in what he had done for Lew.

He watched hopefully as Lew tipped up the glass.

"There's lemon juice and Worcestershire and oregano in it," he said. "Gives it kind of a *tang*, don't it?"

"Betcha."

Charley sensed the tension. At such times he struck an evangelistic note.

"What we got here is sure a hell of a lot better than those fresh-air jobs, huh? Isn't that the truth?"

In that period a one-time star reporter had wangled two jobs through an embarrassed friend in the highway department. Each morning, wearing heavy shoes, carrying tin lunch boxes, they had left Charley's fleatrap for a wide ditch in Des Plaines. There was sobriety in a shovel and an aching back; a foxhole friendship in desperation. But, months later, when Lew moved indoors to offices, they had drifted apart. He had forgotten about Charley. Never, not once—to his shame—had he thought of him after he landed back on the paper. But, strangely, one of John

Ives's rare visits to the office had been the cause of Charley's reappearance. Queer, the way one thing leads to another, the past forever threading through your life. . . .

It had been one of the few occasions he had ever seen Ives face to face. He had been called into Julian's office a few minutes after the Old Man arrived in the building.

"I understand you're an intractable character since you went on the wagon," John Ives had said, giving him an x-ray examination.

"I quit drinking," Lew told the publisher, coolly. "Have I insulted somebody?"

He'd waited, expecting to be fired.

"Mr. Cuscaden wants better writing. Some of the old hands have got to go."

"I'll leave quietly."

"Not so fast. I've been over a list of candidates," Ives said. "You're the only one they've called a 'mean sonofabitch.' That is what I need just now. You're city editor."

The next day's issue had carried a chaste announcement of the promotion in the second section. Charley had used the paper as a blanket in Jackson Park. He had read everything in it.

"You never paid back my two bits, Mr. Lew," he had said, when Lew found him waiting in the reception room that morning. "I sure could use it."

Charley couldn't find a job; and if he stole anything and was sent back to Joliet he was good as dead. The lifer who had given him his scar had been trying for his throat. He wouldn't miss next time.

"I never even had a beer, lately," he had lamented, "but nobody believes me."

That did it. Lew decided to lease an apartment. Quiet evenings with a book, and hot black coffee. Clothes on hangers, socks in drawers, and proper meals. Decided to live like other people.

"Want to be a gentleman's gentleman?" he had grinned.

"I'd take on any job that's done under a roof, no matter what."

There had been a friendly face at home, then, during six months when glances of fear and resentment assaulted him from all sides. He had fired ruthlessly, hired with care, and built a staff. Fired Johnny Richards, whom he admired, and hired Joel McHenry, whom he didn't like; Johnny was often drunk, and Joel was always sober. In those months he had learned what it meant to be an executive with a temperamental staff. Office friendships ended forever; he walked out alone each night. Paula Arnold was Mrs. Boyd Copeland by that time. The men from his younger days had gone to better jobs. The people he knew outside the newspaper business gave cocktail parties, served dinner at nine, or forgot to serve it; too much for the leaping nerves. He was alone.

So, in the Scott Street apartment, at the dinner hour, he and Charley would lift virtuous glasses to the lucky souls who could take a drink and go to the table, wanting food instead of just one more.

A shout came from the kitchen, "You gonna make the salad now, or not?"

Lew took the wooden bowl from the dark cubby-hole Charley had converted into a butler's pantry.

"Not thousand island, *again!*" the tall Negro protested, looking over his horn-rimmed glasses from a *Gourmet* recipe. "That's for them with no palates!"

Charley made fun of *Gourmet,* but the magazine impressed him. Once, he had said, "*Gourmet* is talking about an 'intriguingly delicate little wine' this month. I sure wish they'd advertise a boisterous case of little Old Grand Dad."

By the time he was released from Joliet, he had developed a great respect for the Wine & Food Society. But then, one night, he had waited table at a gourmet's dinner where he discovered the portly gentlemen with exquisite palates got just as drunk as anybody else. He liked to tell about the solemn president who had made poetic speeches about each wine as it was served and all the while he was getting as pie-eyed as any bum on a West Madison corner. "Why," Charley had said, "when the dinner was only half over that high-class old gourmee was a basket case!"

Working at the sink, Lew glanced down at the grocery list on the roller note pad. Very fancy items: *tarragon vinegar, wild rice, saffron, French roast coffee, smoked salmon.* Then he read, at the bottom, underlined: *one box .45 bullets.*

"Bullets?" he mused. "Tarragon vinegar, Charley, and .45 bullets?"

"Yes, sir. I'm down to one bullet." Charley wet his thumb and turned a page. "I was hoping we'd go out to a pistol range and practice. It's been a hell of a long time since we practiced."

"Okay," Lew said. "Some Sunday, hm?"

Charley shrugged. "That's what you always say—some Sunday. Only we never *do* it. Twice—that's all we ever practiced."

And long ago, at that. One morning, while shopping, Charley had encountered an ex-con from prison. The man had been suspiciously friendly and inquisitive; afterward Charley had had some sleepless nights. "A gun of my own," he'd suggested, "would be better'n a sleeping pill." Lew had wangled a permit through Condaffer and Swain of the Detective Bureau. Charley kept the gun in his top bureau drawer and slept like a baby. And the permit lifted his self-esteem. "It shows I

18

associate with folks that have real political *power!*" he had said, and wanted to frame it, like a college diploma.

He was very formal this evening as he served the dinner. Dining-car service. Yes, sir. No, sir. Form.

"Good food is soothing," he said, in response to a compliment. "You can kinda slip away into it, like you do into a drink. I'm sure glad we got interested in food."

For dessert he produced a Baked Alaska. He had made a tremendous hit with Baked Alaska the last time Johnny Richards was in town.

"Better than ever," Lew told him.

Charley had waited for the verdict, standing straight, a creased napkin over his upraised left arm. He wouldn't sit down with Lew—something stemming back to his boyhood in Caddo Parish, Louisiana. He had been offended the first evening in the apartment when Lew had said, "For God's sake, *sit down!* You used to eat with me on Clark Street." Charley had established the relationship then and there. "I *work* here. I'm an *employee!*" On occasions when Lew called for the good silver—which Alice, in all fairness, had divided with him, the day before the divorce—Charley set his own table handsomely in the kitchen—and ate alone. He had certain principles.

Now, in the after-dinner calm, he felt free to ask, "You going on a secret mission, Mr. Lew—or what?"

"No. Croup kettle."

"Oh, one of those. You feel like tellin' me what it is?"

"It's nonsense," Lew said, but the anger had diminished; he told him about it.

"Well, I dunno, it's such nonsense." Charley thoughtfully poured more coffee. "You've got a fine, upstanding effect on drunks, Mr. Lew, for a fact."

But now he was moody. As they were doing the dishes, he said, "You know, I got a friend—Joby his name is, Elwood Joby. He's a butler. He was butler for a bachelor fella. They got along fine. Joby could use the car, like I do, and he was the boss's same size, and got the secondhand suits, including the pants. He dressed real good. And then the boss got married to a mighty fine woman, that pretended she liked Joby—said he was a jewel and stuff like that."

"What about it?"

"Wasn't three months until Joby was out on his ass."

"What's this got to do with anything?" Lew asked, gravely.

"Nothing. It just came into my head."

He quickly changed the subject. But, later, in the car, he asked, "This Mrs. Copeland you're flying up with—she used to be on the paper?"

"That's right."

"Introduced you to your wife?"

"That's the one."

"Miss Paula Arnold," Charley mused. "You got pictures of her in the scrapbook." He drove in silence. "Ye-ah," he said. "It's always nice to meet a old friend. Miss Alice was a few years older, I think you said?"

"When did I tell you that?" Lew asked, surprised.

"Oh," Charley answered, "when we had those fresh-air jobs. The jug had kinda got you mixed up back there—wasn't that the way it was?"

The jug. Yes, indeed. And flattery. Alice had known his by-line; she had been a fan. She had *adored* the little one-stanza verses he put at the top of his features. And the wonderful way he handled dog stories and lost children. And his savage slashing style when he was angry. His writing *thrilled* her!

He had never encountered a fan before and it had affected his judgment. Courting Paula, he had veered away to Alice, who, after all, was more his own age—a mature, poised, charming, wealthy young woman. Alice had lured him into her baronial halls in Ravinia to meet her parents, who examined him warily but indulged her. And that year, during his vacation, a strange thing happened. God only knew how it had been managed, but Paula had seemed to grow daily younger. And cuter. Pigtails, almost. He didn't want to rob the cradle, did he? Alice would say: such a sweet, ingenuous child, isn't she, Lew? So his attitude toward Paula had gradually become avuncular. And, by fall, paternal. Looking back into the fog he dimly recalled that Paula had taken to calling him "Grandpa" with a mocking, humorous lift of the brow. He had been a snob in those days, and Alice was Junior League. Flattery and discreet continual recourse to the jug. Yes, indeed. That's what it could do for you, among other things: lead you into a quaint fieldstone church with the wrong woman. The jug could marry you off, much to your surprise.

Lew grinned across at Charley, and said, to cheer him up, "Want to take the car and stop at your folks' after you leave me at the airport?"

Charley thought it over. His brother and two little bronze nieces lived on the South Side. Whenever he could, he would overload the car with screaming children and cruise for miles along the crowded streets, showing off. But tonight the suggestion failed to brighten him.

"I dunno," he said, glumly, "I got a kinda uneasy feeling for some reason. Suppose you *do* this croup kettle? Well, Mr. Ives might feel so good he'd send you to Europe! Where'll you keep the car if you should ever go to Europe?"

"I'll ship it," Lew said, watching him. Such a nice transparent guy,

Charley. Such an honest, pure-hearted guy. "I'll ship you, too," he added.

Charley was not wholly comforted.

"No matter what?" he asked, and then, embarrassed, said abruptly, "Some of your little lady friends been phoning lately. It's a long time since you been out with the ladies, Mr. Lew. What's the matter with you?"

"Getting old," Lew said, holding the panama with both hands. There was a hard, cold wind from the lake and the top was down. "Getting old and tired, Charley."

"How you carry on!" scoffed Charley. "You're at the dangerous age." Looking straight ahead he made his point. "You watch your step, this trip."

They talked about January third, and the end of Lew's contract, and other jobs and other places; by the time they reached the airport Charley was feeling better. He swerved the car dashingly into the parking lot, made a tire-squealing sweep to the curb and rocked to a stop. Then he went into an exaggerated, Louisiana farewell. Bowed low. Handed over the luggage. Saluted, calling Lew "Cap'n."

Out in public he played Uncle Tom—with a twinkle in his eye. They understood each other.

2 In a few hours these people in the waiting room would step down in Los Angeles, New York, Minneapolis, or New Orleans. Or London. Or Paris. Chicago would be a memory of cold wind and bleak sky. They were getting away. Lew carried his old suitcase through throngs of travelers, and stopped for a long inspection of the arrival-and-departure board.

"Hello, Grandpa Marsh," a shy voice said.

With one shoulder hunched and his guard up, he turned to face the gentle raillery. *Um!* he said. Well, well, Paula! She hadn't gained a pound, nor added a wrinkle: the same diminutive figure, the same golden glow.

"You've been in a deep freeze," he decided. "That's unfair to other women. Everybody else gets older."

"Pretty speech," Paula said, abstractedly. "But I can guess how you felt when you got the order. This is a croup kettle, isn't it?"

"Not now, it isn't. How are you, Butch?"

"L-Lewis, I'm in a mess," she said.

She had stuttered as a child, but had overcome it. Except when she was frightened.

"I heard from Alice last week," she told him, making conversation. "She's in S-Switzerland with her mother. Did you know?"

"Nope," he said. Didn't know. And didn't care.

"She saw Johnny in London. He was sober."

"Many people are, lately."

"I know one who isn't." She saw the pilot waiting near Gate 7 and greeted him warmly.

"Caught any fish yet?" she asked as they went up the steps to the plane.

"We haven't wet a line, Mrs. Copeland," the young man said. This had looked like a great job, in the beginning, but he and his co-pilot had become sky-borne delivery boys. "We're never closer to the water than 6000 feet up."

The plane, a converted DC-6, had a fresh paint job, with the paper's name on the nose, so the total cost could come off Ives's income tax. The six enormous red seats in the cabin reminded Lew of a teletyped order from Ives's winter place at Santa Barbara: WANT SIX PROJECTION ROOM SEATS SIMILAR TO THOSE IN WARNER BROTHERS' STUDIO BURBANK FIRST ROW PROJECTION ROOM #2 FOR MY AIRPLANE BY TUESDAY DELIVERED MINOCQUA. (SIGNED) JOHN IVES. Similar to? These were the very seats. Lew had passed the order along to the motion-picture editor who had phoned the publicity department at Warner Brothers, in Burbank, California, and the first six seats in row one of projection room #2 had been flown in a special shipment to Minocqua, arriving on Tuesday. Mr. Marsh did things right.

The big plane taxied to the line, waited for a signal from the tower, and skimmed the field.

"Here we g-go," Paula said, as if it were a roller coaster.

Lew settled back. Alone in the plane. Very cozy. The lights of the city wheeled below them as they headed north into the windy darkness. Paula cupped her gloved hands and watched out the window.

"Wrigley Building," she reported. And: "The Drake." And: "Edgewater Beach." Apparently she was still going through life like a tourist— interested in everything. The quality that had made her a good reporter. "We're *climbing*! Do you enjoy flying, Lew?"

"Oh, sure," he said. "This is fine."

Grandpa Marsh. Lewis. Lew. He thought: she can't make up her mind what to call me.

"Ravinia," she announced, and watched while the scattered lights moved away beneath them.

She talked with animation about Ravinia, and in her voice was the same pleasant huskiness which had once enslaved him. Her dad still lived in the brown shingle cottage near the Pryor estate where she had grown up, she said. He was sixty-seven and practically retired, though sometimes he filled in with the summer orchestra for concerts in Ravinia Park.

"Clarinetist, isn't he?"

"Lew!" Paula smiled. "Of course not."

"Oh, sure. I remember."

Roger Arnold had been the world's greatest oboe player, a stern, dedicated wisp of a man, a queer duck. He had lived for the moments when

23

he lifted the instrument to his lips and blew odd obbligatos. Once, tight as a horned owl, Lew had imitated him and Paula had been angry.

"I talked to him on the phone tonight," Paula said. "He sent his regards. He remembers you very well."

He waited through an uncomfortable pause.

"You've met B-Boyd?" she asked, at last.

"No."

"He—he's very gifted."

"That so?"

"He could be a composer."

"That'd be nice."

"No, I mean it. He's working on a truly brilliant concerto."

"Tonight?" he asked, drily.

She turned defensively.

"Mr. Ives had the music editor show it to Rafael Kubelik and Horowitz and Bruno Walter. They said it was first rate—if he'd only get it finished."

Lew asked, innocently, "How near done is he?"

"Oh, I don't know, Lew. More than half."

"More than half?"

"Three-quarters, maybe."

He said, "I've written two hundred and seventy-four pages of a novel, Butch."

"Oh, really?"

"Know anybody who wants to buy half a novel?"

She sat back. Then he located a faint nervous clicking. She was opening and shutting her handbag.

"You'll like him," she said, finally.

"Hope so."

"He's a very charming guy."

"When he's sober?"

"Any time. Everybody likes B-Boyd."

He moved closer not so much to look out the window as to catch her perfume. A haunting fragrance. He remembered how she had looked that first day when she came bravely into the office, her knees knocking together. How pretty she had been, sitting beside Julian's desk; how pretty, and how defenseless. He spoke of it, adding, "The first moment I saw you, Paula, I wanted to put my arms around you. To protect you."

"Yes, I know," she said. "To protect me from the foggy, foggy dew."

He laughed. But it wasn't a joke. She had moved away leaving a small, cool space between them.

"Do you remember how mad I was when Mr. Ives sent for me to come

24

to Santa Barbara?" she asked across her shoulder. "It seemed ridiculous, didn't it? Just to get Irene Ives more publicity for a flower show. But that's when I met Boyd. So it was worth it. It worked out f-fine."

"Did?"

"We've had some very happy years."

Past tense.

He liked the clothes she was wearing, whatever they were. A gray suit, tweed, maybe, and an immaculate white blouse, with a wide white collar. And a tam of some dark material with a silver arrow on one side. Very jaunty. He decided she was the prettiest girl he had ever seen, anywhere, in forty-two years. He had been a fool.

"I'm s-sorry if you didn't want to come tonight," she said, "but things are really out of hand. Boyd got into some new kind of trouble. In Cleveland."

Now they were getting down to it.

"Woman trouble?"

She again looked out the window.

"Milwaukee," she announced.

"Woman trouble, Paula?"

"I-I found him in a Cleveland clinic last month. Somebody had knifed him. There's a deep cut in his head and another in his back."

"Does he know who did it?"

"Have you ever tried to get facts from a drunk?"

"I see," he said. "What was he doing in Cleveland?"

"Oh, he's been tight since J-June," she said, unsteadily. "He gets restless and charters airplanes. He's been in Detroit and St. Louis and Cleveland. This is the worst one he's ever been on. I tried to keep it from his family. When I traced him to Cleveland, I went over there, but he ran away. Then I located him in Gary, Indiana, and sent Mr. Price to get him, but he ran away from Mr. Price, chartered another plane and got to Minocqua. Then it all c-came out. Dad Copeland phoned me from the Lodge and I had to admit it's been going on since J-June."

"Who's Mr. Price?"

"He's a lawyer. He handles Boyd's affairs."

"Oh. You have affairs?"

"We're s-stinking rich, or didn't you know?"

"Oh, sure. Copeland money, isn't it? From his grandfather?"

"Emery Copeland. He invented some farm machinery. He doted on Boyd, and left him too much money."

She wasn't telling everything she knew. Not consciously dissembling, maybe. Just reluctant to bring it out. It would be a woman, of course—an assault to her pride. From somewhere out of the past he heard a phrase of Alice's: "And worst of all is what you do to a woman's pride." But, that time, it hadn't been a woman. It had been applause. Alice, the newly elected president of the Junior League, had addressed a convention at the Drake Hotel. Escorting Sid Cohen and somebody from the *Tribune*, Lew arrived at the ballroom in time to hear her speech of acceptance. They'd beamed in the front row, three cheerful drunks, without neckties, with yesterday's beards and a high, last-minute polish on their shoes. The fragrance of silver fizzes had obliterated the mingling of costly perfumes and the house detective had come to get them because they applauded too loudly, slapping their upright palms before their noses, whistling their approval. "Worst of all," Alice had said, "is what you've done to my pride." It had still seemed somewhat amusing when he went to Abe Rouch's bar that evening with Sid and the culprit from the *Tribune;* nearly everybody agreed that the Junior Leaguers were stuffy little dames, and the riotous acclaim from the president's husband and his drunken pals was pretty funny to certain people. Julian hadn't thought it amusing, though, nor had Abe Rouch. "They're nice young ladies," Abe had said, severely. "They do a lot of good. You better kinda taper off, hadn't you, Lew? Go on home, boy."

But he hadn't gone home. Alice had to hire detectives to find him. He had seen her next in Bill Boyden's law office and everything, from then on, happened fast. That's what the jug could do for you: it could take you on a roundabout hilarious way into a quaint old church, and finally into Judge Sabbath's court on a lovely spring morning.

"Butch?"

She was studying the night. There was nothing to be seen but the dark sky and the lights of farmhouses far below.

"How did you trace Boyd?"

She turned slowly. "Through canceled checks," she said. "He sent an Italian shoemaker's family back to Italy for the summer. Then he attended a high-school graduation in Detroit and put three girls in summer school at the University of Michigan. For a while there were lots of checks to colleges. He g-got interested in education."

"Good Lord. How much dough has he got?"

"Even our business manager doesn't know. Lots, that's all. I wish we were flat b-broke. We never will be. His grandfather was so smart not even the Government can get it."

He listened to the insistent clicking of the handbag clasp.

"You went to Cleveland yourself?"

"Yes, I saw him in the clinic. But the next day he was gone."

"Where?"

"He chartered a sight-seeing bus and started for Chicago."

26

"Alone?"

"Except for his dog."

"He travels with a dog?"

"Oh, it's just a one-eyed mongrel he picked up somewhere. Boyd calls him Nameless."

"Well, well." Sounded like a happy drunk. They were a rarity. He had only known three or four. He hoped he had been one, himself.

"Where did he go in the bus, Butch?"

"That's when he stayed at a roadhouse near Gary. I traced him through a check to Lyon & Healy. He bought a grand piano for a bartender. Maple grand piano."

"Open-handed," Lew decided.

"He likes to go to low dives and charm b-bums," she said with warmth. "He plays piano for them and makes them listen. He used to box at Princeton, you know. He makes them listen to classical things like 'La Plus que Lente.' "

"I'm beginning to kinda like him," Lew mused.

"That's his trouble. Everybody likes Boyd and forgives him . . ."

Her voice broke.

"Quite a torch you're carrying."

She took a deep breath.

"I loved him very much."

Past tense again. There was a tightening across his chest.

But he hadn't asked the right question. Sometimes when you came from an interview you knew that you had missed the key, somehow. He found this one.

"Was he alone when he *went* to Cleveland?"

It must have been a full minute before she replied.

"No."

"Who was she?"

It came hard, all right.

"A girl named Maria."

"Maria who?"

"I couldn't find out."

"That's what a cub says," he mocked.

"I *couldn't*, Lew! The charter pilot hadn't paid any attention. Boyd called her M-Maria, but the pilot didn't remember much more." She added, coldly, "She was a Mexican."

"Nothing wrong with being a Mexican."

"I don't mind her being a Mexican," Paula said bitterly. "I do mind her being with Boyd. I mind a lot."

This was it, then. The other woman. All drunks, he thought, eventually turn up with the other woman. And from there it's only one short step to the lawyer's office, and the judge's chambers.

"Did you tell him you knew about Maria?"

"Yes."

"In the clinic?"

"Yes."

"And the next day he was gone?"

"Why are you asking these questions?"

"Do you think it's idle curiosity?"

"No," she admitted.

"What did you say when you told him you knew about Maria?"

"I said I was going to R-Reno—that was before I realized how badly hurt he was—and he said he was tapering off, was sorry about the whole thing and was going to quit drinking forever. But that night he bribed an orderly to bring him a bottle and the next day he was gone."

"*Are* you going to Reno?"

"I don't want a divorce at all," she said, stoutly, "I want to help Boyd— if I can."

"You think a wife can help a drunk?"

"Well, can't I?"

"It'd be a miracle."

"You mean, he's running away from *me*?"

"Foolish of him," Lew said. "But it's possible. Tell me, Butch, did you marry him to reform him?"

"Most certainly not."

"Why, then?"

"Why do you think? I loved him."

"But he drank."

"Some, yes. Very well. But much more, I guess, than I realized."

"Didn't it worry you?"

"No."

"Why not? You knew Johnny and Don Bell and me. Didn't it worry you at all?"

"I thought once he got away from his mother he'd be all right."

"You were rescuing him from his mother?"

"She's a nitwit."

"Does he think so, too?"

"He won't face it," she said, in despair. "His parents live right across the hall from us, on Lake Shore Drive. Boyd was fine all last winter, while they were away, in Europe."

"When did they get back?"

"J-June."

28

"He started drinking in June?"

She nodded.

"After his people left for the Lodge, I thought he'd be all right. But he wasn't. He just got worse."

"Why? Do you know?"

"How could I know?"

"Locked up his liquor, did you, Paula? Talked to him about his drinking? Told him what a fine composer he could be, if sober?"

Alice had done that, in her time. Yes, indeed. Alice had talked eloquently about wasted talents. If she had had one fault, amid her many virtues, it had been ambition for other people. She had wanted to be the wife of an author. She had made a good, hard try.

"What are you angry about?" Paula asked.

"The problem is beyond women altogether," Lew said, bluntly. "You gals ought to learn."

"What do you mean by that?"

"There are no orphan-bachelor drunks, Butch. It's axiomatic that they have a wife, or a mother, or an indulgent aunt." He added, "Or a girl who tries to reform them."

She carefully put the handbag down and folded her fingers.

"You mean it's my fault!"

"Not at all. But you can't help, if you want the facts. I imagine you've tried to help."

"I've tried everything I could think of. We all have."

"Worse than a waste of time," he said.

The silence stretched on and he found himself with memories of Alice that hadn't been in his mind in years. She had done what all good, upright women did to drinking men. She had been patient and brave and obliquely helpful: never missed a chance to say the wrong thing.

"I'll tell you a bedtime story, Paula," he said. "I have an actor friend in Hollywood—you'd know him; I'll call him Carl. Carl drank. He was married to a lovely, strait-laced girl. I'll call her Georgia. One time, when I was in Los Angeles on a story, Georgia invited me to a party. A very gushy girl, Georgia. She said, 'Our life is wonderful now. Carl's quit drinking. He's made all new friends. He's going to New York to do a play and I'm giving a going-away party for all his new friends.' She invited me because I'd quit by then. Well, I went to the party. There were a dozen people there—and all the men were Doctor Somebody or other—and all the wives had a firm grip on the obvious. Carl sat among them, full of vitality, tanned, in blooming health. Then I found out they were all dentists. Their talk ran pretty much to molars. In desperation, bored but sober, lonely for companionship, Carl had wound up at a bowling alley. To keep from having screaming meemies—he was a sensitive guy, you see, and he heard what people actually say in their day-to-day conversations, and that was one thing that drove him to drink—so, to keep from going nuts he'd joined this dental bowling team. Their wives had squatted into domesticity so the men bowled four or five times a week. Well, there we sat, drinking fruit juice, making polite conversation—all of which Carl, with his acute ear, was actually *hearing*. Then Georgia crashed in with the mistake of a lifetime. She said, 'Doesn't Carl look wonderful now that he's sober?' I saw the look go across his face. I knew what would happen. It did. He bought a bottle when he got on the Chief the next morning. He was high as a kite through the entire run of the play."

Paula stared at him.

"Because of what his wife said? A little thing like that?"

"Any little thing. A drunk needs a reason to drink, Butch. His wife, or his mother, or his maiden aunt—some relative, male or female—can usually supply one." He added, "Usually female. We boys kind of understand."

"Well, then, what can I *do*?"

"Nothing. Neither can I."

"But people do stop!"

"By themselves, sure. Usually after they've heard the angel feathers in the county hospital. They make a choice. Then they join A.A. Or get religion—or take antabuse. Or just quit. But it isn't done with a shot in the arm or amateur psychology. That's what I've got to explain to Mr. Ives."

"Then you're not going to even try?"

"No."

"That's negative," she said, producing a twisted grin. "John Ives doesn't like a negative attitude."

"My contract expires January third."

"Oh." She was shocked. "And you're leaving?"

"Unless I get a foreign assignment," he said, grimly. "I'm not a city editor. I've never liked it. Not from the first day."

She slid lower in the seat.

"Look," he said. "I wouldn't worry about what happened in Cleveland. All drunks get beaten up. That's part of it. You choose somebody in a night club, or try to slap down a former heavyweight at the ringside. You get married, divorced and shot at and give away grand pianos. You turn up with a black eye and a gal named Maria. And if you can afford it you send Italian shoemakers to Italy and put girls through college. That's the whole idea. It's a kind of madness, and you work out of it yourself."

30

"Alone?"

"If you do it that way, there's a chance you mean it."

The motors droned steadily. They were passing through a white mist now. Their running-lights flicked automatically against shifting fields of cloud.

"There never were women before," she said at last.

He thought: you could cover divorce court and murderers' row and still be naive about your own affairs. Newspapers were run by fumbling human beings. It was the cold, clean type that made you think there was intelligence behind it. Good girl reporters were no different from other good girls.

"In spite of the drinking—I thought B-Boyd loved me," she said.

"Probably does."

"I'll bet! And Maria, too?"

"Paula," Lew said, sharply, "you can't stay plastered all summer and not turn up with a gal. John Ives knows about this, doesn't he?"

"I didn't tell him."

"Harvey Copeland?"

"I've told nobody. I don't want you to, either, please. I'll handle it myself."

"How?"

"Never mind," she said, and added with spirit, "You're a great reporter. You can turn people inside out. But I won't answer any more questions, if you're not going to help."

"I'd help if I could," he told her and added, "Maybe I have."

"Oh, sure," she said. "You'd recommend d-divorce."

"Probably. Mine helped me."

She caught her breath.

"You really would, then!"

"These things become last year's popular song."

"What does? When you love someone and divorce them?"

"The phrase isn't mine. Bill Boyden said it in his law office. He was right. Alice sent me birthday and Christmas cards for a year or so. Then they stopped. All things end."

Paula folded her arms, deep in thought. Facing it out, maybe. Clearly, it was time. He leaned back, lulled by the drone of the motors. Suppose he had married Paula in that quaint fieldstone church in Ravinia; suppose fate had been with him and he had been sober: Paula, instead of Alice? They'd have a family by now, perhaps—a boy and a girl—ten and eleven. Johnny Marsh, eleven, named for Johnny Richards. Alice Marsh, ten, named for Alice Pryor. By this time he would have finished a novel. Hell, he would have published two or three. Their home would

31

be a paid-for villa in the south of France, and the kids would be bilingual. Bright bilingual kids, both looking like Paula. A fine family, all in bathing suits, with golden tans. But Johnny and Alice Marsh didn't exist. The novels he would have written in the fire of his youth didn't exist, either. He had traded all that for the jug. The jug could cost you a wife and a family and a career. You pay and pay.

He turned abruptly and said, against her lips, "Not from Grandpa," and kissed her hard. There was a surprised answering pressure before she drew away.

"What's that for? My self-esteem?"

"No, mine," he said. "I'm late, but there it is."

"I fought off that whole damn local room all the time I was on the paper," she stormed, with what might have been a trace of humor. "Don't start that again!"

"You never had to fight me off!" he protested. "I was in Abe Rouch's bar at the time."

"Oh, no, you weren't. And don't tell me you've forgotten."

But he had. He glanced past her at a distant flash of silver. Lakes and woodland moved in racing patterns in the moonlight, now. Here they were, in the Wisconsin wonderland, where Chicagoans, getting away from it all, bumped into each other on every dock and trail.

"Just when did I make a pass at you, Butch?" he asked, curiously.

"In Winnetka! In that hot rod."

In the jalopy. Now, let's see . . . You buried such things in your subconscious, but given a prod or two you could sheepishly dredge them up. . . . Oh, sure. Homeward bound from the art exhibit he had swung off suddenly into a dark patch of trees in Winnetka. With the motor still running, he had squared away and made violent love to her, rape in mind. An ardent fool. A happy, pawing, insufferable ass. It had taken an open-handed slap to snap him out of it, and Paula had driven the rattling fenders to her house in Ravinia, while he diluted his embarrassment with quick nips from a flask. Pride, hot coffee and a cold shower had sobered him, and by the time Paula's father got home from a concert he had had himself in hand. He'd stayed to dinner. Oh, sure. That had been the night Alice Pryor dropped in from the big house next door, and he had dazzled Alice. Betcha. He had displayed wit and wisdom for Alice, starting toward the fieldstone church and a wedding, though he hadn't known it, then . . . . Warily, he looked across. What had Paula thought when he suddenly bumped off the highway into the woods?

"Mighty colorful incident," he said, as it came crowding back. "Tell me, were you scared?"

32

"You never scared me. None of you did," Paula smiled. "You were wild but awful nice guys."

The remark disturbed him.

"In your memories," he asked, lightly, "am I lumped with the whole staff? Or do I sometimes stand out alone?"

"You?" She was surprised he'd ask. "Well, you were the craziest." She added, "And the best reporter." Then, as if just realizing, "You aren't so funny sober, are you?"

"No," he sighed. "More like a mortician."

Humorless. Difficult to live with. A sourpuss, according to what Charley said, not long ago, on a bad evening. Grim, humorless, forty-two. And at a dangerous age.

The co-pilot stuck his head in the door.

"Belts buckled? Minocqua coming up!" he called.

A dark patch of pine forest and a wide lake moved under them in the moonlight; and then, over the wing-tip, they saw the headlights of a waiting car, and the runways on a lighted field. Tree tops racing under them, a concrete strip coming slowly up. The wheels touched gently.

Paula said, as she unbuckled her belt, "But you'll help Boyd if you can? There must be something you can do. He's worth s-saving."

"For Maria?"

"That's damn mean!"

She brushed ahead. A red-faced Viking waited near the station wagon with his chin in the collar of his mackinaw. His name was Hjalmar Bojors, and Paula hurried the introductions.

"Is Boyd at the Lodge, Hjalmar?"

"No, ma'am. By golly, wouldn't know *where* he is by this time!" He suppressed a grin. "He played piano at the Muskie Tavern for a while, around nine. I dunno where he went from there."

"Still in the United States?" Lew asked.

"By golly," Hjalmar said, slapping his leg. "You never know!"

It was the admiration of one good drinking man for a better one.

"Cheer up, Butch," Lew said lightly, as the station wagon sped along the highway. "Anywhere outside the continental limits of the United States, and I'll go after him, myself."

"If he's gone again," she decided suddenly, "I am just not going to t-take it."

"Atta girl. Want to come back to work?"

Evidently it was a new thought.

"Was I any good?"

He said, astonished, "Why, sure—you were tops. Didn't anybody ever tell you?"

33

"I'd be rusty. I don't even write letters any more."

"It wouldn't take long. When I came back I was rusty, myself, Butch. Worked out of it."

She adjusted her tam as if about to face into a strong wind.

"Well!" she said, gripping the seat back. "Well, thanks—even if you didn't quite mean it."

"Mean it! Want to start Monday?"

She laughed.

"No, but it helps. Thanks for the offer."

Below them now were the gently swaying masts of sailboats and a long finger of dock with its single night light. Fish were jumping. A big one made a widening circle, far out.

They rolled quietly down a curbless asphalt road through parklike trees. Lew watched for the outlines of buildings against the cliff. The Lodge had been a perennial favorite in the home and garden magazines for two decades: "The House That Climbs a Hill." No floors: levels. No stairs: rises. The architect, reviled in his youth for his innovations, had been imitated beyond good taste by his earlier critics, and probably would die unsung. The planes and angles were now ivy-grown, and a caption under a recent picture had said: "John Cowper Ives's Wisconsin Summer Home Dreams of Past Revolt."

They left the bags to Hjalmar. Beyond the lighted windows of a ground-floor suite a teletype thumped heavily and they heard a ringing telephone. Lew caught a glimpse of Miss Lila, Ives's secretary, who had been lifted to the heights from the information desk in the Ives Building lobby; her shoulders were still bent with the burden of little responsibilities and large self-dramatizations. She was taking dictation, spare pencils in her hair.

Paula hurried across the porch and rang the bell.

"Good evening, Hara," she said to a yawning Filipino who took their things and disappeared down the hall.

Paula moved to a wall mirror, took off her tam, and shook back her hair.

"Lew," she said, alarmed, staring into the mirror. "Come here!"

"What's the matter?"

She turned him toward a better light.

"Lipstick," she told him, snatching his lapel handkerchief. "Get it off!"

He was still scrubbing when they heard the slap of slippers on the ramp.

"Here he is," she said.

The Old Man had once written an editorial suggesting summer togas for businessmen. It had had a facetious, tongue-in-cheek tone; but maybe he'd meant it. Tonight he wore a rustling white robe, and loomed before them like a giant, well-fed monk. His massive face cracked apart in a welcome for Paula.

"My dear!" He caught her in a rough paternal hug. "After this, when you need help—phone *me*. Sitting alone in that apartment! Never again, hear?" His light gray eyes brushed over Lew. "Good of you, Mr. Marsh," he said, briskly. "Glad to see you."

"B-Boyd's gone again?" Paula asked, bleakly.

"Oh, we've found him. He's over at Lac du Flambeau, playing for a wake."

Boyd had escaped at dinnertime, Ives told them. In the Muskie Tavern, a local bar, he had met three sad Irishmen who were mourning a guide named O'Rourke who had been drowned the day before. Boyd had brought the staggering Irishmen to the Lodge to get a book of folk songs, and his dad had gone with them to the wake at Flambeau, following their dump truck in a Cadillac.

"Nothing to worry about," Ives said. "You know Harvey Copeland. He'll hang on." He turned on his charm. He had charm to spare. "I've got quite a plan, Mr. Marsh," he announced.

"Does it include getting out a newspaper every morning?" Lew asked mildly.

"Now, now, now."

Ives raised both arms, slapped open dark draperies, and led them into an alcove where a raised fireplace sent a shimmering glow over a strange array of food. Yogurt and rough health bread and slim carrot sticks on ice. Once upon a time the Old Man had toured Bulgaria, discovering innumerable Bulgars in their nineties who attributed their longevity to buttermilk and yogurt. Coming home, he had tried to change the nation's eating habits. The campaign had failed, but he was faithful to his causes.

"Help yourself," he ordered.

Ives was hungry; all his juices were flowing. He snapped a carrot between his teeth and chewed noisily, his big fingers searching over the table. Cauliflower buds. Radishes. The louder vegetables.

"Told Harvey Copeland about you today, Mr. Marsh," he said, as if this in itself had been an honor. "Told him what you'd done for Ike Bashaw and the other boys. Cheered him up."

"Is it clear," Lew asked, "that I've never cured anybody? You understand, don't you, Mr. Ives, that I hired a few ex-drunks *after* they'd sobered up?"

Ives ignored him.

"Come, come, Paula. You must eat."

35

He tossed stuffed olives in his mouth like a boy with peanuts and then concentrated on the yogurt, making smacking sounds with his lips.

"It's a load off my mind to have you here, Mr. Marsh," he said, and licked the spoon. Homey. Comfortable as an old shoe. "I can handle rational people, but what in hell do you say to a drunk? Quicksilver. Here today, gone tomorrow. Now, Boyd in his right mind is as charming a young fella as you'll ever want to meet. Isn't he, Paula? But when he's in one of these . . ." He broke off. "Where did he get that gash in the head?" he asked her. "Have you any idea? And there's a bad cut in his back, too. Eh? What about it?"

"I'm tired, Uncle John," she said, evasively. "If you don't mind, I'd like to go to bed."

"Hara!" Ives shouted. The Filipino materialized from the shadows. "Take Miss Paula to her room."

She said a quick good night and hurried up the ramp.

"This is hard on her." Ives splashed more creamy stuff into a wooden bowl. "It's hard on all of us. The boy is running away from something. We want you to find out what it is. As I told Julian on the phone today, you're a practical psychologist, whether you realize it or not. Let's get to the bottom. Find out why he drinks. And sober him up." He snapped another carrot. "You're to take time off, if necessary. Let me tell you what I've got in mind . . ."

"Time off?" Lew broke in. "Mr. Ives, two years ago I put in my bid for a foreign assignment. I got back word I couldn't be spared."

"So? This is the first I've heard of it." Busy with his spoon, the Old Man let minutes go by. He put the dish down. "We'll talk about that in the morning, shall we?" He found a cigar inside the robe—togas for businessmen had been designed with cigar pockets—and made a production of lighting it. "In the meantime, there's Boyd." His big lips puffed out. "I'm fond of the boy. I always have been. And I'd do anything in God's green world for Harvey Copeland. Harvey's wife is in menopause and his son is a drunk. It's a tough field to plow, Mr. Marsh."

"Mr. Ives—believe me—this is a job for a psychiatrist."

"Psychiatrist!" Ives snapped shut his lighter. "We've *tried* psychiatrists. I'm ready to blast the charlatans right out of the fog."

"The point is," Lew said, and it seemed to him that he was under admirable control, "there's only one thing that ever cured a drunk . . ."

"Now you keep your pants on," Ives began, and checked himself. Miss Lila appeared in a lighted doorway up the hall.

"Mr. Ives, please," she tiptoed nearer, wriggling her fingers to Lew in greeting: she managed to patronize the local staff in the friendliest sort of way. "Berlin on the wire!"

36

Ives clapped his hands.

"Hara!"

The grinning Filipino appeared again. He bowed and waited.

"Now you keep your pants on, Mr. Marsh." Ives gathered a few last tidbits in his hand. "Don't you suppose I've considered your point of view? We'll discuss it at breakfast." He tilted the cigar and squinted against the smoke. "You were saying? The one thing that will cure a drunk?"

"The sound of angel feathers," Lew said, distinctly. "A peek into the void, Mr. Ives. There's nothing else I know of. It cured me."

The Old Man's pale eyes registered the phrase.

"I see," he said. "Graphic. Angel feathers." It would appear, sometime, in an editorial—you could see him filing it away. He motioned with his thumb. "Take him up, Hara." A moment later his voice echoed against the walls. "There are no hard and fast rules for anything, Mr. Marsh. I've found that out!"

Then a faraway door closed.

Lew found himself in a two-room suite where louvered windows looked out on the asphalt drive, with the lake beyond. He closed the door on the tired Filipino and snaked off his tie.

Beams from a headlight slashed across a wall as he was drifting off to sleep. He threw aside the covers and knelt on the window seat. A car coasted down the road and stopped outside. A Cadillac. Then, below somewhere, a window opened and a woman's pert voice called, "Harvey?"

"Yes, yes. We're here, Dolly."

"Boydie, too? Is Boydie with you?"

Boydie. That was cute.

A tall young man in polo coat and beret was silhouetted in the glare. He stepped lightly across the path.

"Hi, there, Mother o'mine!" he called, articulating perfectly. "How's my girl?"

"Oh, Boydie!" Dolly's voice said. "I've been so *worried!*"

"Go to sleep now," Harvey pleaded, climbing the steps. "Boyd's safe, Dolly. Boyd's safe."

Lew lay back in bed. Dolly, he mused. Dolly Copeland. He had seen her picture on the club pages of every paper in town, but more often in his own. Dolly Copeland leaving for a convention at French Lick. Dolly Copeland leaving for a convention at Niagara Falls. Dolly Copeland—leaving—returning—leaving—returning. Nobody had roots. . . . The more money, the more they traveled—scurrying around like ants.

He fell asleep.

3 He awakened to an insistent buzzing. Sunrise stained the sky and a shaft of pale September light glowed weirdly on a gallery of framed photographs on the north wall. Lew rolled over in bed.

"Yes?" he said, picking up the phone.

"Mr. Marsh?" Ives's voice was slow with weariness. "Will you come to the drawing room at once, please?"

"Yes, Mr. Ives."

At once, Mr. Ives. *Roger!* Over and out, Mr. Ives. On my feet!

I sounded like Julian, he thought. Yes, yes, Mr. Ives.

Windows were still shuttered; doors were closed; dim, quiet halls—a sleeping house. He tied the cord of his robe as he scuffed along in the semi-darkness, his knees buckling a little on the downward ramp. In the serving alcove a silver coffee urn sent up a rich aroma. John Ives was eating; just out of bed, and eating—turning to food, perhaps, as some men did to whisky.

"Boyd's at it again," he muttered, lifting his sleep-wrinkled face from a steaming cup. "Help yourself."

A distant piano gave forth something heroic from Beethoven; talent displayed at an ungodly hour.

"You didn't answer my question last night," Ives grumbled.

"Sorry, Mr. Ives." Lew turned the spigot. "I've forgotten what it was."

"I simply asked you—what does one say to a drunk?"

"Well," Lew mused, "you don't get anywhere when you argue with them, Mr. Ives."

"You are right."

"And there's no point talking sense."

"You are right there, too."

38

Lew shrugged. "You improvise as you go along, I guess."

Ives thrust his hands deep in his pockets. This morning he wore a blue toga; wool, snug and warm—a winter toga.

"I want him back in bed before he wakes up the household. His mother's in there with him. I can't manage her, either." He slapped aside the heavy draperies. "I've sent for Harvey. Come along."

Boyd Copeland wore a tweed jacket, flannel slacks, argyles and brogues—trig as a new sail. A black beret gave him a jaunty Parisian air; a bottle and shot glass indicated that he felt no pain. He sat at a concert grand piano near the wide shuttered window, back straight, his handsome head uplifted, playing brilliantly. Light from a copper floor lamp with a flowerlike copper shade glowed down on his lean, dancing fingers. He suddenly abandoned Beethoven and trickled out precise patterns from Debussy. A one-eyed mongrel pup, legs braced, was greedily lapping milk from a wooden salad bowl, splattering the carpet. There was a wet, white trail across the floor.

"S-h-hh," someone whispered.

Dolly Copeland sat far forward in a big chair, pride and worry mingled on her oddly pretty face. Rings glittered as her busy hands fussed with a bobby pin; rings, at dawn. Nervous glances from her slightly protruding eyes swept from her son's broad back to the untidy mongrel. "S-h-h-h," she hissed, with a slender forefinger against her pouting lips. Lipstick, too, at dawn.

"Dolly," Ives insisted huskily, "this is Mr. Marsh from the paper. He's going to put Boyd back in bed for us."

"Don't interrupt, now, please! It *shocks* Boyd when you interrupt!"

Then, ignoring her own admonition, she explained: she had locked Boyd in his room last night. But sometime this morning he'd dressed and shaved—he always looked tidy; no matter what was happening—and —where was she? Oh, yes, he had climbed right out the window! Imagine! His dog was hungry. He had to get his dog some milk.

Another sleepy figure appeared in robe and slippers and here was Harvey. His face, too, was red and wrinkled; and he was tired, dead tired. And boiling mad. He'd spent last night at a wake, and he was sick of it. I'm sick of it, I tell you, sick of it, Dolly.

"Goddam it, Boyd," he shouted, "can't you let decent people sleep?"

The keys crashed. The concert ended. Boyd closed his eyes and sat, hands folded, as if taking a nap.

"Shame, Harvey!" Dolly's negligee fluttered about her dainty slippers. "Boydie's going to play us his concerto!" She pressed her little face against his cheek, and said, beguilingly, "Boydie, please play Mother your concerto? Is it finished, dear? Have you done more work?"

39

"Work?" Harvey made a series of scoffing sounds in his nose. "Now, there's another thing I'm goddam sick of. I'm sick of that goddam unfinished symphony. . . ."

"Now, now, Harv," Ives said, soothingly. "Let Mr. Marsh handle this. He'll put him to bed."

Lew, leaning in the doorway, returned his cup to the saucer. Heigh-ho. Putting a drunk in bed, he thought, was like poking a cork under water. He'd rolled Don Bell into bed in days gone by, and Sid; and others. They always got up. Time slipped its belt when you were drinking; nights were minutes and minutes were nights.

He put the cup down and fought back a yawn. Paula would turn up before long, maybe. Paula would be mighty attractive in the early morning. She had always looked like a girl who would wake up pretty: dewy-eyed and fresh—that would be Paula.

"Boydie . . ."

Boyd, standing now, smiled down with tolerant amusement, cupped his mother's face in his hands, and kissed her nose.

"You've met Nameless, Mother?" he asked, picking up his drooling dog. His enunciation was faultless; you'd never know he was drunk. "Nameless doesn't know who I am, either. That's what makes us so congenial." He frowned at Harvey. "Both anonymous, both wandering the highways and byways . . ."

"Oh, son!" Dolly pursed her lips pleadingly. "You're ill. Go back to bed, dear. Take just a little nap for Mother?"

"Mr. Marsh!" Ives prompted from the window bench where he had joined Harvey. But Boyd silenced him with an imperious, half-humorous lift of his palm.

"Quiet, please," he ordered and made a slow circle, inspecting Lew. "A tall, hard-eyed stranger," he mused, and now he had a Spanish accent. "And who are you, Señor?"

"I'm the joker in this deck, son," Lew said. "Why in hell don't you go to bed? You're plastered."

Boyd beamed.

"A man of discernment!" he cried, delighted. "El señor speaks the simple truth, madre mía! Refreshing, isn't it? Name, Señor?"

"Lew Marsh."

"Ah, but yes! The editor!" He swept a bow. "My former wife has spoken highly of you, amigo. You know my former wife, Señor? She was Paula Arnold. A newspaper reporter. And very good, I'm told. Recall?"

Harvey Copeland shouted, "Former wife! What's he talking about, now?"

40

"He's ill, Harvey," Dolly protested. "He doesn't know what he's saying." And then, inspired, she said, "He has a headache."

Ill. A headache. Or biliousness, perhaps. Or insomnia. Anything but what it was. Lew thought: mother-smothered. No wonder he drank. He heard himself say, "Mrs. Copeland, leave him alone."

The negligee swirled.

"You were speaking to *me?*"

Boyd stepped in, knuckling Lew's chest.

"You are forthright, *Señor*—I find it charming. But have you been screened for background?" He shifted the dog in his arms. "Backgrounds are important, are they not, *madre mía?*" Suddenly, he opened his palm. "The guest-room key, please!"

Dolly's rings glittered as she fussed with a knotted handkerchief.

"Mustn't lock doors!" Boyd waggled a reproving finger. "In case of fire, then what? I should be compelled to vault from the window." The notion briefly amused him. He kissed her nose again and took the key.

"Where in hell is he going now?" Harvey demanded.

His son ignored him.

"*Señor*, as you so wisely suggested," Boyd said, throwing an imaginary bull-ring cape over his left shoulder, "I shall now retire. I am, indeed, in a condition. I can feel it, myself."

He touched his beret as if to remove it, changed his mind, and bowed with an elaborate Spanish downsweep of his arm.

"*Adiós, señora y señores!*"

Dolly fluttered after him up the ramp.

"Boydie," she was saying, "wouldn't you like a bromide for your headache? You must get more rest, dear. Why, you scarcely sleep at all!"

Lew thought wearily how often he'd seen her, how many times she was multiplied, all up and down the social scale—a Mother's Day mother who never quite knew what was going on.

But there was a new and happier atmosphere in the room. Ives had brightened.

"Lewis!" he said, promoting his city editor to the family circle. "You see, Harv? Notice how he handled that? Boyd's gone to bed!"

Harvey's bloodshot eyes reflected amazement. A struggle dating back to the time Boyd was three had now been resolved—and it was a miracle, that's what it was. Nobody—nurses, his parents, his relatives, psychiatrists —nobody, mind you, had ever got Boyd Copeland into bed until he was damned good and ready. The wonder of it grew on them.

Dolly's voice was shrill in the upper hall.

"Boydie! Wait, dear! Let me tuck you in!"

41

That would do it, Lew thought. That would arouse the thirst in him if anything would. He studied the two happy faces.

"Ever occur to you people to keep her out of it?" he asked.

Not to Harvey, certainly. Keep her out of it? It struck him as a revolutionary notion. Clearly he had lost an important fireside struggle long ago. You knew the type. Harvey Copeland had weathered many a trying year with his frivolous little wife; she wasn't what she once had been, or what he had thought her to be, and he no longer saw or heard her.

"Well," he said doubtfully, and called up a spurt of courage, "I'll see what I can do."

"Now we've started, son!" Ives said as Harvey trudged away. "Please see to it he gets some sleep. And talk to him when he wakes up. Bring him out of it. Sober him up."

Yes, Mr. Ives. Wet nurse a drunk? Certainly, Mr. Ives.

A phrase for his resignation burned uncensored through his mind, as he said, "You say you've tried psychiatrists?"

"The best," Ives said. "All incompetent."

"What do they suggest?"

"Oh, all sorts of ridiculous things. Psychoanalysis. Ranch life, for instance. Shipping out on a boat. Or into the woods with the lumberjacks. Do you think he'd go? That boy can't even sit still for an intelligent conversation. Last winter around New Year's I flew a celebrated professor, a psychologist—Dr. Donald Wilson—all the way from California. He didn't get to first base."

"Did Dr. Wilson have any suggestions?"

"They were utter nonsense."

"Such as?"

"Oh," Ives scoffed, "he used campus words like 'getting him away from the negative milieu of the home.'"

"What's that mean?"

"Who knows? The man refused to lift his hand unless he could take Boyd with him to California and work on him there—away from the 'negative milieu of the home.' Release him from the pressure of his mother! His wife! Mrs. Ives! Me! He gave me high-flown talk about tolerance and aspiration levels and frustration, and how certain personalities impinged on his adolescent psyche—that sort of mish-mash." Ives dug inside his toga and produced a long Havana. "Get him away, they all tell us. Well, he goes away, all right! Mentally, he's away right now, isn't he? We want him back." His eyes iced over. "It's in your hands, sir. Get on with it, if you please."

Lew felt a throbbing vein in his temple. An obtuse, high-handed old

42

man, wasn't he, now? Flew an expert three thousand miles—and ignored his advice! You couldn't compete with stupidity on such dizzy upper levels. Indeed, you couldn't compete with it anywhere. It whipped you every time. Rolled over you. Smashed you down. It ran the world.

Harvey and Dolly Copeland came back down the ramp and Harvey seemed bewildered by an unexpected victory. The vanquished Dolly was sobbing wildly but stepping right along at her husband's elbow. She tossed her head petulantly as they passed Lew.

"Boyd's broken my heart! He won't sleep at all, Harvey. He'll just drink and drink and *drink!*"

Lew thought: *Maybe I will, myself, if this keeps up.*

But his anger dissolved in an amusing memory. He recalled a caption under Dolly's picture on the club page. Mrs. Harvey S. Copeland, vice-president of the Mothers for Temperance, leaving for the convention at Topeka, Kansas. Oh, fine. She had been among the well-meaning ladies who had applied pressure on the Pentagon to withdraw the daily issue of beer from the soldiers dying in Korea—thus sending a hot, dry flash, if not actual rebellion, into the foxholes and the stinking rice paddies. These dames! Wonderful, weren't they? Why, of course! Dolly was up to her hips in temperance meetings and prohibition fol-de-rol. He recalled the club department's hilarity when they reported her talk to the annual gathering of the Women's League for Voting Dry. The club department had never heard of that one: the W.L.F.V.D. Grinning from ear to ear, the picture editor had come to Lew's desk with a wet print from the dark room, and there were the Hattie Carnegies and the Lilly Dachés and the crow's feet and the double chins of the board of directors of the W.L.F.V.D.—seven pod-dry little women, all preened for the occasion, wearing orchids at noon. Don Bell had looked over Lew's shoulder. "And not a face among 'em that wouldn't drive me right back into the gutter," he had intoned sadly. Very amusing, when you looked back on it. Wonderful world.

He stopped at the wide window halfway up the ramp. High in the sunrise the geese were flying, going south. A speedboat slashed the dark blue water, sending creaming waves along the shore. Then the sunlight silvered the wing-tip of a plane; moving, going, leaving, returning, on land, water, in the air; man and bird and fish and beast; the restless, universal movement; going somewhere, going away. Something John Ives had said came into his consciousness with a little shock: *Away? He's away, now, isn't he? I want him back.* You took a train. Or a plane. Or a boat. Or you took a drink. Or went to a movie. Or a meeting. You sat in your own dark living room staring at the television set. Somehow you got away. From what?

43

The dog barked in the hall ahead. Turning the corner Lew encountered a scene that would make a likely anecdote for his five ex-drunks when he got back to the office: a dipsomaniac engaged in idiocy.

Boyd Copeland, an alcoholic perfectionist, was repeatedly flipping a Navajo blanket to place it just so on the floor outside his bedroom. The mongrel, tongue lolling, his one eye bright with anticipation, sat poised on his haunches, ready to leap, thinking it all a game.

"What goes, pal?" Lew asked.

Boyd flipped again. Wasn't satisfied. Another flip. Very intent on the job.

"My room, *Señor*," he announced, "is crowded with unpleasant associations." He smoothed the blanket. "We are camping out."

He lay down, snuggled the dog beside him, and rested his head wearily on a bent arm.

"*Buenas noches.*"

"Don't be a chump." Lew grinned. "There's an extra bed in my room if you want it."

"So? No inconvenience, I trust?" he asked, instantly on his feet. "No discombobulation?"

He walked steadily beside Lew into the suite and examined the exits.

"Two doors, wide windows." He nodded with satisfaction. "*Gracias, Señor.* I'll stay."

His gratitude was pitiful. Starved for love, maybe, like Sam Prisk. Everybody was starved for love. And bottled up with conversation, too. Full of travel stories. Boyd bustled around, getting settled, phoned downstairs for the transfer of luggage; and, then, making himself at home, like a college roommate, cocked his feet on the chair and told of bars he had liked and bartenders; of an ambulance he had hired to go from Indianapolis to St. Louis because he had actually felt a little queasy one time. He was entertaining. A happy drunk.

"I understand you had a slight concussion in Cleveland," Lew said, laying out his shaving things. "How'd it happen, sonny?"

"I don't know." Boyd was thoughtful. "Fisticuffs, I imagine. In a Democratic mood I encountered a Republican, or vice-versa. Unusual for me. Know why?"

"Why?"

He snapped an airy finger.

"I just don't give a damn." He swore cheerfully at the dog. "We've got it worked out so all is gaiety, eh, Nameless?"

"How's your hangover?"

Another airy snap.

"Never had one. Never feel a thing."

44

"Don't kid the shock troops," Lew said. "Let's see your wound, pal."

Boyd took off his beret and bent his head.

"Unwholesome, isn't it?" he inquired, with an upward glance. "A turning of the stomach?"

It was a puckered, red scar with eight-nine-ten stitches. Unwholesome was as good a word as any.

"I keep it covered," Boyd whispered. "My sweet mother is a shade on the hysterical side, swoons at the sight of blood."

"Knife?"

"Wouldn't know. It's possible. I have a slight scratch between my shoulders, also." Boyd frowned in thought. "Intellectually, I accept a trip to Cleveland, but Cleveland itself has slipped my mind."

Lew wondered: had Maria also slipped his mind?

"Were you alone?" he asked, casually.

Boyd's face assumed a dramatic sadness.

"Always alone." The accent came back. "A lone wanderer on the highways and byways since early childhood, Señor." And then he said, surprisingly, "I believe you know Ike Bashaw?"

"What about him?"

Boyd got up, turned down the sheets on the bed, and carefully adjusted the pillow. Then he folded a card and wedged it in the telephone to muffle the buzzer. His mind had gone away.

"I must improve my appearance with sleep, sweet sleep that knits the raveled sleave of care," he said. "I wish to look my best. They tell me my ex-wife has arrived."

"You got a divorce somewhere?" Lew asked.

Boyd drew himself up.

"Painful subject," he chided, sternly. "Prefer not to discuss it with a total stranger. But it's the consensus, Señor—Paula is too good for me."

"You're right!"

"I have, however, found a woman who isn't."

"Named Maria, Boydie?"

He lowered his chin, belligerent now. The fighter. Ready for fisticuffs.

"You will refrain from the diminutive, if you please." He ripped off his shirt, tossed it aside, and turned his back, flexing his shoulder muscles. Lew glimpsed another puckered scar. Boyd swung around and swelled his biceps. "Feel, please," he ordered.

"Why?"

"I used to box at college." He glowered, murderously. "Call me Boydie and I shall have to lay you cold, Señor."

"You're drunk," Lew said. "You'll lay nobody cold."

Boyd rebuked himself with a gesture.

"Why, yes, so I am. I'm in a condition."

An affable dipsomaniac, sure enough, Lew thought, ducking his head into the shower. Seven years ago he'd have made him a boon companion. A great little guy to encounter after work, at Abe's . . .

Abruptly, the shower door opened.

"It's good of you to take me in, old man," Boyd shouted into the steam. He now wore red-and-white striped pajamas. "It indicates an open-handed generosity of spirit, rare in our day."

Then he was gone.

Lew found him changing the bed a few minutes later—folding the fresh sheets away, putting on the used ones from his own room. The logic was woozy, but he himself was brisk, neat and efficient. Servants had brought his luggage, including a leather hand-trunk with padded compartments from which he took a fifth of Scotch, placing it under the bed. Then he slipped a shot glass beneath the pillow and with frowning concentration set the clock for 4:47. A sound program had settled into his befuddled head; he would sleep now and be bright and cheery for the cocktail hour.

"A pleasant encounter, *Señor*," he said, smoothing the sheet over his chest with his long, artist's fingers, "I trust we shall meet again."

He drifted off into a smiling sleep. Away. Unconscious. And there'd be no qualms when he came back; the jug was his insurance. A classic hangover was in the making here but, like any foresighted dipsomaniac, he'd postpone it as long as he could. The day would come when his tongue would thicken, and his fingers stumble on the piano keys; when a barroom brawl would mar his handsome features, and people would turn their backs, or sidle away; when a doctor would say, "You'll quit, or else!" Then he would decide, and fight his way back, if he had the courage. Dark visions of death might cure him and the dark murmur in his ear—nothing else. You turned from the jug at last because you were afraid to die. You ran from life; but you also ran from death. In the end it was sometimes easier to live: and thus—a cure. Wouldn't you think such a simple idea could penetrate John Cowper Ives's massive head?

Lew went into the suite's living room to put on his shoes. The framed photographs on the wall caught his attention; pictures autographed to the boss, with affection and admiration; with gratitude; with respect.

To John and Irene Ives, gratefully, Kenneth Watson. And: *To John Ives, with admiration, Louis DeBeck.* There were a score of them in the proud gallery. Here and there Lew recognized co-workers from the days of his own apprenticeship. Johnny Richards, interviewing Churchill at No. 10 Downing Street; Ernie Walsh with Harry Truman on the new

46

balcony at the White House. All of 'em right on hand wherever things were happening. All except Lew Marsh.

Someone knocked lightly, he called: "Come in!" and there was Paula. He finished tying his shoe, said "Hi-ya, Butch," and studied her. He had been right. She woke up pretty.

"I hear I missed a dawn recital."

She wore a plaid skirt and a light blue cashmere sweater, and there were wet curls where her shower cap had failed her.

"Is Boyd all right?"

She had looked like this many a morning in the old days when she came to work; fresh and alive and utterly feminine. You wanted to take her in your arms, reassure her, and protect her—and not just from the foggy, foggy dew. You always wanted to do something about Paula.

"Lew?"

"He's fried to the eyes, Butch. But sleeping. No telling how long."

He caught her faint perfume as she made sure the bedroom door was tightly closed.

"Did you find out anything?"

"Nothing."

"That's what cubs say," she smiled chidingly. "Didn't you try?"

He had always loved her. He had known women by the dozens, scores, hundreds; for years now, every well-dressed, gloved and hatted girl who caught his admiring eye instantly had been compared to Paula. What the hell, he thought. Let's start.

"Paula, will you marry me?"

It should have been a surprise flank attack but she wasn't startled. He caught a friendly, scoffing look and then drearily remembered the office ritual; mornings, when she had come in looking especially appealing, everybody had proposed to Paula. "Will you marry me, Butch?" the men would say. "I have a wife and three children and we're a little crowded, but will you marry me?"

"You know," he said lightly, "if I had married you when it first crossed my mind—assuming you'd have accepted—we'd have two kids by now. We'd be sunbathing somewhere in the south of France. I thought about it all night."

"I'll bet."

"No, I mean it."

She seemed puzzled; he wasn't smiling. Lew went on, seriously, "You can't go on with Boydie and Mommie and Uncle John and Harvey."

"Why can't I?" she demanded. Then she whispered, alarmed, "Lew, what did Boyd say?"

"About what?" he asked in surprise.

47

"Maria."

"Wouldn't discuss Maria."

She paced the room, her arms locked across her chest, head down and shoulders hunched; sometimes, returning from an assignment that had excited or engrossed her, she had paced like this beside her typewriter. She didn't see him; he wasn't there.

The door opened abruptly. Boyd, barefoot, in his red-and-white striped pajamas, refreshed and cheerful, spread his arms to Paula.

"My lovely!" he cried. "I *heard* you were here! How've you been?"

"Hello, B-Boyd," she said, warily. Her eyes misted. "I hope I didn't wake you."

"Slept like a top!" he announced. He ticked off on his fingers, "If anyone cares to play tennis, ride horses, go fishing, flying, hiking, hill-climbing, or frog-hunting, I'll be ready in a flash!"

"You've slept five minutes," Lew said, bluntly.

"Ah, yes," he blinked, orienting himself. "The hard-eyed stranger. How've *you* been, *Señor?*"

"Bored. You're a first-class bore, Boydie. Go back to bed."

Boyd placed his right toe behind his left heel, and did a brisk about-face.

"*Señor* Marsh," he purred, playing a game—he was a Spanish don, perhaps—"I have twice warned you. Find something else to call me, *Señor.*" He snapped his fingers. "Or I'll bat you around like a jai alai ball."

You didn't argue with a drunk. Or rationalize. Or hope to make sense. Or even react. You waited. You agreed.

And sure enough, the silence brought on a new and happier notion.

"Oh, but of course!" he cried, shuffling memories in his tired mind. "You're *the* Lew Marsh! An intellectual, Paula, a brilliant conversationalist, no doubt." He dug in with his bare feet. "Sir, I should like to discuss world affairs sometime—when I'm sober."

"Any particular date in mind?" Lew asked.

"How about a week from Tuesday?"

"I never make plans with a drunk," Lew said. "Why don't you let me try to catch you sober?"

"*Touché!*" Boyd.cried, staggering back as if wounded. He focused and advanced on Paula. "My lovely, you heard that *riposte?*" He rested an elbow on her shoulder. "I said I would like, and *he* said . . ." But it was too complicated. He took both her hands: "I want us always to be friends."

"You're pretty darn t-tight," she said, breaking away. "You don't know where you are or what you're saying. Go to bed."

48

Hurt, he rested one bare foot awkwardly on the high arm of a chair. "How was Reno, Paula? Dull this season? Did you stop at a dude ranch?"

She whirled from the window. The blaze in her eyes had no effect on his politely inquiring air.

"Boyd," she said, "I didn't go to Reno. There's been no divorce."

If she had expected him to be relieved his reaction was a disappointment. He flicked a mental calendar prodding the top of his beret with one stiff finger.

"Somewhere, perhaps, I have put the wrong construction on your own suggestion?"

"You begged me not to go, so I didn't. Does it change your plans?"

Nothing blurs time like the jug, Lew thought. Believing his wife to be in Reno, Boyd had spent the summer in carefree, drunken travel, and now he had to poke at the months with his fingertips.

"Sometime in July," he mused, "or August . . . ?" but it was gone. He straightened. "This might be awkward, Mrs. Copeland."

"Why?"

"I am hopelessly entangled, I do believe. I have made certain commitments."

"With whom?" Her eyes glistened.

"With a woman I'm too good for. Of the earth—earthy. It's a change."

Lew caught his shoulder, spun him around, and sent him running into the bedroom.

"The woman doesn't live you're too good for, pal," he said, following him in. Boyd lost his balance and sprawled across the bed. The dog leaped up to lick his face and they wrestled joyously. Lew pulled aside the covers and rolled them both in.

"Tired," Boyd said, smiling sweetly. "Exhausted, *Señor*." He held out one palm as if testing for rain. "Is it drunk out this morning?"

Paula was racing down the sloping hall when Lew returned. She didn't hear his call. A moment later, a distant door slammed and when he reached the living room she was taking the steps to the beach two at a time. Then she ran headlong into the wind, hair flying, skirts whipping about her legs. He momentarily lost sight of her as she crossed a rustic footbridge near the boathouse. Boydie had lost a wife, he thought; he'd gone too far.

Watching the diminishing figure on the sand he couldn't remember, now, the final scene with Alice. It had been early morning, something to do with a cat—a temperance talk with a cat. . . . Oh, well. But he knew how she had looked in Judge Sabbath's court. She had worn a prim blue suit with a starched collar and cuffs and she had been gentle and unhappy and bewildered; the tiny mole on her neck was all that had reminded him he had once loved her. *If* he had loved her; if it hadn't all been a product of the jug.

Their divorce had been the end, and a beginning. Tensions had eased for him when he locked the apartment door for the last time. The simple act of breathing had taken on its true importance in the hospital, and he was free of Alice, free of the jug. Was that it? You escaped an emotional mix-up, had a preview of your tomb, and God in his heaven finally cured another drunk. Maybe so.

Someone nudged his elbow. It was Hara.

"I have been looking for you, sir. Mr. Ives wants you. I'm to sit with Mr. Boyd, if you wish."

"Guard the doors and windows," Lew said and followed the coffee fragrance to the breakfast room.

4 The Old Man was sitting alone with his back to the windows, hunched over his plate, eating again with vast enjoyment. Maybe even John Ives suffered the winds of apprehension and quieted his leaping nerves with food. This was breakfast now, for sure; this was official. He was huge in his blue toga, ruddy, comfortable, hungry.

"What's Paula doing down there?" he demanded, staring out toward the beach, his jaws working.

"Running."

"What from?"

"Had a bellyful of Boydie."

Lew turned to the chafing dishes on the sideboard. A Filipino butler suggested creamed chicken. Sold, he said.

Ives mopped gravy with the soft side of a biscuit.

"Is the boy asleep?"

"Well, he's in bed with his eyes closed."

"Getting along, aren't you, Lewis?"

Lew drank his orange juice. "I wouldn't bet on it if I were you."

Fall colors in severe angular vases recalled years when the paper had been overenthusiastic about flower and garden shows. One spring Irene Ives had won first prize for a rock garden display in the exhibition halls of the Hotel Sherman, and the feature pages veered noticeably toward garden clubs and the Midwest's native flora. Apparently she'd been busy this morning: red maple leaves and sprigs of sumac were scattered artistically to make a centerpiece on the round breakfast table.

Ives scrubbed his lips with a napkin.

"Y'know, Lewis, when you're away from the city desk there's always

51

a problem. Sam Prisk won't do—not for very long. We must find somebody to fill in while you're away."

"I'm to be away?"

Ives reached across for another biscuit and settled back to strop it. His ego was an inch-thick armor and he was snug in it. Ignoring Lew, his glance played over the table as he talked, or out the window, where Paula was now a tiny figure far down the beach. "Now, Ike Bashaw has imagination," he said, chewing. "I've been watching his work. How is he doing? Is he drinking at all?"

Ike and his birthday. Ike and his shaky trips to the water cooler.

"He hasn't missed a day in fourteen months," Lew said.

It was true enough, wasn't it? He'd been there yesterday, hadn't he? Not worth a damn, of course. But he'd been there. Maybe, along about now, a promotion was what Ike needed.

"Glad to hear it." Ives saluted humorously as Harvey came gloomily in. "Where is everybody, Harv? Where's Irene?"

Harvey Copeland's eyes were puffed. He needed his sleep, and he hadn't had it. He fought down a frog in his throat.

"She's with Dolly," he growled, waiting while the butler served a tray at the sideboard. "They're in the solarium. Dolly thinks she can eat, now. I'm taking her something. God, what a night!"

Ives shot affectionate glances at his friend's broad back. "You get a little nap, Harv," he said. They bantered with broad, Rotarian humor until Harvey dutifully made off with his tray.

"That Harvey!" Ives's big face creased with wrinkles. "You'll love him, Lewis. A man's man. He spits on his hands and finishes things, the way you do. And he's always had a potful, but it didn't spoil him. It's funny how things go."

He pushed aside his plate, put out a pad and pencil, and settled down to business.

"Now," he grunted. "When we're young we get hold of a dream, and that's what starts us. Eh? But it's a mistake to hang on beyond the time it's useful. You tell me you're restless in the best job in town. City desk. Why, man, the desk is the heart of a newspaper. Fact is, I've always said a paper's as good as its city editor—no better, no worse."

"I'm a reporter," Lew said, steadily. "I've had all the desk work I want."

"You're an executive if I ever saw one," Ives announced, and it was final. "Your trouble is, you let little things bother you. Julian tells me the Guild gets under your hide."

"Way under. It's no secret."

"Well, son—we've *got* the Guild. We have to make the best of it."

"We wouldn't have it," Lew observed, embracing a heaven-sent opportunity, "if you boys at the top had seen it coming and split up a little dough."

For years he had been saying this, with the bitterness aroused by stupidity at the top—saying it in Julian's office, in the B/G Sandwich Shop downstairs and at council, but he'd never expected to have a chance to say it here. He waited cheerfully for the explosion.

Ives's toga quivered.

"That's a bull's eye," he laughed, and shouted, "Harvey—come here!" But Harvey didn't hear him. "Well, well, well!" He gazed at Lew thoughtfully.

Then he turned on his charm; it was in everything about him, like an aura around his massive face and head, in the jolly way he worked his cigar between his lips, and in the amiable rumble of his voice. Why, his affection for you was an almost tangible warmth across the table, Lew thought. Julian once had described it: John Ives could wring charm out of his clothes.

"Lewis," Ives flicked a speck of tobacco off his tongue and bit down hard on his cigar, "starting January fourth you'll be the highest paid city editor in America."

Apparently, he was all set for lively expressions of gratitude. Lew forked aside a red hyphen of pimiento.

"You hear me? I'm ready to draw up a new contract."

"I like the one I've got." Lew thought of the croup kettle; and of Boyd. He'd had enough. "I'm leaving Chicago on the first plane out after five o'clock on January third."

And not alone, either—if luck were with him. He saw Paula coming along the shore. She stopped to skip a pebble. Then she moved on, like a woman with a destination. Reno, maybe? Faced it, had she? Made up her mind?

Ives wore the crafty look of a trader.

"Twenty-five thousand," he said, grandly. "How's that?"

Taxes. The day had passed when a large sum could quicken your heart or send you dreaming. Washington was in your pocket up to the elbow.

"I won't dicker with you," Lew said. "I'm not interested in money. What's your plan for Boyd?"

The Old Man stared. Why, this was heresy. *He* was interested in money, whether you paid high taxes or not. Everybody was interested in money. Money was what made the wheels go round.

"Not mine," Lew said. "Not when I can't keep it."

The Old Man promptly took another tack. "An able city editor, with his heart in the job, could do quite a job in Chicago. The crooked gambling. The clip joints. The phony hoodlum unions. And I've often

53

thought the town should do something about the bridges." He tapped the table, watching Lew warily. "I'd back an able man to the hilt, if I could find one. Been looking for the right man for years."

"From here?" Lew asked.

The pale eyes froze. A vein in his forehead swelled and throbbed. But then, surprisingly, the charm returned.

"Y'know, I forget, sometimes," he said and the toga again was quivering across his chest. "I get a tough guy for my desk and then I'm shocked when he ain't a pantywaist, like everybody else." He chuckled, savoring the joke. "From *here!*"

He crossed his legs, and talked, father-to-son.

He had built the Lodge, he said, for a simple, sound reason of health. His eardrums were thinner than other people's. Twenty years ago he had made the alarming discovery that the noise at the Lake Street corner of the old Ives Building, if increased by 1/6 more decibels of sound, would have driven the tenants mad. Scientists from Northwestern University had measured the bedlam: the screech of the elevateds, clanging street cars, the incessant piercing shrill of policemen's whistles, the high-pitched clatter of riveting machines, the snarl of trucks, the whine of taxis—all the tumbling tumult of a lusty, expanding city had hammered against sensitive membranes and he had groaned through days with migraine headaches. But during his first summer in Wisconsin he had discovered he could run the paper even more effectively *in absentia;* his very absence had increased his power.

Yes, sir! Stumbled on a technique of management, and afterward appeared in the new Ives Building only when displeased; the next voice you hear is the voice of God. It worked. In spite of taxes, the paper made money and, in his maturity and detachment, he had learned that the public mainly wanted entertainment from a newspaper. Readers' surveys showed they preferred the comic pages to anything else. Simple? Yet it was the sort of discovery an old man makes, in his growing wisdom, when his blood is cooling and the ardent crusading days of his youth are gone. But he would welcome among his editors a man who was willing to accept the challenges; he'd watch and guide him, and take pride in him, and pay him well.

"Now, then," he said, doodling on the pad. "Write your own ticket, within reason. What do you want?"

Maybe you couldn't reach his mind, sensitive as his ears were said to be; perhaps he had learned to hear only the words that pleased him. Lew pushed his plate aside, "Sorry, sir. Not interested."

Ives drew a deep breath, jerked the toga, straightened it on his shoulders, and settled more firmly in his chair.

54

"Once and for all, sir," Lew interrupted, "I'm not an executive. Don't tell me in January that I didn't give you notice. This is September sixteenth. I'll put it in writing today."

"Very well," Ives growled. "We'll drop it."

But he was faithful to his causes and he had a new one; it hadn't been dropped for long. He exuded geniality, poured coffee, chatted about the days when he, himself, had been a city editor. He was a gifted raconteur. When Irene Ives came to join them they were laughing heartily, the contest forgotten.

"Irene! Come in!" Ives waved with a jolly, full-arm motion. "We're giving Ike Bashaw a promotion. Lewis tells me he's doing well!"

"How nice to hear!" And she asked, warmly, "How is Travis Ashbourne? He's another of my boys. His mother and I were classmates at school."

She had freckles on her nose, honest streaks of gray in her straw-colored hair, and pale eyelashes innocent of make-up; not pretty, but her bones had a patrician structure. Lew liked her instantly and said what he could for her boys.

He had forgotten, if he had ever known, that she had sponsored Ike Bashaw. Oh, yes, indeed, she said. Ike had grown up in Minocqua, a stalwart lad; she was interested in boys. If her son had lived—he'd died at birth—he would be a man by now. . . .

"John!" She turned excitedly. "Have you told Mr. Marsh our plan?"

Ives beamed.

"Now, listen to me. . . ."

Winters were spectacular in this Wisconsin countryside, he said, drawing a word picture: the first snowfall would be coming soon, sifting down over the fir trees and the lake, and the fields and fences—a beautiful sight from these big windows. Boyd could chop wood, wear high boots and plaid mackinaws—put out traplines and do a little hunting. A few weeks with Lew and he would finish this what-do-you-call-it concerto, the best thing he'd tried to do, and he'd have his health back. A vacation, you might say, eh, Lewis? It had been a dream of his own to be snowed in here for a while. He would enjoy it vicariously while sweating out his sinus in California. You see, what Boyd needed was the companionship of another man who understood the liquor problem. Someone, if you'd pardon him, who'd been a drunk, himself. There was a direct wire to the office if anything important came up. . . .

"How do I keep him here?" Lew asked. "Lock him in a closet?"

Hjalmar Bojors appeared in the doorway, bringing in a mingled smell of alcohol, boot oil and the great outdoors. He smoothed his yellow hair, waiting sheepishly to be noticed.

"Is Mr. Boyd ready?" he asked.

Lew choked back an explosion of laughter.

"Ready for what?" Ives came roaring from his chair. "Isn't he in bed?"

Hjalmar shifted his big shoes and addressed Irene.

"All I know is, he phoned for the station wagon. He's got a reservation on the noon train to Chicago because, by golly, he sings a duet somewhere tonight."

The cork had popped.

Mrs. Ives swept ahead of them toward tumult and shouting in the solarium.

"Listen to this damn fool, John!" Harvey bellowed. "Boyd's talking about a divorce! He's trying to make us believe the marriage is over!" He glared around, distractedly. "Where in hell is Paula?"

Boyd leaned on his cane, dressed for travel, listening, as if to distant music. Two embarrassed houseboys had carried down the luggage. Lew sensed a rustle and whisper beyond the heavy drapes and around the corners. The staff had been alerted. Mr. Boyd was off again. Leaving. Here we go. Away. Away.

"I'll get Paula," Irene Ives said soothingly, and the draperies swirled.

Dolly, on the chaise, seemed surprisingly unworried. She nibbled daintily at a crust of toast.

"Let Boydie speak!" She pursed her lips over a cup and twinkled at her son, "Boyd and Paula know what's best." Taking a complacent sip, she said, "Speak right up, dear."

Boyd spun his cane, braced it behind him, and spoke right up. "I am thinking of Paula's happiness," he said, nobly. "I believe it is Father, is it not, *madre mía?*—who so often remarks, in his quiet way, that Paula is too good for me?"

"She's too good for a drunken bum!" Harvey shouted. "Why don't you sober up, Boyd—act like a man, that's all I ever asked." There was loneliness in his cry. "Now, listen to me! You let that girl get away from you, and I'll never forgive you!"

"Noisy here." Boyd removed a glove, put two fingers between his lips, and whistled shrilly. Nameless slid in on his haunches and looked adoringly at his master through his one good eye.

"*Avant,* men!" Boyd signaled a brave advance, topping Harvey's protest. The servants bent doubtfully to the luggage. "*Adiós,* everybody!"

Lew felt a quick jab.

"Keep him here!" John Ives ordered.

This little shambles, Lew thought, would make another lively anecdote for the dayside rewrite battery when he got back to town. And that would be today. Right now. Today.

He flipped Boyd's tie.

"Think the glow will last, sonny?"

That was what you worried about, the one rational thought in the fog: must keep the glow. Keep it, or you woke to the terrors, with your mind racing through unsavory memories of yesterday, and the day before; of idiotic conversations, of witless behavior. But the jug would erase all that. You had no worries when you kept the glow.

"Kid, you're a basket case," Lew said, with a mental nod to Charley. "You'll have sod in your eye before you know it."

Boyd wet his lips.

"Think so?"

Lew looked coolly past him toward John Ives. "I'm going back to Chicago today. Want a ride?"

"With you?"

Boyd had brightened. Companionship!

Lew thought: the need for companionship was probably a hunger in him. He'd lost his friends by now. And soon his wife.

"*Muy bien, Señor!*" Boyd grandly tossed the imaginary cape. "When?"

Lew made a mistake. "I'll call you at two."

Later? Boyd cocked his head. So often new friends floated into his misty orbit, made alluring suggestions, and somehow vanished while he tied a shoe.

"A pact?" he asked, craftily. "Your pledged word, *Señor?*"

Lew offered his hand, and, after shaking it, Boyd embarked on a polite, cane-swinging circle of the room. *Adiós*, everybody! A change in plans! But then he saw Irene and Paula talking earnestly on the terrace and considered joining them. Yet there was space to negotiate, and fresh air to encounter. He decided against it and focused his attention on John Ives. "I shall return to bed," he said, solemnly, "and shortly journey to Chicago with the hard-eyed stranger. But I prefer to be sky-borne whenever possible, Uncle John. The air is swifter. Your plane, *Señor*—would you mind?"

Ives muttered uneasily. He never knew what to say to drunks.

"He means yes," Lew said.

"*Gracias, Señor!*" Boyd adjusted the Homburg and pointed his cane toward the hall. "And so, once more, to bed!" he cried. "To one and all, once more, *buenas noches!*" But his purpose shifted. He doubled a fist under Lew's nose. "Throw a curve, *amigo*, and when next we meet I shall do the Mexican hat dance around your prone figure."

"My pledged word," Lew said, gravely.

But now Dolly was tugging at Boyd's coat.

"Boydie, dear?"

57

Boyd fixed a look of fondness on his face. "Yes, Mother o'mine?"

A crumb of toast had caught in a tiny wrinkle at the corner of her mouth. A tenacious crumb; pouting failed to dislodge it. Coquettishly, she drew him closer.

"If Paula is going to Reno," she murmured, "why don't you and I take a little trip? Just Mother and her boy." She yearned up at him. "Wouldn't that bring back old times?"

It might not bring back old times, Lew thought savagely, but it sure as hell would arouse the hot, dry flash. Mother and her boy! He could guess what "old times" had been like—for Mother and her boy. You saw Mother and her boy in watering places the world over: lonely, dissatisfied women and dutiful small boys practicing the arts of feminine conversation while they passed teacups and snapped cigarette lighters like little men, their hearts in hot rebellion.

Memories of some such earlier travel shocked Boyd out of his aplomb and he broke away in a welter of excuses: sorry, Mother o'mine, sorry, sorry. He ran wildly toward the porte cochère.

"Wait!" Dolly screamed. The tray slid from her lap and she raced after him. "Don't go, Boydie! You never stay! You never stay and talk to Mother!"

John and Harvey both were shouting, one to the servants, the other to his wife. Hjalmar! Dolly! Confusion boiled along the hall. Hara! Guardo! Dolly! Stop, all of you! Hold on! Stop him! Stop him!

A stiff breeze blew through the open door and Lew stalked into it, hands deep in his pockets, his shoulders hunched. There was a milling group on the driveway, gowns billowing in the wind.

Boyd had crawled behind the wheel in the station wagon and managed to lock the door. "Good-bye," he shouted, pawing the dashboard for the ignition key. Dolly shook the door handle, sobbing hysterically. John and Harvey kept getting in her way.

"Wait, Boydie, kiss Mother good-bye."

Lew, standing on the top step, sniffed an unmistakable aroma. Hjalmar, flushed by a recent nip of his own, dangled the car keys in his hand. He, too, was shouting, "I got 'em, Mr. Ives, I got 'em. He'll go nowhere! I got 'em."

A family affair, Lew thought. Mighty pretty. The sort of thing you saw sometimes in the corridor outside the domestic relations court. Ives mounted the steps clutching his toga and Lew asked coldly, "Did Dr. Wilson see much of this before he hit on that diagnosis?"

He left Ives open-mouthed. Damn. This, for sure, was the "negative milieu of the home." This was "personalities impinging on childhood memories" and no mistake. But you didn't need an expert to point it out;

any fool could see it. Hadn't Ives noticed that fixed look of fondness? How obtuse could people be?

He found Miss Lila in the library.

"Well," she said in her easy, patronizing manner, "and what can I do for you?"

"You can help me make it official," Lew snapped, and dictated his notice, as of January third. "I'll sign it when I come down."

He had wadded his pajamas into the suitcase when Ives came in. His gown, open at the front, revealed a tanned mound of stomach, thus indicating that togas for businessmen were impractical, after all.

"Sir," he growled, planting his fists on his hips and thrusting out his chin, "what do you mean by walking off from me?"

Lew said, carefully, "Dr. Wilson was right. You'd better call him back."

"You're not giving me an argument, surely?"

Lew banged shut the suitcase. "I can, if necessary. I just dictated a notice to Miss Lila. I'll move up the date, if you like. I can leave at once."

"Now, now, now! Everybody's upset this morning. That's what drunks can do to sober people."

"And vice-versa."

Ives tugged at his lips. And vice-versa, he mused and opened the attack from a new direction.

"Last Sunday," he said, backtracking, "Bill Derek, on our science page, had a story about a new drug, piromal. Why don't we try some, eh? If this boy of ours can get twelve hours' sleep, by-pass his hangover, I'm sure you can straighten him out. There must be a way. I put it in your hands. Try piromal."

He would go on forever, seeking a palliative, a miracle potion, some necromancy.

Lew sat on the window bench and talked quietly about Don Bell, and Ike Bashaw, and himself, and other dipsomaniacs he'd known. But the words failed to convey his meaning; Ives listened glumly, and finally said, "No hard and fast rules for anything, Lewis!" He spread his hands on his knees and got up. "I make you fully responsible." Then he added brusquely from the doorway, "My son, you owe me this."

That was putting it on the line, wasn't it, now? You owe me this. Lew listened to the receding slap of the slippers. The jug was sure as hell expensive, it sure as hell was. It was never paid for. The cost came out of the past, ran through the present, and raced ahead of you into the future. You pay and pay.

He went looking for Paula and found her comforting Harvey on a balcony beyond her own bedroom. After repeated failures to catch her eye, he finally whistled.

"Reno, Butch?" he asked, when she came out.

"I g-guess so."

"When?"

"Oh, I don't know." She glanced unhappily back at Harvey, who sat staring stonily out at the lake. "I can't go right now . . ."

"Why not?"

"Dad Copeland."

"What about him?"

Well, she said, Harvey Copeland had always been her friend; she had hunted and fished with him, and they'd been pals. He had begged her to stay, at least for a while. A day, two days; over the week-end, anyway.

"But you're coming back to work!"

There was longing in her eyes.

"Yes, Lew—as soon as I can."

"See here," he said, eagerly, "I've got a judge in my pocket. I can get you a divorce in Calumet City in an hour and a half. Desertion. Calumet City. Clean it up quick."

The suggestion startled her.

"Oh, no," she protested. "I'd like to get away, Lew—I'd much rather go to Reno."

Then, to his surprise, she was on tiptoe; warm lips briefly brushed against a corner of his mouth.

"You've helped."

He heard himself saying, "Hey, wait, Butch! Listen . . . " But she had gone back to the balcony. "See you, Lew!" she called. "And thanks—thanks *very* much."

As his knees buckled on the downward ramp he tried to recapture the flavor of that surprising moment. Well, well! She had kissed him. There had been something like a first kiss about it; he couldn't remember, now, who the girl had been, but long ago, back of the high-school auditorium after a play rehearsal one spring evening, he had kissed his first girl; the surprise and wonder and special delight of it had been with him for hours. Well, this was like that. Forty-two, and he had recaptured something. Recaptured? Hell, an improvement. Things were looking up.

He hummed his way down the hall. She'd come out of it, whatever it was she had felt for this charming bum; she'd emerge, intact, one fine day and this dizzy marriage would be last year's popular song. And then! Why, then they'd be married on a week-end late in December, and he would line up a job in London, or Paris, or Rome, or Japan. And they'd have two little kids, after all. He'd be a father. He'd be only forty-eight or nine when Johnny Marsh joined the Cub Scouts somewhere. A new young father, forty-eight or forty-nine.

Miss Lila was waiting for him in the library. The notice had been written on the electric typewriter and looked like print. Very official. Very final. He put it against the wall and scratched his signature.

But Miss Lila said, her thin face pert with superior knowledge, "Think you're leaving us, do you?" She produced her irritating little laugh. "Be sure to see Mr. Cuscaden this afternoon."

"Why?"

"Never mind. Just don't do anything foolish." She adjusted a pin in her piled-up hair and made his flesh crawl as she wiggled fingers, " 'Bye, now, Lewis."

Hjalmar sat at the wheel in his mackinaw, a stolid Nordic with a drunk asleep on his shoulder: Boyd, having agitated the household into a froth, was now content to catch forty winks and build up strength for his next endeavor. Dolly had gone—in hysterics, no doubt. Only Ives was waiting, the chill morning breeze tossing his ridiculous gown.

"Now, then," he said, winding up for another effort—never-say-die, that was John Cowper Ives. "I have one more suggestion, Lewis."

Afterward, in his soul searching, Lew would know that the tragedy had its beginning then, in the decision he made when Ives suggested taking Boyd to California, or Florida, or New York. He might have gone. There were to be six dull weeks until Paula came back from Nevada, and he was tempted. But you can't keep a cork under water, and he saw himself haunting the bars and night clubs in distant places, searching for a will o' the wisp, and in the end he prevailed on the Old Man to let him go back to Chicago. He said, "Oh, hell, Mr. Ives, now let's be honest. Let's face the facts. I'll take him to Chicago. . . ."

An icy north wind rippled the water, and the cattails in the low places had a frosty look in the morning sun. Boyd roused, sat up and gazed about with lively interest. They heard the recess bell in the white country schoolhouse, and saw children pouring onto the playground. Boyd bowed to them in solemn condescension, his fingers touching his forehead. He was Walter Mitty now, a visiting notable.

But the glow was fading. Before long he would need a nip from his flask, Lew was sure; there would be guile, and transparent strategy. How about a cup of coffee, gentlemen? he would say. Pardon me, old boy, but I must stop at the nearest gas station, if you don't mind. Or he might be more forthright: Cold this morning. I need a nip. Long ago Lew had tabulated the fat-headed counterfeit phrases of the drunk: Beer is food for me. I never touch a drop before five o'clock in the evening. I never drink more than one at noon. I can take it or leave it. I like a highball or two every night—it erases the day. Make it a double, I'm tired tonight. I never drink on Sunday. It's the soda that does the damage. Drink? Oh, well—one, just one, for my cold. . . . Wonderful phrases to delude the onlooker and lull the conscience. He'd been expert at it, himself. I'll have rye, he used to say, it's better for me.

By the time they reached the airport the frosty morning air had blown Walter Mitty out the window. Boyd managed to strike a gay note in his farewell to Hjalmar but his mind was somewhere else. The glow was gone. He furtively felt his pocket. His flask was still there. Then he covertly located the washroom—gentlemen to the right. When the clerk behind the counter said Mr. Ives's plane would not be ready for forty minutes he suggested:

"Like to look over the town while we're waiting? I'll watch the luggage."

"Just *take* the drink," Lew said. "That's simpler."

The Chicago papers were on a wire rack near the counter. Lew scanned them quickly to see if the opposition had beaten him anywhere. All was well. No exclusives except his own: Achilles-called-Kelly's battered face stared out dully from a page of his own paper, and the story was what he had expected it to be: stodgy, straightaway, written by a nightside commuter with his mind on a rose garden. But the paper looked all right. Good, in fact. He was proud of it. He turned to the *Tribune* for a more careful reading and Boyd sat down beside him.

"Go on, Boydie," Lew said, absently. "Take the nip. You're going to need it."

"The name is *Boyd*, I keep telling you—Boydie is a nursery endearment. '*Boyd*,' if you don't mind."

But the belligerence was gone.

He laid an overnight bag on its side, braced his cane on it, put his hands on the hook and lowered his chin. The grandiose manner had disappeared. He sighed.

"Sir, just why did you come up here?"

A clerk left the office. Nameless investigated interesting smells in the corner and lay down. A feature on page two of the *Tribune* looked like an exclusive and was momentarily disturbing until Lew remembered that he'd had the story. It had been rejected in council yesterday afternoon.

He said, turning a page, "John Ives has a crazy idea I might sober you up."

Boyd twisted the cane, darting a shrewd sidewise look. "Oh? What made him think you could?"

"Because I'm a drunk."

He sat up.

"Drunk now?"

"No."

"Drunk yesterday?"

"No."

There was a pause.

"Lately?"

"No."

He sighed.

"I see," he said, disappointed. "Reformed."

"No, retired."

The distinction struck him as irresistibly funny.

"Are you going to try?" He grinned as if the challenge intrigued him. "When do we start?"

The *Tribune* stories were all routine; Lew started through the *Sun-Times*.

"I passed up the chance, kid."

"Why?"

"Can't be done."

The clerk in the leather jacket came back for time sheets and went out again. An army trainer raced down the field and took off in an orange flash outside the window. The motors faded away in the sky.

"You could declaim," Boyd suggested amiably. "You could tell me what a famous composer I'd be—sober."

"Um."

"Or tell me how I'm breaking everybody's heart."

"Yes, indeed."

"You could describe the human kidney, and wet brain, and alcoholic psychosis and cirrhosis of the liver."

He managed the difficult words without stumbling and was openly pleased, repeating the sentence to make sure Lew had noticed, adding, "and delirium tremens."

Lew finished the *Sun-Times*, stacked the papers together, and hooked an arm over the back of the bench, crossing his legs.

"Like to hear what I told Mr. Ives just before we left?"

Boyd nodded eagerly.

"He tells me your mother thinks you drink because you're not happy. . ."

"She's right," Boyd said. "I'm a lonely figure."

"I told him happiness makes no difference whatever—not to a drunk. A drunk—when he's happy—drinks to celebrate his happiness. When sad, to drown his sorrow. When tired, to pick himself up. When excited, to quiet down. When ill, for his health. When healthy, because it can't hurt him. Drunks shouldn't drink. That's the hell of that."

"Witty," Boyd said.

Lew went on, "I told him you were a well-bred bum and your manners were pretty, and you couldn't do anybody much harm. I said that in my opinion your wife was well rid of you. I finally convinced him there was just one thing that would cure you, Boydie."

"What?"

"Death."

The cane slipped.

"Or the fear of it." Lew added, "That's what sobered me up. It comes with a whirring sound. You hear it in hospitals."

Boyd tapped the cane thoughtfully against the edge of his shoe.

"You don't like me?"

"No. Not a hell of a lot."

He spun the cane between his fingers like a juggler, balanced it, then put it head down on the overnight case, resting his chin on his hand, contorting his body. It was a ridiculous position, but he seemed to find ease in it.

"So what are you going to do?" he asked, at last.

"Go back to work."

A toe had cramped. Boyd got up, pressed his foot steadily against the floor, gritting his teeth. Eased, he sat down. But the cramp moved to the calf of his leg. He got up again and walked in a circle, stamping his foot.

"Ever have those?" he wondered.

"Oh, sure."

Finally, he sighed with relief. It was gone.

"Well," he said, very much interested, "what *did* you decide to do about me?"

"Nothing."

His lips parted.

"Nothing at all?"

"I said I'd bail you out when you got in trouble. I'll visit you in the hospital when they extract what's left of your kidney. In another few months, they'll be feeding you intravenously. I'll bring you flowers."

Boyd nodded. "That will be thoughtful. Books, too. I'm an omnivorous reader."

Taking a business card from his wallet, Lew wrote his home address and telephone number.

"I said I'd spring you when you get in jail—unless you kill somebody—and if you wake up some morning married to a whore, I'll get it annulled. I said you can drop in for a drink." He thought back. "I guess that's all."

"You could sort of keep an eye on me," Boyd hinted.

"How?"

He sat now with his elbows on his knees, suddenly depressed, staring moodily at the floor. Nameless sniffed at him curiously.

"What's the matter?" Lew asked.

"You are forcing me to drink alone," he said, defensively.

Great, wasn't it? The fat-headed counterfeit phrases. Put another on the list.

"Oh, hell," Lew said. "Come on—I'll buy you one."

5   The Muskie Tavern on a nearby side street looked promising enough. There were birch trees in the parkway and whitewashed stones along the drive. A large fish was outlined in slender neon tube, the name *Muskie Tavern* spelled out in Spencerian script. At night, with shining cars under the glowing sign, the music and laughter to greet you when you opened the door, it would have a festive atmosphere, but in the cold morning sunlight the half-logs of the facade were a shabby deception, and cigarette butts and match covers and dead leaves littered the walk. The drive had not yet been hosed down. Some convivial soul had been sick last evening in the comforting darkness, spilling out his gaiety on the brown grass beside the gravel pathway.

"Step over it, Boydie," Lew said.

It took a moment to accustom their eyes to the gloom. Nameless slapped his tail against the old upright piano and sniffed loudly in the shadows. Familiar fragrances. Homecoming. Lew felt a savage satisfaction. He hadn't been in a bar at ten o'clock in the morning for—for seven good years. He was beyond this, sure enough. The hot dry flash was still with him, but he could weather it; he was free and he had time now; that was what you discovered when you sobered up—time stretched like rubber—there was more and more of it; you had morning hours that had been lost in hangovers and hours in the evening that had once slipped away in senseless laughter. He looked around. He had never felt steadier.

The chairs were still upside down on the tables. The odor of yesterday's beer and this morning's disinfectant mingled into something more than an odor; it became an acrid taste in his mouth. A half-finished highball had been forgotten on the juke box. Disintegrating cigarette

66

butts floated dismally in it, like small dead fish. In a shadowy corner a shuffling figure pushed listlessly at a floor brush, moving scatterings of red sawdust toward a door—the bar's bum earning his morning drink. When the bum moved into the pale sunlight under the window they saw his matted gray hair, the stubble of beard, and caught the sour smell of him. He was an ancient in cracked shoes, with red-rimmed watery eyes. He went on sweeping.

"Dan's havin' his breakfast," he mumbled. "Ya gotta wait."

Lew caught up a dirty napkin and brushed off a leather-cushioned stool.

"If you can't wait, kid," he told Boyd, "take a belt from the flask." He jerked a thumb toward the bum and lowered his voice. "Don't look now, but there's a pal for you. *Salud*, Boydie!"

Through the open door Lew could see Dan, the bartender, at breakfast in the kitchen. He wore a clean white shirt and sat at a red-checked table, gustily eating ham and eggs.

"Hold your horses, fellas," he called with his mouth full. "Be there in a minute."

Dan supped coffee loudly from a white cup. He was a big man, ham-handed, with a hairy dark chest, and a look of vibrant health. He came strolling out a few minutes later, picking his teeth.

"Well, boys, what'll it be—here for the breakfast club, are ya? Name it." There was fleeting contempt as he peered closer. "Oh, Boyd. Hi. Straight Scotch?"

His big soft fingers took down two shot glasses. Lew put a bill on the bar and lined the glasses, rim to rim.

"Get the glow back, kid," he urged Boyd heartily. "Drink 'em both and there's more where that came from."

Boyd didn't move.

The bum was sweeping wistfully around the stools now. There was nothing to distinguish him from other bums, except his feet, which were enormous.

"Want a drink, *Feet?*" Lew asked.

The bum glanced nervously at Dan. The bartender reached for another shot glass and filled it not quite full. Feet leaned his broom carefully against a table and rubbed his fingers together.

"To your health, gentlemen!" he said, lifting his glass with a courtly gesture. "To your very good health."

He gulped noisily. Boyd tossed down two drinks in quick succession. Glow? He waited expectantly.

"Nothing for you, mister?"

"Not this morning," Lew said. "Fill 'em up."

The bum took his time, savoring this second windfall. He leaned his back against the bar, hooking the heel of one big shoe over the rail, and gave himself up to solid comfort, marshaling his credentials. There had been great days in his life, days of work and daring, of sobriety and success; he wouldn't want you to think he'd always been what he was now. Though he would never see you again some remnant of pride compelled him to bring out the tattered achievements. He studied Boyd uncertainly and finally fixed the rheumy eyes on Lew.

"Mister," he said, "I used to . . ."

"I know."

His open mouth revealed yellow, broken teeth.

"You didn't hear what I was going to say!" he protested.

"Sure I did. You used to. You don't now."

A great, choking laugh caught in the bum's throat; at his time of life, and in his condition, laughter was the safest reaction to insult. He slapped his knee.

"Hear that, Dan? Good, wasn't it? Yeap—that was real *witty.*" He nudged Boyd. "You heard it, partner? Ain't he a card, though!" He told it from the beginning to end; where he was standing, what he said, the flashing answer. He'd have to repeat it to Ole Hanson when Ole came. Remind him, Dan. Make a note of that one. It was real witty, when you got right down to it; quick as a wink.

Dan huffed a warm breath on a highball glass, held it up to the light, and rubbed in a circular motion with his white cloth. Lew pulled out a handful of change and went to the juke box.

"Ever see Ike Bashaw these days, Boyd?" Dan asked, curiously.

Lew looked back. Boyd was dropping pretzels into the mongrel's waiting mouth.

"I said," Dan repeated, "do you ever . . ."

"No, I don't, Dan."

Lew decided on a rumba. The nickel rattled into the metal throat, the records shifted, and the music began with a barbaric rattle of gourds. Jungle music. Great stuff at ten o'clock of a brisk Wisconsin morning.

"*I* see him, Dan," Lew said. "He works for me."

Dan held the glass to the light again, squinted, and gave it a final polish. Lew lounged with his elbows on the bar.

"Oh? Mr. Ives's paper?"

"That's right."

Boyd dropped three pretzels in quick succession. Nameless got them all.

"Why?" Lew asked.

"Oh, just wondered." Dan was watching Boyd.

68

Lew mused. "Ike came from this part of the country, did he?"

"Yeap. His daddy's still the best guide around here, ain't he, Boyd? You ever want to catch muskie you ask for Ted Bashaw."

There was something special in the bartender's manner, an undercurrent of contempt. He chuckled but his eyes were sharp.

"Remember the thirty-pounder you little fellas caught—that shrunk to twenty when we weighed it?" He laughed and explained to Lew, "Bet me five dollars, Boyd did. Paid it, too—right off. Always quick and easy with his money, Boyd was. Any little trouble and he could run four or five miles and phone Mr. Price."

Boyd took an experimental bite of the last pretzel in the dish, found it tasteless, and gave it to the dog.

"Yeap—always paid right up, Boyd did—even as a young fella. Shelled out his dough, I'll say that for him."

Finding himself excluded from the conversation, Feet, the bum, put his glass down with a gusty sigh. He waited a few seconds and moved reluctantly away with his broom. Inside the juke box the voice of a hot-blooded contralto chanted of love in Brazil. The gourds rattled. There was a monotonous backbeat of tom-toms. Nameless opened his jaws, snapped, and missed a fly.

Dan was polishing busily, smiling at a reminiscence.

"Them two kids was thick as thieves, wasn't you, Boyd? They sure lied good." He laughed again. "Once when they was young squirts they come in here with a pocketful of cash and ordered drinks. Remember that time, Boyd? Freddie Johnson was workin' for me then, and damn if they didn't convince Freddie they was twenty-one. I coulda lost my license."

Boyd left the stool abruptly.

"Shall we go?"

"The night before they'd swiped somebody's motorboat and run it on the rocks over to Baker Lake. Wild kids. No harm in 'em, you know—just wild."

"Tell me about it, Boydie," Lew said.

"Oh, he's probably forgotten," Dan said easily. "It's just one of them things a fella's apt to remember when he lives in the same town all his life."

"I paid for the boat," Boyd said, defiantly.

"Sure. Worked out fine for everybody. You paid for the boat and Ike faced the music. So Ike's back on the paper, is he, mister. How's he doing now?"

Boyd stretched out his hand to Dan in a stylized gesture that Lew thought had gone out with the market crash in '29—elbow raised, one

69

shoulder higher than the other, right foot forward, ready for the stock-broker's cordial grip. The aplomb was back—not what it had been, of course, but rapidly rounding out.

"Nice to've seen you again, Daniel," he said, with mannered warmth. "A pleasant encounter."

Then he shot his cuffs, pointed his cane and walked out. Lew turned to the ancient with the broom.

"What was it you used to do?" he asked, gently.

The bum said, turning away, "I was a lumberjack." He went on with his sweeping. "But that was long ago, so never mind."

"For the lumberjack," Lew said, putting a dollar bill on the bar. He found Boyd at the roadside. Very impressive in his well-fitting clothes. Very intact-looking. All put together now.

"Got the glow back, Boydie?"

Boyd tightly gripped his cane and raised it.

"I used to box at college," he said, furiously. "Call me *Boydie* once more and I'll let you have it."

"You *used* to box at college." Lew reached for his necktie and flipped it up. "Past tense, Boydie—like the bum in there."

Boyd looked away.

Nameless, intoxicated by the fresh air, loped joyously across the highway, barking at grasshoppers and Boyd, welcoming the diversion, whistled shrilly between his teeth. Lew walked on.

But with a quicksilver change of mood Boyd caught up to him and strode along at his side, whirling the cane.

"Beautiful morning, isn't it?" he asked, all unpleasantness forgotten. "A wonderful day!"

"Oh, sure. God's in his heaven. All's right with the world."

Now he was severing petals from the faded sunflowers with deft slashes of the cane.

"Tell me, what else did Uncle John say about me?"

"Nothing. We were talking about drunks in general."

About the ex-drunks on the rewrite battery who had made it, and others who had tried and failed. About men like Amos Dorrance on the copy desk who hadn't drawn a sober breath in fifteen years—nor missed a day's work. And about Pud Davis who couldn't handle a glass of beer. It had been a post-graduate course in the realities, most of which the Old Man wouldn't face.

"Lovely, lovely morning," Boyd repeated, slashing another sunflower. "Notice the tang in the air?"

And they'd discussed Freddie Wright of the rewrite battery, who once had submitted to a three-day revulsion treatment at a quick-cure joint on

South Clark Street. He had regained consciousness fifteen pounds lighter but no more cured than Gambrinus himself. Freddie hadn't wanted a drink right then—he was too weak to open his mouth—but he wasn't cured. He'd been brought up short later on by the angel feathers. There was no cure but a man's own decision. Lew had said it over and over again; he'd said it five times.

"Boyd?"

"Sir?"

"Want to try a thought in your muddled head?"

"Yes, *Señor?*"

"When you start dying, which won't be too damned much longer, send for me, will you?"

"But, of course," Boyd said, remembering. "And you'll bring me books. We'll read aloud."

The plane was waiting near the hangar with the landing steps in place. The tall work ladder was being wheeled away and the pilots, squatting under the wing, were playing mumblety-peg, like small boys.

"Tell me something about Ike Bashaw . . ." Lew began.

But Boyd was bowing to the pilots.

"*Señores,* if you'll excuse me, I shall go aboard and take a little nap." His fingers brushed the pocket where he kept the flask. "*Hasta la vista, mis amigos!*"

He went carefully up the steps and into the plane with the dog bounding after him.

"We can leave any time, boys," Lew said.

"Sorry," the pilot told him, wearily. "The Old Man called. The Cadillac is coming in with somebody else. We're to wait."

Paula? Lew strolled around the plane, across the field toward the road, and back again. The minutes dragged. Had Paula thought it over, decided Calumet City was more sensible after all? How could she comfort Harvey Copeland at this late date? The bands tightened pleasantly around his chest. It would be Paula in the Cadillac. It would be Butch, all right.

And it was, too.

He found himself running to meet her when the car swirled in with Harvey at the wheel.

"I've d-decided to go with you," she said, but couldn't trust herself to go on—to explain why. She took the steps two at a time, some sort of self-discipline: she didn't want to climb them at all.

Harvey squeezed Lew's arm companionably.

"Paula has always been a very sensible girl," he said, approvingly.

"That so?"

71

A fat, fatherly chuckle bubbled from his throat.

"I tell you, it was touch and go this morning. Why, she's the only woman in the world for Boyd." He trudged along at Lew's side toward the plane. "It's an ideal marriage—if you can only sober him up."

"Sure, sure."

At the steps Harvey warmly wrung his hand.

"I've talked her into giving Boyd another chance. So do what you can to help them both, Mr. Marsh. We'll all appreciate it."

The sky turned red.

Afterward, he couldn't remember if he had released the shout; perhaps the rage had caught in his throat. Proud of yourself, are you? You're quite the salesman, Harvey. Your drunken son has been whoring around all summer, so now you send Paula back to him! You're a great little guy. . . .

He remembered the startled face of a pilot and heard his own voice as he climbed the steps, "Let's get the hell out of here! Come on. Let's go!"

6   It hit you harder when you'd been away: Chicago was a dirty town. Refuse in the gutters, crumbling asphalt, faded billboards, tattered awnings. And the choking stink of the stockyards, carried today on a strong south wind. A dust storm skittered along the street and pedestrians shut their eyes or turned their backs to walk against it. No animation in the crowds, though sometimes Negro faces brightened at the sight of Charley, spruce and proud, at the wheel of the car. Charley had arrived at the airport with the top down, defying the gray, threatening September afternoon.

"Seems like you've been away a week, Mr. Lew," he said, driving languidly. He was watching Boyd and Paula in the rear-view mirror, trying to add things up. "Glad you're back."

You were aware of cops, too. Wherever he went in Chicago Lew encountered cops he had known as a young reporter. Now he recognized Jimmy Enders at a busy intersection. Officer Enders would go off duty soon and pick up a little extra money ushering customers to tables in a strip-tease clip joint on West Madison Street. In uniform, too.

"Hi, Lew," Enders said as they drove by. "Hi, Charley."

Bracing himself with one hand on Paula's shoulder, Boyd rose from his seat, and bowed to the policeman. Paula ducked her chin, and slumped lower in the seat.

She had started the trip with the determined cheerfulness of a practical nurse with a difficult patient, but at the airport the cork had popped and all her doubts returned.

On the flight from Minocqua, in some secret fashion—under observation the whole time—Boyd had recaptured the glow, and improved on it; he was first down the landing steps at the Municipal Airport, making a

73

dramatic visit to Chicago in Chesterfield and Homburg, bowing right and left. A crowd of bobby soxers, awaiting the arrival of a movie star, had mistakenly swarmed about him. With Paula looking on in tortured embarrassment, he had climbed a ramp to make an impassioned speech in heavily accented English, accepting the keys to the city on behalf of what he called his *gobierno*. When the delighted youngsters begged autographs he had signed: *Alvarez Obregón, assassinated July 17, 1928.*

Charley had been enchanted.

"Man, oh, man," he'd breathed. "Why, it's just like old times!"

It was, at that, if you had the stomach for it. Like the time Johnny Richards had invaded a hotel ballroom during a Rotary luncheon, presenting himself at the speakers' table as a Washington bureaucrat; or the Saturday Sid Cohen had made a coast-to-coast broadcast of an all-star game at Soldiers' Field, because a pal, the announcer, had been taken drunker than he was. The sort of performance that became legend in the better bistros.

Sid's performance had amused everyone who knew him—except his wife. The heroes of the bistros rarely amused their own wives. Wives were oddly humorless.

Angry and ashamed, Paula had said desperately, "Lew, please help me get him home. Let's get him out of sight."

She now sat as far from her husband as she could; head down, humiliated and apprehensive.

"No gaiety these days," Boyd complained, brightly. "No *joie de vivre!*"

Charley swung into Michigan Boulevard from Roosevelt Road and here a shifting wind blew pedestrians around the corner, swirled their dresses, or lifted their hats; a sheet of paper floated from an office window and glided in prolonged flight over their heads. Tires sang on the asphalt. Michigan Boulevard was cold.

"Brisk," Boyd said, digging into his pocket. "Brisk afternoon. Proper weather for a nip. Join me in a nip, my lovely?"

She didn't answer.

"Charley?" he invited, offering his flask.

"Sorry, Mr. Boyd," Charley said, but he was deeply flattered. "I had to give it up." And a moment later, he whispered, "He's a nice young fella, Mr. Lew. Might be we could cure him if we'd just be patient."

"You can have him."

Charley gripped the wheel and lifted himself an inch to see Paula's face in the mirror. Then there were quick sliding looks. Pursed lips. The frown. Very thoughtful now. Thinking of his friend Joby, no doubt— Joby and the bride. Quick on the uptake, Charley was. Nobody's fool.

74

"Yes, sir," he murmured, "I'll betcha I could cure him. I found out a coupla things I never told you, Mr. Lew. I got the *perfect* cure."

"Later," Lew said, sharply. "Later, Charley."

In a sudden, unnatural quiet on the avenue, with only the whisper of tires and the murmur of motors, Boyd burst into song. *"La Cucaracha"* floated out into the stillness in a rich baritone and a rumor seemed to run through the sidewalk crowds. When the car stopped for the light at an intersection they drew a straggling audience.

"Gracias, señores y señoritas!" Boyd acknowledged an uncertain patter of applause and climbed up on the seat back where all could see him. As they drove on he continued to accept imaginary plaudits with his condescending Walter Mitty salute.

"He probably forgets to *eat*," Charley muttered, intrigued by the problem. "Betcha I could put him to sleep with a roast-beef sandwich."

Two motor cops, recognizing Lew, ranged up beside them.

"Who've you got there, Mr. Marsh?"

Lew studied their thick, red necks.

"The late Alvaro Obregón," he told them solemnly. No glimmer from the cops. No humor in them.

"Want an escort?"

"No, thanks. He's traveling incognito." And he added, "Keep it to yourselves, boys, but he's drunk just now."

"Amigo," Boyd purred, as the motorcycles roared away, "for decades politicians have talked about the good-neighbor policy. Tonight we shall do something about it. You will dine with me?"

"Where?"

He bowed graciously to two startled old ladies on the curb.

"You, *Señor,* may toy with an enchilada while I enliven the occasion with a Mexican duet in which I sing a sort of backbeat."

"Who with?"

"With the Little Singer of San Juan Capistrano."

"Who's she?"

But now he was kissing the back of his glove to three stenographers in a second-floor window. Delightful *señoritas.* Provocative creatures you have here in *America del Norte. Hasta la vista, muchachas!*

"Who's the Little Singer of San Juan Capistrano?" Lew persisted. Paula, eyes still down, waited intently.

As though she were not there, Boyd said, "Of the earth, earthy, *Señor.* A product of Old *May-he-co*—slender of limb, warm of blood, delightful."

"Name?"

He boxed with the dog.

"I have offered her mine. Yes. I have offered her the protection of my exalted station. We harmonize beautifully together."

"When is the wedding, Boyd?" Paula asked, bitterly.

He blinked. Little alarm bells seemed to ring in his mind. With a drunk's transparent cleverness he diverted their attention, lifting a lordly hand to the cop at Dearborn.

"How's your pistol, officer?" he inquired pleasantly, as they drove by. Paula grimly adjusted her tam. There was no stuttering now.

"Be sure to send me an invitation," she said bitingly. "But let's get rid of the divorce first, shall we? I won't want alimony. And cruelty—will that do for grounds?"

Boyd recoiled with both hands at his heart.

"*Mea culpa, señora!*" he cried, sitting again beside her. "Have I said something to offend you?" An elfin appeal played over his face. "Let's dine together, and be friends," he said, "and I'll let you good people try to sober me up."

Paula drew breath to speak. Lew cut in sharply, "You're talking to the jug, you know."

Charley chimed in, "That's right, ma'am. It don't mean a thing!"

The car swung around the block and pulled up at the Ives Building, headed east. Paula was frankly crying now.

"I'm going upstairs a minute," Lew said, gently. "Want to wait?" She nodded.

"Want me to phone Harvey you've had enough, Butch?"

No answer.

"You can take still more, maybe?"

"P-please, Lew," she begged. "I'll handle it."

Boyd drew his knees up, whirled around in the seat, and lowered his head to her lap.

"Need forty winks," he told her, smiling up.

"You're a stinker, aren't you, Boydie?" Lew asked, getting out. "A born stinker."

"Tired, too," Boyd agreed, shading his eyes with his hat. "S-h-h-h-h, don't wake me."

Charley carefully closed the door and came around to join Lew at the curb. He was Uncle Tom again.

"What instructions, cap'n?" he asked.

"Keep him there."

"Don't look too good, though, a colored man wrestling around with a white man, if it should come to that."

"Then call a cop."

76

Julian was sitting on the edge of his desk, one arm through the sleeve of his trailing overcoat, promising the F.B.I. to make a speech to the police school in December. He looked washed out, tired; needed a haircut.

"Nice trip?" he asked when he had hung up. "Where's Paula?"

Lew told him. Raising the window, Julian looked down. Paula had moved to the front seat beside Charley, who was fussing with the radio. Alone in the back, Boyd toyed with an open, flat wallet which appeared to be full of colored knitting needles.

"What's that he's got?" Julian wondered.

"God knows," Lew said. "This has been nonsense from beginning to end."

Resting one foot on the low window sill he brought Julian up to date. The green dwarfs marched endlessly, around and around, and back into the cave. The running red letters still were promising good health. As he talked, he saw Boyd insert a knitting needle into the flask and bend over. Oh, sure. Not knitting needles, though. They were colored straws. Atta boy, Boydie. Nobody saw you, kid. Got away with it. Hold that glow.

"Mr. Ives expects some definite action, Lew," Julian was saying. "Thought of anything?"

Lew asked, without turning, "He wants me to move that bum into my own home, is that it?"

Julian didn't know quite how to phrase it.

"I quote," he said, embarrassed. "He thinks Paula would be agreeable to the experiment, and he'd appreciate it very much."

"Sorry."

"Well, it is asking a hell of a lot."

"Isn't it, though?"

Charley and Paula turned their heads to the radio, trying to hear a program over the beat of the traffic and Boyd had relaxed again—this time with his head on the dog.

"January third will be quite a day," Lew said. "Celebrate it with me? I'll buy you a lemon coke."

"You even wrote out notice, did you?" Julian asked, glumly.

"In black and white. I was kinda stirred up."

"Going to chase stories when your legs get tired?"

"I've heard that one, Mr. Cuscaden."

Julian tugged at a ravel on his coat sleeve.

"You're moving Ike Bashaw up to day assistant, I'm told."

"I guess so."

"He had a birthday hangover yesterday, as I presume you noticed. Did you mention that to Mr. Ives?"

"No."

Julian was thoughtful. He hadn't, either. And it was foolish of him. He knew where his bread was buttered.

"I gathered as much," he confessed, "so I didn't. Well . . ."

He started toward the door but felt around in his pockets as if he'd forgotten something. He hadn't—there was more to say. He returned to the desk, opened a bottom drawer and shuffled long-forgotten, dusty papers.

A clock over the entrance of the building across the way jerked its minute hand:

3:45. Cavanaughs, Homburgs and imported numbers were bobbing toward the station. These were the 3:45 felt hats. No limp crowns. No sweat stains. The hats of commuters who could say, "Take my calls, Miss Smith," and leave Chicago early. You would see cheaper hats on less successful heads a little later on. Lew spun his panama, waiting.

"Lew," Julian said, finally, "when Miss Lila worked downstairs I did her a favor once, and she hasn't forgotten. You're not to repeat this, understand?"

"Die first."

"She tips me off, sometimes."

"Does?"

"Don't do anything hasty about getting another job."

Lew turned around.

"Why not?"

"John Ives will give you a foreign assignment rather than lose you. Good night."

Lew let out a long breath as the door closed. Good old Julian. Not a bad sort after all, was he, now? This was nice to know: a foreign assignment. Fifteen weeks to go, and a foreign assignment! Things were looking up.

He savored the news a moment, and went on into the local room.

"Yes, Mr. Marsh?" Ike said, turning from his typewriter with extravagant courtesy as Lew stopped beside him. "Something on your mind?"

Ike had had time to recover. Eyes clear, hands steady. He had figured his severance pay, of course, and totaled his assets—that was the first thing you did with a hangover. Whatever he had saved might not be enough to see him through to another job; the courtesy masked his concern.

Let him worry, Lew thought. Let him sweat a minute.

"How's the family, Ike?"

"Okay," Ike said, bending a paper clip out of shape.

"The kids?"

"Oh, all right." He worked the clip into quite a tangle. "Colds. But they're okay."

He had three straw-haired children with rosy Nordic faces, two boys and a girl. One of them was named Lewis. Lewis Bell Bashaw. The boy would be eleven or twelve now. Same age as Johnny Marsh, the bilingual kid who might yet make his appearance, however late.

"Ike, this is none of my goddam business, but I'd like an answer."

Ike tossed the paper clip into the metal wastebasket and braced himself.

"Sounds serious."

"I covered for you at the Lodge this morning."

"Why?"

"You didn't toss away those fourteen months because it was your birthday," Lewis said, coldly. "You must have had a better reason. What was it?"

"What difference does it make?"

Lew lowered his voice.

"The next city editor has to be dependable," he said, grinning. "You know? Dependable, Ike? Like me."

Ike whistled softly, and untied a shoestring. Then, like a ballplayer stalling for time, he carefully tied it again.

"What about Sam Prisk?" he asked.

"What about him?"

"Oh."

Ike glanced across.

In his prim, busy fashion, Sam was being city editor for all he was worth. They could hear his clipped words into the phone. "Sam Prisk, city desk . . . I'm sending over a crew . . ."

Ike saw visions of a house in the country, and a maid, maybe—no sitter trouble—and a new car, so he could get away from Chicago week-ends; he saw college for his kids, and an annuity, and himself retired with fly pole and hip boots at sixty-five. The rosy future broke in on him; you could read it in his eyes.

"Well, Lew," he said, at last. "I guess the reason I got drunk that night was because my wife . . ."

In Ike's drinking days Sarah Orwin Bashaw had come to the cashier every Wednesday to pick up what was left of her husband's salary, usually with a child in her arms, and another hiding, big-eyed, behind her skirts. Everyone had liked her.

"What about Sarah?" Lew asked, narrowly.

And here was news. All these years, and he hadn't guessed.

"You ever lived with a jealous woman?" Ike asked quietly. "You can't cope with it. There was a girl—Thelma Briggs—who lived next door to me when I was a boy—I haven't seen her for years." He leaned forward with his elbows on his knees and huskily poured out the story of an old frustration. "Thelma's happily married—two or three kids, lives in Pittsburgh. There's no more romance between us than you'd have with a sister. But, damn it, is there anything wrong with *liking* a girl you've known all your life? Well, Sarah won't have it. Thelma sent me a necktie for my birthday and when Sarah found out I'd written Thelma a few letters, she threw a whing-ding. Next thing I knew I was drunk."

Oh, sure. You got back into a man's world with the gurgling of the jug; you erased the little woman, and grew hair on your chest. Free and manly for an hour.

You tried to explain, Ike went on, but whatever you said was twisted out of context and you found yourself with your back against the ropes, weaving and bobbing to escape a rain of verbal blows, a lot of them below the belt. There was no use talking to a jealous woman, no reason, no logic in her. You thought, oh, hell, I'll go to Abe Rouch's where everybody talks the same language.

"You know, Lew? You can take just so much, and something gives." Ike expected sympathy and understanding. He didn't get it.

"You're telling me you let Sarah get you down?" Lew asked slowly. "Is that it?"

"Well, sure, I . . ."

"Ike, you're still a drunk, making excuses and offering me alibis."

"Well, what do you do? In a case like this?"

"Kick her pretty ass," Lew said. "It's a man's world, pal—didn't you know?"

He pushed a chair aside and walked away. Sam Prisk, shirt sleeves neatly folded above his thin white elbows, stopped him as he passed the city desk.

"Nice trip? Here's a good feature for tomorrow. Don Bell wrote it. There's a horse out in Barrington that's actually forty-five years old. We've verified it."

Animal story.

"Oh, fine," Lew said. "Oh, fine, Sam."

He started on but Sam caught his arm.

"Have you heard? The President of Mexico flew here incognito. We're trying to find him. I just got a tip."

"Don't bother."

"Why not?"

"I started the rumor."

Lew grinned, and glanced out the window. Julian had reached the street now and stopped beside the car. Boyd was sitting up, and all four were chatting. A jolly little group. Someone must have said something amusing; they were laughing. Even Paula smiled.

Lew turned away and came face to face with Ike.

"You wouldn't have to worry about me," Ike said.

"Wouldn't?"

Ike made it firm, "No. You wouldn't, Lew. That's on the level."

Their eyes locked. Sarah Orwin Bashaw would have to grow up now, Lew decided; her husband just had. Didn't take long when it happened. In the tick of the second hand on your watch.

He led Ike to the window.

"Know them?" he asked, pointing down.

"Paula!" Ike breathed. "Why, there's Paula." He squinted. "And Boyd!" He wasn't concealing anything as he told Lew, warmly, "We were kids together. Nice guy."

"See much of him?"

"Not lately. He's a lush nowadays, I hear."

"He skips the hangovers."

"That bad, is it?"

"Object lesson," Lew said. Julian had left the car and was moving into the crowds. "Go down and keep Boyd interested, will you, Ike? I've got one more guy to see."

"Glad to."

Lew called to Sam Prisk, "Ike's going out for me, Sam."

Sam had rocked far back in his chair with his hands locked behind his head hoping to hear what they were saying. Poor Sam. He'd be back on the nightside tomorrow. Once again, he'd go home on the el at three o'clock in the morning, and explain to his wife that Ike Bashaw, another ex-drunk, had hurdled him at the desk. No reward for virtue in this hard world. No justice.

Lew thought: now's the time to smash these boys—as good a time as any. Keep the reputation fresh. Let 'em have it. He moved to the city desk, jolted Sam with the bad news, coldly bumped the day assistant back to the County Building, said, "Is that clear?" and turned away. He could feel their eyes burning into his back. An executive. Yes, indeed. An efficient, well-paid heel.

He moved down the corridor through murmured questions: Just get back? Nice trip, Lew? How was the Lodge? Typewriters clattered beyond the glass partitions. Literary editors. Drama critics. The church editor. The society department. Quieter, here. Leisurely. Journalism.

They even had their names on the glass panels in neat black letters. And here, too, was the council room. John Ives and the architects had dreamed out a room for weekly meetings of department heads: oak-paneled, book-lined walls, a fireplace, brass, copper, tooled leather. It had housed a single meeting of the department heads—the first and only. They had talked to each other in subdued voices until Julian asked, "What in hell are we doing *here*? I'm busy at my desk." Thus it was a well-nigh virgin meeting room, in every sense. When foreign-service men passed through town they hid their bottles behind the books; and during the Christmas holidays, when gift liquor bubbled up everywhere like mountain springs, the reporters sometimes kidnapped ink-stained stenographers from distant floors and cornered them in there; but some prude had had the couch removed, and the doors wouldn't lock, and the leaded windows, on a winter afternoon, gave the place a depressing, cloistered air. It hadn't turned out to be of much use for anything, not even assignations. The Chapel, the reporters called it. They would say, irreverently, when someone griped too much: tell you what to do, boy— go in the Chapel and say a little prayer.

Lew stopped before a glass door on which the letters proclaimed: "Hal Ortman—After Dark in Chicago." Ortman, a cadaverous young man with a touch of jaundice which he called his night-club tan, was hunched over his typewriter breathing hot fumes of burning shellac from a for-gotten cigarette on his desk.

"Hi, Lew? Nice trip?" He made a series of dots to emphasize an innuendo. "How's John?"

Hal knew everybody. He knew Harry and Tom and Bea and Gertie. He had even known Winnie. He had been in England during one of the wars.

"Hal," Lew asked, leaning in the doorway, "who's the Little Singer of San Juan Capistrano?"

Hal tilted back in his chair. He enjoyed answering questions. Once he had won a home-freezing unit on a radio quiz show because he knew so much trivia.

"Maria? Why, that's Maria de Diego."

"Good?"

"You mean talent? Fair. Good, no."

"Where do I find her?"

"Huarache Club. She made a hit last spring. She's playing a return engagement."

"Has she been in Cleveland lately, do you know?"

Hal considered. Yes, he knew that, too.

"In June. At the Patio Lounge."

"Anything else about her?"

"Just that I wouldn't touch her with a ten-foot pole."

"Why not?"

"She's Lenni Garr's girl."

"Again?" Lew invited, coming slowly into the room.

"Oh, sure. That hood's all hot and bothered. He quarried a big diamond for her. She can hardly lift her hand."

Lew spun around a chair and dropped into it.

Hal was asking, "Is there a story? I had a hint about 'em in the column but I didn't think it was worth much."

Lenni Garr's girl. Oh, fine. The town teemed with unattached little dames who had their noses pressed against Y.W.C.A. windows looking for anything in pants—but Boyd had picked out a gangster's mistress. Good, good.

"Lenni might even marry her." Hal was in prize-winning form this afternoon. "He wants her to be the mother of his kids. He divorced his wife, y'know. Yeah, got custody, remember? His wife was a tramp. He's a sucker for bums."

There were smoky-eyed skirts storming the public dance halls, all boy-crazy, and forlorn stenographers and lonely grass widows—all round of limb, warm of blood, eager and willing—but they wouldn't get you a gash in the head. He should have suspected. He was too old to be naive. Instinct should have warned him that this would be no ordinary croup kettle; this one was a Stanley Steamer.

"Is there a Boyd Copeland among the people you know, Hal?"

"Boyd? Why, sure. He's a talented amateur pianist. I heard him play some Debussy for Ernie Byfield, one night, just before Ernie died."

"He's playing for Maria de Diego these days, Ortman."

Hal's mind didn't work fast enough. Memory was all he had; information danced on the tip of his tongue, but he had no brain.

"Who says so?" he asked, vaguely worried. "I'd've heard of it if there was anything . . ."

"He got a beating in Cleveland. Lenni been to Cleveland lately?"

Hal sat up suddenly.

"Yeah, he was! Hey—wait a minute. *Boyd Copeland!* They're friends . . ."

"Of John's," Lew said, harshly. "John Ives."

A night-club columnist who tended to business would know who was squiring whom to the bright spots. When the dipsomaniac son of the Old Man's best friend stumbled into trouble, a night-club columnist worth his salt would pass the word along. You might not win a deep-freeze with it, but such information could do more for you than talent.

Hal said, nervously, "I don't see how I missed this!"

"Shall I tell you?" Lew let the chair legs touch the floor. "You squat in the Pump Room and the Buttery too much, maybe. You lap up too much free liquor in the better parts of town. You appear on too many TV programs." Then he snapped, "Get to Lenni Garr. Let him know we're interested in Copeland. Make it clear to the son-of-a-bitch. If he talks back, give me a ring. I'll be home."

He stopped at Bill Derek's desk. Bill, the science reporter, understood Einstein's theory of relativity and the hydrogen bomb. He was brilliant. He had been a Communist party-liner until Korea. Now he was lost and wrote long letters to Henry Wallace, who was also lost.

"What's piromal good for, Derek?"

"Powerful sedative," Derek said, sensing Lew's mood, and making it clipped and short. "Effective with alcoholics. You sleep away the hang-over."

"How long?"

"A day, two days."

"That's for me."

Lew turned to the switchboard. Lil Claussinius cracked her gum and listened brightly.

"Call Dr. Homer Waterfield," Lew said, and she looked sly and knowing. "He's to meet me right now in the lobby at 1360 Lake Shore Drive. Tell him to bring a quart of piromal and look surprised to see me. Make it clear—*surprised*."

Dr. Homer Waterfield's clinic was in a brownstone house on the near North Side. A large clientèle of rich hypochondriacs had brought him prosperity, but he was always happy to do little favors, on the cuff, for newspapermen: among his patients were women who really had something to worry about. The reporters knew it, and he knew they knew it.

Jed Brooks, the night managing editor, came through the swinging gates as Lew went out.

"Nice trip, Lew?"

Nice trip, Lew. Didn't they ever hear their own voices? Nice trip, Lew. How are you, Lew? Raining, Lew. Nice day, Lew. Windy. Cold. Cloudy, Lew. Skim a greeting off the top of the mind. Don't think, don't see, don't feel! Five o'clock shadows came a little early to darken his corner of the elevator as he went down. The only drink you don't take is the first one. It's not for you, boy, it's not for you.

7 The skies had darkened. A gentle, steady rain soaked into the dust in the gutters. Traffic was heavier. The nightly exodus had begun. Lew found Ike standing under the awning, collar up and hands in pockets, looking moodily toward the car. Charley had put the top up.

"Wow, he's fried," Ike said, sadly. "And what's that Spanish accent all about?"

"That? Why, love, Ike. You know? Love? He's courting Lenni Garr's favorite whore—a Mexican dame."

Ike gave a low whistle.

Hal Ortman hurried down the alley in a borrowed raincoat, one size too large. He was hell-bent for Abe Rouch's bar—to nerve himself up, no doubt. A quick one for courage.

"See you, Ike," Lew said, and ducked across to the curb. But as he slipped behind the wheel, traffic everywhere came to a throbbing halt. Bells clanged. Much unnecessary blaring of motor horns. The bridges lifted, one by one, as a Navy freighter, moving in from Lake Michigan, inched between the buildings. The city stopped.

Paula, beside Lew in the front, had started to speak when Boyd's bright face came between them.

"What now?" he asked, expectantly. "Tavern Club? Buttery? Saddle and Cycle? Where?"

"Now let's leave all that to Mr. Lew," Charley said soothingly in the back seat. "I was going to tell you about one time I served dinner to a bunch o' gourmies . . ."

The traffic edged forward once more.

"What took so long?" Paula asked.

"I had a couple of chores for Walter Mitty."

"Anything I should know?"

"Not now."

A tug blasted its throaty warning and along a parapet on Wacker Drive the freighter's brightly painted stacks glided slowly by.

"Did you find out who Maria is?"

"A tramp, Paula." Lew asked, pointedly, "When do you leave for Reno?"

Both gloved hands came up to shield her eyes.

"I j-just don't know," she said, unsteadily.

Charley, in the back seat, developed a theme in soothing cadences. Another practical psychologist was hard at work. Drunks were starving men, he knew. Suddenly, in the fog, you came upon your hunger. Then you ate ravenously. The blood left your tortured head, and you fell asleep. He talked about food in melodious, seductive phrases, and the effect was hypnotic. Boyd dozed off.

"He's a fine young fella," Charley whispered. "He *listens!*"

That was Charley's measure for a man: whether or not he listened. Colored people listened to each other, he had once pointed out. Many white folks didn't. White folks' minds were busy with what they were gonna say. But you watch on street corners out in Englewood, people chatting, and they were attentive to one another. He had long ago made estimates of Lew's friends in this fashion. Don Bell listened. Johnny Richards had listened more intently than anybody and he had liked Johnny best of all. In the early days he had insisted that Lew had been much too hasty in firing Johnny. A little more patience would have brought him around.

"We had a fine talk, waiting for you," Charley said. "Didn't we, ma'am? Mrs. Copeland and I, why, when we get to the apartment we're going to cook up some protein, vitamin food for Mr. Boyd. Yes, sir, I got a pretty good idea of what he needs: *red meat!*"

Lew pulled up at 1360 Lake Shore Drive. Under the long red canopy Dr. Homer Waterfield, with his little black bag, was waiting, ready to look surprised. An elaborately uniformed colored doorman materialized at the curb with an open umbrella. Charley called him by name, " 'Evening, Mr. Easter!" Charley said, respectfully, and you knew that somewhere on the South Side Mr. Easter was a man of substance.

"Why, Mr. Marsh!" Dr. Waterfield said. "And how have you been?" He was nervous. This was a croup kettle for the good doctor, too. Not a word said, but the pressures were on.

"You have a patient in the building, doctor?" Lew asked, drily.

The doctor cleared his throat.

"Why—yes."

86

"In a hurry, are you?"

"Why, no," he said, uncomfortably. "Not especially."

"Boydie," Lew suggested, avoiding Paula's puzzled gaze as he introduced them, "let's buy Dr. Waterfield a drink, shall we?"

The Duke of Alba couldn't have been more gracious. Jauntily twirling his keys Boyd led the way from the elevator on the thirteenth floor.

The entrance to the adjoining apartment was not ten feet away and there, in a bronze bracket on a blue-gray door, an engraved card read: "Mr. and Mrs. Harvey S. Copeland." Oh, fine. All cozy and intimate; mother o'mine and father o'mine right at hand.

"Dolly drops in often?" Lew asked, pleasantly.

"Guess," Paula said, smiling faintly.

Boyd bowed them in, charming the doctor, *"Está Vd. en su casa!"*

An oil painting of Mother o'mine, pretty as an April cover on a magazine, hung above the fireplace, dominating the spacious room. Dolly, pink and white and honey-colored, sat in a bower of roses with her lips parted as if to call: Boydie! Lew gave her a quick inspection, winced and turned away. Tall windows faced Lake Shore Drive. The Avenue, awash with gleaming lights in the gentle rain, curved gracefully northward. There was a sweeping view of sandy beaches with the lake beyond; white sails raced for harbor, far out. It was quiet here; homey, comfortable, and, if you stood with your back to the fireplace, in good taste. From the way she moved about as she took their things it was clear that Paula loved these rooms. Lew thought: it must have been a heady adventure to step from the tumult and tension of the local room into such surroundings. Well, she'd had it; and it hadn't worked out.

"What about piromal, Doc?" he asked, when they were alone. Paula had preceded Charley and Mr. Easter to the bedrooms with the luggage and Boyd was rattling ice trays in the bar. Furtively, Dr. Waterfield opened his bag and palmed a tiny vial.

"It's a remarkable drug," he said, nervously. "However, it's still experimental. Ah—the little lady. You've told her?"

"No."

"I don't really like to do this unless she . . ."

"For John Ives," Lew said.

Waterfield cleared his throat.

"Oh, well," he said, "if it's for Mr. Ives!"

Boyd called from the bar, "Join me, *señores?*"

It was no ordinary bar. Ship models in bottles. Chromium railings. Teakwood. Tubular stools. It had been decorated by Marshall Field & Company. On the day it was finished a riotous unveiling had left certain blemishes, Boyd said, explaining a crack in the glass front of the liquor cabinet.

"I invited people of varying backgrounds." He was busy with ice cubes. "My then wife . . ." he paused, thought it over, corrected himself, dropped a cube, and went on, "No, no—my *present* wife—Paula. Where was I? Oh, yes—she feared *my* friends mightn't blend with other people. But they came together like beaten eggs. In fact, quite a number stayed several days."

The room was further marred by trophies from his alcoholic safaris. Pictured in a battered advertising sign, a red-coated rider, taking a hurdle, conveyed the notion that good whisky made for good horsemanship. And thumb-tacked to the wall was an original colored photograph of a Man of Distinction, a hale, rugged fellow; he was a well-known actor who had once told Lew he had acquired a permanent tan lying drunk in the sun at Palm Springs. And in a Four Roses fish bowl, lighted from underneath, small, hungry guppies swam frantically behind the red lettering. Lew found a tin of food, dusted some over the water and the fish fought for it like diminutive trout. There were beer steins from Heidelberg and innumerable plastic bar spoons with "Pump Room" embossed in gilt letters. Nailed to the teakwood bar itself was a metal sign, reading: "Danger: Men Drinking!" And there were slot machines. And a juke box. The slot machines were old and battered—Lew could dimly remember when John Ives had spoken for them after a sheriff's raid—but the juke box was brand new. The polished plate on the front said: "Garr Music Corporation, Leonard Garr, President."

"How are you getting along with Lenni Garr these days?" Lew asked.

Their host had opened a fresh bottle of Scotch. He measured an exact jigger for the doctor's highball.

"*Señor,*" he said, with dignity, "I refuse to be intimidated by anybody." He squirted soda. Not too much.

"I presume Lenni gave you the juke box along with the gash in the head?" Lew asked.

No answer. He was preoccupied with a jolly business: two jiggers in the next one; his own. A mere whisper of soda. He scowled at Lew, "Nothing for you?"

"I've had mine."

Boyd explained to the doctor, "Señor Marsh is a celebrated ex-alcoholic, Doctor. They now use him for a good example." He gave Waterfield a highball and lifted his own. "*Salud!*"

Lew dropped a nickel in the box. Lights went on. Records shifted. A frantic, rhythmic rattling of pellets underscored a hurrying, catchy little tune. Nameless, ranging far and wide through the rooms, came scamper-

88

ing joyously into the bar at the sound of the music; he recognized the aroma of whisky and settled down; he was at home.

Then Mr. Easter went by in the hall. A distant door closed. Boyd, hearing Paula's approaching step, frowned until she appeared.

"Charley and I will be in the kitchen," she said, avoiding Boyd's unfriendly gaze. "Call me if you need anything."

"I'll be there in a minute," Lew told her.

She hesitated, looked unhappily at Boyd, and hurried out.

Waterfield's half-closed hand concealed the vial. *Now,* Lew thought. He leaned an elbow casually on the juke box.

"Boyd."

"*Señor?*"

Lew peered down at a list of song titles. "Come translate this Spanish for me, will you, please?"

Boyd was flattered. Spanish, he said, was the language of his heart. But he didn't leave his drink where Waterfield could reach it, as Lew had hoped he might; bringing it with him, he cried, "*Con mucho gusto!*" and glibly began reciting titles.

"Let me smell?" Lew asked, easing the highball from Boyd's fingers. Pretending fascinated interest in the titles, Lew moved the glass gradually around behind him. There were faint, repeated clicks as the emptying vial touched the rim.

The doctor, returning to his bar stool, forced innocence into his face and cried, "*Prosit!*"

"*Señor!*" Boyd brought his heels together, found Lew sniffing the drink, and took it back with a bow.

Lew said, encouragingly, "Wish I could join you."

"First today!" Boyd announced and downed it in five big swallows. But something was wrong. "*Caramba!*"

He smacked his lips. Wet them. Ran his tongue around inside his mouth. "Hm," he said, staring at the oily residue in the bottom. Greatly outraged, he emptied the contents of the Scotch bottle into the sink.

"No integrity," he lamented. "Eight dollars and ninety-seven cents a throw, *señores,* and no integrity at all. *Qué les parece?*"

As Boyd occupied himself mixing new drinks the doctor moved around to the corner of the bar where he could catch him when he fell.

The sweet-voiced singer chanted a patter lyric. Boyd sang with her, in his rich baritone, not missing a note, not slurring a syllable. In round Spanish phrases he toasted the doctor, and drank again. The rustle and rattle shuffled under the melody to a pattern climax. Boyd executed a few dance steps on the parquet floor. He was feeling fine.

A new record dropped. The singer chanted. The gourds rustled and rattled. Guitars twanged. Boyd went out, got a top hat, put it down, and danced around it: the Mexican hat dance. High over his head he held his glass and didn't spill a drop.

"Any time, now," the doctor whispered.

But nothing happened.

"*Dígame!*" Boyd asked the doctor, "*Está usted divirtiéndose?*" And translated, "Are you enjoying yourself?"

"*Sí, sí,*" said Waterfield, feeling his own drinks. "*Mucho, mucho, Señor. Bien. Bien.*"

Boyd approved of him.

"We'll have another!" he decided.

Three minutes. Five. Ten. No collapse. Records dropped. Pellets rattled. The catchy little tunes hurried on and on.

"This singer," Boyd said, first in Spanish, then translating, "is a dear, dear friend of mine with whom I sometimes sing duets well into the rosy dawn."

"Not bad," the doctor pronounced. "Not bad at all. Excellent."

Boyd was now conducting the orchestra. Lew whispered "*Piromal,* doctor? You're *sure?*"

The doctor was gay.

"Different effects on different people," he said out of the corner of his mouth and airly began to hum the tune.

"Well," Lew said, "you can start making notes for science."

The doctor pulled himself together, explaining his own drinking habits. His tongue was thickening. Now, gentlemen, he said, he rarely drank before six. Never touched a drop after dinner. Nor did he ever take more than one at lunch. Of course, he considered it improper to imbibe so much as a glass of wine before performing an operation. He was under compulsion to explain all this at considerable length.

Lew interrupted.

"When can you expect results, Doctor?"

"From what? Oh! Why—instantly!" the doctor said. "As a rule, instantly, Mr. Marsh. I looked it up. At once. I don't understand this." He pulled the string of his pince-nez, put his glasses on and peered at Boyd.

Boyd, warmed by the doctor's sudden interest, threw a friendly arm over his shoulder, his mind going back to an earlier remark: Maria de Diego was not bad. Indeed, not, Doctor! Bad? She was *terrífica!* Gifted. And yet of the earth—earthy. And, why, say! Why don't you join us for dinner, Doctor? Will you join us in a little while? A drink or two—the first today—and then meet Maria de Diego, of the earth, earthy—slender of limb, warm of blood, delightful. Maria never angrily locks her bedroom door, Doctor. Maria is a friendly, charming bum of a girl, Doctor.

You are too good for her, Doctor, as aren't we all? Too good, Doctor, too good, too good.

"You're repeating, Boydie," Lew said.

A warning was all he needed. He checked himself. No more repetitions, then. No more slurring. The alarm bells were ringing in his mind.

"I've a dinner engagement with friends, *señores*," he said, dismissing them with an air of urging them to stay. "Forgive me while I shower and change?" When they made no move to leave he played the perfect host. "Please make yourselves at home. I won't be long."

Blowing the juke box a kiss on his fingertips he whistled down the hall on a good straight line. Whistled beautifully, too—double notes, his own obbligato.

"Waterfield!" Lew blazed into the doctor's flushed face. "Didn't you give him *enough*?"

The doctor examined the empty vial, shook it, and said, thickly, "A dram, by George! Enough to fell an elephant!"

Boyd bounced "*La Golondrina*" against the walls of the shower stall. Scientific interest came into the mist in the doctor's mind and he pompously led the way into the bedroom. Boyd had hung up his clothes, racked his shoes, laid out his dinner coat and a handsome ebony cane. His watch had been placed at the apex of a geometric arrangement of other articles from his pockets: car keys, the wallet of colored straws, a fountain pen, a notebook and a silvery money-clip bulging with new bills of large denominations. Everything right at hand. Functioning at top speed. On his toes.

"Dear me!" Waterfield formed his words with care. "Our patient must have the constitution of an . . ." He reached out and found a wall. ". . . elephant. As for me, sir, I've had rather too stiff a jolt on an empty stomach. I'd like a breath of air."

Two cocktails were all he ever, *ever* drank, the good doctor said, making his way cautiously along the hall. He spotted a door leading to a little balcony over the alley and went out, opening his mouth to the fresh air. Lew left him there still explaining his drinking habits to the darkness. He never took a drop *after* dinner. And, certainly, never more than one apéritif at noon. And *six* o'clock was his cocktail hour, ordinarily. He rarely touched a drop of anything before six o'clock.

In the kitchen, Paula and Charley were working busily, side by side at the sink, preparing a culinary sedative. A thick steak from the deep-freeze had been put out to thaw; and Charley, in a barbecue apron, was whipping up a marinade. Chatting with Paula. Relaxed. Much at ease. Coffee had begun to perk on the stove.

"Come right in, Mr. Lew," he said. "I got good strong coffee coming up."

Paula brushed at her forehead with the back of her hand.

"What's going on in there?" she asked, uneasily, as Lew sat down on a corner of the kitchen table. "Where in the world did you dig up that doctor?"

But Charley interrupted. "Listen, folks!" he said, admiringly.

Something from *Rigoletto*, now. Boyd had moved into the bedroom and, from the sounds, he was hammering his chest as he sang.

"The doctor," Lew said, "was Uncle John's idea." He poured a bubbling cup of coffee and told them about piromal.

"But, Lew, is it *safe?*"

"Up to now," he said, returning to the table, "it's had no effect whatever. Boyd's fine. The doctor's plastered."

Paula disappeared for a moment and came back. "He's made of iron, that's all." She picked up a peeling knife and went back to work on a large Idaho potato. *Rigoletto*, under hammer blows, echoed still louder through the halls. "The things he does would k-kill other people. But, Lew, I think you might have. . ."

Another voice joined in the aria. Dr. Waterfield was a tenor if he was anything.

Paula jerked the peeling knife angrily along the potato and Charley held forth on the virtues of Vitamin B-1 and proteins. He wasn't in favor of drugs, he said. Nothing would knock out a gowed guy quicker'n a red beef sandwich. He was still talking when the singing abruptly stopped.

"*Lew!*" Paula cried and dropped the knife.

They found Boyd, his body still wet, lying naked across the foot of the bed. He had pillowed his damp head on his arms and drawn up his legs like a child.

"Don't worry," Dr. Waterfield intoned, counting a pulse. "The reaction is normal, Mrs. Copeland." He peered at them owlishly over his pince-nez. "Body chemistry, y'know. Different effects on different people."

Paula watched the arm fall limply and put her ear to Boyd's tanned chest. He was breathing quietly. As she drew the covers over him he stirred and the glassy eyes opened. "Maria, Maria," he murmured. *"Vamos á la cantina."*

Paula jerked her hand away.

"Thank you, Doctor," she said coolly, and the doctor, in elfin humor, hummed "Japanese Sandman."

"I'll finish the marinade for Miss Paula, anyhow," Charley said, gloomily, closing the bedroom door. More to himself, he added, "I sure wish they'd let *me* handle it. I've got some *theories*."

His back was stiff with disapproval as he stalked to the kitchen.

"Beautiful, beautiful rooms," the doctor said. He held his arms stiffly while Paula guided up his topcoat. "Are they not beautiful, Mr. Marsh?" he asked. "Beautiful, beautiful rooms." He searched around for his bag. "So often, in my profession, I see beautiful, beautiful rooms. And yet I meet so few happy people in them. Odd, isn't it? Isn't it odd?"

He hesitated in the doorway, rephrasing his drinking habits to Paula. One at noon, never more—except beer, of course. Beer was food for him. *I'll be damned,* Lew thought, *Waterfield's a lush.* There were long minutes of polite palaver before Paula could close the door.

"Lew," she said, angrily, leaning back against it, "I think you might have told me. Wasn't this drastic?"

She was wearing an apron, too. She thrust her hands deep in the wide pockets and spread her feet apart, in a fighting pose.

"I was right here," she said, hotly. "You could have asked me first. Why didn't you?"

He gently bumped her chin.

"Orders, Butch," he said.

He moved on to the phone, dialed the office and asked the night operator for the direct line to the Lodge. Paula sat on an arm of a love seat with her feet straight out, watching doubtfully.

"Ever hear the Mexican records in your own bar, Butch?" Lew asked as he waited for his connection.

"I never go in there," she said, shortly. "Why?"

"They're Maria's. Her name is on them." He heard the voice of the distant operator. He added, "And the fish are dying, pal. You really ought to tend the fish."

"Well, who *is* she?" Paula demanded. "Maria *who?*"

"De Diego," Lew said. "Lenni Garr's girl. She's a bargain. Along with Maria you get a good deep slash with a knife."

It became last year's popular song, that old love. Then you couldn't remember the tender moments, or why you had carried a torch, or how you had suffered. He told himself this when he saw the pain and worry in her eyes.

"Yes, Mr. Ives?" He straightened when he heard the Old Man's voice. "I'm at Paula's apartment." She listened intently as he explained, "Yes, sir, Lenni Garr . . ." This was Mr. Marsh again, doing things right. Yes, sir, I sent Ortman to warn him. Yes, I'll have a report tonight on his talk with Garr . . . No, I anticipate no trouble. No. Yes. No. Yes, Mr.

Ives. He wound up, "I'd suggest an ambulance at once, Mr. Ives. Let Boyd wake up in a hospital."

There was a consultation at the other end. Paula, at the window now, dully watched the endless headlights moving on the outer drive. Lew could hear Harvey's voice. And Dolly's. And Irene's. Waiting, he tried to guess what Paula might be thinking. Surely this would wind it up. A gangster's whore . . . This should be plenty. Hurt pride. And misery. A broken heart? That was nonsense, a broken heart. Work would mend it. You could sink into work. It could become a healing obsession; and the day would come when all this would be a distasteful memory, the worst of it forgotten. Gently does it, he thought. This is down near the end. Easy does it, now. Take your time.

He heard John Ives's rumbling voice approaching the phone. Then the Old Man was saying, "Lewis? Dolly wants you to do *nothing* until we all get there. Understand? We're flying down tomorrow."

And here, again, he would think later, the tragedy might have been averted. Dolly had fate in her bejeweled little hands.

"Right, Mr. Ives," he said, crisply, and waited for the receiver to click at the other end. But there was further consultation. Then Harvey came on.

"May we speak to our girl?" he asked.

Paula took the phone. Listened. Tried to speak, and couldn't. Her throat had closed.

"Good night, good night," she managed to say at last and put the receiver down.

Lew opened his arms. She came into them and her fists were clenched tightly at her breasts. He pressed spread fingers against her shoulder blades. She shook back her hair and looked up at him. She was thin, he thought. Done up. Exhausted. Thin.

"Damn, damn, damn," she said. "Oh, Lew!"

He allowed his fingers to stray gently through the curls at the nape of her neck. Her eyes were dry and bright. She was crying, inside.

"Want us to stay here with you, Paula?"

She slipped from his embrace and moved restlessly around the room. Wanted to run. Wanted to run sobbing in grief and anger. When she could trust herself, she said, "No, Lew, no, thanks. I'd much rather be alone."

8   The rain continued to fall quietly through the early evening but the wind, brushing the corners of the building with a tired sigh, gave promise of heavier rain to come. Lew sat before the fire thinking of Paula's weary resignation: No, Lew, I'd rather be alone. That was the word: alone. Boydie was away again. This time, though, you'd know where to find him: in bed. Felled, like an elephant; pegged down. Twenty-four, thirty-six, forty-eight hours. A relief to everybody.

A hurrying, catchy tune persisted in his mind as he skimmed an early chapter in a dog-eared manuscript. Charley had said, after dinner, "If you got nothing to do, well, why don't you work on the book?" The book. How many years had he been working on this book? And what for? These pages were not half a novel. They were nothing but an old bitterness brought painfully up to date; even the bitterness was fading out. The thinly disguised story of his marriage to Alice, a nice, humorless, devoted girl. Mish-mash, that's what it was; stream of consciousness.

And to hell with it!

The phone rang.

"Lew?" Ortman's voice was shrill. "I finally located Lenni at the Ajax. I told him what you said."

"Well?"

"He dead-panned it."

Big for their tailor-made britches, these second-generation gorillas. Give them a bank account and they thought they were citizens. Dead-panned it, had he? The murderous bastard.

"He talked back to me," Ortman said, sheepishly. "So I told him he'd better come to the office and see you. He promised he would."

"*When?*"

Hal hesitated. "Well," he said, and he was loth to repeat it, " 'When he gets around to it.' I told him he'd better get around to it at nine o'clock tomorrow morning."

"We'll do better than that," Lew snapped. "I'll do him quite an honor. I'll see him myself. Where is he?"

"He's left the Ajax but you'll find him at the Huarache Club around eleven. He gets there in time for the second floor show."

Lew glanced at the clock. An hour to kill.

"Right," he said, and banged up the receiver.

He would lay it on the line, and that would be a pleasure. Lenni Garr. You saw him at opening nights with his well-dressed pals, manicured and combed and shaved, trying to look human; a mild, suave little man, avid to be seen and admired, with a rat's alertness in his shuttered face. Nowadays he said, "Hi, Loo," with an edge of patronizing humor. He owned a factory on the South Side. Yes, indeed. A million-dollar operation. President, no less. Bankers spoke to him. Certain hotels and night clubs welcomed him. He had even tried to get into the Tavern Club. And had been turned down.

Charley appeared in the doorway.

"Mr. Sam Prisk, was it?"

"No."

Charley had been moody again. He looked pointedly at the neglected manuscript, flicked a rebuke with the polishing cloth and went into the dining room where he did a good job on the table, using both hands.

"What's the matter?" Lew asked.

The mood, until now, had been marked by monosyllabic answers and meticulous attention to duty. Charley decided to ease his mind.

"Don't seem right you didn't bring Mr. Boyd Copeland over here where *I* could work on him. I could cure a drunk, even if *you* can't."

Lew said, "First thing you know you'll talk too much about it."

"Make sense, though."

"But talk too much."

Charley withdrew. A freshet of rain struck the windows with a metallic sound; a few drops came down the chimney and hissed on the log.

The kitchen door swung open. This time Charley advanced on the dining room with the carpet sweeper. He tried to force it under the horizontal table-brace, failed, and got down on hands and knees to pick up a crumb.

"Look here," Lew's voice startled him, "are you thinking about your friend Joby?"

Charley sat back on his heels.

"No, *sir!*" he said, stoutly. "I was thinking about piromal from a plas-

96

tered doc. I wouldn'ta done it, Mr. Lew. No, sir, not me. I wouldn'ta wanted the *responsibility*."

"You can't reach a drunk's mind, Charley. You have to be rough."

"That's right, if you say so."

"You have to knock him out."

"If you say so, that's the way it is."

Charley pushed the sweeper in long, rhythmic motions. Suddenly, the wind whistled mournfully in the areaway and thunder rolled somewhere in the sky. Lightning, wind, rain, sleet—snow, too, probably. Chicago could give you weather in a package deal.

Lew rapped out, "Come on! What's eating you?"

Charley worked his way into the living room, dusting things at random. All steamed up tonight, wasn't he, now? Damned if it wasn't a little like living with Alice.

But there was no answer.

Lew reviewed his own pre-dinner behavior. The Yorkshire pudding had been slow to brown.

"Charley," he said, "I guess I was a little rough about the Yorkshire." He added, "But it took you so damned long."

Charley silently dusted a book and put it back. No doubt about it now: he was thinking of Joby, that perfect jewel.

"How'd you like Mrs. Copeland?" Lew asked, gravely.

Here was a nice surprise. He had liked her.

"*Fine!*" he said. "Yes, sir—there's a *lady!* I don't blame you for being fond of *her!*"

His face was honest.

"All right, then." Lew sat forward in his chair. "What's on your mind, then? Shoot. Let's have it."

Charley stalled.

"You'll take off," he predicted.

"Hell, I won't take off!"

"Give me your honor?"

Lew masked a smile. "Yes, I give you my honor."

Charley stood with his back to the mantel, scrubbing the toe of his right shoe against the carpet, deep in thought.

"Didn't hear the typewriter this whole last hour," he announced.

"No. Before you write a new chapter you have to think. A painful process, pal. You aren't sore about that?"

"Hm?" Charley said. "Oh, no." Then, not looking up, he asked, embarrassed, "Mr. Lew, you remember the first time I made a Baked Alaska?"

That one came in sideways, Lew thought. Leaning back, he locked his fingers around one knee.

"Big success. Sure. But what about it?"

"I haven't even *wanted* a drink since then. Not since my Baked Alaska."

"What's this?"

"That *did* it."

"Did what?"

"The final cure," he said. "*I'm cured!*"

"Well, this is great news." Lew was still bewildered. "What am I supposed to do?"

"You could be, too," Charley said, meeting his eye, briefly, "and then you wouldn't carry on and insult your good friends, like you did me, tonight, about the Yorkshire pudding, ranting and raving and all that crazy talk. That was nerves. I always forgive you because it's just screaming nerves. *I* know. But you could be cured."

"By helping Boyd, you mean? Is that it? Like Alcoholics Anonymous, is that what you're getting at?"

"No," Charley said. "Not you. You're a rugged individualist. Not you."

"Then what in hell are you trying to say?"

"I *said* you'd take off!"

"Damn it, I'm not taking off! But make it clear! I don't like double-talk."

"I'll make it clear."

"All right, then. Do it."

Charley bumped his shoulder blades against the mantel and fixed his attention on the far wall.

"Every night you come in, jittery, with the screaming meemies, and fight the old battle right up to dinner," he said, gravely. "Well, I used to, too. But I've been over it longer than you think. For six-eight months now I've had it licked completely. Since I made that Baked Alaska—why, I wouldn't *swallow* if you poured whisky right into my mouth. I'm completely cured."

Lew stared at him.

"I've missed the key, somewhere," he said, contritely. "Want to start again?"

"I've talked to Mr. Abe Rouch about it and he says I'm right. Mr. Abe Rouch says I've got it figured to a T."

"Abe?" Lew broke in, surprised. "When do you see Abe?"

"Oh, on my day off, sometimes. I jest drop in if I'm going by. He gives me a lemon coke, and we chat, in the back room. He likes to hear about you. His feelings are hurt that you don't drop in. Once he heard you went to the Ajax with the boys and had a coke there. He feels if you can go to the Ajax, why . . ."

"Don't get off the subject," Lew said. "What's this miracle cure, Charley? What is it? You've been babbling about it but you don't tell me anything."

"I'll tell you."

"I wish you would."

The night Charley had taken that Baked Alaska out of the oven—*baked* ice cream, he said, if you could imagine that!—why, there it was, perfect, with the ice cream firm and the egg whites brown and—well, a thing happened, inside him, in his heart, such a swelling of pride as he'd never known before. Egg whites had kept the heat from melting the ice cream as the book had promised. He had written the recipe down and tried it, taking a big chance because it was a party, and there were guests. But that wasn't all. The *book* had made a mistake; it hadn't said how *long* to cook the Baked Alaska. A most important item had been left out. He had read it sixteen—seventeen times, thinking he wasn't getting it, but the cookbook hadn't given the *time* anywhere—all the recipe said was: *nicely browned.* You had to use your own judgment. So he had. He'd guessed at it, holding his breath. And then he'd opened the oven door at precisely the proper second, and there it was: *perfect.* Wow! Man, oh, man! He had never heard such praise. Why, by the time he got back to the kitchen, after the tremendous success of the Baked Alaska, he knew he was as good a cook as you'd find on the near North Side. Or in Chicago. Or maybe in all of Illinois. Don't you see? An empty place inside him had been filled full with the praise he'd earned for something he, himself, had done. There on the kitchen shelf were the wine bottles and the brandy bottles and the Cointreau. But he didn't need a drink. He didn't even see the bottles now. Wherever he looked all he saw was that browned Baked Alaska.

"I'm beginning to catch on," Lew smiled. "What else?"

Charley stopped bumping.

"Mr. Lew—are you *afraid* to go to Abe's?"

The question struck with a delayed impact. Lew sat back to think it over.

He remembered the softness of a spring night at Abe Rouch's long ago. It had been a Monday night, along about sunset, and the bar was almost empty; the river sounds and the hum of the city came pleasantly through the screens. Don Bell and Ike had drifted in, then Sid, and some of the others. There had been hours of good talk and laughter. An affection for the men of his craft swept through him, gripping his throat. So many of them talked well, drunk or sober; so many abstracted more from

99

life than other people; so many wore an armor of cynicism but were sensitive, enthusiastic, kindly men at heart.

Afraid to go to Abe's?

"Yes," he said, at last. "What of it? Yes, I am."

"Mr. Lew, like you mentioned a while ago, I got a—a key from my Baked Alaska. Like you say—a key!"

"Let's have it."

Charley tightened his belt, and buttoned the jacket again.

"Well, when you do something you can be proud of, when you make things—like Mr. Bell's gadgets with his scroll saw—or collect first editions, like Mr. Sid Cohen, and find an old book that makes you proud—well, all of a sudden you've got a empty place filled up, and then you don't have to fight the booze all the time. That's the way *I* figger, anyhow. Then you're solid, Mr. Lew, you're easy in your mind."

Charley moved to the refectory table and idly riffled manuscript pages. His big gold ring glowed in the light from the fire.

"Well!" Lew said. "That was a great wind-up! You mean, a man should do something creative?"

"Yes, sir." Charley kept his back turned. "That's exactly what I mean —like a book, for instance."

"Charley," Lew said, "I've had a hell of a day and I'm going out. I haven't time to work tonight and I don't feel like it."

"I didn't mean just *tonight!*" Charley instantly protested. "It's all the time, more wound up, and edgier and edgier. I don't even care about Tahiti, if you'd stay here and calm down. Well, nothing's going to calm you down but doing a thing you can be proud of, like that book."

"All right, Charley, you've got a point."

"And while I'm talking," Charley said, facing him again, "if you should marry some mighty fine young lady—and, say, she didn't like me— which is her privilege—because—well, she might not want me around her kitchen—I'd understand that. I wouldn't be sore. If that happened, I'd leave happy, if you were cured. You treat me finer, except for some blowups, than any man, white or black, I ever met. I appreciate it. I'm your friend. But it hurts to see you, night after night, still going through it, when all you got to do is find yourself a Baked Alaska. And finish one little old easy book."

It was a long speech and it came from his heart.

"Not every night, Charley," Lew said.

"Damn near."

The wind made a last high protest and died away. The cold rain washed steadily against the windows. Charley stooped down and put another log on the fire.

"You took it real good," he said. "I'm proud of you, Mr. Lew."

The phone was ringing again.

"Well, you made it clear," Lew said, gently, and lifted the receiver. At first it sounded like Evelyn Southern, the night operator in the local room. The wind and rain had done something to the wires. But then, when he heard the girl's voice struggling with a troublesome consonant, he knew with shock that it was Paula.

"I went over to the Ambassador for the papers and I had a s-sandwich at the B-Buttery and when I came back B-Boyd was gone!"

"That's impossible!"

"Oh, no. He's gone. Easter says he took his car, the L-Lincoln, and wore his d-dinner jacket . . ."

"All right, Butch," Lew said, soothingly. "I know where he'll be." Piromal. Body chemistry. Different effect on different people. Fine, wasn't it? Great little drug. He found himself pawing through the dark hall closet, shouting, "Charley! Where in hell is my raincoat? *Charley!*"

But by the time Charley came, he had found a winter overcoat and put it on. He went out and slammed the door behind him.

Send for Mr. Marsh, he thought, *he does things right!*

In red light bulbs on the roof a Spanish dancer jerked her arms in the rain and clicked her silent, incandescent castanets. Lew drove splashing through the puddles into the parking lot. Nearby, under a motorport, a blue Lincoln convertible straddled two spaces, parked with its front bumper a good four feet from the wall, the luggage compartment awash in the downpour. Parked with infinite, alcoholic care.

A shivering Mexican in shawl and sou'wester handed Lew a damp claim check. Lew asked, "Mr. Copeland's Lincoln, I presume?"

"*Sí, sí!*" Chattering teeth flashed. "He is a gay one, isn't it so? You are his friend?"

"No."

Lew bent his head and ran into a wet wind. Shaking off his coat under the marquee, he studied a life-size tinted photograph of Maria de Diego. The Little Singer of San Juan Capistrano had a flat nose, a bedroom prettiness and dark, predatory eyes. No lady, of course. But warm of blood. Of the earth, earthy. Delightful. And dangerous. He moved through a shabby foyer into the smoke and music.

Sounds of eager scratching came from the other side of a Dutch door in the cloakroom. Nameless leaped high in the air and fell back sprawling, tangled in his leash.

Lew moved on.

Seventy-five tables crowded a room large enough for sixty; thirty-five people twirled like grunion in the moonlight, bumping and sweltering on a midget floor. The air was heavy with tobacco, Chanel Number 5, and the smell of bodies. A matronly woman, with bursting bosoms, stumbled on the steps in the semi-darkness. Lew caught her as she fell. Her fat arms were damp. He braced her against an upright and waited for her husband who arrived with tears in his eyes and a hot, strong breath, and conversation. He had income-tax trouble. It was killing him. He was as good as dead, a suicide. He was here tonight to get away from it, away from it all. Well, Lew thought, this is the way to fix it. Cry in your beer. That's how you solve the tax problem, old boy. With tears. That'll do it.

"Go home, Buster," Lew said.

At once the man was belligerent. "Whom do you think you're talking to?" he demanded, breathing straight bourbon. "Whom do you think you are?"

His wife clung to the upright.

"Oh, Willoughby," she begged, "come *on*! Mama's *tired*!"

Willoughby staggered away with a sullen glance over his shoulder.

Lew could see in the dark now. And there was Boyd at the piano on the bandstand. Near him, tilted comfortably back in a gilt chair, a Mexican pianist was taking a siesta. He had relinquished the keyboard to a better man. Boyd's fingers flew. Maybe the blend of piromal and Scotch had the same effect as marijuana. Make a note, doctors. Boyd was fine. Spruce in black tie and dinner coat, glowing with health. Much noise. Much gaiety. Much laughter. The massed dancers swayed on the tiny floor.

Pedro, the head waiter, tucked parchment menus under his arm.

"Señor Marsh! How nice to see you!"

Lew searched back in his mind to the week-end riots and remembered: Pedro Ceséna had been an eager beaver with a butter pat and ice pitcher, a busboy in the old College Inn. They shook hands.

"Pedro," Lew smiled. "There's going to be a business recession."

"How are you sure?"

"I'm taking Boyd Copeland home."

The Mexican sighed heavily.

"We shall miss him," he said, with humor.

"Lenni Garr here?"

"Not yet."

"Soon?"

"It is inevitable."

The number ended. The dancers squeezed and jostled back to their chairs. Light from tiny table lamps glowed on their moist faces. The women smudged lipstick on highball glasses, the men dusted ash into their chicken à la king. These were the things you saw when you were sober.

"Bought a juke box yet?" Lew asked.

Pedro shrugged.

"We have a new one in the men's lounge."

"That's good. It wouldn't do to get too quiet."

The Little Singer of San Juan Capistrano came into the spotlight. There was a patter of applause. Resting her spangled breasts on the piano, she gave the audience a smoky-eyed, seductive look. Boyd sauntered up beside her, swam down into her melting gaze and they sang. It wasn't bad.

"How long has this been going on?" Lew asked, curiously.

"Oh, this is special for tonight," Pedro explained, delighted. "Mr. Copeland sang with her in Cleveland, so she has told me. Now that she is back, he has promised to sing here regularly. Let us hope he remembers."

A remarkable character, Pedro said. Last spring Boyd had come often, sitting at a ringside table, all alone; at a late hour one night he had joined the orchestra, and conducted community singing. Sensational. One could not but like him. The musicians liked him, and the cooks and waiters and busboys. And the Little Singer of San Juan Capistrano, she liked him, too.

"And Lenni Garr?" Lew asked. "Does he?"

Pedro mopped the inside of his hands.

"But there has been no trouble here, Mr. Marsh. We run this high class. Very high class."

He darted away. A moment later Lew saw him escort Lenni Garr and two companions to the ringside. Boyd and Maria were singing that hurried, haunting little tune. Lew inched between the tables. He had recognized Lenni and Cully Yates, but not the other one, the one in tweeds.

He reached the table as Pedro hurried off. No gaiety here. No conversation. They were watching the bandstand.

"Gentlemen," Lew said.

Three polyglot faces looked up at him.

Nobody moved. This season, Lenni wore thick, honey-colored bifocals. And in his lapel was a ruptured duck. Like everybody else, he was a veteran. He belonged. And he wore tailored suits like everybody else. And had regular haircuts and manicures, like everybody else. He was a business man. Betcha.

"Well, well." Lenni decided to be witty. "If it isn't the Fourth Estate, second time tonight," he said in his queer, taut voice. "Hi-ya, Loo. Where you sitting?"

"Here."

Bumping a chair hard against Lenni's knee, Lew suggested, "Mooch over. Where's your manners, kid?" Lenni gave an inch. "More." The chair bumped again. "Let's be comfortable." Cully Yates hitched aside sheepishly. Lew sat down, saying, "Hear you boys have nice places out in River Forest. Regular gentlemen farmers." They didn't answer. The beautiful blending voices sang a patter lyric. The band was hot. The audience was hot. Corks popped. Gaiety everywhere, everywhere but here. "Cully," Lew said, "do you happen to know a Greek named Achilles, called Kelly?"

"Never heard of him."

Lew asked, "You know him, Lenni?"

"No."

"Got a beating and bought a juke box," Lew explained. "I thought you might have heard."

"Friend of yours?" asked Lenni.

"No," Lew said, "but he's got one somewhere. He was in the hospital. Some kind soul sent him flowers."

"What about it?"

"Just making conversation. It's my social sense, pal. I was brought up not to allow embarrassing little pauses."

Tweeds was suffering. Tweeds had been ignored; nobody had introduced him. He had credentials, too; he'd distinguished himself in some dark alley.

He, too, produced a voice: "I'm Kip Zunches."

He had won gold watches in amateur fights in his youth and the effort had taken the usual toll. Plastic surgery hadn't helped his nose, and a hundred punches had dulled his eyes forever. But he knew he was there, and wanted to join in.

"Kip Zunches," Lew mused. "Pretty name. Don't wonder you're proud of it."

Kip glowered. Nothing could be done to disguise Mr. Zunches as a businessman. He was what he was. Lew wondered what unprincipled tailor had made him a double-breasted suit of tweeds.

"Get my message, Lenni?" Lew folded his fingers on the table. "And was it clear?"

Lenni said, evenly, "You're out of your territory, Loo."

Feisty, wasn't he? Big for his pants.

"That's where you're wrong, Leonard. I'll make you a promise."

"Yeah. What?"

"If anything else happens to young Copeland I'll run you bastards right out of town."

Lenni's associates waited. They had confidence in him. It was his show. He didn't let them down.

"Listen, Fourth Estate," he said, in quiet fury, "I been pushed by you guys for the last time, see? I don't take lip from a cadger like Ortman in public or any place else."

"Oh? Where'd all this happen?"

"At the Ajax Bar, that's where," Lenni snapped. "Picked a good spot to work me over in public. Smart guy. Big newspaper guy. There's a limit to what you stinkers can get away with. You already passed it."

So that was it! Hal had nipped too much courage before he delivered his message. Got carried away. *I'm a hell of an executive*, Lew thought. A lousy executive. A good executive can get things done without doing them himself.

"So how've you been, otherwise, Leonard?" he asked, coldly.

"No complaint."

"Business okay?"

"Yeah. Elegant."

"You have charts and graphs, I suppose, just like anybody else?"

"Sure, a thriving, legitimate business. We know how to get out and push."

"Pushed many Greeks lately?"

Kip opened and closed his war-scarred fists. Cully took out a package of gum, extracted a stick, folded it into his mouth. Lenni's eyes devoured Maria on the bandstand. The second encore now. A little number called *"Mi Corazón Sólo Sigue un Camino."* Something about a one-way heart.

"Lenni," Lew said, pointedly, "you'll be pushing yourself in the can shortly. Think it over, palsy."

The smoke swirled in a storm of applause. Maria took three bows and kissed the audience good-bye on the heel of her palm. Boyd changed places with the pianist, tilted the chair, and dropped off into a siesta of his own. The gourds rattled and the strings twanged; the same thirty-five people, with a few added, jammed together on the floor, jiggling rhythmically, perspiring. Then, as Maria, in a sequin-spattered shawl, came toward them, Lenni's thin lips parted hungrily. The Little Singer of San Juan Capistrano bounced her breasts as she hopped between the tables and patted bald heads in passing.

"Hi, baby, hi!"

Lenni yearningly lifted his face. She kissed him with an open mouth, toyed with his ear and said, in a too-cute accent, "Sore at Maria, my Lenni? Please, no! Please."

Everybody moved politely and she snuggled down into a chair beside him. "Lenni, I could not help it—in public, you see? Tonight Señor Copeland—well, he turns up! So! What can I do? In public?"

The poor mug's in love, Lew was thinking as he watched Lenni's wandering hands. The spatulate fingers smoothed Maria's shawl, touched her thigh and explored under the table. She squealed in pretended delight. Nausea had attacked Kip and Cully. An involuntary exchange of glances said: bad business to have the boss in love with any little dame. They turned their pained eyes away as Lenni kissed her again.

Maria settled back, gave her breasts an uplift and twinkled her limpid eyes at Lew. He twinkled back.

"And who is our new frien'?" she asked, prettily.

"I'm Señor Copeland's bodyguard," Lew said bluntly. "I came to make it clear to these monkeys that one more pass at young Copeland and you'll all find yourselves living in old *May-he-co*—if you run fast enough." He turned to the heavy lover. "Or would you prefer the can, Leonard? You're a cinch for the can. Even the paid-off cops are kind of embarrassed you're still out, pal."

"Yeah?"

"Lenni—use your imagination," Lew snapped. "You must have *some* imagination, kid. Dig it up and use it."

"What on?"

"John Ives. He packs a hell of a wallop. And he wants Boyd healthy."

"Mr. Ives should keep the squirt home, then. It's wet out."

Lenni basked in Kip's relieved laughter; he adjusted the knot in his tie, and produced still another crusher. "He should keep his feet dry to stay healthy." In sudden rage, he grasped an ash tray and banged it repeatedly on the table.

"Now, listen to me, Fourth Estate," he snarled, "you kept my old man scared all his life. 'What's in the papers?' he'd say—worrying about us kids—about you guys, crucifying his whole family, so we couldn't get in any decent school. Well, it's different now, see? I got a country estate. I got my boy in St. Matthias, see? I'm a public-spirited citizen. I contribute big to politics. Yeah, bigger'n you think. I make campaign contributions—both parties. I'm impartial. I got my income taxes paid, even got a refund. I got all my employees on social security. I got a factory doing war work. I'm *in!* I got there."

"Yeah," Kip said, heartened by this sound behavior. "And we got another public service. Sonsabitches want their eardrums shattered with juke boxes and we accommodate 'em, don't we, Lenni?"

That was no ab lib. He was repeating one of Lenni's quips. No doubt it had got a big laugh when he first heard it. But tonight his timing was poor. Only Lew smiled.

"Great slogan." He suggested to Lenni, "Why not use it in your ads, pal?"

"You think this is humorous?" Lenni scoffed. "Listen—you guys got a racket just like anybody else. Ever pay to see a ball game? Or a first night? And what's your take at Christmas? Jees, the airs you guys put on and all you got is a racket. Listen, I pay for ball games, season box, see? I notice you at the Cubs' park with that nigger of yours. On passes. Last time I was at an opening I paid eight-eighty. *Each.* Six people. You had Annie Oakleys. And I don't *take* stuff at Christmas. I'm the guy that gives it."

"And I'm the guy that sends it back," Lew told him. "Up to now I haven't made you eat it."

Lenni hammered the table.

"The point is, I go first class." He twitched his hands in abortive, angry gestures. "I'm past the place I'm scared." Cully's eyes warned him and he lowered his voice. "I'm fat, Mister Marsh. And I got friends— V.I.P.'s. I know 'em intimately."

Kip admired the word. Intimately. His lips moved as he added it, temporarily, to his vocabulary.

"So," Lenni preened himself under Kip's uncritical regard, "you stay in your territory and I'll stay in mine, and everybody's gonna be happy. This is Chicago, Mr. Marsh. I know my way around Chicago."

Maria nodded her head firmly, and in her too-cute accent, said, "That is true. You listen to my Lenni."

"And Cleveland," Lew ignored her. "You know the alleys in Cleveland, too."

Lenni had been two-timed by his girl in Cleveland. Lew knew from the quick fear in Maria's eyes.

"Yeah," Lenni said, furiously, "and this'll show you what a panic I'm in, Fourth Estate." He leaned across, his face contorting. "I warned that drunk before he *went* to Cleveland. I got tired of warning him, clear back last June. So I and Kip went to Cleveland, also. And I don't give him any more warnings, see? How do you like that for frank and honest? You guys don't scare me. Not a goddam bit."

Lenni looked around the table with immense satisfaction. In Cleveland, he had been a cuckold, but his self-esteem was back. *That's telling him, isn't it? You heard me, Maria. If anybody wants to know what I told Lew Marsh, well, you were there. You can prove it.* He whistled at a waiter.

"Get some food here," he ordered. "We don't drink, we eat."

"That was a great speech, Leonard," Lew said. "It impressed the little lady. Now, get this into your thick hoodlum head and sleep on it. You make one more pass at Copeland and all twenty-eight floors of the Ives Building will fall on you. You'll be up to your ass in masonry. That's a promise, palsy. And we never break a promise. Now, be a good boy."

Smoke floated like a fog as he moved between the tables to the bandstand. Boyd was dozing now, with elbows on his knees, his head down. Lew shook him.

"We're going home, Boyd," he said, quietly.

No surprise. No question. Boyd was lost in time and space. Patting a yawn, he rose.

"You do not wish to hear me play, *Señor?*"

"When we get home."

He bowed. But then he prodded his temples.

"Sorry," he said. "I have invited guests for dinner."

"They couldn't make it, Boyd."

"Oh, too bad." All at once, he had trouble focusing. Something was creeping up on him. Piromal, or Huarache rot-gut. But he kept on a straight line to the check stand, asking over his shoulder, "No one ill, I trust?"

After collecting his coat and the dog he made a wide circle of the foyer, calling good night to startled strangers. And outside, when the cold air reached his lungs he was momentarily on top of the world again.

"I'll drive my own car. I can always drive. Drunk or sober. Never had an accident."

Stepping over puddles he meandered purposefully toward the Lincoln, twirling his keys. But Lew caught his arm, altered direction, and took him past the Lincoln to his own maroon convertible under the motorport. Boyd plopped down in the seat and poked the radio buttons until he found a musical program. As Lew backed the car out Boyd rolled down the window and leaned far out, staring at his Lincoln. A cog had slipped. Confusion in time and space.

"Isn't that *my* car?" he asked, puzzled. He studied the car keys in his hand. "That's odd, *Señor*—how did my car get there without these keys?"

All the way home, his tired brain wrestled with it, and when he'd worked it out, he said, gravely, "But, of *course!* We are in *your* car? How stupid of me! Do you suppose I am now approaching an alcoholic psychosis? How interesting that will be, *Señor,* is it not so?"

9   Washington Irving's *Legend of Sleepy Hollow* had a sedative effect on Charley and nightly he read a paragraph or two before he turned off his light. His fingers still marked his place in the book when he came from his bedroom in his pajamas and slippers; seeing Boyd he rushed off for his robe.

"Mr. Boyd, sir," he called, "I got a surprise for you out in the kitchen. Dutch beer and a snack." He beamed on Boyd as he looped the cord. "Come along."

"Dutch beer?"

"And a snack," said Charley.

"Beer is food for me," Boyd said, and followed Charley to the kitchen.

Lew heard them in animated chatter as he dialed the phone in the hall. Ah, what beer, Charley! And jest taste this roast beef, Mr. Boyd! Beer. Beef. It would be a contest.

Paula's voice said, anxiously, "Yes? Hello?"

"I've got Honey-Bun here at home with me, Butch," Lew told her. "Want him? Or shall I let Charley have him?"

He thought she hadn't heard. At last, she said, "Charley can certainly have him."

"You all right, Butch?"

"Yes."

"Except for what?"

"I've d-decided."

"Calumet City?"

"No, Reno."

"Calumet City is quicker," Lew protested. "Why stall around?"

She said, "Pardon me," cleared her throat, and then spoke too loudly.

"With Dolly coming, there's just no point in trying, Lew. And, anyhow, I can't stay in this apartment another day."

Charming place, though. Beautiful, beautiful. The ink-stained gals at the office envied her that greener field. Dreaming of some such cave they tapped their little fingers to the bone; it was the pumpkin and the coach and the glass slipper and the wand. But Paula couldn't stay there another day. Heigh-ho. You wanted it, you got it, you didn't want it: where to now?

"Butch," he said, "come six weeks, will you marry me?"

There was a brave attempt at lightness.

"That's the best offer I've had lately."

Damn, he thought. That office gag. He was forming phrases to lift it to a higher level when she asked, bitterly, "I suppose Boyd's still on his feet?"

"Oh, sure. Upright, but practically embalmed."

"Well, I—I just can't t-take any . . ." Her voice trailed away. "Thanks for everything, Lew."

Butch, he thought, hanging up, someday you'll try to remember what in hell Boyd *looked* like! Why, *sure*. Take Alice. He couldn't remember much about Alice, except the tiny mole on her neck, and the slow way she smiled. Her face was a blur in his memory; gone. All things end.

He turned off the lights in the living room, adjusted the night bulb in the bath, and moved on. Boyd, at the kitchen table, was wolfing a huge slice of roast beef, holding it dripping in his hands. His eyes kept fluttering.

"The man was half-starved!" Charley said, winking. "I've fixed him, good." He arched his secret smile. "Better'n piromal." Lew went along the hall to his bedroom as Charley followed.

"He's so gowed, Mr. Lew," he said, sadly. "So awful, awful gowed."

Lew snaked off his necktie.

"Put him on the living-room couch."

"Yes, sir," Charley said. "You see, all you *ever* need is patience, Mr. Lew." The rebuke was gentle, but he faced him with it. "I should think, all you went through, that time I helped—why, you should have a little patience."

"Mrs. Copeland just gave him to you." Lew hung his coat in the closet. "You can have him, Charley."

Charley bumped his shoulders against the doorjamb.

"And do all I can for him?" he asked, deeply pleased.

"All you can."

But he wanted the last word if he could manage it.

"All the time, your raincoat was in the closet plain as day," he said, his voice melodious with continuing rebuke. "All that was *nerves*, Mr. Lew. You didn't see it on account of nerves."

"Sorry if I took off, Charley."

"That's okay," he smiled. "There was only one picture fell when you slammed the door. Good night."

Sometime during the night the rain briefly changed to sleet and Lew roused from his pillow to hear the scattering icy pellets against the windows. Once, from far away, he heard the murmur of voices, Charley's voice. And Boyd's. And into his sleep came the sound of a door, opening and closing. He sat up on his elbow. Nameless was romping in the outer hall. Rain water was awash in the alley. The sky outside was black. He sank luxuriously into sleep again. . . .

The phone shrilled, awakening him with a jerk. He reached out blindly, located it, and cut it short.

"Yes?" he said, lifting his head uncomfortably.

It was Jim Gregg, on the lobster shift. His voice was faint.

"Lew?"

"Yes, Jim?"

A humming on the wire. Lew threw aside the covers and sat on the edge of the bed.

"Jim, I can hardly hear you."

"Brace yourself—I've got bad news."

Lew felt with his toes along the carpet until he found his slippers. The room was cold. Water ran in the wall pipes. Someone was in the shower stall. At four o'clock in the morning, someone was taking a shower.

"All right," Lew said. "What is it, Jim?"

"Here's the way it looks: a home-made bomb in a Lincoln outside the Huarache Club in Plymouth Court. Colored man in the car, Lew. I just talked to the City Press reporter. He says it's Charley—Charley Donahue from your address."

I'm not awake, Lew thought. *Now I'll begin to dream I've got a hangover. This is one of those dreams of being drunk.*

But the receiver was solid in his hands. His feet were in his slippers. He could hear the steady drip of rain as it fell in the areaway outside the open window. He could hear the water in the wall pipes. He was cold. He was awake.

"He is badly hurt?"

"He's dead, Lew."

But Charley's horn-rimmed glasses were on an open book beside his bed table. A hooded reading lamp glowed down on the white pillow on his bed. His pajamas and robe were there. And the fat pocket edition. In a group photograph on the bureau a thin Negro stood on a narrow, unpainted porch, his skinny arms around two little girls in pigtails. Lighter faces. Kinky hair skinned back. Charley's nieces. Imogene and Janie. Charley's brother, Fred. They loved Charley. They would cry.

Lew stood in Charley's doorway a moment longer. In the bathroom the shower was suddenly turned off. Boyd was humming *La Golondrina*.

Lew went back to his own room and picked up the receiver.

"Jim?" he said.

"Yes, Lew?"

He hung up.

God damn it to hell, he thought, *I felt worse about a broken bicycle.*

He had been a reporter too long. And an editor. He had delivered too many messages. Death was in the day's routine by now. Your husband is dead, madam. Your little girl was run over, madam. Have you a picture of your husband? A picture of your little girl? Maybe that explained this frightening lack of grief. Charley was dead. Okay. Everybody has to die. You go right on. You tick off Monday and Tuesday and Wednesday. Wednesday was done. Mark it off the calendar. This was Thursday. What the hell!

Once he had had a crying jag at Abe Rouch's. Yes, sir. In those days he'd had a great capacity for emotion. Easily touched. Very sentimental fellow.

He jerked open a bureau drawer.

"*Cómo está, amigo!* Chilly morning, *sí, Señor?* Shall we go for a drive? Charley's gone to get my car."

Boyd stood naked in the doorway, scrubbing his lean athlete's body with an oversize towel. An amiable drunk. Beautiful manners. Dolly Copeland's boy.

"When did Charley leave?" a voice asked.

"Sir? Oh, just now. Just went out the door."

What was the passage of time to a drunk?

Lew thought: *Now take that bicycle.*

He had been eleven years old—young enough, then, to feel a sense of loss. It had represented a supreme achievement: he had earned it himself. A blue bike, very shiny, a very glittering blue bike. He'd possessed it all one summer morning and never had he known such happiness. He'd gone sailing down the hill near his grandparents' house in Winnetka; walked up, coasted down again: undiminishing rapture, all morning long.

But he had left it for a moment in a neighbor's driveway.

And everything in the world had shattered. The sunlight shattered. And the summer morning. And his heart.

"Charley's dead, Boyd," he said, reaching into the closet for an old suit.

Lew could even remember where he'd bought the suit: in the basement of Carson, Pirie, Scott. A bargain. The stripes were too loud for the upstairs trade.

"An accident?" Boyd was saying, his mouth stupidly open. "In *my* car?"

Clean shorts. A dozen clean ironed shorts in the drawer. Charley had put them there. That ought to do it. Something would crack now. It would be a hell of a thing, wouldn't it, if the loss of a bicycle was the last thing in his life he would feel?

Boyd was crying. There were tears welling up in Boyd's eyes. The jug helped, of course. No end of emotion in the good old jug.

"Lew—wait for me," he sobbed. "I'll get dressed, Lew. Charley *wanted* to get my car for me. He'd never driven a Lincoln. He was afraid I'd wake you up, Lew. He'd always wanted to drive a Lincoln. Wait for me, Lew."

Wet, naked, crying, repeating and drunk.

Now, you see? Look, you see? The raincoat was *not* in the closet. Charley had been wrong about that. Charley could make mistakes, too, you know. He wasn't infallible. He could be as wrong as anybody.

While Nameless wagged and watched, Lew carefully laid coats and jackets over the back of the chair. He moved every hanger. It was not there. He put on his heavy overcoat for the second time. Then he closed the door behind him, pushing the button for the automatic elevator. The cables creaked loudly in the sleeping building.

In the lobby an old woman with her skirts pinned above her knees was mopping the marble floor.

"Good morning, sir," she said.

It was necessary to move four cars before he could get to his own. When he turned on the headlights, Boyd was in his path, trying to knot his dress tie. No coat. No hat.

Lew reached across and opened the door.

"You didn't see my raincoat anywhere?" he heard himself ask.

"No, no, I didn't, Lew."

"Get in."

Boyd got in carefully. Lew said, "It's funny about my raincoat. Charley said it was in the closet."

"I didn't see it."

"Well, it's funny about it. If Charley said it was in the closet it ought to be there."

"I didn't look in the closet."

"Well, I did. It wasn't there."

The streets were slippery. A newspaper truck skidded around the corner. There were scattered lights in the Loop buildings. They passed an all-night restaurant with steam on the windows. A bum or two walked through the rain. The city before dawn.

"What're you crying about?"

"I don't believe he's dead."

"What're you crying for then?"

"Oh, Jesus, Lew. If he *is* dead . . ."

"If he is dead, what?"

"I don't know, Lew. I just hope he isn't dead."

No Spanish dancer, now. No bright lights under the marquee. Water was deep in the gutters. Two police cars, with motors running, were pulled up at the curb, their radios chattering monotonously into the stillness. In the headlights from another car, a tow-wagon was jacking up the Lincoln. The hood was gone. There were ragged holes in the top. The glass in the windshield was a web of cracks. Boyd put both hands over his eyes.

Lew rolled down his window. Four policemen huddled on the sidewalk. Water ran down their necks.

"Where's the body?" Lew asked, and they peered at him. "Officer, where'd they take the body?"

"Emergency hospital, mister."

Another one said, "No, Dan. They moved it to the morgue."

A big cop came over rubbing his nose with the back of his leather glove. "Who are you?" Then he peered closer. "Oh, hi, Lew," he said. "This don't amount to much."

"What kind of a bomb?"

"Just a home-made gadget hooked up with the starter. We figger somebody laid a trap for a nigger car thief. We just got identification. It was Charley Natchitoches. Had a record as long as your arm."

Their big faces were huddled at the window. Lew heard his own voice saying, calmly, "That's the way you figure, is it?"

"Yeah, Lew."

Big, bland, thick-necked cops. They all contributed.

"Yeah. We're gonna check on him." And: "It's Boyd Copeland's car. He's a playboy." And: "It might be he knows some practical jokers." Another added: "We're just getting to work on it, Lew."

A voice, his own, said, "You aren't going to fumble this one, pals." It was the first time he had thought of Lenni Garr. "You're going to solve this one—so don't lose any of the pieces." Then he was shouting, "Don't mislay any of the evidence, you dumb bastards."

"What's eating *you?*" the cop demanded.

Lew jerked the gear shift and drove a block in low. He was thinking about the bicycle again. How he felt when he heard the wheels of the gravel truck smash over it. How it looked crumpled on the concrete ribbon of the driveway, with its twisted spokes and broken frame. There had been no saving it. There had been nothing left that anybody could use.

He knew every inch of the morgue. Once as a young reporter he had sauntered in eating a candy bar and found a dead policeman lying on a stretcher in the lobby. He'd been sensitive in those days. He had felt everything. It made him ill. He had retched.

Boyd tagged at his heels across the walk and stood politely aside in the office. Then they were moving down a corridor behind a uniform. The smells of formaldehyde caught their throats. Boyd gagged. The quiet, covered bodies frightened him. He held back.

The officer chewed a cold cigar.

"There he is, Mr. Marsh." He lifted the sheet. "A piece of metal came up through the floorboard and went right through his raincoat. It's in his heart, Doc says. We got the raincoat out there in the office. It has your name sewed in it."

There was a cut on Charley's cheek. And one in his forehead. His eyes were closed. But surprise was in his face, surprise and horror. His last thought hadn't gone yet. He was gone, but his last thought was there.

"Sure is a rainy night," the cop said, covering Charley's face again. "Letting up any?"

Lew followed the uniform down the aisle, through the door and into the office. Boyd, too, looked at the raincoat. There was a jagged, bloody rip along the front.

"You know," Lew heard his own voice in a normal, conversational tone, "I was looking for this coat tonight, Officer. It wasn't in the closet. It had me bothered. But now I understand. Charley wore it."

"We'll have to keep it until after the inquest, Mr. Marsh."

"Oh, sure," his voice said. "You do that. You keep it."

No sound but the car motor purring at the curb. No movement but the forgotten windshield wipers busily flicking.

"Lew," Boyd stopped him before he reached the car. He said, brokenly, "Lew, I don't know what to say . . ."

He didn't know what to say. Charley had a cut in his cheek and a splinter of metal inside him, in his heart. He was dead. He was on a slab. He was in a morgue. And Boyd didn't know what to say. I know what to say. I know many things to say, you worthless little son-of-a-bitch. We'll start with that. Many things to say, many things I can do. I

115

can begin by killing you, you harmless, polite, stupid little bastard. I could beat your goddam brains out. I could spatter them on the wet sidewalk and there would be another quiet dead body on a slab in the morgue.

He listened, with detachment, to the curses, watched curiously as his own fist smashed into the drunken face. That bomb was meant for you, not Charley. That was for you and Charley's dead. You killed Charley, you no-good drunken little son-of-a-bitch. Dolly's boy. Lew flushed his mind of obscenities, tasted them in his mouth, spewed them out. This happy drunk, the well-bred dipso who'd never do much harm— why, there was no fight in him, he wouldn't lift his arms.

Lew watched the head rocking and began to feel the sting against his open palm. Stayed on his feet, didn't he? Tough. Yes, indeed. Used to box at Princeton. Suddenly Boyd shuffled his feet, doubled his fists, and squared away. Then there was violent satisfaction in the onslaught. He beat him to his knees and hit him again and again. A body stretched out on the wet sidewalk and lay still. Better than piromal. Better than roast beef, Charley. He's asleep. We finally put him to sleep.

But part of his mind said: beating up a drunk. Senseless and cowardly, I'm a grade-A heel. But all drunks get beaten up. You choose somebody in a night club, or take a girl away from another drunk, or kill a friend. That's the whole idea. It's all in the name of fun. You get away. You get away.

Alone in the car at an intersection he tried desperately to remember where he had planned to go. The red light had stopped him. He stared at his hands. His knuckles were cut and bleeding. There was blood on his wrist and the sleeve of his shirt.

The signal changed. A flurry of wind and rain swept the dirty street. A heavy produce truck splashed past and crossed on the green light. Lew sat at the wheel watching the sweeping windshield wipers, studying the wet half-moons. The motor idled through four light changes. Couldn't remember where he had planned to go. Another truck went by. And another. Then it was as though a hand rested on his shoulder. Nobody there. *He's helpless, Mr. Lew.* The light turned red again. *He's a nice boy. He's a big-hearted young fella.* No traffic now. No cars were waiting. His mind was playing tricks on him, of course. *You got to be more patient, Mr. Lew. He listens, Mr. Lew.* The light turned green again.

The motor snarled and ran smoothly in reverse; he backed up a block, two blocks, three. Boyd sat on the curb, hunched over, his head on his arms. Muddy water swirled over the toes of his shoes. Lew opened the door.

"Get in."

But he missed his footing. An apologetic grimace brushed his battered lips. He caught himself, sank down in the seat and buried his face in a sleeve. Lew drove toward the Avenue.

Five-forty-five now. More cabs on the wide street, more lights in the hotel windows. Early tourists watched unfamiliar street signs through the sheets of rain. An Arizona license plate, far from home.

They drove silently south and presently the cars at the intersections were driven by Negroes and only Negroes were on the streets.

Boyd lowered his hands.

"Where are we going?"

"Charley had a family," Lew said. "That's where we're going, Boydie. To see Charley's family."

"Oh," Boyd said. "Oh, yes."

Lew's voice said, "You must tell Mother o'mine about this adventure. She'll be sympathetic. You can always count on Mother o'mine. Spill it to her. Cry in her lap."

He had forgotten the street number. He rolled quietly along between rows of sleeping brownstone houses.

"I—I'd like to do something for Charley's family," Boyd said.

"You have, kid. You did last night."

Charley's family. They lived right along here, in one of these brownstone houses. At Christmas time there would be wreaths in the window. They made a festival of Christmas. They were from Caddo Parish, in Louisiana. The sleepy old South. Fred Natchitoches could say "Caddo Parish" so that it became a place of romance with placid bayous and cypress trees and rich, lazy living. They were homesick for Caddo Parish.

Two tricycles, a rocking chair and a sagging lawn swing crowded the narrow porch. Lew stopped the car. Boyd got out, took a notebook from his pocket and wrote, stiff-fingered, with a ball-point pen.

"What are you doing?"

He managed his lips.

"Noting the address."

Lew heard him shuffling behind him on the walk. Breakfast smells were in the air, and lights in the windows, and voices. The old-fashioned doorbell clanged loudly and inside he heard a child's eager footsteps racing down the hall. Then a small hand struggled with a stubborn bolt. "It is, too, Mr. Lew!" a happy child shouted. "Let me alone, Imogene! It's Mr. Lew!"

Boyd spoke a second time before he made it clear. "I shall send them a generous check." Tears rolled down his cheeks and into the corners of his lips.

117

"Do that, Boydie," Lew approved, harshly. "Pay your way, kid. Always take care of these little expenses as you go along."

He looked down into scrubbed, welcoming faces. Pigtails. Ribbons. Nice, clean dresses. Imogene. Janie.

"'Morning, Mr. Lew," Imogene said, shyly. Then: "Mr. Lew! What's the matter? I'm sorry . . ."

On that morning in Winnetka he had raced around a corner of the neighbor's house, and around a fragrant lilac hedge, to find the driver of the gravel truck getting slowly out of his cab. Together they picked up the broken bike.

"I'm awful sorry, kid," the driver said, and the morning shattered.

10 The green dwarfs jerked steadily in the swift September darkness. The red letters ran around and around. Ike Bashaw, the new day assistant, hurried to the washroom, escaping from the desk a few minutes early. Sid Cohen went out: temperamental tonight—speaking to nobody. Travis Ashbourne, the apprentice, studied the bulletin board to see if he had won the fifty-dollar weekly award for the best reporting. He hadn't. He never would. The night staff, starched and shaved, was now arriving from the suburbs—returning reluctantly. Been away. Lew tossed a sheet of copy into the wire basket, reached for another and glanced at the clock: 4:40.

This is the night to go to Abe's, he thought. Yes, indeed. *Charley Donahue was murdered, Abe.* This was the night. This would be the test.

He worked numbly through the last pages of copy. From the open window to his right came the beat of increasing traffic. A fugitive breath of September escaped the monoxide fumes and drifted in, reminding him sharply of a boyhood evening in Winnetka, of wood smoke and Indian summer, and the snug room under the eaves in his grandparents' house. He had discovered the public library while he lived there and the third-floor room with its old Morris chair had been a sanctuary for his books and dreams. Looking down from that narrow window, he had tried to see into the future; in those days, he had thought the ultimate achievement would be to become an editor, as his dad had been. Well, here he was.

Bobby, the copy boy, hovered nearby.

"Mr. Cuscaden wants to see you before you go home."

"Okay."

Ike came back with red, clean hands.

"Quite a day," Ike said.

The floor around the new assistant city editor was littered with half-smoked butts. Ike's chair had been a hot seat since early morning. And this afternoon he'd had a run-in with a pal. Twice Sid Cohen had been told to rewrite a story.

"Oh, sure." Lew tossed a sheet of copy into the basket and penciled through the next. "You'll learn to like it, Ike, my boy."

Quite a day. Yes, indeed. Four o'clock phone call. Charley's body in the morgue. Smashing fists into a weeping, drunken face—quite a day. "I dented that croup kettle, Julian," he had said. Julian had been shocked.

"Where'd you leave him?" he'd asked anxiously. "Lew, where's Boyd?"

Charley was dead. Charley's two nieces were heartbroken youngsters; Charley's brother had been sick with grief. Tears had trickled through his warped black fingers as he sat with his shabby elbows on the fumed-oak dining table.

But Julian had worried about young Copeland.

"At my apartment, Mr. Cuscaden. I took him back so he could get his goddam dog."

"Where did he go then?"

"I haven't the faintest idea. I lost interest."

"You should have kept the boy with you. There'll be trouble."

Trouble? Charley was dead. Tough break, Lew, everybody was saying. Nice trip, Lew? That was yesterday. Tough break, Lew. That was today. The ex-drunks, one by one, invited him to dinner. Corner-of-the-mouth invitations had been issued all day long. Nice guys. Wonderful guys. Worried about him. Not Julian, though. Julian was worried about John Ives and repercussions. There was a notice on the bulletin board:

TO THE STAFF

Boyd Copeland, (son of Harvey S. Copeland,) intimate of Mr. John Ives, was seen early this morning on Scott Street with his mongrel dog. Any member of the staff encountering Boyd Copeland, or anyone who has seen him, report to me at once.

Julian Cuscaden,
Managing Editor.

This was journalism. Not what they taught the students at Northwestern, the bright, happy boys who tossed aside the cap and gown and turned up full of beans and knowledge, but journalism, nonetheless. It would be a feather to find young Copeland. Better than an exclusive; it would do more for you than talent. You'd be a star.

The red and green lights reflected on the desk now, shimmering, making a moving technicolor pool. The green dwarfs were inexhaustible, became brighter and busier as he became more tired. Nearly five. Nearly time for Sam. If Sam were ever late, this would be the night. Sam Prisk late tonight! The hot, dry flash.

He felt in his pocket for the telegram. It had come at noon. A boy had brought a paper carton of black coffee, and a yellow envelope. He read it again:

LEW I WILL STAY OVER IF I CAN HELP I AM HEARTSICK FOR YOU PAULA

He had wired back:

GO IF YOU CAN I WOULD

He hadn't phoned her. He was afraid she would say, "I'm sorry, Lew."

Ike was yawning. Nervous yawning. Stretching. Nervous stretching.

"Drag it," Lew said.

Ike got up at once.

"Where's the decompression chamber?" he asked, sardonically. "Aren't you ever afraid you'll get the bends?"

He gave his hat a rakish slant, threw his coat over his shoulders and went out alone. Lew looked after him: an executive now. He would often leave alone.

A copy boy stood at his elbow. This one was named Villegas. Pete Villegas. He had a face like a bulldog and some day he'd be good. Alert—jumped when you spoke. He dropped a new piece of copy on the desk and said, "Mr. Marsh?"

"Well?"

An odd note in Pete's voice. The round blue eyes were clouded. He sidled closer, started to speak, broke off in misery.

"Say it."

He blurted, "I'm awful sorry about Charley." He'd been nerving himself to these remarks since early morning. "We had long talks a coupla times while he was waiting for you downstairs. He gimme a knife once."

Lew's throat constricted.

"You'll do, Pete," he said, roughly. "You're okay, son."

Peter went away.

4:47 now. He was half down the page of copy before he thought: In Memoriam, Charley:

> . . . . the bomb that killed Donahue, crudely fashioned from a six-inch length of two-inch pipe, was filled with high velocity powder and wired to the car's battery. The police now believe it had been designed to frighten, injure or kill someone else. Boyd Copeland, clubman, 1360 Lake Shore Drive, owner of the demolished car, could not be located today for a statement.

He had no known enemies, according to Sgts. Bert Condaffer and Herman Swain of the Homicide Bureau, who reported that two other convertibles of similar style and color had been parked at the Huarache Club last evening. It is hoped their owners will come forward to aid the investigation. The inquest into Donahue's death will be held Saturday at 10 A.M.

Lew looked up to see Sam Prisk well into his strip-tease at the lockers: once again unwinding, unbuttoning, slipping off, folding things away. Neat as a pin.

"Too bad about Charley," Sam said, giving Lew's back an awkward, friendly pat. "What's back of it, do we know?"

"Oh, sure," Lew said. "Lenni Garr killed him."

He saw Hal Ortman coming nervously into the room.

"Got a theory, Hal?" he called.

A trace of color appeared under the columnist's night-club tan.

"Matter of fact, Lew—I have."

"What?"

"Kip Zunches."

"So? Why?"

"Well, Kip's punchy, y'know? Used to be a fighter. The way I see it he was buttering up to Lenni. Thought he'd scare Boyd off. A firecracker in a new Lincoln would be his idea of a practical joke. I don't think he meant to kill him—I figure he balled it up—put in too much powder. That's the way it looks to me."

Lew asked, harshly, "Have fun throwing your weight around at the Ajax last night, Ortman?"

Before the days of the union, Hal would have been fired this evening. But he was safe now. You didn't discharge a man who had built up twenty-two hundred dollars in severance pay: it would take an earthquake to dislodge him. His defenses were ready.

"You said to tell him off."

"Did I ask you to get an audience?"

"You didn't say not to."

"That's right. Overestimated you. My mistake."

When the silence had unnerved him, Ortman moved on across the room.

"This isn't much of a story for us," Lew told Sam bitterly. "The P.M.'s gave it all it was worth. A Negro killed in a clubman's convertible—a comedy of errors. We'll carry a straightaway follow."

He left the chair. But Sam didn't take it. He waited warily beside the desk.

"The roust is on, Sam," Lew said, putting on his suit coat. "I've talked to the Chief, the Sheriff, Homicide, State's Attorney—everybody. Lenni's going to get one hell of a pushing around. The works. Maybe I can get him killed."

Lenni hadn't been found. He was away. Yes, indeed. Out of town—on business. There was a coin-machine association convention in Indianapolis, maybe he'd high-tailed it there this morning. His secretary didn't know. But he'd be back. After the inquest he and his boys would come drifting into their favorite haunts. But they'd see cops. Honest cops. Crooked cops. They'd bump into cops in their dreams. Even the thick-necked, red-faced cops who took a little on the side would be tough now. Orders. From the top down. Tickets for speeding. For parking overtime. For spitting on the sidewalk. There were a million laws on the book. You broke a federal law if you didn't rip off the tax stamp on a package of cigarettes, if you failed to smash a whisky bottle; there were laws enough. For one hundred and fifty-seven years now legislatures had been passing laws; there were whole libraries full of books, all full of laws. There were so many laws, statutes, codes, ordinances you could drive a thick-skinned hoodlum to suicide. Lenni would get the treatment; the Ives Building would fall on him. It had been a promise. We never break a promise, Lenni.

"We'll pin that bombing on the bastard," Lew said, "but meanwhile it's the roust, Sam. Put that down as policy. Pass the word along. The roust is on."

He had been shouting.

He went into Julian's office.

"Want me?"

"You okay, Lew?"

"Certainly."

"Damnedest thing happened," Julian said. "Travis Ashbourne got into a cab downstairs and asked the driver if he'd seen Boyd Copeland. Travis says this driver was with Boyd all day. What d'you know, Lew? That boy's on his toes."

The boy wasn't on his toes. The boy was stupid. But maybe he could draw to an inside straight. It made no difference. Luck or brains, one as good as another.

Travis and a little square-shouldered Yellow Cab driver named Barney Youssetter came in a moment later. Travis was proud.

"I just happened to mention Boyd Copeland and his dog . . ."

"Sit down, son," Julian said, tenderly. "Sit over here, my boy." He handed the cab driver a dry cigar. Lew sat dully on the window sill, as Barney talked. Barney was loquacious and observant. He'd once sold a

123

story to a pulp magazine and had always wanted to be a newspaperman, himself.

"Get on with it," Lew said.

"Well, sir," Barney began. "I pick up this drunk at 8:30 A.M. on Scott Street, only then I don't know he's got the jits, see? He's kickin' it out, but to me he's just a drunk. He give me twenty bucks. That's just the start.

"He's been in a fight—really fixed up, with a mouse on his eye and his lips puffed and blood on his tux shirt and no collar. He's got a little old one-eyed dog with him and he says just go and roll around the park— Lincoln Park. I expect him to take nips like any drunk. Only he's not taking nips. He's kickin' it out—or trying to. He's off the booze, see?

"Well, inside an hour he's sitting on hot sparks with his legs twitching. He says—*stop!* So I stop. He pops out like crazy, flags down another hack and transfers the dog. This is a hacker named Joe and the drunk tells Joe he can't stand nothin' against him, like a dog leanin' against him. So Joe tails us—two cabs now, one for the dog. Joe's grinning from ear to ear. He got twenty, too.

"Well, from then on it's really something. We go to three Turkish baths—only the drunk don't stay long enough anywhere to take off his pants. And to some barber shops—only when we arrive the drunk don't go in. He keeps givin' us dough whenever we stop—fives, ten and all like that. We say you shouldn'ta done this but he says don't argue: voices drive him nuts.

"So we shuttle. Along about noon we're out in the country near the Des Plaines River when he lets out a yell and says he can't take it. If he don't have a drink he's gonna go off the track. So we rush him to a road-house. Well, sir, he don't go in the roadhouse, either. He runs around the parking lot maybe ten-twelve times like he's gonna blow up, like it's spontaneous combustion. Then he gives us each twenty, and says it's okay, he's quit drinkin'—and take him to Gary, Indiana. So we start. By now he's got the window down and he's leanin' out with his mouth open, drinkin' rain water. He begins to look screwy as a toad.

"Well, we go to a truckers' hangout near the mills at Gary. He don't wait for the hack to quit rollin' before he's up the steps and into this Gus's Place. Then it's old home week if I ever saw it. Gus and the truckers give him the big hello. The drunk tells 'em how he quit drinkin' in the middle of a snort in the shower this morning. They say that's fine and ast him to play the piano.

"This Gus has a big maple concert piano, looks like a million, all shined up and polished, with snapshots of this guy, in frames, on the wall. It seems this drunk give Gus the piano. He's rich as hell, see? Good story, huh? Anyhow, he's hot stuff there, damned if he ain't.

"They call him Mr. Doakes. Well, he sits down at the keyboard with the dog beside him and Gus says, impressive, 'Quiet, you guys!' and won't even draw a beer. So then it's quiet. Hushed, like a church.

"Mr. Doakes—what's his name, you say? Copeland? Well, Copeland lifts his hands like José Iturbi and comes slamming down on a discord. His fingers don't track, see? It's strictly booby-hatch, right from the start. The dog howls. There's sour notes and confusion until some guy lets out a laugh and Gus looks around like he's gonna kill somebody.

"'What you need's a drink, Mr. Doakes,' he says, kinda sad and disappointed, but Doakes don't take it—the poor, desperate bastard. He keeps tryin' to play until Gus himself can't stand it anymore and pushes a nickel in the juke box and turns it full blast. But it's not so much to drown him out—it's more, well, hell, it's embarrassing, see? It's sickening. Gus makes him a present of a bottle and a shot glass but the guy says, 'No, Gus, I quit.'

"And now he's cryin'.

"The truckers turn their backs. Joe and me, we can't look, neither. He cries how he quit because he killed a guy by accident—somebody borrowed his car, or something like that. Then—all of a sudden—he's sobbing like his mother died. He's gasping.

"Next thing he bolts out of there, him and the dog, and he tells us to get him to the Ives Building in Chicago. He gives us more dough, I forget how much—twenty, maybe, maybe it's another ten—and we get started.

"Well, it takes us hours. Three—four times he gets out and runs along the shoulder until he's winded—you never saw nothin' like it. Then he rides starin' at his hands. He can't play piano sober, see? But drunk he could play piano. He keeps chanting this, and he's shakin' like a tree fulla owls. He wants to die.

"Well, by now, I'm on his side, see? I want to help. So I lean back and talk to him, soothing, about how he's sure got plenty of the old moxie, and tomorrow it won't be so bad, and the next day'll be better than tomorrow. I laid it on heavy but it wasn't phony because—oh, I dunno—I had the guy with me all day, and not account of the dough but something—I dunno—the guy's got guts, see? He's likable.

"Well, he quiets down now. Never mind the Ives Building, he says, take him to 1360 Lake Shore. That's his home. I says, 'Who's gonna be there?' He says, 'Nobody.' I says how about the wife, has he got a wife? Yeah, he's got one. Where is she? Well, he don't know. He can't remember. He thinks she's away. Then after a coupla blocks he remembers she's up in Wisconsin. So, figurin' he shouldn't be alone, I say how about his folks, has he got folks? Yeah, he's got folks—only they're in Wisconsin, too; and he gets the twitches again.

"I tell him about a guy in the Sunday science section that floated around in some new drug and got past the jits and if he'd go to a hospital and get himself knocked out, I offer to sit with him until he falls asleep. It's pitiful, he's so grateful—lonesomest bastard I think I ever saw; it was like I was his oldest friend. 'That's it, Barney,' he says, movin' to the jump seat for maybe half a minute. 'Take me to Passavant!'

"So I wheel around and start for Passavant and so does Joe.

"Now, this shows what kind of a guy he is—in all that agony he thinks of the dog. Suddenly, he says—stop! So I stop. He's gotta leave the dog with Mr. Easter, the doorman at 1360. So we turn around and start back north once more. Joe, too.

"Well, sir, then a thing happens that makes you believe in miracles. We park at this classy apartment and in the middle of some kinda crazy business with Doakes pushin' out the dough, some to Easter for dog food and more to me and Joe—we each got twenty again—why, all at once a big chauffeur-driven job comes rollin' to the curb. And guess who's in it! It's his old man and old lady. Hot damn. Is that a relief!"

Lew left his place on the window sill.

Oh, fine! Dolly and Harvey, at the end of a long, hard day? Oh, sure. That would fix Boyd up. He'd be drunk again, of course, by this time.

"Did he run to the nearest bar, or what?" Lew asked, fascinated, pulling around a chair.

"No, no," Barney said, beaming. "His mom jumps out and grabs him and gives him a lovin'—she's cute as a bug, mink coat and jewelry—and keeps sayin', 'Oh, thank God, Boydie, it is only just a colored fella that got killed!'—and how she was sick-worried, and how she's gonna tuck him in—and nurse him and stuff like that. And his wife comes down from upstairs lookin' sad and sympathetic and beautiful and I take my hat off and say a prayer. You guys can laugh if you want, but when you're sick or in a jam it's a comfort to know you got a mother. I miss mine, God rest her soul."

"And how did you happen to come over here?" Julian asked, smiling fondly at Travis.

"Oh, I dunno," Barney said. "After I left 1360 I didn't get a fare and I just sort of come over this way. I read your paper every day and a few times I picked up reporters here and got in on real good ones. A murder once, and two suicides. So I pull up at the stand outside and the first fella that gets in asks me have I seen a drunk with a dog. Ain't this the damnedest thing? If I put it in a pulp story they wouldn't believe it, but I've seen coincidences like that in real life, plenty of times, and I probably could get away with it if I could write slick. But I can't write slick. I only got to eighth grade."

"Travis," Julian said, writing a voucher, "I want you to take this to the cashier for Mr.—for Barney. And here's fifty dollars for yourself. You're getting the award this week, son. That was excellent work, Travis, excellent work, my boy."

Julian ignored Lew's heavy sigh. He put in a call for Mr. Ives, and when he got him said quietly, proud of himself, "Mr. Ives, I thought you might like a fill-in on Boyd's activities during the day."

After he had hung up Julian sat for a moment with the fingers of both hands pressed into the pit of his stomach: nervous indigestion. He shook out a bromide.

"That's the fifth time I've talked to him this afternoon," he said, splashing water on the blotter as he poured. "This tragedy gave them a bad scare, Lew. It might have been Boyd, you know."

"I wish to Christ it had been."

"Now, Lew."

Julian drank before the tablet had quite dissolved and chewed the last of it.

"I had to get a ticket for Paula on the Reno plane for tonight," he went on. "The plane was full up. Sometimes I wonder what happens to people we bump off airplanes."

"Was this all you wanted to see me about?"

"No. Didn't I tell you?"

"What?"

"Oh. Mr. Ives is coming here. He said he's just leaving."

"Want me?"

"He might." Julian pressed his stomach again. Then, though the room was cool, he mopped his forehead with his handkerchief. "I wish you hadn't beaten up young Copeland. The boy's face was marked. They were afraid Garr had got to him again today."

"I get it," Lew said. "He does want to see me."

Julian grumbled.

"I either had to tell him—or lie to him. Sorry, Lew."

They sat in silence while the electric clock jerked away three minutes.

"Mr. Ives has always thought a lot of you, though. I don't think you'll hear too much about it. I explained how much Charley meant to you."

"Upset him?"

"Now, now. It was just one of those goddam things. Don't be bitter."

It was 5:45 now. Nothing worse than waiting. How much of his lifetime did a man spend waiting? How many years, if you added it up?

Some sixth sense warned Julian.

"He's in the building!" he said.

A kind of telepathic shock always preceded John Ives's arrival. Rumor sped along on telephone wires, echoed in the elevator shafts; the news would promptly reach remote places such as the washrooms and the building superintendent's oily domain underground. Even tired, indifferent charwomen would hear it, too: The Old Man's here!

Julian's phone rang sharply.

"Yes?" He listened, hung up and straightened his coat. "He wants me alone," he said. "Stick around."

Julian strolled calmly through the local room toward John Ives's private office, the picture of a man at ease. But he was dog-trotting inside.

Lew idled at the stairwell until he saw him hurrying back along the hallway from Ives's office.

"He's in a good mood, Lew. Anti-psychiatrist campaign." He waved a sheaf of papers. Didn't have to fire anybody. Just another crusade. Big relief. "We're going to blast psychiatrists out of the water. And I think he wants to talk to you about Charley. He feels very badly about it."

A happy man, Julian. Lew moved on.

Miss Lila had been weeping.

"You'll have to wait a moment," she said, brokenly, powdering her red nose. "He's on long distance now—we're going to Washington tonight."

"What's the matter with you? Hard day or hay fever?"

She bit her lip. "Oh, Lewis! Isn't it just *crushing* when Mr. Ives gets angry?"

"Who's he mad at?"

"Me. We're going to Washington tonight and I asked if I couldn't stay home just this once, because I hate flying. I *hate* it. I feel sick all the time but I never let him know. So I asked if I could stay, and that made him angry, and then he found a mistake in a memo, and he's been brutally uncivil ever since."

The dictograph light flashed. Ives's voice said, crisply, "Send me Lewis Marsh."

The light went out.

"You see?" Miss Lila pressed her handkerchief against her eyes. "Not even *please!*"

Hand outstretched, the Old Man came around his desk. He wore a dark business suit with a knitted tie and a wide-collared shirt with long tabs. No toga. He kept his togas for Wisconsin.

"My boy! That was a shocking affair last night. I'm taking care of the funeral expenses."

"I've already done it, thanks. And Boyd gave the family a check."

"But I don't want you paying for the funeral. I can afford it."

"So can I."

Ives pursed his lips and raised himself to his toes.

"Oh, I see," he said.

There was a momentary outthrust of his chin as he returned to his chair.

His personal checkbook, with "John Cowper Ives" in bold letters on each check, lay open on his desk. There were odd, unlikely people from coast to coast, misfits he had encountered in his travels, to whom he sent money and instructive books and pamphlets—treatises on yogurt culture and farming, or bee-keeping, or sheep-raising. This, apparently, was his night to write checks. He searched through a little stack of envelopes, found one, and carefully tore it up.

"Yes, yes," he said. "A shocking, disgraceful thing. I'm going to do an editorial on hoodlums called 'Aborigines in the Suburbs.' How's that?" He didn't wait for an answer. "Why weren't we warned, eh? Didn't Ortman know about Boyd and this Maria de Diego?"

"No. He hasn't been making that end of town."

Ives sealed a letter, running the flap back and forth over his tongue, giving it a good wetting.

"I'll speak to Mr. Cuscaden," he said. "We'll fire Ortman."

"Fine." Lew added, "He's built up twenty-two hundred in severance."

"How much?" Mr. Ives held an envelope at his lips. "Twenty-two hundred!" He slammed his open palm on the flap. "Oh, well, that's different. Give him a stiff warning. Bawl him out."

"I have."

"Sit down, sit down!" He pointed smilingly at one of the leather chairs. "Lots to talk about. No hurry, are you? Any engagement?"

"No, sir."

"Good. You moved Bashaw up, I understand? Will he do?"

"Hope so."

"You know," Ives said, busy with his checks, "when Ike was a small-fry, he showed great strength of character at a church once, in Minocqua. My wife was teaching Sunday School there, summers, and I'd gone all-out on the temperance thing—this was when I still thought Prohibition might work." He slammed his palm on another letter. "The churches had a fellow going around, a broken-down preacher, getting boys' Sunday School classes to sign a pledge, the Lincoln Pledge, not to take a drink. You know—on your honor? A very solemn thing."

He kept occupied, licking envelopes, sealing them and slamming them against the desk. There was about him something to warm your heart;

129

his complete unself-consciousness, maybe—his vitality. Lew drifted into an almost hypnotic spell.

"Well," Ives was saying, "the most terrific pressures were put on those kids. Mothers, fathers, Scout leaders, the preacher, everybody—they made it crystal clear that a boy was a heel, a no-good and a bum, if he didn't sign. Yes, *sir*! The town was inundated by a wave of righteousness. One Sunday every youngster in church marched up front like little men and dutifully signed the Lincoln Pledge. Boyd Copeland, Tommy Beeker's boys—the Sears, Roebuck Beekers—Herb Pratt's boys—all of 'em." He paused dramatically. "All—all but one."

Lew waited.

"*Yes*, sir." Ives pointed vaguely north. "Young Ike Bashaw, twelve years old or so, stood up there in that church and, in his high choir soprano, said he liked a glass of needle beer with his dad on hot summer days, after fishing, and he wouldn't sign on his honor—his honor was an important thing, he said—and he advised the other boys not to sign, either." Ives threw back his head, roaring at the memory. "I was furious with him. I sat there raging while he made his speech. He told those kids when they got older they'd like a glass of beer, sometimes, and they'd take it, and there would be their honor all shot to hell."

"He said 'shot to hell'?"

"He did, indeed. Yes, sir—*in church*. Well, you never heard such a rinky-dink. Dolly Copeland marched Boyd home and said he was never to play with Ike again—he didn't, either, and they'd been fast friends—it was quite a blow to Boyd—and overnight young Ike Bashaw turned into the pariah of Minocqua." He leaned back, chuckling. "Well, sir, a couple of years later, when Irene took an interest in him—Ike was doing odd jobs around the Lodge, y'know—I told her, certainly send him to Cuscaden. By then I had decided any kid with that much iron in his back might make me a good city editor some day." He slammed another letter. "That's why I'm interested in him, y'see, Lewis? A man shows what he is from the time he's born and that boy had the first requisite of good citizenship: conviction and the courage that goes with it. The priceless ingredients in a republic." He was about to make a note. There was an idea for an editorial which would offend nobody; and now and again you needed a few of those. He clicked the dictograph. "Remind me—editorial—conviction and courage—Ike Bashaw." He snapped the key closed. "Well, Lewis, I hear the roust is on."

"That's right."

"Tell you what I figure," Ives said. "If we can, we'll get Garr on a murder charge. Failing that, we'll nudge the grand jury on the juke-box racket. And while we're doing that, you can have the authorities roust him around. He might get shot."

"It's in the works."

"Good. Now, then—next." He put his letters in the mahogany *out* box and tilted a cigar. "I'm sending you to London in January—Miss Lila will draw up a contract. I ask only this: leave a good man behind you. If Ike doesn't make the grade, find somebody else." He snapped his lighter. "If you're not happy in your job, Lewis—very well. But *think*. There's nothing sadder than an old reporter when his legs are tired."

"So I've heard."

The Old Man threw one well-tailored knee over the arm of his chair and blew a smoke ring. "Now, then—about Boyd. He didn't have a drink all day. He's fighting it out. Feels guilty, don't you think?"

"Perhaps."

"Hm? Yes. He never in his life felt guilty about his drinking—until last night. That got to him, Lewis. It's a great step forward."

"Expensive, however," Lew said, coldly.

"Yes, yes," Ives said impatiently. "But that's just one of those irremediable things, you know. That's Fate."

Lew sat forward, experiencing the strange feeling of having lived through this before.

"What about Boyd, Mr. Ives?"

"Eh? I had a long talk with him. He'd locked himself in his bedroom, but he let *me* in . . ." His eyes widened in horror. "My God, that's a terrible ordeal, that hangover, isn't it? He couldn't sit still. Actually in physical agony. It's a frightful thing. Where was I?"

"You talked to him."

"Oh, yes. He seemed principally to be concerned about *you*. Yes. He likes you, wants your good opinion."

"He'll get drunk again and forget it."

"No, no. I told him *you* wanted him to come to work on the paper, and he—well, he lit up, Lewis—much as he could, y'know, in his condition."

"Mr. Ives," Lew said, wearily, "if he's shaking out on it, the place for him is a hospital . . ."

"*Hospital*! What are you talking about? He's been in hospitals—they'll turn him over to a goddam psychiatrist and there we go again, fifty bucks an hour—and for what? No, Lewis. You're the man to cure him, just as I said yesterday." He frowned. "If you'd followed my advice and taken him to Florida or New York your Charley Donahue might be alive tonight. Don't forget that."

A low blow. What was all this? The loaded velvet glove?

"*So*," Ives went on, "he's to come to work down here tomorrow."

131

"Okay," Lew said, resignedly. "I'll chain him to Ortman and they can wander around together."

"No, no. Dayside, Lewis. He's got to work directly under you. He can be a leg-man. He can help trace down this Garr thing. Let him call on plumbers—find that pipe, locate where they got the powder. Regular assignments . . ."

"Mr. Ives, we keep trying to get out a newspaper. . . ."

"Now, now, now! This is an order. I dropped a hint yesterday. This time it's an *order*, sir."

"Fine," Lew said, angrily. "If he can stand up, fine. If he can't I can always spare Travis Ashbourne to push him around in a wheel chair."

Ives clamped down on his cigar.

"I don't like your attitude."

"Mr. Ives, that's a busy desk out there. I haven't time to wet nurse a drunk . . ."

Ives came around the desk.

"Mr. Cuscaden didn't have time, either," he said, sharply. "But we took a chance on you once. Remember?"

"I was a trained newspaperman, Mr. Ives, and I'd been sober for years. It isn't the same thing."

"You giving me another argument?"

"Okay." Lew shrugged. "I'll do the best I can."

"That's the way to talk." Ives beamed at him. "Now, what I want you to do is this: go to Boyd's apartment right away, get him, move him in with you, bring him down tomorrow—and *put him to work*. Live with him, eat with him, talk to him, work with him—cure him."

Lew jumped up.

"Did you say—*move him in with me?*"

"Certainly."

"Where?"

"Why, in your apartment!"

Anger could be as soothing as a shot of rye.

"Just what kind of a peasant do you think I am?" Lew shouted. "That's my home. I'll be goddamned if I'll do it."

"Now, now. Just calm down."

"Honest to Christ," Lew said, stalking up to Ives. "You go too far sometimes, you really do. Did you know we have a name for the chores we do around here, chores that have nothing to do with getting out a newspaper? They're called 'croup kettles'—that's for a week-end assignment of mine you've probably forgotten. We spend one hell of a lot of time running down croup kettles—it's a miracle the paper is as good as it is."

132

Ives had moved away. Lew followed a step, shouting, "I'm going to be up to my ass rousting Lenni Garr—*that's* what I'll be doing between now and January—so I'll pass this one. If you want Boyd stumbling around here, okay—but live with me? No, sir—that's just too goddam much."

Ives stopped, raised himself on his toes.

"Croup kettles, eh?" he said, rocking up and down. "Very clever. And do you imagine there's a job anywhere that doesn't have 'em? Including mine?" He scowled into Lew's face and said bitingly, "You're an able fellow, Lewis. You'll be a world beater when you grow up. Make it soon."

"Is that all?"

"No. If you want to go to London in January you'll follow orders— now. Make up your mind."

"That's easy. I've got a contract until January. We'll skip London." The ice came into Ives's eyes again.

"You want to get Garr, do you?"

"Plan to."

"You talked to the State's Attorney, did you, Lewis? Sheriff? Chief of Police—all of 'em?"

"Today."

"Put the screws on, did you? Made it strong?"

Lew braced himself.

"Yes, Mr. Ives."

"I see." Ives was crisp. "But you talked for *me*, sir. *I* was talking. It's my newspaper. I've got the power." He emphasized with sharp thumps on his curved fingers against Lew's chest. "Everybody comes right into line when you've got the power. And I'm the one that's got it. I'm *sharing* it with you, d'you see? I'll give you the time you want, the men you want, the power. *Carte blanche*—men, time, power. And just how far could you get alone, without it? If I jerk the desk out from under you tonight—where will you be, Mr. Marsh?"

The knee, the elbow, the thumb in the eyes, the bludgeon. Nicely done, too. Nobody ever said John Ives was a pantywaist.

Well, that was that. He wouldn't hesitate. Miss Lila would order a fifteen-week salary check, and Mr. Marsh would be on a curb looking around for a job. Other publishers would say, John Ives's ex-city editor? Let's check, shall we? Hard to handle, is he? Tell him, sorry, we're full-up right now.

And the bombing? The investigation would dwindle off. No public interest in this one, boys; just a nigger died, boys; wipe it off the books, boys, we're short of manpower.

Squeeze play.

"You win," Lew said, at last.

The Old Man walked him to the door.

"I don't mind a man getting mad if he just doesn't lose his head," he chuckled.

Miss Lila's tense face hoped for a kind word as they passed her desk in the anteroom. In the elevator lobby Ives brought a small white envelope from his pocket.

"Will you give this to Paula when you're at Boyd's apartment, please? It's for the nine o'clock plane."

Lew grimly tucked the ticket in his wallet.

"Croup kettle," Ives chuckled again. He held out his hand. "Good night, Lewis," he said, warmly. "Good luck, son."

September, October, November, December. Three and a half months. Lew went down the marble stairway, two steps at a time. The newsboy on the corner displayed a headline in an afternoon paper, shouting, "Car bombed at night club! Read all about it! Clubman's car bombed. Huarache Club bombing. Read all about it."

11 An engraved card in a bronze bracket said: "Mr. and Mrs. Boyd Copeland." Doors and windows were open; the beautiful, beautiful rooms were being aired now. A stiff lake breeze billowed the drapes.

Rooms to depart from, Lew thought, walking in. Yes, indeed. Rooms to leave. Boyd and Paula had often left them for Santa Barbara, Virginia Hot Springs and Cape Cod. For Cleveland. For St. Louis. For Florida. For Hawaii. They were terminal rooms. They were leaving them now, forever.

Furniture tags spun wildly on short white strings. Alice, too, had tagged items for the movers. Like Paula, she had been generous, taking only her fair share, plus the wedding presents her college friends had sent. *Take. Leave. Give Away.* Boyd was to keep the piano. Paula was to keep the phonograph. And the portrait of Dolly? *Boyd,* said the card, in Paula's neat backhand script.

"Hey, Butch!" Lew called.

She came from the bedroom dressed for travel in a trim gray suit, a jaunty toque with a half-veil.

"Thanks for the telegram," he said.

Then they were standing side by side looking out at the endless flow of traffic. He closed the windows, but his fingers ached for the feel of her. Take it easy, he thought. Wait it out.

"Charley was so sweet about Boyd, out there in the kitchen," she began. "He was . . ." But she didn't go on.

The headlights moving along the outer drive were bright moving asterisks. Oh, sure. Charley was dead, but you could always think of phrases.

"Johnny Richards wrote me a good line in a letter once," Lew said.

135

"Writers have certain compensations—while you're being beaten to a pulp you can always get some material out of it if you'll remember to take mental notes."

She smiled faintly.

"Johnny's wonderful."

"Yeah. And too damned far away."

Nameless came from somewhere and rubbed against Lew's leg, like a cat, went off, sniffed the carpet, and stopped to point. Had some bird dog in him.

"Where's Boyd?" Lew asked.

"At his mother's."

"Sobering up?"

"Not now."

Of course not. Cute as a bug in her mink coat and jewelry, she would have said all the wrong things and brought on the hot dry flash. He thought of Alice's mother and her temperance talk with a cat. At parties, Charley used to say, "Mr. Lew, tell the folks about Mrs. Pryor and her temperance chat with that cat." It had been Charley's favorite anecdote.

But Charley was dead. Everything went right on, though. Conversations, love, divorce, news and disasters. After a few years the name would come into your mind at odd, idle moments and you'd remember you'd felt pretty damned badly about the sudden death of a man named Charley, just as you'd felt grief-stricken about a smashed and twisted bicycle when you were a kid. All things end. You can't hang onto grief forever.

He gently slapped the airplane tickets into Paula's hand.

"Have a quick trip."

"Oh. I thought a copy boy would bring them. . . ."

"No. Me."

"Oh. Thanks."

He flicked off the light on Dolly's portrait as he went by.

"See you in November?" he asked at the door.

"Yes, Lew."

"I'll write."

"I'll answer."

He found himself across the room again, with his arms around her.

"Oh, Lew, I'm so sorry about Charley . . ."

Then he was knocking on Harvey Copeland's door, knocking hard, like a policeman.

He caught the fragrance of oil of peppermint. Dolly lay on an oversize divan with a damp cloth over her eyes. Here, too, were beautiful terminal rooms and another glowing portrait: Boyd, sober, dressed for polo, looked down from another fireplace. Not playing polo right now, though. No. Drunk right now.

"Mr. Marsh," Harvey said stoutly, "I can't permit you to take the boy into your apartment. John, God bless him, is a little high-handed sometimes. I shall have my son committed . . ."

A running start carried him ducking and dodging like a broken field runner through Dolly's hysteria but he was brought down into grim, hard-breathing silence in the end.

"He doesn't mean it!" Dolly screamed. "We're going to try John's way, Harvey. Don't listen to him, Mr. Marsh."

Lew walked away from it, looking for Boyd. There would be a discreet game room, no doubt—called "Rumpus Room," or "The Playroom . . ."

Heavy doors opened into a handsome library where thousands of leather-bound books waited to be read. Beyond, he found a Dutch door marked "Ship Room." And here it was. But it was locked.

"Lew Marsh, Boyd," he said, knocking briskly. "Open up."

Inside a chair scraped the floor. He knocked again.

"I'm looking for the key, Lew. . . ."

From far away he heard Dolly's sobs suddenly muffled as if by a hand clapped over her mouth. The voice went on, shrill as a fishwife. This library, too, Lew thought, was a terminal room. This was a terminal apartment. Dolly had often left it for temperance conventions. He thought of her pretty, composed face on the club pages: leaving, returning. Mrs. Harvey S. Copeland, regional director of the Mothers For Temperance, leaving for the convention at White Sulphur Springs. Mrs. Harvey S. Copeland, chairman of the Symposium Committee of the Mothers For Prohibition, returning from the convention at Louisville, Kentucky. She was like Mrs. Pryor, Alice's mother, damned if she wasn't. Was there always one, with banners, in a jug-boy's background? Mrs. Pryor, by all reports, still uttered phrases that could drive a man to drink. Alice's mother had marched on bars out in Pasadena, California, one year —her picture, along with pictures of other well-meaning busybodies had appeared in *Life*. "My temperance work keeps me busy now that my daughter has grown up and left me," she used to say. Perhaps the day would come when Dolly, having watched in vain for her potted lily on Mother's Day, also would invade the taverns, carrying banners. These dames! Was there no way to reach their minds? Motherhood and sainthood were somehow confused in their fuzzy thinking; it never occurred to them they made a major contribution to the evils they were trying to right.

Harvey, also smelling faintly of oil of peppermint, came trudging in, trying to give defeat the air of victory. . . . Well, if you're willing to *try* this, Mr. Marsh . . . If you don't mind too much, sir . . . My wife hasn't been too well these last few years, a woman's nerves, you know . . .

Dolly had won again.

"What can we do?" he asked. "I want you to be frank, Mr. Marsh. What can we, as the people most concerned with the boy's well-being—what can we do for Boyd?"

"Thought of a world cruise?"

"Yes, we have. But I doubt if he'd go."

"I mean you, Mr. Copeland—you go," Lew said, bluntly. "You and Mrs. Copeland—both of you."

Lew fished a bent cigarette from his pocket. When the astonishment had firmly settled on Harvey's face, he looked around for a lighter and saw one on the massive library table. A knight in armor, handsome, bronze and heavy. It didn't work. Harvey held a match.

"My ex-mother-in-law," Lew said, musingly, "the only one I've had, was high in the Prohibition Party, always nominating a candidate. She once carried on a temperance talk with a cat. I'd been on the wagon three months but she knocked me off with it. Like to hear about it, Harvey? Can you spare the time?"

"Why, yes," Harvey said, agreeably. "Yes, indeed, Lewis. A temperance talk with—what did you say? A cat?"

"Kitty," Lew said.

A temperance talk with Kitty, the cat. It had been a hard three months. The first week had been a horror of screaming nerves, and apprehensions; but he had got through the days, a week, and then the second week; and a month, two months, and three. He was going great. He would stop at Abe's with the boys after work and order a coke, with a sprig of mint and a twist of lemon, and tell people how much better he was feeling; and that, this time, he thought perhaps he'd probably, possibly, stay on for good. "Liquor, for me, has reached the point of diminishing return," he would say. "What'll you have?" But then, one winter midnight, he turned up at Abe's fried to his unhappy eyes. Abe was shocked. "How'd it happen, Lew?" he'd asked. So they'd traced it back.

A dinner party for friends and relatives and Alice's mother, Mrs. Pryor. The good lady's lips had thinned with disapproval when Lew served cocktails to his guests; not even the sight of his own tall glass of tomato juice had interrupted her crusade; she had been holier-than-thou and carried on a temperance talk with the cat. "You and I don't need stimulants, do we, Kitty? No, we're just fine the way we are. They don't know what they're doing to their insides, do they, Kitty? But *we* do, don't we, Kitty?" A drunk needed a reason for drinking and Mrs. Pryor could always provide one. The gurgling jug would diminish embarrassment, screen vision, deaden voices, get you away from stupidity. He had dumped two jiggers of vodka into the tomato juice and hours later turned up at Abe's roaring and unhappy, with three hard months undone. Lew summed it up for Harvey.

"An alcoholic isn't man enough to be amused by these idiots," he said. "You let them bother you. There's no means of communication. In a frenzy of frustration you get plastered. See?"

"I see!" Harvey said, unoffended. "My word! A little thing like a temperance talk with a cat!"

"Any little thing," Lew said.

There was no sound now in the Ship Room, no movement whatever; Lew drew back, banged against the door with his shoulder and snapped the lock. Then he saw coiled hawsers, and distress flags and gay gadgets. Boyd was huddled in an officer's chair at a captain's table, with bottle and shot glass.

The bruised face lifted.

"Man of action," he intoned thickly. "No privacy any more."

"Hi-ya, Boyd?"

But help had arrived. Dolly was in the doorway.

"Oh, Boydie . . ." she began.

A nudge electrified Harvey. He whipped away like a fireman to a blaze. They heard Dolly scream, "Harvey, you're hurting my arm!"

Boyd put one hand behind his ear.

"Dissension?" he asked, interested, when his parents had gone. "Trouble in the home?" Carefully, through swollen lips, measuring his words, he said, "I gave those colored people a check, Lew. Five thousand dollars."

"I know."

A cut above his eye had been daubed with mercurochrome; there was a spreading bruise on his cheek. That had been an admirable performance this morning, now, hadn't it? Smashing fists into a weeping, drunken face, beating a sodden misfit into the sidewalk; quite a performance.

"How about a little nip at my place, Boyd?" Lew asked gently.

He steadied himself.

"Right," he said, and led the way.

But Dolly had thrown herself full length on the couch in the living room and at the sight of her he veered off, brushed by his father, and circled the piano.

"Must play one soothing sonata," he announced, taking his place at the piano. "First things first. One soothing sonata, Señor."

He rubbed his fingers briskly, afraid to begin. Lew brought him a drink and his eyes misted with gratitude. "Thank you, *Señor*, thank you, thank you!"

He downed it, readied himself for the glow that didn't come, and concentrated his attention on the keyboard. With a teeth-gritting effort he steadied his shaking hands, fluttered them lightly over the keys and produced a rippling jaunty passage that seemed to hearten him. Then in high, spurious confidence he launched off into Beethoven and ran into a shocking series of discordant, crashing, unmusical sounds.

And here it was, Lew thought, sooner than you might have expected; the wild notes crashed into Dolly's shrill hysteria. "Oh, Boydie! Oh, Boydie, darling. Play us some of your concerto!"

"Harvey," Lew said. "Please, Harvey—out, both of you, out!"

Boyd screamed, "I can't play! I can't play!"

Tears ran nakedly down his face. *Sick*, Lew thought. *Twisted, mixed-up, sick.* The brimming eyes followed his parents as they moved toward the library. I tried to quit today, Lew, he was sobbing, I can't play, I tried to quit, I can't play.

Lew filled a shot glass.

"Bottoms up, kid. We'll go to my place. There's plenty more there."

"Why your place?"

"To get the hell out of here," Lew said.

A brilliant suggestion. Boyd up-ended the glass, held onto the piano, and got up. The freshet had passed; all was sunny now. He was off and away to his own apartment, calling, "Paula? Where's my dog?"

Oh, sure, Lew thought, following along to Paula's bedroom; your wife packed for Reno but you were concerned about a dog. It was like his own final evening with Alice: in the spring twilight he had dropped in at the apartment—sentimental, mellow—hell, not mellow, fried. The dear little girl was leaving, and they'd had happy times, hadn't they? Many happy times. It would be uncivilized to part in anger; what was a little divorce between the best of friends? But, when he found Alice busily packing, his interest had fixed on a lost copy of Emerson's essays. "Alice, where's my Emerson?" he had asked, pawing through the books. That was the way the marriage had ended—in a fine, alcoholic turmoil, looking for a book.

Paula snapped the lock on an overnight bag.

"Mr. Easter has your dog, Boyd," she was saying as Lew came to the doorway. And because Boyd's attention had wandered now to the bare hooks in her closet, Paula repeated, patiently: "Your dog is tied downstairs, somewhere, Boyd."

Probably, she, too, Lew thought, would offer friendship as a parting gift, and say, "Come to me if I can ever help you." Like Alice, surely, she would cling to the remnant, and offer friendship.

But she made it simpler. "Good-bye," she said.

Then an ineffable sadness touched Boyd's face.

"You've called a cab, my lovely?"

"Yes, Boyd."

"Can't permit it," he said, one hand uplifted in dignified disapproval. "No, no. I'll drive you to the station, Paula, my dear."

Lew heard his own weary sigh in the silence.

"I'm flying," she said.

"Then I'll drive you to the airport. I insist."

Paula said, brokenly, "I must see Dad Copeland now."

Boyd stared after her. Here was a fresh, bright, alcoholic project; the best foot forward. He would drive his wife to the airport—yes, indeed, he would; he would wave sadly to the departing Reno plane. Lew could see it grow into a fixed idea.

"Let's go, now, Boyd."

Boyd dug in and took his stand.

"A slight alteration in plans, Señor," he proclaimed. "If you'll excuse me. I must get my car . . ."

"You have no car."

He focused.

"No car?"

Forgotten, had he? Slipped his mind?

"Blood, remember, Boydie?" Lew heard himself shouting. "On Charley's raincoat? Of the blood, bloody. Lenni Garr. Your car blew up, recall it?"

Lew spun him around and shoved him violently down the hall.

"Yes, Lew, yes. I remember," he said.

He was sobbing again.

12 A four-motored plane climbed westward in the night sky, became a triangle of lights and disappeared. Paula's plane, Reno-bound. Lew, in the parking lot, braced his hands on the wheel, too tired to drive. A dog's hot kiss slobbered his ear. *Damn.* No place for dogs in this civilization; they had evolved for the woods, the campfire, the open trail. They'd vanish some day like the dinosaur.

"Get down," he said, too loudly.

Boyd, in the back seat, murmured, "Maria!" and turned over. He had slept through the farewells and Paula's departure. Typical, she had said.

"He's seeing me off," she'd said. "It's t-true to form."

At the gate she had murmured a last word about coming to work in November, and how grateful she was, and how sorry about Charley. She had clung tightly for a moment. But they had shaded their arrival at the airport to only three minutes to spare. . . .

The dog scrambled over into the front seat and plopped down, his long tongue lolling through a wide smile.

One dog too many.

Children laughed in the nearby darkness. Twins, in the next row of cars. They were around seven years old, if a tired man was any judge of ages. The period when every boy should own a pet.

"Want a dog?" Lew peered in at them with Nameless in his arms.

"Oh, golly, yes!"

Oh, boy, a real dog, they said. Oh, boy, wait 'til Daddy sees him. Daddy was buying an airplane ticket. The boys were going to Grandma's in New York, tomorrow—for a whole, long six weeks' vacation. Oh, boy, what's his name?

"Think of one," Lew suggested.

That was that. You could dust your hands. Reduce the minor irritations. *I don't drink,* he thought. It was easy. It also helped to give away a dog.

"What's the matter, mister?"

He had been staring off into the parking lot.

"Good night, boys," he said absently.

A black Cadillac sedan rolled through the gates from the street. Hawthorne Race Track sticker on the windshield. Shiny fenders. White-walled tires. It was hard to get white-walled tires. Low license number. They, too, were hard to get.

Lew leaned against his own car, waiting. Three minutes went by; four, five. He felt less tired. No one had got out of the Cadillac. Why not? Waiting to make a run for a plane, maybe?

He circled the cars. There were two men in the black sedan. One was the uniformed chauffeur. The other was Cully Yates.

An airport policeman slouched against the counter, near the phone booth in the waiting room, picking his teeth.

"Any cops staked out here, Officer?" Lew asked, handing him his card.

"Yeah," the cop said, studying it. "A couple of 'em, Mr. Marsh. Look in the baggage room, near the gates."

And sure enough, on a baggage truck in a shadowy corner, he found Bert Condaffer and Herman Swain, from Homicide.

"Who were you kissin' good-bye?" Swain asked, with heavy humor. "How's the boy, Lew?" He had known them in the old days. They were cards.

"Cully Yates is outside in a Cadillac," Lew told them.

"The hell he is!"

They'd been hanging around since noon, bored to death, watching for Lenni. Another plane was leaving for Indianapolis in two minutes now. They'd been waiting for that.

Lew walked with them through the terminal.

"We hear the roust is on." Herman fixed his gaze on the Cadillac. "Who's going to stop it?"

"Nobody."

Their skeptical glances slid together.

"All the way up the line?"

"Count on it."

Well, well, they said, this might be fun, you know it?

Herman Swain had once been an acrobat on the Gus Sun Circuit; he still looked professional in his well-creased double-breasted suit. Bert Condaffer sang "Holy City" at Police Benefit shows, yearned for the return of vaudeville, and wouldn't take a dime on the side. Honest cops. Comedians, too. Witty.

"Why, look, Bert," Herman said, peering in at Cully. "Here's a convention delegate with no badge."

"Oh, dear me!" Bert minced. "He really oughta have a badge, Herman!"

"Look, boys," Cully protested as they hauled him out, "I'm vice-president of a legitimate business, see? I got a board meeting in Indianapolis. . . ." But he saw Lew and dwindled off. "I got to make a speech . . ."

"He sings, too," Herman winked.

"Is that so, Herman?"

Bert was the straight man.

"Oh, yes. Shall we take him where he can give us an aria?"

"Let's," Bert said.

They bundled him into an unmarked Ford sedan, not bothering with the chauffeur.

"We've been studying telepathy, Lew," Herman chuckled, sliding in behind the wheel. "It's a big help down at the bureau. When they don't talk we just read their minds."

They were talented. Cops often said there'd never been anybody in the department who could relieve the monotony like Bert Condaffer and Herman Swain. Their questioning of prisoners was better than a gag show on television, you really ought to hear it! The Chief, listening to playbacks on the wire recorder, always doubled up with laughter; sometimes he invited friends over. The Chief said they were a rare team, for sure. He liked their brand of humor.

The overture was playing now. They were in the wings. Excited. Happy as boys.

"Lew, why don't you come along?"

"I'll come for Lenni," he said.

They promised cheerfully, "We'll get him for you."

Cully loudly spat out his gum.

"Why, that was *rude*, Cully!" Bert said, as they drove away. Herman couldn't resist giving the hidden siren a little touch. No marks on the sedan. People might not know they were cops.

Three shadowy figures appeared suddenly in Lew's path as he returned to his car. The twins, and Daddy.

A small finger pointed.

"*He* gave us the dog, Daddy," a boy sobbed. "This man. He *gave* him to us!"

Daddy said, "That the story, mister?"

It seemed a very long time ago. Lew rubbed his face.

"That's right," he said.

The man stooped down and hugged his sons.

"Cripes, mister," he said, in self-rebuke. "I thought they'd gone off the rocker. They told me one man gave 'em a dog and another guy came and snatched it."

Lew raced to the convertible. The lap robe was a tangle on the floor. The seat was empty.

Boyd had gone.

Oh, fine. Oh, sure. The cork had popped. The Stanley Steamer. Oh, fine. Great, wasn't it? The hot, dry flash.

"Boys," Lew said gently, "where did the man take your dog?"

"In a cab." They pointed. "That way!"

A light changed. Somewhere far ahead the siren snarled. The traffic was heavy; there were no cabs in sight.

Childhood tragedies left a mark, sometimes. A lost dog. A broken bike. You could feel such losses when you were young. In boyhood, it could break your heart.

"If you want them to have a dog," Lew told the man, wearily, "I'll get them one." He gave out another card. "Come and see me. Sorry, kids."

And to hell with Boyd, he thought. *To hell with dogs.*

Rolling queues stopped dutifully at each intersection. A block, a stop, another block; the drivers were conditioned to frustration, listening to their car radios, their minds away.

Where shall I go?

Not home. Not right now. And yet . . .

"In the sum total," Charley had once said, "when you get right down to it, you gotta fight it out, alone, Mr. Lew. That's how we all do it—bang, smack, up against a wall, *alone.*"

And aren't you right, Charley. Ain't it the truth!

At Eleventh Street he swung off with the wind at his back and parked in front of the Detective Bureau.

The lobby smelled and looked familiar. Smelled of Lysol and looked outmoded. It always had, from the morning it opened. The same people who had been here in the old days were here now; the weeping woman, the bewildered child, the gesticulating immigrant with a blanketed baby in his arms; the bail-bondsman with his pocket nail file, and the covetous shysters. All still here.

Two detectives led a shabby bum through the lobby. One of them said, "Hi, Lew." Nothing had changed. Familiar faces swam up out of the past: the bright, the stupid, the honest, the crooked: detectives. He had known most of them. "Hi, Lew," they said. "Well, this is an honor! Hey, boys, whadya know, we got a real, live city editor with us tonight!"

He found Jimmie Kessler, one of Sam Prisk's nightside photographers, playing canasta in the press room. In other years it had been poker; but otherwise everything here, too, was just the same. Jimmie was amazed to see him.

"Get a good picture of Cully Yates, Jimmie?"

"Not too hot, Lew." Jimmie grabbed his camera. "He covered up."

"Let's uncover him."

Photographers from the *Tribune* and the *Sun-Times* tagged along. Good boys. On their toes. Rumor would now travel like gossip over a back fence: *Lew Marsh visited the Detective Bureau tonight.* Other city desks would be alerted; they would try to beat him on his own story. If they could. He shouldn't have come.

Condaffer and Swain were questioning Cully in a stuffy, windowless room.

"Well, look who's here, after all!" Herman said, relaxing.

Lew asked, "Stand him up, will you, Bert?"

"Why shore," Bert grinned. "But cut us out of the background."

Bert jerked Cully to his feet and Herman pinned the arms back. They swung him around into a clean-cut, open-faced pose. Bulbs flashed.

Herman twined his fingers in Cully's hair.

"Want a nice profile?" he asked, twisting the head around. "How's this?"

"Full view, boys," Lew said. "Full in the face with the mouth wide open. I want him aboriginal."

"You bastards!"

Bert Condaffer opened a threatening palm. "Now, Cully-boy," he said, mildly. "Watch your language, Cully-boy."

They pushed him back in the chair. Cully unwrapped a stick of gum. Sizzling, wasn't he, now? Full of righteous indignation, yes, indeed. He had a forty-thousand-dollar home and a pretty wife who joined garden clubs; he, himself, was vice-president of a million-dollar corporation and subscribed to high-class magazines. He was a solid citizen. This was a great indignity. He knew his rights.

"I'm on record, you guys," he snarled as the photographers trooped out. "I asked for a lawyer."

Lew watched him, wondering what made him tick.

"You guys know I'm laughing atcha," Cully went on. He folded the stick of gum and popped it into his mouth. "I don't know a thing. You can't hold me. I'll get a writ."

Bert, sitting on the edge of the table, tossed elephantine humor at his partner.

"Hm, gonna get a writ, Herman," he said, and asked curiously, "Just how will you get in touch with your lawyer, Cully? Any idea?"

Herman had a suggestion.

"Telepathy, maybe, Bert?" he inquired in mock seriousness, and asked Lew, "You want to read a good book on telepathy? Get one called *Mental Radio,* by Upton Sinclair."

They were having a wonderful time. The overture was over. The curtain was up. Hams.

"You guys better let me phone," Cully warned them. "I know my rights."

"But, Cully," Bert asked, thinking, no doubt, of the wire recorder, "don't you want to do your bit for science? You sit in a cell and experiment with telepathy, huh? Don't you want to, Cully?"

They kept their ruddy faces straight, with effort. Great gag, wasn't it? This was a laugh.

Bert snapped a kitchen match under his thumb nail and watched it burn down.

"That sure scares the hell out of me," Cully said, and spat his gum toward the cuspidor. It missed.

Bert was grieved.

"Ill-bred!" he chided. "*Tsk-tsk-tsk.* Pick it up, please, Cully." He struck another match.

When Cully was back in his chair, Bert asked quietly, "Who bombed the Lincoln?"

Cully folded a new stick of gum in neat squares. "I quit smoking," he said, conversationally, chewing hard. "Mrs. Yates read an article in an old *Reader's Digest.* It was called 'Man or Smokestack.' She tried to quit, too. But she didn't make it. There's a new kind of liquid you can spray your mouth with, and it gives tobacco a unpleasant taste. Mrs. Yates tried that. But I said just chewing gum I could quit any time I wanted to. I get along fine. This is my sixteenth day."

He offered the package to Bert. "Gum, Bert?" he asked. "Herman?"

He ignored Lew, and shoved the package back in his pocket. Not much in the way of an insult, but the best he could manage with the material at hand.

Bert fussed playfully with Cully's necktie, fixed the knot, patted it, and stepped back, regarding him thoughtfully.

"A natty dresser," he observed. "I'd hate to see his suit mussed up, wouldn't you, Herman?" Then he snapped, "*Who bombed the Lincoln?*"

Cully worked his jaws. Folded his arms across his chest. Stared. Spat toward the cuspidor.

Bert sighed sadly. "Oh, dear, oh, dear," he said, "oh, dear me! *You* want to ask for a while, now, Herman?" he inquired innocently.

Herman hitched his pants with spread fingers.

"Well, I can at least *try,*" he said, sweetly.

Cully grasped the chair and braced himself.

"When you start the rough stuff," he wavered, "keep in mind I can sue hell out of you. That's a promise. I'll sue you bastards for a hundred thousand dollars."

"Rough stuff?" Herman, astonished, gazed at his big acrobat's hand. "You planning rough stuff, Bert?"

Bert's long face was shocked. He minced extravagantly, "Why, it never crossed my mind!"

Herman sat back comfortably on the table and swung his legs.

"Cully," he murmured, "the roust is on, pal. It's okayed right up to the Governor. Nobody has to buy juke boxes any more—or have them serviced. Lenni's going out of business. Why don't you retire, while it's easy, lad? Anything you say here is safe, see? You're right at the place where you can make a lot of friends. That right, Lew?"

"Or enemies."

"Yeah. Like Lew says—you're kind of at a turning point in your career."

Cully planted his feet. "Too much talk. Why don't you start it?"

"The papers are always sounding off about police brutality," Herman complained, turning to Lew, "but people like John Ives don't know how provoked we can get. That right, Bert? Aren't you *provoked?*"

"I sure as hell am," Bert said. And Cully muttered an obscenity.

Herman whisked his open palm by Cully's nose.

"Watch your language."

Bert Condaffer was on his feet now.

"Maybe we better *both* ask it, Herman." He walked slowly around behind Cully, hands on his hips, poised for fight.

"Let me," Lew said abruptly.

You could watch cops just so long and it turned your stomach.

"Why shore," they said, surprised.

Cully's eyes were scornful. But the first question stopped his jaws.

"How's your boy Eddie doing in school this semester?"

Cully's mouth opened.

"How's his new car?" Lew asked.

Reached him. His teeth came down hard on his gum. The jaws worked again, and faster. He was an up-and-coming family man. Betcha. A solid, home-loving citizen, like anybody else. The Cully Yates folder from the paper's morgue had been filled with pictures of Cully and his wife and son, and of the trim green lawn and rock garden. Mrs. Yates had once joined a P.T.A. She had bought uniforms for a Little League baseball team. All for Eddie. Eddie was their pride and joy. He was a junior in high school, first string halfback; a good-looking, athletic, dark-eyed kid.

"The sports department says Eddie's all-American material. Planning to go to the University of Illinois." Lew explained to the detectives: "Weighs 190 pounds, five-feet-ten. Cully gave him a car for his birthday. One of those right-hand-drive British jobs."

"Is that so!" Herman was impressed.

"Eddie's been picked up for speeding once or twice," Lew said. "Nothing serious. Boys will be boys."

"If he's been cited for speeding too often," Bert mused, "maybe we ought to bring him in and have a fatherly talk."

Herman had brightened.

"That's not a bad idea, Bert. We could bring him here and let his own father talk to him. I always like to get the parents in on these things when I can."

Cully jumped to his feet.

"You sonsabitches," he screamed. "You leave Eddie outa this. He's a clean-livin' kid. He's never been in no trouble."

There was much more.

"Tsk-tsk-tsk," Bert said, "watch your grammar."

But nobody smiled.

"Just where *is* his school?" Herman asked.

"River Forest," Lew said. "A fine high school. Eddie's there with the better people."

"Why, a father-and-son picture in the paper would shock the kid's friends, wouldn't it?" Herman mused. "Isn't it funny, Lew, how these hoods get to be such social climbers?"

Cully spewed a flood of obscenity.

"I'll tell you what we'll do," Herman said. "We'll let Mr. Yates go downstairs now and think for a while and see if he can remember who bombed the Lincoln, shall we, Bert?" He went to the door and called the sergeant. "Take Mr. Yates where he can refresh his memory."

The sergeant was an old man. "Come on, Cully," he said, and his smile was tired.

Cully spun around at the door and said, with honest passion, "If you start pushing my kid, you'll wish to God you hadn't."

Bert got a good laugh.

"Rebuke him!" he cried, mincingly, with a downswept palm. This time the old sergeant threw back his head. Weren't they cards, though?

"Hey, Lew," Herman said as Cully was led away, "that kid stuff got to him. I hear Lenni's quite the father, too. Oh, yeah—Lenni's got a very bright boy—Anton, his name is, sixteen, seventeen. We can sure as hell keep these kids from speedin', can't we, Bert?"

"This is psychology!" Bert helped Lew with his coat. "Yes, sir, this is what might be called applied psychology, Herman!"

Too bad to roust the kids, Lew thought. Clean-livin' kids, were they? Maybe so. Too bad.

"Take it a little easy on Eddie, will you?" he asked.

"Take it easy! Why, you opened the doors for us, Lew!" Herman slapped him on the back. "We won't do anything if he *behaves*. But you just gave us a brilliant idea, pal. We appreciate it."

Not actors at all, Lew thought, going out. Cops. Born cops.

An officer at the radio panel was broadcasting into the mike. Teletypes, new glittering gadgets; everything but radar. Lew paused to inspect the panel, thinking: when it's all over and my legs are tired, I'll lecture in a journalism school. . . . Lewis Marsh, Ph.D. A Course in Croup Kettles. *Never succumb to an independent impulse,* he would tell the eager young faces. *Embrace all nonsense with enthusiasm. Do things right.*

"Officer," he asked. "Send out an all-points call right away, will you?"

"Certainly, Mr. Marsh."

He wrote it out: Boyd Copeland, clubman, dipso, cane, topcoat, Homburg and a one-eyed mongrel dog; scar on top of head, fresh new bruises about lips and eyes; mercurochrome on right cheek.

"If you find him, bring him to my place. Eighty Scott Street."

So that was that. Julian would say: Did you send out an all-points call, Lew? Julian would need affirmative answers. There would be repercussions. "Yes, Mr. Ives," Julian could say, "we sent out an all-points call." Yes, yes, yes, Mr. Ives.

Condaffer and Swain walked him to the elevator lobby. They were full of ideas now. And grateful. And animated.

Good night, they said, good night, Lew, boy. Mention some names around here, will you, Lew? Mention Condaffer and Swain. We'll go to town! Nice to've seen you again, boy. Nice to be working with you again. Good night, good night.

You heard what people actually said in their day-to-day conversations, and saw what dubious triumphs pleased and inspired them; you found yourself engaged in a shabby business, and you knew, when the day's work was finally over, that the worst of it could be erased with a quick drink at Abe's. There was absolution for your own daily sins in a good, stiff slug. Bottoms up, boys.

But not for me, he thought. God damn it. Never. Not for me.

A warm breeze from the prairies came stealing down the quiet canyons as he drove north. 10:15. No dinner, but he wasn't hungry. Tired, but he wouldn't sleep. Charley's robe and slippers would be where he'd left them when he went out to die. The leftovers from Charley's last dinner would be wrapped in waxed paper in the refrigerator. Lew thought: I'll go to a Greek restaurant. He would order a hot roast-beef sandwich and a glass of milk.

But he drove along the upper Avenue, turned left past Eighty Scott Street, and found himself parking the car across from the Ambassador West.

There was laughter coming from the dimly lighted Buttery. That's what he missed nowadays—the laughs.

He dialed the pay phone in a lobby booth.

"What is it, Lew?" Julian's voice asked, husky with sleep. But he awoke at once and asked all the right questions. "Lew, have you sent out an all-points call?"

Yes, Julian.

Morning papers were stacked on a corner of the room clerk's desk. He bought one of each and went into the Buttery. Jimmie Hart, who had once been a room clerk and was now weighted down with impressive titles, came from a table to greet him warmly. They were old friends.

A moment later Lew slouched at the bar to skim through the opposition columns to see if he'd been beaten, anywhere. The bartender's face came up out of the past, fatter, ruddier, a familiar face. Oh, sure, from the old Bismarck Hotel. Dave, his name was. Dave somebody. Made a fine martini.

"Heard you've been away, Mr. Marsh," Dave said. "Have a nice trip? What'll it be?"

13 Last night's hot wind had brought re-enforcements from the prairies. The doorman at the Ambassador mopped the inside of his hat. A sizzler, Mr. Marsh. The cop on the corner: wow, *humidity!* The attendant in the parking lot: Jeez, this'll be a day! And in the elevator: "How hot is it, anyway?" the girl operator asked.

"I'll tell you how hot it is this morning, Eunice," Lew said. "It's so hot that level sidewalks become an uphill climb."

She gave him a quick look.

No razor at the Ambassador. He hadn't shaved. No shirts. So he hadn't changed his shirt. No pajamas. So he had slept in his underwear. Coffee hadn't helped. The cold shower hadn't helped. And dressing late, he had lost a button. Hey, Charley, there's a button off this shirt!

He'd never say that again.

But you came alive at the city desk when you rolled up your sleeves. Here was the day, the obsession. You were a juggler here, with nine glittering balls kept spinning day and night: the staff, the news, the crusades, the croup kettles, the special features, overtime, hiring, firing. Don't drop one, boy, don't drop one.

Ike glanced once at the stubble and said, "I've got a prize-winner, Lew."

"Yeah?"

The first sheets of copy were already on the desk. And a note from Sam Prisk on the spindle.

"I had a croup kettle before I got my tail in the chair."

"You'll learn to love 'em, Ike."

"We're to book passage on the *Ile de France* for Mr. and Mrs. Harvey S. Copeland, sailing Saturday from New York."

See how far a little thing could go? Mrs. Pryor once indulged in a temperance talk with a cat and therefore Mr. and Mrs. Harvey S. Copeland sailed Saturday on the *Ile de France*.

"No cabins available."

"Make one, Ike. Swing on it, boy."

Sam's note said: *Lew: Cully Yates got a writ. He's out. Condaffer and Swain tried to reach you. Cully didn't talk. Sam.*

Cully hadn't needed telepathy, Lew thought, and pulled up the first pages of copy. Some furtive, plain-clothes cop, at a pay phone, had tipped off Cully's lawyer; you could see that without wizardry of any kind. A leak in the Detective Bureau. No surprise to anybody.

He surveyed the staff: Jerry Weintraub, a crime reporter, had come back from his vacation, tanned and fit.

"Jerry!" Lew called.

A break. Nobody better than Weintraub. Nobody quicker on the up-take, no harder worker.

"Jerry," he said, "find a Greek restaurant owner named Achilles— everybody calls him Kelly. See if he'll file a felony complaint against Cully Yates. I want Cully picked up again—and charged this time. Get all the bail the judge will stand for. Fifty thousand. Seventy-five. Hop to it, kid."

He raised his head from his penciling to see a swift exchange of glances. Jerry was embarrassed.

"Sorry, Lew," Jerry said. "Can't do."

"Why not?"

Ike interposed, "Julian wants him for something else."

"To look for Boyd?"

Yeah, they said.

Oh, fine. The best crime reporter on the staff, a roust on; but Weintraub would cruise the city in a Yellow Cab looking for a drunk. Great, on a hot morning. There was a new, nervous bulletin on the board: *Staff: Keep your eyes open for Boyd Copeland and his dog. Again missing. Very important. Julian Cuscaden, Managing Editor.*

Okay, okay, Lew said, and called the next best man.

At ten o'clock Julian made his morning, eye-shuttered tour of the local room. But he broke stride as he passed the desk and spent only a moment at the teletypes.

"See you, please," he said brusquely as he returned to his office.

He pointedly studied the soiled shirt and the stubble.

"I tried to call you back last night," he said, narrowly. "Didn't you go home?"

"No."

"You all right?"

"Certainly."

A querulous old man's note came into his voice. "I don't see how in hell you let Boyd get away. You know what this means to Mr. Ives. Boyd's the one thing he has his mind on. Goddam it!"

A glittering ball. You kept them all in the air or you went out of business. "Never give me alibis," he told his own reporters.

Dropped one, he thought.

"I missed, Julian."

Julian mopped around inside his collar.

"Missed bad."

"That's right."

Julian wasn't looking at him, either.

"Well, I've decided not to tell Mr. Ives until I have to. I want that boy found."

"Weintraub will find him. If he doesn't, I'll tell Mr. Ives myself—if he has to be told."

"I hope it won't be necessary." He pressed his ribs with both hands, took a deep breath, and the querulous note was higher. "I've been trying to work out a date for my vacation. Mr. Ives has offered me a guest cottage out in Santa Barbara and my wife's all steamed up about it—California clothes, the whole works. I've got a month this year—or more if I want it. And I'd planned to go Sunday."

"Well, why not?"

"How in hell can I go if you've lost Boyd again?" His hands had made a damp mark on the desk blotter. He dried them on his pants. "Today of all days," he growled, "the cooling system went on the blink. All right, all right."

Even Julian: the nerve-ends flaming under the skin; the breaking point.

"That's all, Lew."

Thoughtfully, with a mental grin, Lew rubbed the stubble as he went back to the desk. You should have asked me, Julian, if you were worried. I do, I ask the reporters. An ex-drunk has no sanctuary. *Were you drunk last night?* It's a fair question. You should have asked.

An hour blurred away. Copy fluttered down. Flimsies. More copy. Lew penciled, cut, sent back for rewrite. The phones rang. Mr. Achilles, having recognized several hoodlums from photographs, co-operated bravely and swore out a felony complaint against Cully Yates. A Lenni Garr salesman named George Gappan was picked up for running a red light on Division Street. Another, Blue-Jaw Vincente, was hauled in for interrogation after making a left turn from the outside lane. It had begun. Where are you, Lenni boy? Away? We'll bring you back. Are you braced, kid? Here it comes.

An AP flimsy came to his desk: FLASH PLANE CRASH NEAR RENO NEVADA ALL DEAD

Westbound? Eastbound? What airline? These questions would be answered later. Any Chicagoans on the plane? Any children?

A girl named Paula Arnold Copeland—was she on the plane?

All would be answered as soon as the news could be gathered. It wasn't Paula's plane, of course. If it had been the shock would have greeted him when he walked in. But he called the airport, even so. No, last night's nine o'clock flight to Reno had landed on schedule. All was well. Not Paula's plane. Not tragedy. News, that was all. Just news.

Phones rang. The tempo built up. Ike answered calls for the city desk, taking on the crackpots, the complaints, the public. Lew listened with half-attention as the copy piled up. Ike handled the calls pretty well. No, madam, we're always pleased to hear from our readers, may I switch you to someone who can handle this better than I? And he had assigned with courage this morning. There weren't enough reporters to cover everything. You sifted out what you thought might be news. Yet balconies sometimes collapsed where there were the dullest speakers. A good city editor assigned as well as he could and kept his fingers crossed. Ike, maybe, would be all right.

I'd have chosen Don Bell, Lew thought. But Ike Bashaw was sitting across from him because he had once made a sturdy, honest speech in a Sunday School, back in his boyhood. You earn and earn, just as you pay and pay.

New flimsies came in: four Chicagoans aboard the plane.

He ripped open a telegram; glanced at the signature and felt a quickened pulse-beat.

PLANE CRASH HERE FOUR CHICAGOANS ABOARD SHALL I COVER PAULA

He wired back: OKAY BUTCH

A bulletin came through the City News tube, beating his own reporters: Cully Yates picked up again.

"Look," he shouted into a telephone to a reporter at Central, "this is our story and the city press beats you in with it. What is it? Canasta again? Couldn't you meld?"

Good pictures of Cully came down from the morgue. Cully Yates in his suburban rock garden. Mrs. Yates, wide-bottomed in slacks, with hoe and sun hat. Young Eddie Yates in a football helmet. Where the hell are pictures of Lenni? He hadn't *asked* for pictures of Lenni? All right—get them. A boy brought them: Lenni Garr, his ex-wife, his children, their cars, their boat. Check with legal, run what we can. Lenni Garr wanted for questioning—run that. Tomorrow, the restaurant owners who had bought juke boxes they didn't want would begin phoning; anonymous, helpful voices on the wire. Tips would creep in. Unsigned letters. Citizens, gathering courage, now would begin to report the strong-arm stuff. Other papers would jump on it. The roust would be news. But when you had a head start the competition wouldn't catch up. There would be exclusives. You could beat the town again and again when you'd pegged a story for your own. . . . Cully was arraigned before an honest judge. Bail was set at sixty-five thousand. *Deposit boxes will be emptied before this is over, Lenni. Bail-bondsmen will run their fat legs thin, my hoodlum friend. All twenty-eight floors, Lenni. Just starting, kid.*

Condaffer phoned. The department's experts had been over the remnants of pipe from Boyd's car; no clues. The car itself had been examined. No clues. Looked bad, Lew. Looked like no dice.

"We'll crack it from behind, Bert."

The afternoon blurred. Julian came out with Paula's story. The testy mood had passed and he was smiling.

"I've put a by-line on it. Should it be Paula Arnold, or Paula Copeland? What do you think?"

"Paula Arnold."

Paula Marsh. That's what it should have been. He wrote it out on a scratch pad to see how it would look: *By Paula Marsh*. It looked fine. He tore the sheet into small squares and dusted them into the basket.

The story deserved a by-line. A group of people who had never met before came together in an airport, sat quietly together in the dark night sky, and died together in a blazing instant just at dawn. Her lead began: "All the dead were strangers . . ."

The four Chicago women had wanted divorces. Got funerals instead. Six weeks in Reno, or an instant on a hillside: their husbands were free. Yesterday's bitterness, today's sorrow. She had written words that hurt as she put them down.

By Paula Arnold.

All the dead were strangers. . . .

"Ike?"

Lew tossed the copy across the desk and watched covertly as Ike read it. The assistant city editor began drawing deeper on his cigarette. Proud. That's what anybody's good writing did for you: it made you proud.

"Hasn't she got it, though?"

"She's always had it."

Phones rang. Tension was a current in the room. Kip Zunches was picked up. Mr. Achilles-called-Kelly obligingly put the finger on him.

He would be arraigned tomorrow. Seventy-five thousand dollars bail for Kip; it was in the bag. The judiciary was co-operating.

These would be great days for Lenni. He couldn't hide out forever. He would have to dig up cash, stand by his muscle boys, come back to town. Soon cops in squad cars would follow him whenever he went out, from home, to office, and back again. He would be frisked in restaurants. House detectives in hotel lobbies would tell him to move on. As his notoriety increased, police in other cities would push him along whenever he turned up. He would join the gypsies. *Imagination, Lenni; you should have used it, pal.*

Charley. See? It had been an hour since he'd last thought about Charley. See how it was? You lived, you died, your best friends were busy; nobody remembered. Your name floated into an editor's preoccupied mind like a shiny, broken bike. . . .

Another hour blurred.

Ike asked, during a lull, "Break your razor?"

"Didn't go home. Had a four-room suite at the Ambassador."

"The hell you did. Complimentary?"

"Jimmie Hart."

Jimmie Hart, the manager, had watched him with friendly concern. He knew. He had said, You stay here tonight, Lew, I'll compliment your room.

"I was sober, Ike," Lew said.

Ike grinned.

"You look bad, pal, but not that bad. I didn't doubt it."

"You're a liar."

He hadn't taken a drink. Never closer, though. Never closer . . .

Ike had left the desk for a moment and now someone was at Lew's elbow. So this would be Travis Ashbourne III bringing himself to his city editor's attention. They never learned.

"Mr. Marsh, I was just thinking about the holidays. When you make out your schedule I'd like to work the holidays. All of them."

This was September. The next was Thanksgiving. Ten weeks off. Painful to be underestimated by stupid people. No reaching their minds.

"Very generous of you, son." Lew passed copy into the basket.

"Well, I'm not married," Travis explained, moving right in with all his boyish charm. "I know the married fellows like to—be with their families."

Lew leaned back.

"Got anything to do between now and Thanksgiving?"

Travis flushed, explaining, "Ike only gave me two little assignments today."

157

"Sometimes you must feel that you don't earn your money."

"Yes, sir. Sometimes I do."

"Ever think of creating work for yourself?"

"I don't understand, sir."

"Try," Lew said. *"Think."*

4:45 now. He had meant to phone the clerk at Eighty Scott Street and have his rooms cleaned up. It was too late now. Phones. More copy. Ike came back. Ike had washed up on the paper's time. But he didn't take as long as the last day assistant, you could say that for him. Nor did he get as clean.

"Lew," Ike said, "why don't you come home with me for dinner? Sarah told me to ask."

Lew declined. "Rain check?" he asked.

They both watched the beer sign. Talked about the weather. Other Septembers. Other heat waves.

"Ike," Lew said, "the other day in Minocqua I heard something about you and Boyd and a motorboat. What's the story?"

"Hell," Ike said, irritably. "Funny about little towns, isn't it, Lew? People never forget anything."

In little towns the past threaded into the present, as if everything happened concurrently. It always surprised Ike, when he went home, to find people remembering the details of old picnics and hayrides and how thick the ice was in 1929. Of course, the motorboat accident had been a local sensation.

Boyd had been forbidden to play with Ike and Thelma Briggs along about then, Ike said. Dolly Copeland hadn't approved of either of them. No background. But every summer Boyd had managed to steal away from the Lodge sometimes, and they went fishing or spearing frogs or target shooting; once they had built a raft. But one night, early in September, just before Boyd was to leave for prep school, they had stolen a power boat and, racing it through the channel into Baker Lake, had smashed over a rock. Later, in the struggle to free it, Thelma foolishly had thrust her hand too near the churning propeller. She had lost two fingers. Ike had applied a tourniquet in true Boy Scout fashion, and awakened a farmer to take her into town. Boyd had raced ahead across fields and over fences to phone Mr. Price, who paid the bills and tried to hush things up. The story had come out eventually; the people at the Lodge had been the last to hear it.

"Boyd ran out on you?"

"Oh, well," Ike said. "Sure. He was a harassed kid, Lew. Always pretty scared."

"*You* took the rap?"

"Well, we tried to keep his name out of it." Ike was defensive. "His mother always raised such a stink. He was mixed up, Lew. But I always liked him."

The nightside staff was drifting in from the sweltering suburbs. They wore older suits this evening, older shoes, shirts on which their thrifty wives had turned the collars.

"Well?" Ike looked at the clock.

"Yeah. Drag it."

Five, on the dot. Sam Prisk arrived with his coat over his shoulder and a box of Kleenex under his arm. Hay fever tonight. He always came down with hay fever in September. Some sort of pollen in the air.

Julian stopped at the desk as they were running through the schedule of tomorrow's news.

"Heard from Jerry Weintraub?" he asked, nervously.

"Not yet."

"Be sure Sam understands our problem, Lew."

Sam understood it. It would be a feather for the nightside if they located Boyd; Sam would assign on it. He'd scatter his men like bird shot. Trust Sam. This was his meat. He'd overdo it.

"If Mr. Ives should phone in from Washington," Lew said, tossing his coat over his shoulder, "don't tell him about Boyd unless he asks. Is that clear?"

It was clear; yet covering other men's mistakes made Sam uncomfortable. So many problems at the desk. So many painful decisions. Still, yet, on the other hand, there was no need to worry the Old Man unless you had to, was there? He could see that.

5:15 now. Lew went slowly down the stairs. He was crossing the lobby when, like a hard blow to the solar plexus, he saw Charley, standing near the street door. *"Charley!"*

But it wasn't Charley. It was Charley's brother, Fred. Little rivers of perspiration ran down from Fred's black, tight hair. He wiped a pale palm across his face.

"I was hoping to catch you, Mr. Lew," he murmured. "I didn't want to come upstairs and cause a bother."

His voice was easy and melodious, like Charley's voice. Lew had once heard him sing a solo at the African Baptist Church on a snowy Christmas Eve. Fred worked in the stockyards and stood in pools of blood all day, swinging a heavy mallet, wielding sudden death; he took care of his daughters, sang in choirs, and that was his life.

"I got a problem I never thought I'd have," Fred said. His fingers groped in a stained chamois sack. "I got too much money." He brought out a check. "You know that five-thousand-dollar check the man gave me?"

"Well?"

"It's good. I took it to the bank."

He pointed to an entry in his bankbook. There were seven deposits of one dollar each, and one deposit of five thousand dollars.

"Okay, Fred. So what?"

"Well, sir, last night, along about midnight, the doorbell rang, see, Mr. Lew? I get up and it wakes up Imogene and Janie. Well, who's there but this same fella, this Mr. Copeland, with a colored cab driver, both had some drinks, quite a lot. Well, they bring in four cases of dog food, and this dog—Nameless. Mr. Copeland, he gives the girls the dog."

"Go on."

"And then he give us *another* five-thousand-dollar check, to feed the dog with, and take care of it for him. I don't know what to do with all this money."

"Shall I tell you? Bank it, Fred. Then you'll have ten thousand and seven dollars."

"But is it *right?*"

"Certainly, it's right."

"But he was gowed, Mr. Lew. I don't think he remembered the other five he gave us. He was loopin', you might say. He'd lost track of time."

"Fred," Lew said, studying the check (it was correctly signed and dated), "any time Boyd Copeland comes around and gives you a check for anything at all, slap it into the bank, pal. He can afford it."

"I won't get in trouble?"

"I'll guarantee you won't."

Fred repeated it, his lips moving: he'll guarantee I won't. Then, suddenly, the money became his; the money in the bankbook and the check in his hand. His head came up and he was dreaming; he was going away. Where?

"Man, oh, man," he said, and he sounded like Charley. "Man, oh, man. Poor Charley and lucky me. Thank the Sweet Jesus."

Hal Ortman hurried across the lobby to the elevators. White dinner jacket tonight. Fresh haircut. Powdered jowls. Nothing weighed on Hal's conscience. Nothing worried Hal, not even the heat. Big evening ahead. Loved his work.

"Was it a private cab, Fred?" Lew asked.

"Yes, sir. Private cab."

"Get the number, by any chance?"

"No, sir, I didn't."

Jerry Weintraub would have checked the cab stands by this time. If a driver were missing Jerry would find him. That, surely, was where he had begun his search, at the cab stands, near the airport.

"Fred," Lew said, "sometime soon—not tonight—but this week-end, say—I want you to come and get Charley's clothes and things."

"I could come Saturday after the funeral."

"Do that."

"He's got some nice clothes there, Mr. Lew."

"He would want you to have them."

"Yes, sir. I'll take everything but his gun."

"Want a lift anywhere now?"

"No, sir. A friend drove me down in his truck."

"Good night, then."

"God bless you, Mr. Lew."

Lew went up alone in the sweltering elevator, unlocked his door, and snapped on the light. And there were the rooms as he had left them; everything the same. Charley's robe. Charley's slippers. The manuscript on the refectory table. He put it away on a lower shelf with old phonograph records. Swept by an enveloping loneliness he thought of Don Bell who had been home alone one night when a kind of madness had seized him. Don had come out of it three days later in the La Salle Hotel. Afterward, he couldn't explain what had happened.

If it had caught Don, it could catch anybody.

Lew called the office, got the dude-ranch number in Nevada and dialed long distance, waited, and heard the cheerful voice of a Reno operator. The Bar-3-7? There was laughter in the background, and then Paula's anxious, husky tones.

"Good story, Butch," he told her. "Julian gave you a by-line."

She released a long breath.

"How nice of you to call me!"

He heard the scrape of a chair as she drew it to the phone. A new, blood-warming intimacy ran along the wire. She had had to borrow a typewriter and rewrite the story two or three times, and she would do better when she got into the swing of it again, she told him. She had felt sorry for those four women; not just because they had died so tragically; she'd tried to express what she felt, hadn't been satisfied, and had sent the story anyway, her knees knocking. It was wonderful to hear there'd be a by-line on it.

"That lead," Lew said, "'All the dead were strangers.' That's quite a title, Paula."

"For what?"

"Oh—a short story. You used to write short stories."

"And get them back."

"You're better than you ever were."

"Why, Lew!" she laughed. "I can feel this going to my head!"

"Rent a typewriter. At the worst, work will pass the time." He added, grimly, "I've got a way to pass the time—until you get back. The Garr story is going to be a hell of a thing. Lenni had his fingers in every dirty pie in town. We'll smoke him out."

"Save some of it for me," she said; and then she asked, very casually, "Is Boyd with you?"

"Does it matter?"

Gravely, after a pause, "No, I guess not."

Hard knuckles sounded a peremptory triple knock on the outer door. Startled, he lowered the receiver. You could recognize a policeman's fist; it hammered, "Open! In the name of the law!"

"Just a moment," he said, and put the phone down. God, I hope not, he thought; not tonight. Not Boyd. Not now. I'm too tired to handle Boydie.

But he was prescient.

There were new bruises on Boyd's face; one eye was closed. Somewhere, in the last hours, he had been in another fight; his collar was torn and his knuckles were bloody. He was swaying this time.

Lew gazed at the dramatic tableau in the hall: two uniformed cops and Travis Ashbourne III, looking proud.

"I found him," Travis said, modestly. "Want him here?"

Lew stepped aside. He said savagely, "You're just in time, Boyd. You're wanted on the phone."

Boyd pulled himself together, wet his lips and meandered across the room.

"Hello?" he said, thickly.

The receiver slipped from his fingers. Lew caught it, and said, "Paula?" He thought: *that was a heel trick. I'm a goddam heel.*

"What's happening there?" she asked. "Is he all right?"

"Why, sure. He's in great shape," Lew said. "He's been missing again. One of my reporters just found him."

When he had hung up, he carried Boyd, with the cops' help, into Charley's room and roughly disrobed him. When he tried to roll him into bed Boyd fought wildly, flailing his arms, twisting his naked body against Charley's sheets.

"Not here!" he sobbed. "The couch, Lew—not in here!"

The short, hard struggle exhausted him. He lay back, breathing hard. Lew brought a bottle from the bar.

"Travis," he said, putting the bottle on the bed table, "you remember Charley?"

"Yes, sir."

"Those are Charley's nieces." Lew pointed to a photograph on the wall. "Cute kids. They loved Charley very much."

Boyd sobbed, "I'm going to quit." He pushed the bottle aside and rubbed the back of his hand across his open mouth. "I gave up. I'm going to quit."

"Not you, sonny," Lew growled. "You're Boydie. You're Mom's boy. You'll never make it. Help yourself."

He snapped off the light and locked the door.

"A drink, gentlemen?" he asked.

Well, why not? the cops said. A nip, maybe, Mr. Marsh. Just one. A touch against the weather. Bourbon, please. Travis lined up with them.

Lew sniffed the sharp fragrance, studied Travis' manly handling of his glass, watched the whisky go down, strike, and spread its warmth. A few minutes later, lifting his voice above the clatter of loosening tongues, he phoned Julian, loudly giving credit, "It was Travis again, Julian—on his toes. Yeap—Travis found him." When the cops had gone, Travis lingered in the hall; having heard applause, he was now insatiable.

"I was more or less lucky," he said, yearning for another pat.

"All right, son," Lew said, "how did you do it?"

"Well, remember you said to *make* work if I didn't have any?"

"I see. Going to cut me in for a share of it, too, are you?"

"No, but that's what you said, Mr. Marsh. So I got to thinking about Mr. Copeland. I noticed all day how worried Mr. Cuscaden was."

"He's in love with you now, pal."

The boy laughed.

"Well, I remembered the cab driver said Mr. Copeland had been to Gus's place near Gary—so I phoned over there, my own expense. And he was there! So I took a cab to Gary, at my own expense. When I got him back inside the city limits I called the cops. I'm lucky, I guess."

"Or a genius," Lew said. "Time will tell."

He held out his hand.

"Good night, Travis. I'll okay your expense accounts in the morning."

"Yes, *sir*," Travis said.

"Overtime, too."

The boy flushed.

"Thank *you*." He swaggered away. Lew watched him until the elevator doors had closed. Be surprising, wouldn't it, if that spoon-fed kid became a newspaperman, after all?

A sudden cold wind came through the darkness with a fresh, sharp tang of fall. Chicago weather. You never knew what to expect. Lew pulled up a blanket. I'll sleep in a moment, he thought, I'm damn tired.

What was this—Thursday? A great week, so far. Yet soon he would find himself off the time belt moving through soft clouds of slumber into Friday. Wet nurse a drunk around the office on Friday. There was a laugh. Sleep, sleep; you longed for sleep, ached for it; and your mind went around and around. Travis Ashbourne, not Jerry Weintraub, had located Boyd. Julian would give Travis the award again. . . . Sleep . . . Suppose you had a drink and ate something? Then you'd sleep. Death-like, dreamless, drunken sleep.

He heard a splintering crash far below in the alley. A party some-where? Someone's guests, passing through the cocktail hour into happy abandon, were now tossing things out windows? He lifted his head from the pillow listening for loud, idiot voices. No idiot voices. No sound whatever. Nothing but the wind. He lay back. Colder than hell. Freeze the brass monkey. What a town! No wonder the talented men and women all left it as soon as they could raise the carfare. Artists, actors, writers—they all scurried away. No wonder the leading citizens raced nightly to the commuters' trains. A foul, dirty, wind-blown miserable town.

Give me sleep, give me sleep.

Help me sleep.

He was drifting off when a high-pitched scream from somewhere in the alley brought him upright. A man's desperate voice cried, *"She's bleeding. There's blood. There's blood. Oh, Christ, oh, Christ, oh, Christ!"*

He threw aside the covers. It had been Boyd's voice, in Charley's room.

Charley's gun lay near Boyd's twitching fingers. Light from the bed lamp glowed on his naked, glistening body, spread on the floor. No blood; not a mark on him. Lew turned him over. Not a mark.

"What in hell are you trying to do?"

The cold wind whipped the curtains. "I want to die," he said, "I want to die. I tried to quit, Lew. I've quit, Lew. I want to die!" The shakes. His right leg jerked, twisting in a cramp. "I've quit. I want to die."

Lew broke the gun. A single bullet lay ready in the firing chamber. "All you had to do was pull the trigger," he growled.

"I did!" Boyd screamed. "I did pull the trigger. Five times. *I pulled it five times!*"

"Pointed where?"

"In my mouth!"

He lifted himself on shaking arms and crawled, twitching and sob-bing, toward the door. "In my mouth, in my mouth, in my mouth!"

Lew tossed the gun on the bed, picked him up, and dragged him down the hallway into the bathroom. He spun the faucets, got a roaring flood of water, and tumbled him in. Boyd screamed, covering his face with his hands, "The propeller, oh, Christ, she's bleeding!"

"You need a drink, pal," Lew said, and went back to Charley's bedroom. The bottle wasn't there. The screen had been unhooked. The curtains lifted into his face, swirling in an icy breeze. Lew got another bottle from the bar and went back to the bathroom. Boyd was quiet now. The tub was full.

"Boyd!"

The twitching legs splashed water over the side.

Lew held out a brimming shot glass. Boyd's hand struck out, slapped hard and the whisky swirled in dark streaks in the water. "I've quit," he sobbed. "I've quit, Lew." His body jerked convulsively. Withdrawal convulsions, maybe. That's what they called it at the sanitariums: withdrawal convulsions.

"I've quit! I give up. I've quit!"

"Great news."

Lew brought hot coffee, held the wobbling head and helped him drink it. His gratitude was pitiful. "Oh, thank you, sorry to trouble you, sorry . . . sorry . . . please, sir, the light hurts my eyes, sir. Will you turn it off if you don't mind? Oh, thank you, sir. You see, there was blood in the water," he said. "Thelma lost two fingers." He had run to phone Mr. Price. He had run, and run, and run. . . . He was tired. It was not a dream. It was like a dream but not a dream. A nightmare, and not a nightmare. It was a mad vision, unrolling like film; he couldn't stop it.

Lew braced both hands behind him and leaned back against the basin, hearing without listening. Boyd was still talking; it was all about Charley now. "*He wanted to drive my car. He had never driven a Lincoln. It was his idea, Lew. He begged me, Lew.*"

"Sure, kid, sure."

I didn't know where I was when I woke up, Lew, and I turned on the lights and there was that picture; and when I put it away in the bureau drawer there was that gun. The bottle. The gun. I dropped the bottle out the window, Lew.

Yeah, I know, I know.

And then there's this nightmare, when I try to quit, there's this nightmare. I fought it all day. Lately, whenever I try to sober up, there is this dream, this nightmare.

I'm sick of it!

"Yeah," Lew said. "Yeah, Boyd, sure."

Boyd sat up, soaped a washcloth and scrubbed his face furiously; scrubbed his neck, and his ears, kept on scrubbing.

"I pulled the trigger five times!" he screamed.

"Then what, kid, then what?"

Then he had broken the gun, found one bullet in the firing chamber . . .

"Heard the angel feathers, did you?"

"What?"

"Never mind."

Lew brought the phone on its long extension and sat wearily holding it, trying to remember the Passavant Hospital number. Superior, what? Superior 7. . . .

He couldn't remember, and dialed o.

"Who you calling?" Boyd asked, peering through soap. "My wife? Are you calling my wife?"

"You have no wife."

"Where is she?"

"Reno."

"She decided not to go to Reno."

"She changed her mind."

"I give up, I give up, I give up. I don't want another drink. I won't take another drink. I'm through."

"You're late," Lew said, and asked for the Passavant Hospital number, got it, and dialed. "You've lost a wife."

Boyd splashed a gallon of water over the sides of the tub. His shaking hands couldn't quite reach a towel. Lew tossed one.

"It's cold," Boyd whimpered, rubbing his twitching body dry. "I shouldn't go out in the cold, Lew. Not after a hot bath."

"You didn't get far with the gun. Let's try pneumonia."

"What?"

"Death staring you in the face—that might do it for you, sonny. I can't think of anything else this side of hell that'll sober you up."

In the living room while they waited for the ambulance Lew wrapped mufflers around Boyd's neck until he looked like Sam Prisk on a winter day. He was feeling sorry for him now. The weak-kneed little bastard was really trying to quit. Twitching, chattering, trying to quit.

Later, sitting beside him in the ambulance, Lew said, "Now, listen to me. Are you listening? Don't count on me from here on, see, kid? Have you got that?"

He was awake. He was listening.

"They'll shoot you full of vitamin B-1 and saline solution. They'll patch up your body. But the rest of it you'll have to do for yourself. You'll lick it by yourself, or you'll never lick it. Have you got that? Do you understand?"

Boyd's fingers clutched his wrist.

"But where will I go?"

"If you mean it—back to your own apartment. Want to try a thought in your head?"

He seemed willing.

Lew said, coldly, "Take down Dolly's picture, hold it in both hands, knee-high, draw back your right foot and put your toe through the canvas."

"What are you talking about?"

"It's a substitute," Lew said, "for a kick in the ass. It's long overdue."

"What are you saying to me?"

"It's advice," Lew said. "Are you equal to some more?"

"I'm listening."

"I've never felt that a man was justified in drinking himself to death because one of his parents happened to be a fool."

Boyd's hands covered his face.

"I can't go back home," he whimpered.

"That's up to you," Lew said. "I'm pulling out of it."

"But you had help," Boyd chattered, accusingly. "Charley told me. Charley told me all about it."

"That's right." Lew watched the dark, empty streets slipping by and in the night shadows there was something of the past, of the days on Clark Street. "Charley would have helped you, too, Boyd. But he can't now. Charley's dead."

Thirty minutes later, after a competent nurse had injected a needle into Boyd's arm, an eager young doctor confided to Lew in the hall, "We have a new drug which we find very helpful in these cases, Mr. Marsh."

"Named?"

"Piromal."

"Put a guard on the door," Lew said.

In the pre-dawn darkness Lew felt the cold air going deep into his lungs and sensed, rather than heard, the urgent ringing of the phone. He raised himself to one elbow. A far-off voice growled, "Julian tells me you've put Boyd in a hospital against my orders, Mr. Marsh."

Here we go again, Lew thought. John Cowper Ives and his limitations.

"Did he also tell you I found him playing Russian roulette with Charley's gun?"

"We've got the anti-psychiatrist campaign starting Monday," Ives said, grimly. "I don't want him in the hospital. Get him out."

Words. You convey ideas with words. You find the right words and sometimes you do wonders. Always worth a try.

"Boyd's in a bad way, Mr. Ives," Lew said, bracing the pillow behind him. "He seems to be trying to quit. If he is—then he needs doctors, nursing, shots, saline solution. That's out of my line."

There was heavy breathing. Thought, maybe, and heavy breathing.

"Very well," Ives said, at last. "But I want him out of the hospital as soon as the doctors will release him."

"Yes, Mr. Ives."

"And back with you."

Lew threw aside the covers.

"I'm giving you an argument now."

"Well?"

"Mr. Ives," he said, hotly, "I can't do the quitting for him. You say I'm a practical psychologist? Take it from me then—he'll do it alone, or he'll never do it. You don't lean on anybody. You don't run for cover. You face into it, and you quit. Alone."

He said it all carefully: alone. You destroy your marriage and lose your friends. You come out of the hospital and go back to a shambles. You stand in the wreckage and begin meeting the expenses, the costs that come forever out of the past. You fight down your frenzy and start paying for your jug.

"This is the test, and if he doesn't make it this time he'll never make it. You'll do him a kindness if you let him fight it out—alone."

"Is that all?" Ives asked, sharply. "Are you through?"

"Not quite," Lew said, and he had considered this, off and on, all night long. "I'm going to marry Paula if she'll have me, Mr. Ives. That tempers my enthusiasm for this croup kettle. If you think my judgment is warped, then you'd better handle it some other way."

And now, Lew thought, he'll jerk the rug.

"Mr. Marsh?"

"Yes?"

"I want daily reports while Boyd is in Passavant."

"Yes, sir."

"I want him out of there as soon as the doctors will release him."

"Yes, Mr. Ives."

"Then I'll want to know where he is living and what he is doing."

"Yes, sir."

"You will—ah—drop in on him occasionally?"

"No, Mr. Ives. I will not."

Now, Lew thought, *the rug.*

The breathing filled a long pause. Then Ives said, "Alone, you think?"

"Yes, Mr. Ives. Alone. You quit alone. It's the hard way, but the only way."

"Well," Ives said with an I'm-a-reasonable-man tone in his voice, "you seem to have done pretty well with him so far. I rather thought you would."

He hung up.

Nothing about Paula, either assenting or opposing, Lew thought, reaching for his robe. A deliberate omission, of course. Clever, maybe. Nothing to complicate the situation. You had to hand it to him. The Old Man knew when to keep his mouth shut.

And that, he thought, was that. He put coffee to boil on Charley's stove, thinking: not too long to wait, now. One bright day in November, Paula would come back to work in the local room. . . . She'd be part of his life again, as she had been in the days when he veered away and went down the long aisle in a fieldstone church with the wrong woman.

14 This was the hour: the pile-up, the crush, the shrilling phones, the typewriter barrage, the copy. Lew worked toward the deadline, deep in the obsession. November this was, and a great day. Paula had been in his mind all morning, but now he had lost the pleasant daydream. You couldn't keep up with the copy, continually stacking inches high on the desk. Copy from the City Hall. Copy from the courts. Copy from the Federal Building. Copy from the hotels. Copy, copy, the last run of copy before the first edition.

3:30.

The electric clock jerked its minute hand. 3:31. Too much to do, Lew thought, too little time in which to do it. 3:32. Four o'clock deadline.

Boy! Boy! Here, boy! Lift your feet!

Coffee in paper cartons. Smoldering, forgotten cigarettes. Shoulder to shoulder, elbow to elbow, and everybody a million miles away. A note fluttered down. The first edition editor asking: *Lew, when in hell do I get the lead on the Garr story?*

Don, give me a start on the Garr story, break it off, and give me a start!

Where's the weather? Who's got the weather story? Goddam it to hell, why are we always late with the weather? Joel! Joel McHenry! Get the weather over here, get it here!

The phone. No time for phones. Let the phones ring.

Lil Claussinius screamed:

"Lew—your phone!"

It was Ollie Trask, the picture editor, on the phone. "Lew, there's a mix-up in names on that Englewood story. Which is right—the story or the photog's caption?"

Jerry Weintraub. Oh, Jerry! Mix-up on captions. Fix it, fix it.

3:34.

Bobby Ferrig, moving his heavy shoes with speed, came up, moved on, and a teletyped memo spiraled down:

> *Kindly get two plane tickets for Mr. and Mrs. Rexford Robb McCrary of Atlanta, Georgia, now at Congress Hotel, leaving for Los Angeles on United ten o'clock tonight and send orchids to Mrs. McCrary from me.*
>
> John Cowper Ives,
> Santa Barbara.

Ike, here's one. Drop everything, boy. Croup kettle, snap into it.

"Lew, your phone!" Lil called again. *"Lew, answer your phone!"*

How do you like this? A rewrite man from St. Louis *Globe-Democrat* asking for a job.

"You called at a good time, buster, you called at a hell of a good time."

Hang up in his ear. Bang it down. Shatter his eardrum. To hell with rewrite men from the *Globe-Democrat* looking for jobs by telephone.

Copy. Pile it up, pour it on, let's have it. More, more, let's have it, bring it on.

A touching, fey suicide story, badly written. Who wrote this? *Ashbourne.* Oh, sure. Travis Ashbourne III. I'll cut that III off his name someday. I'll whittle Travis down to size.

> Jossiah J. Cosson of Princeton, Illinois, leaped to his death from the twenty-fifth floor of a Michigan Avenue hotel late yesterday afternoon. He left a note to his wife written on a Canasta score pad:
> *Maudie: I can't play Canasta with the Withers next Wednesday or any other Wednesday. I keep telling you I don't like playing Canasta with Bert and Margie Withers.*
>
> Josh

No time, now, to coach Travis. No time to ask: Was Jossiah J. Cosson drunk? Sober? Insane? Or just tired. Too late now. Have it rewritten for the next edition. Send it through sloppy.

Boy!

Give Sid Cohen the dupe on this one.

Sid, rewrite for the next edition.

This is it, he thought. This is the hour. This is when it's best. The tension, the scurrying, the noise, the racing clock, the ordered confusion. You're drunk now—drunk with work.

171

Joel McHenry's long, sad, ex-dipsomaniac face came up with the weather through a fog of smoke. 3:36 and we finally get the weather! Colder. Possibly early snow. Good story, well-written—but always late. Boy!

Goddam. McHenry, president of the Guild, always late with the well-written weather. Joel had the Guild on his mind, maybe. Thinking about his obligation to the men and women of his craft. Craft, hell. Tradesmen. "There may be a strike, Lew," he had said this morning. "The reporters won't cross the picket lines if there's a printers' walkout. The printers haven't settled their new contract, Lew." A union man, heart and soul; the weather could wait.

That's all we need, Lew thought. Reporters dutifully staying home while printers pace the streets in the wintry breezes. These aren't the good old days, boys. This is now. This is the brave, new regulated world and to hell with it.

Sid's voice came floating up in a passionate, humorous, affectionate tenor over the rattle and shuffle, "Paula! Hey, Paula! Will you marry me?"

The noise diminished. Nothing but the thumping teletypes. Lew belatedly looked up. Dreaming? Hearing things?

In the hurly-burly of this hour he had forgotten. This was the day. This was it. *Paula!*

And there she was in the doorway, wearing a tweed suit with a sable fur, and one of her jaunty tams, the one with the silver arrow. Here she was, home from Reno. *I'm not going to fly, Lew,* she had written. *I'll not go on proving that I'm not afraid to fly. I'm coming on the most comfortable train I can find, in a drawing room, with a pile of books. I'm afraid to fly. . . .* God, what a pretty girl, what a pretty girl! Butch. She's here!

As she went by the rewrite desks the old-timers said, "Hey, Paula—will you marry me?"

That goddam office gag.

"You'll have to ask the boss," she said.

The bands tightened across his chest and he was looking into a blur of beauty. He thought he detected an extra pressure from her gloved fingers.

"I came at an awful time, didn't I?" she asked, contritely, trying to edge away. "That shows how long it's been. I'd forgotten what it's like around here."

The five ex-drunks crowded to the desk and even Julian came hurrying from his office. "Butch, honey," he said, and kissed her. Phones rang, teletypes thumped heavily; but everything else had stopped. You could

172

always waste a minute. You'd work faster to make up time you'd lost. Time? It was nonexistent. Time stretched like rubber. Time was what you had a hell of a lot of, when you worked fast enough to make up.

3:40.

Rewrite men went back to work. Julian returned to his office. Lil Claussinius topped the noise with a greeting, "Hi, Paula! Lew, your phone!" Ike answered three phones at once. Hello, hold it; hello, one minute; hello, hold it. The crush was on again.

"Dinner, Butch? At the Tavern Club, tonight?"

"Dad's expecting me in Ravinia," she said, worrying about Lew's phone. "I just dropped in because I couldn't wait."

Dad. Ravinia. Roger Arnold. The cottage. Oh, sure. Relatives. There were always relatives.

"But you're coming back to work?"

She nodded. "What time tomorrow?"

"Nine," he said.

But that was far off. 3:41 until 9:00 tomorrow. That was a stretch of time. Much too long.

"How about sticking around?" he asked. "I'll drive you home."

"I'll phone Dad," she said, delighted. "You'll have dinner with us, won't you?"

3:42.

Two phones, Lew. Two calls for you, Ike said.

The first edition editor: "Lew, where in hell is the weather?"

"It's on the way, Ollie. You've got it, Ollie. On the way down."

The other phone: "Mr. Marsh? This is the public-relations office at the Santa Fe . . ."

Ike, take it—take this, Ike. It's a press agent, Ike. Take it. For God's sake, don't give those calls to me.

"I didn't know," Ike said, "he asked for you, I didn't know. Hello?"

Five, ten, fifteen, nineteen minutes blurred away.

4:00.

Let out your breath. The copy was all down. How the hell do we do it, day after day? Seventy-five per cent of tomorrow's paper down, now, in the first edition. Made it. We always make it. You wonder how. And, with the release of pressure, you thought: I sure as hell could use a drink.

Council. Time for council.

The editors trooped into Julian's office and sat at the big, scarred table. From Lew's place on the far side he could watch the local room through the glass partition. Paula had found an unused desk in the corner near the teletype. She threw her coat over a chair, swung around to the typewriter and began busily tapping.

173

Writing what?

Letters to the girls she had met in Reno, maybe. The lonely ex-wives and the lonely bums. *Some of these girls here at the ranch*, she had said in an October letter, *are just plain tramps, Lew, but we've all promised to keep in touch. It's like making shipboard acquaintances in a stormy sailing. People love one another when they're in danger, or when they're lonely. I even like the tramps.*

Council, where it was decided what would be done with the news of the day in later editions, demanded his full attention—and didn't get it. Paula was back. He had read and reread her letters, searching between the lines for a verbal equivalent to the extra pressure of her fingers. He had screened paragraphs like the one in late October in which she had said, *This is a quietly frantic place and I'm trying to put what I feel about it into a short story. I've never known women who wanted so much to be married—and here we all are, getting divorces. I saw a sad sight today: six divorcees on horseback jogging along a windy trail, all trying to charm an ungrammatical cowboy who was wondering, no doubt, which of the six lost dames would be easiest to make. If he had said, 'Marry me,' he could have had a harem.*

The voices at the table dropped into a familiar drone. He was thinking: all these years, and all that had happened in the time between, and now once again Butch would arrive with the commuters, bringing into the local room her freshness and enthusiasm, her perennial curiosity and her beauty. Turn back the clock. . . .

I've got somebody to stay sober for, he thought.

A voice said: Lenni Garr.

Julian was talking about the Garr story.

He looked up to find eyes twinkling at him.

"Yes, Julian?"

Wool-gathering, that's what I'm doing, he thought. Come back, come back. Yes, Julian? What in hell were they talking about? Where are we?

He sat straighter in his chair.

Julian was speaking calmly. Not so jumpy these days. Needed fewer bromides. His vacation in a guest house on John Ives's estate in Santa Barbara had done something special for Julian. "Mr. Ives was on the phone this afternoon," Julian repeated. "He didn't give me a flat order, but I gather he feels we'd better taper off the Garr story for a while."

Why?

Lew left the word unspoken, staring at him. When they gave you foolish orders you accepted them in silence.

He listened in growing disbelief. Jed Brooks agreed, and the news editor.

"Here's the point, Lew," Julian insisted. "Until there's an indictment the other papers are sure to taper it off. Of course, if you can *find* Lenni . . ."

Lenni was out of town. Yes, indeed. Lenni was away. He had been reported in Cleveland, in Detroit, St. Louis, and in Las Vegas, but the thick-fingered cops couldn't seem to put their hands on him.

"Let the police push his boys around much more," Julian said, "and this story may boomerang on us, don't you see? People will begin to sympathize with them. On the other hand, when Lenni's found . . ."

"You agree, don't you, Lew?"

"Whatever you say."

He thought: running, are you, Lenni? Away, are you? I'll bring you back. I'll have you up to your ass in masonry before I'm through. In the meantime, you bastard, how do you like travel?

In the local room the tempo had stepped up again. Copy . . . New inches of copy. He pulled up the first sheet. *Cohen* in the upper left corner. He read with relaxed enjoyment.

Jossiah J. Cosson, 47, of Princeton, Illinois, a lumberman, tumbled his twenty-five floors to the alley in a more graphic fashion, struck harder when he landed, lay quieter under blacker cloth. He had escaped. His farewell note, surrounded by Sid's gentler words, was more poignant; it would arouse fellow-feeling in the breasts of other tired businessmen who played dull games with dull people on regular evenings to please the little woman. The death of Jossiah J. Cosson was now a little classic in less than two hundred well-written words.

Lew thought: I'd better give him a lovin'.

Sid!

Sid Cohen turned from his typewriter.

"Nice going," Lew said.

The sallow face took on color, the lean fingers moved faster on the keys. Lew studied the back of Sid's flushed neck. Even Sid was starved for love. Everybody, apparently, listened with an inner ear for a warm patter of applause, all starved for love.

I'm even listening myself, he thought.

For weeks he had waited for a word from Julian. From John Ives. From somebody. He had wanted to hear it: good going, Lew!

Copy thinned down; he was getting on top of it. There were hushed areas in the room now, less confusion, fewer ringing phones. He swung around in his chair, remembering Paula. After a moment, sensing his eyes upon her, she waved briefly and went on typing. Hard to believe, wasn't it? Paula was back.

Ike, scrubbed and clean, returned from the washroom and propped his heels on the low window sill. One of the red letters in the sign had dropped out tonight—an "R" was gone. Such things worried the staff in their idle moments. Where was the electrician who fixed beer signs?

"Paula looks swell, doesn't she?" Ike said, over his shoulder.

"Yeap."

"Good to have her back."

Understatement, Lew thought. Good? You don't know, Ike, my boy. It's the foundation.

Ike said, "I talked to her for a minute while you were in council."

"Did?"

"Yeah. She didn't ask about Boyd."

Lew propped his own feet on the window sill.

"You tell her anything?"

"No."

"Why not?"

"Well, she didn't seem curious. I didn't know whether to bring it up."

Not curious. Odd, he thought; odd that she wouldn't be curious. He himself always had asked about Alice whenever he encountered a mutual friend. How's the gal doing? How's Uncle Edward? How's Mama Pryor? Some happy day you might learn that Mrs. Pryor, carrying her temperance banner, had slipped on a barroom floor out in Pasadena—and broken a hip. You'd want to hear about that.

She'll ask *me*, Lew thought. She'll ask about Boyd on the way home. 5:00.

Sam Prisk was fur-lined for November. Fur-lined hat, fur-lined gloves, fur-lined overcoat. Even so, he seemed to be coming down with one of his winter colds. He laid out eight mentholated cigarettes. His voice was husky.

Lew walked away from his throaty "Good night" and joined Ike and Don Bell at the water cooler.

"Get a good night's sleep, Bashaw."

"Why?"

"I'll be moving you to the nightside. The antihistamines have no effect on Sam. He'll run a temperature tomorrow."

Don said, "Don't be too hard on the poor bastard. His winters have been hell for him since he lost his hair."

Paula, timing her movements with his own, met him smilingly at the switchboard.

"Gee, Paula," Lil said. "It's gonna be swell to have you around again, honey."

Lew thought: ugly as a duck herself, but Lil admired beauty in other women. A nice old gal.

"Good night, Lillian," he said, with surprising warmth.

Paula's gloved hand, a butterfly touch on his elbow as they crossed the lobby, was better than a massage for the tension in his neck and shoulders. At night, Ike Bashaw often growled, "Okay, now where's the decompression chamber?" Well, here it was: gloved fingers in the crook of your arm, a quieting hour with Paula. He was light on his feet tonight and walked too fast. She skipped to keep up. I forget how tiny she is, he thought, and grinned down at her.

She was saying, "Sid looks older and more solid, doesn't he?" But Don, she said, was the same. And Ike, with his sandy hair, would always look young, probably. She'd noticed that Julian seemed less tense, in better health. She liked newspaper people best of all; why, today she'd even rather liked Joel McHenry. It was wonderful to be back. This time she'd stay.

The beer sign, Lew thought, as they moved through red and green shadows in the parking lot, needed only an apostrophe to boast a southern accent: IT'S GOOD FO' YOU.

But not fo' me!

He matched coins with the parking attendant for the day's fee, lost, and gave the boy a dollar.

"What are you so happy about?" Paula asked as the car nosed into the traffic.

Everything was better now, it sure as hell was; everything was perfect now. He'd made this same long drive with her in the days of the rattling fenders—three sheets in the wind, hair in his eyes, a flask in his pocket, young and foolish. Perhaps the Fates would be kind enough to let a sober man start his life all over, give him the same pretty girl along with his growing wisdom, say, Now, boy, you've earned it, do what you can. Second chance.

"I bought the Chicago papers every day in Reno. You really whopped 'em, didn't you, Lew?"

"Betcha."

He, too, had been starved for love, and this was, unmistakably, a patter of applause: she had counted the exclusives. She'd felt a rush of pride every time she picked up a new headline. The Garr story had been superbly handled, Paula said. In Reno she met a newspaperwoman from Providence, Rhode Island, who was sweating out a divorce from her second or third husband, and Lois DeWitt had remarked that John Ives must have a good city editor in Chicago. Paula had said proudly, "It's Lew Marsh. I know him very well."

They had caught the opposition flat-footed, stayed one full lap ahead, but not once had he heard a word of commendation from Julian or John

Ives. No hosannahs. JUKE BOX RACKET TERROR BY GARR GANG TOLD JURY. No heart-warming memos. GARR SEEN IN ST. LOUIS: ESCAPES TRAP. No cheers. CRIME COMMISSION AIDS IN FIGHT ON GARR GANG. No bells. No paeans . . . He had sent Jerry Weintraub on a quiet trip to Washington and the next exclusive headline read: KEFAUVER COMMITTEE TO INVES- TIGATE GARR. And Julian's only comment was, "Lew, how long do you plan to keep Weintraub in Washington? The overtime is running pretty goddam high." And Ives had wired: KINDLY HAVE SOMEONE BID UP TO ONE THOUSAND DOLLARS FOR TOM SAWYER FIRST EDITION AT TAYLOR- DUELL AUCTION LAKE FOREST TOMORROW.

No cheers, no patter. No nod of approbation. Five exclusives—and no lovin'.

"Well, I think it was a great job, Lew," Paula said.

Yes, sir, here were the long awaited kudos.

"Oh, well," Lew said, not wanting to flash his press badge, "we got out ahead on it—because of Charley."

You could mention Charley now and not bring on a silence. Charley had been dead a long time, nearly eight weeks; he was a fading memory in other people's minds. Charley? Oh, yes, that colored fella who used to work for you. I remember Charley. . . .

"Do you have enough to indict Lenni when you find him?"

"Not enough to make it stick."

They were nearing the Wrigley Building now. She leaned over, close to him, looking up. The Wrigley Building, always white and clean under the night lights, was a smiling rebuke to the smoke-begrimed town.

"Where d'you imagine Lenni is, anyhow? Mexico?"

"He found a good cave somewhere," Lew said, drinking in her elusive perfume. "But we'll dig him out."

She sat back, watching the lighted windows along the wide avenue. "You never did tie him to the bombing."

"There's time," he told her. "I've got until January third."

Now, he thought, I'd better tell her she's going with me on January third. But up from somewhere in his mind came Alice's voice, her esti- mate of him as a lover, "You're so darned precipitate, Lew. You don't know the first thing about women. You've no idea how a girl's mind works." He pulled up short, and thought: take it easy, now; *watch* it! Paula sat as if relaxed beside him, but her fingers moved nervously and he heard the faint repeated clicking of the handbag clasp. He decided she was thinking about Boyd.

But, apparently, she wasn't.

"Are you really leaving in January?" she asked.

"January third, at five P.M. Why?"

She reached over into the back seat for the lap robe. When she had tucked it carefully about her knees, she ventured, "Nobody should ever tell another person what to do. But I'd hate to see you go."

"Why?"

"Because," she said, half-facing him, "you're the best. I knew today, just watching. And you like the desk better than you think you do. I'm afraid you'd miss it."

It was another hosannah. Warmed the heart. Maybe that's what the boys rushed home to when they high-tailed it out of the office in the evening: the fireside cheering section—appreciation that nobody else had time to give them. Did Mrs. Sam Prisk say, "You're good, Sam. You're a careful, painstaking, efficient night city editor, Sam, in spite of your colds." And Sarah Bashaw, "Oh, Ike, you look so tired. They don't appreciate you down there. Put your head on my lap." Of course! That's what brought the eager light to their five o'clock faces . . .

"Say some more, Butch," he laughed. "Build me up. Pour it on."

He had decided to drive the old route along Sheridan Road through Kenilworth and when they reached Willow Street in Winnetka he searched curiously for the patch of trees into which he had bounced the jalopy on that far-off day. But the trees were gone. The town had changed, grown up.

Butch had stalled long enough, he thought.

"Heard from Boyd?" he asked, bluntly.

"No," she answered without hesitation. "And I don't want to."

She pressed the dashboard lighter and held the glowing end for his cigarette. Then she snuggled the lap robe about her knees and squared her shoulders.

Lew said, "We sent John Ives daily reports while Boyd was in the hospital."

No interest. She was fascinated by the street signs, apparently. Liked to know where she was.

"The Old Man sent the reports on to you, I suppose?" Lew said, harshly.

"Why, no. What made you think that?"

"Well, you haven't asked about Boyd."

"D-do you think I'm heartless not to?"

"Aren't you curious?"

"No, I'm not," she said, emphatically. "Lew, do you know what I want to do now? Work, that's all—work and work and work. What is it you call it—the obsession of work? Well, I want that. I've finished a short story, 'All the Dead Were Strangers'—I've finished that—and I want you to take it home with you and read it. It might even be good. I'm going to write fiction in the evenings and eight hours a day you can give me the hardest jobs you can find, and the grubbiest . . ."

"Torch still flickers."

"It's out," she told him, flatly.

Well, that was nice to hear. But work was like whisky—you could escape into work. You could get drunk on work.

Takes years, sometimes, for songs to die, he thought.

"You don't want to hear if he's sober?" Lew asked.

"No."

"We've dropped it, then," he said, relieved, "for good."

They drove the last ten minutes in a flat, hard stillness. Glencoe, too, was all built up; and Ravinia. He failed to recognize the turn-off.

"In there . . ." Paula pointed hurriedly.

He made a tire-squealing sweep off Sheridan Road and climbed a winding asphalt drive through wintry trees. Bare branches snapped in a sharp, cold wind from the lake. They passed the old Pryor estate, dark now—he didn't bother to look at it—and drove under tossing branches toward the warm windows of Roger Arnold's cottage. When he stopped the car in the gravel turn-around near the rustic front gate, Paula made no move to get out.

"Lew," she said, angrily, "how is he, anyhow?"

"Who?"

"B-Boyd, how is he?"

Boyd. Then he'd been in her mind, all along, hadn't he?

"There are dupes of the daily reports," he said, grimly. "Ike has them. You can read them tomorrow, if you care to."

"I don't care to. What's in them?"

Lew settled back. Travis Ashbourne III, he said, had been told to call Passavant twice each day. Lew remembered phrases from a few memos: "Boyd Copeland is showing 'startle patterns.'" And: "Boyd Copeland is responding to treatment . . . Boyd Copeland has gained five pounds. Boyd Copeland has returned to his own apartment at 1360 Lake Shore Drive." And Ike Bashaw, calling almost nightly on Mr. Boyd Copeland, had also made reports. It was doubtful if any drunk's recovery had ever been more carefully documented by a newspaper. The dupes were locked away in Ike's drawer in the desk. Quite a fat folder.

"Sure you don't want it tomorrow, Butch?"

"But how is Boyd *now*?"

"Sober, so they tell me," Lew said. "I haven't seen him."

"Does Ike still visit him often?"

"Some, I guess—evenings."

"B-Boyd's living all alone?"

"I guess so."

"In our—in his old apartment?"

"We passed it tonight. Why didn't you look? Lights were on. Didn't you notice?"

"No." She added, hastily, "Is he writing music?"

"I haven't inquired. Want me to?"

"The more I think about last summer, the madder I get," she said. "When I found out about M-Maria, I should have gone to Reno right then, and had it over with . . ."

"*Paula!*"

Her father stood in the doorway, with the warm light behind him. He wore an old corduroy jacket, slacks and tennis shoes. She scrambled from the car.

"Dad, you remember Lew," she said, as Lew came up.

"Indeed." Mr. Arnold's handshake was a cool offer of limp fingers. "I've never forgotten Mr. Marsh. Good evening, sir."

Well, well, Lew thought, here's a thumb in the eye.

He followed them into the music room where they awaited the call to dinner. An animated father-and-daughter conversation excluded him momentarily and he sat on the piano bench recovering his balance under Paula's pleading, apologetic glances. It was as if she were saying, "Give me time—I'll bring Dad around." She busied herself being a hostess with a martini shaker and a pitcher of tomato juice and Lew, looking idly at music manuscript on the piano rack saw an arresting signature, scrawled in pencil: *By Boyd Copeland*. Roger Arnold's pale hands reached in, gathered the sheets together and stacked them away before Paula had noticed.

"D-Dad," she said, as he returned to his chair by the fire, "I'm going back to work on the paper."

The white Van Dyke seemed to bristle. Mr. Arnold surveyed Lew without warmth.

"And you're city editor now, they tell me, Mr. Marsh?" he asked, as though he couldn't believe it.

"And g-good, too," Paula insisted.

Stuttering, Lew thought: frightened. What about?

"Your guest will need more tomato juice, presently," Mr. Arnold said, and the twitching of the Van Dyke indicated a small, forced smile. He brought the pitcher. "More, sir?"

Lew felt the jolt that preceded an unpleasant memory. He gazed at his shoes uneasily as he sipped; a jagged, gray jig-saw piece from the past drifted into his mind.

The oboe!

The fireside conversation bubbled along without him and Japanese lanterns came floating up from somewhere; soft lights, party dresses, chamber music. Musical instruments fitted in somehow. There was an oboe on the piano. A hooded bass viol in the corner. A violin in its case beside the bookshelves . . . Chamber music; now, let's see. . . . He recalled sitting on a rustic fence just out of the range of a garden spotlight, with an imaginary oboe at his lips. And what had happened? Now, let's see. . . .

During dinner while Paula talked of Reno, the picture formed in small uneven sections; he sorted the pieces as they sat before the fire with their dessert and coffee. . . .

No memory was ever lost. Oh, fine.

Back there, on a summer day:

"We don't hear enough first-class music, that's our trouble," Johnny Richards had said, refilling his shot glass in Lew's apartment. "What we lack, pal, is culture." So they had rounded up Don Bell and Sid Cohen at Abe Rouch's that Saturday afternoon, and nipped their way to Ravinia Park in the rattling jalopy. They'd arrived too late for the concert, but had beguiled the time with a healthful swim in the lake. They had nipped and sunbathed in a sandy cove, until, inspired by the jug, they had decided to call on Paula.

Butch, they said, dear, frightened, courageous, good-hearted, beautiful little old Butch, the prettiest girl ever to walk into a local room—she'll be glad to see us.

Deciding with a drunk's woozy logic that she might be in some sort of trouble—beset, perhaps, by rapists, hungering for her youth and beauty —they had meandered along the asphalt drive through the trees to her father's house. A wonderful sight had greeted them there—cocktails, an outdoor buffet, and Japanese lanterns. And chamber music. The place swarmed with musicians and symphony patrons in their summery best. Paula, the gracious hostess, had tried to persuade them to eat something. Sandwiches, hot coffee, anything. *You must eat, boys.* But they'd been fascinated by the music. Roger Arnold had composed something, hadn't he? It was a first public performance, wasn't it? It would have been rude to munch sandwiches when all those Fine Arts Building characters were so enraptured with the quaint music of the viola, the piano, the clarinet, the bass viol and the oboe. They had staggered into the garden, stumbled over folding chairs, sniffed the citronella. "Mosquitoes don't bother *us*," Don had explained loudly to a bosomy matron as she splashed the repellent. "We *scare* mosquitoes."

Unseen by the musicians but in full view of the audience, Lew had mounted the rustic fence to display his gift for mimicry. With an imaginary oboe at his lips he had waited primly for the exact moments to blow brief obbligatos, imitating Roger Arnold, his host. The guests had managed to control their anger. His companions had rolled off the folding chairs in laughter.

And there it was—fresh as yesterday in his mind.

"Mr. Arnold."

"Sir?"

"I made an ass of myself here one night," Lew said and Paula was startled. "I've owed you an apology for a good many years."

No response under the Van Dyke. Mr. Arnold said, gravely, "I had worked very hard making arrangements of some seventeenth-century pieces by a forgotten man named Emil Roget. It was an important occasion to me. And it was beautiful music."

He turned the talk to Reno and later, giving Lew the same limp fingers, said a civil, "Good night, sir."

Alone with Paula on the porch, Lew asked, "Didn't you once say he'd sent me his regards?"

She quickly reached behind her to close the door.

"He's never liked newspaper people," she whispered, embarrassed. "I always try to make amends, Lew. I guess that's what you'd call a social f-fib."

"Well, I apologized to him," Lew said, with gathering warmth. "What shall I do next?"

Relatives. Alice had always said, "You never make an effort with my relatives." Well, he'd make one this time. He'd put in a standing order with Vernon Grear, the music critic, and twist passes from Vernon's reluctant fingers for every musical event in town. He'd take Roger Arnold to dinner at the Tavern—nightly, if necessary. He'd charm him.

"I used to be afraid of Dad," Paula said. "I stuttered like crazy whenever he walked into a room. But I can handle him now. He'll forgive you —when he really knows you. He's a very friendly sort of man, really. You see, that time, he'd worked a year on the Roget music. It was a pretty darned important night for him."

Lew tilted her chin and lightly kissed her lips.

"I'll apologize every time I see him," he promised. "I'll wear him out, apologizing."

Usually when you faced up to ancient sins people were kind enough to laugh and say they'd forgotten; or they said, "Think nothing of it, old boy, water under the bridge." Roger Arnold hadn't come halfway.

"Look here," Lew asked as they walked to the car, "your father must have met up with drunks before. What about Boyd, for instance?"

"He likes Boyd," Paula said, steadily and quietly. "He believes Boyd has great talent." She smiled. "Musical talent is the only kind Dad's ever recognized."

It was cold. She hadn't brought her coat.

"Good night, Lew."

Check, please, Lew thought. I'll charge it, boys. You bought your jug on credit, so much down and the balance in driblets all the rest of your life.

This one's on me, he thought. He'd been a drunken fool.

15 But, at six o'clock that Friday evening, he exulted: here's Paula, here's the Tavern Club, here we are. They had driven over from the office at five-thirty and he'd said, "Taking you to the Tavern for dinner makes it official, now. You're home." He'd dreamed of this.

He had a favorite table near an east window, but they paused first in the lounge, looking down on the glittering sweep of the upper Avenue— a Tavern ritual. The white, clean Wrigley Building, the river, and the *Tribune* tower: it was a *view*. "Best in town—at night," the reception committee proudly told out-of-towners. And it was, too. A sparkling, cloud-reaching, busy, lusty town.

He propped her manuscript in its big manila envelope in the window ledge, took out his new reading glasses and gave them a trial run over the menu. Forty-two—and glasses. He was getting old.

Paula cocked her head.

"But I like you with them," she told him. "They give you a distinguished look."

Just the thing to say.

She had a distinguished look herself, he thought.

"What's that you're wearing?" he asked. "It's quite a dress."

"I had it on all day. It's called sheer wool."

"Not sheer enough," he smiled. "I didn't notice." But this remark, too, failed to amuse her and he added, "I had quite a day."

There had been a fumbling, bloody murder in a walk-up on Wilson Avenue. A train wreck near Peoria. An AP report that Lenni Garr had been seen in Laredo, Texas. And Ike had been sent home at noon to take a nap because Sam Prisk's wife had phoned in with Sam's temperature: 103°. Joel McHenry had called a meeting of the Guild in the Chapel to see how many of his fellow reporters would refuse to cross the picket line, if it came to that. Quite a day. It was still whirling in his mind. Even in the Tavern, with Paula, it took a while to emerge from the obsession; a drink, of course, would anesthetize the nerve ends, erase the worst of it . . .

"You wish to see the wine list?" asked the waiter.

No.

No, we do not wish to see the wine list, he said, and thought: nor your hopeful smile, waiter. Nor do we wish you to be obsequious, waiter. None of that. We wish to roll back the years this evening, roll 'em back to the exact moment when I should have had the wisdom to court this gal in sheer wool twenty-four hours a day. Good-looking, isn't she, waiter? A damn pretty girl, isn't she, waiter? And as nice as she looks, boy, as nice as she looks.

"You wish to order, now?"

Yes.

And carefully, too. Giving thought to it. Alice had often said: Lew, darling, must you *always* order prime ribs? Where's your imagination?

But that had been in his loose-ends period; the heigh-ho, lackaday and "Old MacDonald" period. He knew about food now. Charley had taught him. He ordered with deliberation.

There was an awkward little pause when the waiter had gone.

"How's your Dad, Butch?"

"I told him he'd been rude," she smiled. "He's sorry."

"Send his regards?"

She flushed.

That wasn't a very damned thoughtful thing to say, now, was it? Paula looked steadily out the window, though nothing could be seen but the reflection of the nearby tables and a few distant lights along the river.

"Your father sees Boyd occasionally, does he?"

"Now and then, I guess. Dad always helped Boyd with orchestrations."

There was another and longer pause.

"How *is* Boyd, does he say?"

"I haven't wanted to ask." Her teeth caught her lip. "I never expect to see him again."

"Did you ask Ike for the dupes?"

"No," she said. "What's the matter? Has something happened?"

"I'm jealous," he told her, flatly.

She laughed.

"Do you remember, years ago, telling me about Adelaide?"

He didn't. Adelaide? Adelaide who?

186

All these years, Paula had remembered a long dissertation on the subject of jealousy. The lecture had been delivered in the B/G Sandwich Shop in the Ives Building one morning when Lew was trying to sober up. He had been very funny. In high school, he had said, he had been green-jealous of a girl named Adeline or Adelaide—the name had slipped his mind. He'd haunted the street in front of Adeline's or Adelaide's house. On spring evenings, in the fire of his passion, he had roamed Elder Lane to see if boys' bikes were parked in her driveway. Not until many years later had he realized that Adeline, or Adelaide, must have been grateful for his shy attention; there had never been a bike in her driveway. Nobody had ever taken her anywhere. He had been jealous because of his own bewilderment, his own ineptness. Women were a separate species, from a separate world. He had vividly described his tortures and ended, "Now what in hell was that girl's name?"

"Imagine your remembering," he said.

"I guess I hung on your words in those days," Paula smiled.

Maybe so. He had been a swashbuckling figure, with a cocked hat and high confidence, when Paula first came to work on the paper. But even then, striding through his clouds of glory, he'd had the good sense to recognize her as someone special. He had thought, when he first saw her pacing beside her typewriter, arms folded, deep in thought: there's my girl, I'll marry her. In those days she had always looked up with a frightened smile when he paused at her desk. She'd been grateful for the help he had given her—blushed when he spoke, stuttered more than usual, said, "H-Hello, Lew," in a throatier way. Then he had been at ease with Paula. He wasn't now.

She was saying, "We went for a horseback ride in the mountains once this fall—two other girls, a cowboy and myself. There was a sign on the trail. It said: 'Deer are very fond of aspen leaves.' Just that—nothing more. And I thought then it would be a helpful remark to drop into the pauses that come at dinner tables when the host and hostess and the guests can't think of anything to say. You could toss it toward the centerpiece and see what happened. 'Deer are very fond of aspen leaves.'"

Lew laughed. "It might just lie there, though."

"I know, but it would s-show that you were t-trying."

What was happening here, he wondered? What had gone wrong? Sitting at this table through the empty October evenings he had pictured their first evening together; they were to laugh, and reminisce, blur sentences together; flirt some, maybe—*begin*. There was to have been no awkwardness this evening. Damn. He didn't know how a woman's mind worked, hadn't the faintest notion. Alice had said, "You come at me as if we lived in a cave and shopped with stone hatchets. Lew, darling, try to

187

finesse!" Well, where did you start? When you were on your best behavior, avoiding old mistakes, where did you begin? Perhaps a girl just
home from Reno, with no intention of seeing her ex-husband again,
would expect you to say: Look, Butch, I love you. I always have. I'm
older, creak a little, maybe, wear reading glasses, but I want to marry you,
when you're ready, and that's no office gag. . . . On the other hand,
that was a blunt instrument, for sure. The girls he had known in the
years between, the little "lady friends" whom Charley had so approved of,
hadn't expected a serenade or the oblique approach; they'd settled for
stone hatchets, any time; they'd say yes or no, and that was that. But
Paula was different.

They both spoke at once, and stopped.

"What were you going to say, Paula?"

"Oh, nothing. It wasn't important. What were *you* going to say?"

"Mine wasn't important, either."

But the air cleared a moment later with her blurted question, "Lew—
aren't you ever going to tell me what you think about my story?"

"Good God," he said, under his breath.

That was it. She'd been sitting on the edge of her chair, trying not to
seem too anxious, making conversation about deer and aspen leaves,
waiting for a verdict. She had molded fog, made something out of nothing, worked for weeks with cobwebs; a writer, in his secret heart, lived
with his doubts.

"I'm sorry," he said, contritely. "I read and liked it. In fact, I read it—
three times."

"Why?"

"Impressed, that's why," he said, and heard an indrawn breath.

"Is it good enough for the Sunday section?"

"It's too good for 'em."

He couldn't be sure, of course, that his wanting to like it hadn't
warped his judgment. But it had seemed superb to him, better than anything she had ever written. There was emotion in it, and cool-headed
craftsmanship, and atmosphere—an intact, well-written story, saying
what it had to say with economy and style. He told her this and she
sighed a breath of relief.

"But I'm a newspaper editor, Butch," he said. "I'm flattered you'd want
my opinion, but I don't write the checks. Suppose I send it to an agent
in New York? Harold Ober. He sold a story for me once—the only one I
ever finished. He'll tell us."

Suddenly she had come alive.

"You know something?" she said, leaning earnestly across the table. "I
feel as though a *crust* had broken in my mind. I can't explain it. It hap-

pened the day I arrived in Reno. A kind of cool breeze came up in my brain. When you suggested on the phone that I might pass the time by writing a story, I knew right then I'd be better—more fluent, and all that. Well, I was, too. You see, all these years I lied to myself about Boyd. I kept telling myself there weren't any other women, and that he didn't drink more than many men, and that everything would be perfect—in the future. Well, you can't lie to yourself about a big thing like that and see anything else very clearly. It's all opaque, and distorted. Something about arriving in Reno freed me—of Boyd, of all sorts of stupid fears. So I faced into things when I wrote that story. And now I have a compelling urge inside me, and I want to *really* write." Work and work and work, she said. Day and night.

Running away from what? he wondered.

She thoughtfully watched the waiter as he served their dinner. When he had gone, she said, "It will take a long time to get over Boyd, of course. You can't live with somebody—and love them—and forget it in a minute-and-a-half. But it will help—if I write. You know, I felt sorry for those girls at Reno who had nothing to do except look for another husband . . ."

"What's wrong with looking for another husband?"

"Oh, you know, Lew. If you're *busy*—well, you can bring yourself together again. If you can write, or paint, or compose music, or make ceramics—well, you can get past the wanting."

Very frank, he decided. Confiding in me. Grandpa Marsh and his new reading glasses. D'you suppose that song will be dead by January third?

"Deer are very fond of aspen leaves," she said, and he wondered how long he had been looking at his plate in silence.

"Paula," he began.

But Gilbert, the Tavern manager, hesitated at his shoulder.

"Your office is on the wire, Mr. Marsh."

Sam, making sure . . .

No, Sam had a cold.

Ike.

It would be important, then.

He excused himself and walked slowly between the tables to the foyer. Alvin Burke, a *Tribune* editor, glanced up curiously from where he was dining with his wife at a corner table. A casual, speculative look from Alvin. Henry Weaver of the *Herald-American* had just come in. A casual, speculative look from Henry, too. There were four or five opposition editors in the dining room tonight; Lew took his time. Once, years ago, Don Bell, in his cups, at Abe Rouch's, had rushed to a telephone and rushed out, alerting everybody. An opposition reporter had phoned his city desk: "Don Bell just tore-ass outa here after he got a phone call—what's he working on, do we know?" That had been enough. Don's exclusive sprayed over onto every front page in town.

Lew carefully closed the phone booth.

"Lew, I think we've stumbled onto one," Ike's voice said quietly.

"Yes, Ike?"

He knew that Ike had swung around in his swivel chair with his feet on the window sill, his back to Sam Prisk's night assistant. Ike spoke softly, his hand cupping the mouthpiece. Not that he didn't trust Sam's assistant. But copy boys had long ears; they'd been known to boast to opposition copy boys on the beat: hey, you, wait'll you see our midnight edition, you're gonna get a whopping, wait'll you see. It didn't take much to tip off the opposition.

Ike said, "It's Maria de Diego, Lew. She phoned Boyd tonight."

"From where?"

"Here in town. She's scared to death, apparently. Hiding out."

"What did she want?"

"Dough."

"Sounds fine."

"Yeah. Boyd says she's desperate. Wants to get to old *May-he-co* all in one piece. So she suddenly thought of palsy's checkbook."

"What did he tell her?"

"Kinda smart. Told her he had people there and would call her back. She's at a Superior number which can't be too far away."

"He's at 1360?"

"Yeah, waiting. I didn't know who to send from this goddam night-side. Shall I call in Jerry Weintraub?"

"I'll go myself."

"Thought you might. I'll tell Boyd to expect you."

Maria de Diego. This would be the tip-off, maybe. In Laredo, are you, Lenni? You're coming back, you hoodlum sonofabitch.

Lew idled away three minutes buying cigarettes in the foyer, paused to chat with Gilbert in the doorway so that Burke would see how unhurried he was. Then he dawdled away another minute at Bill and Sarah Boyden's table because, across the room, Frank Newman, also of the *Tribune*, had looked up thoughtfully from his dessert. The competition was all laying for him, of course. Five exclusives, a phenomenal run of luck. They were on their toes.

"Anything important?" Paula asked.

Into a lull, in a normal tone, he said, "Just Bashaw. He's the worrying type."

With his knees jumping to get out, he went through to dessert, ordered a second cup of coffee, lingered over it. Burke had forgotten him. And Newman. And Henry Weaver. They would all watch covertly when he left, of course; they'd give him the eye. These evenings, since the run of exclusives, they lifted haggard faces from their highballs with steadily diminishing cordiality in the Hi-Lew-hi-ya-boy. Notes had fluttered onto many a city desk from upper levels: *Are you all asleep down there?* They'd been catching hell. Their grim glances had been a kind of dark applause.

He said to Paula without moving his lips, "Table-hopping on the way out, Butch."

They spent a good seven minutes moving across the room. "Take your time in the powder room," Lew whispered. He ambled around the foyer, showing the proper impatience. Burke gave him an understanding grin, man-to-man. Waiting for a woman, pal? Don't we all!

This could be it, Lew thought. *This could be a big one!*

Maria's bullet-riddled body might have turned up, long before this; he'd half expected someone to find it in an alley somewhere. You couldn't sleep with a hoodlum and not garner a few important items along with the sweet nothings in the moonlight. Kip Zunches, with his singleness of purpose, must have considered how comforting it would be to have Maria safely dead. And Cully, too. They were among the muscle boys who had been taking the rap for Lenni in his lengthy absence. Cully had been hauled in for questioning a dozen times. Kip had been arrested for left-hand turns from the right-hand lane; for parking overtime; for spitting on the sidewalk. They had been frisked in restaurants, tailed, pulled back whenever they tried to slip out of town. Out under heavy bail for their part in the juke-box racket, with a possible grand jury indictment hanging over their heads, they must have been wondering how much Maria knew and where she was. There had been unverified reports of her being seen with Lenni in scores of places—St. Louis, Cleveland, Los Angeles, Acapulco. While the bail-bondsmen were running their fat legs thin, sucking Lenni's treasury dry, the muscle boys who hadn't got away had had some bitter thoughts about her; maybe, now, if he could work on her a little, Maria would be scared enough to talk.

Paula came to him unhurriedly, drawing on white gloves. She withheld the question until they reached the street.

"Mrs. Newman was in the washroom," she whispered. "I didn't want her to be suspicious. Did I stay too long? What did Ike say?"

Lew flagged down a passing cab.

"Later, Butch," he said. "Better take a train home. Doubt if I'll be back tonight."

"I wouldn't put in an overtime slip," she told him, wistfully. "Are you sure you won't need me?"

The driver held the cab door.

"Northwestern Station," Lew said, and paid him. " 'Night, Paula."

Blood pounded in his veins. Taper it off, Julian? He sauntered to his own car—sauntered, just in case, thinking: NIGHT CLUB SINGER IN CUSTODY—that's how we'll taper it off. GARR ARRESTED, that'll taper it, Julian. LENNI GARR JAILED FOR TWENTY YEARS—that'll wind it up. November, this was. November, December, and January third. We'll taper it off in plenty of time. . . .

Paula's cab made a U-turn on the almost empty avenue. He saw the fading tail light in the rear-view mirror as he drove north across the bridge. The bells were ringing. No ships in the river, no tugboats. The lake would soon freeze along the shore line, and small icebergs would cut off the river traffic; but sometimes, in the winter, they raised the bridges, anyway. Or rang the bells for practice.

Testing, maybe.

What a town!

Maria had phoned Boyd. Fine, fine! And why not? Into her crafty, predatory little mind had popped the chump she'd known last summer; the playboy with the fat bill clip and the open checkbook. Boydie. *Señor y Señora, como están ustedes* and *gracias, Señor*—that one, the chump. I am so frightened, Boyd, dear, she had said, no doubt, will you give me some money? This was the break, maybe. . . . How would Boyd look? Ike kept reporting: The guy's made it this time, Lew. Sober for good, Lew. Not interested, pal, he had said, not interested. But seeing him, he would know if he'd sobered up for good. He could tell. Some sixth sense reassured you when they meant it. The ex-drunks who came to him asking for jobs might be spruce and combed, shaved, polished, and clear of eye but, in some half-mystic way, he could peg the ones who'd slip. Yesterday the rewrite man from the St. Louis *Globe-Democrat* had been in the local room, arriving at a sensible hour; a handsome, gray-haired, aristocratic-looking bird, with gloves and a bow tie; steady of hand, square of shoulder, with health in his cheek. But he would pop the cork when he'd saved four dollars and had half his debt paid. You *knew*. He had been too sure, too self-confident. The solid converts had the grace to show their nervousness, to hint their inner shame; they flushed, or glancing out the office window at the beer sign, quickly jerked their eyes away—and sighed. That was it. The converts *sighed*. There was the slide rule. You could measure with it. No sigh, no cure.

The elevator climbed with agonizing deliberation toward the thirteenth floor.

Music. The rippling keys again—this time in an unfamiliar melody. Something by Copeland, maybe. *Dad thinks he has great talent.* Musical talent. Roger Arnold had never recognized any other kind. . . .

The door was ajar.

And here were the beautiful, beautiful rooms again—sparsely furnished now. Exactly half the books were gone. The refectory table—gone. Half the chairs—gone. Coffee table—gone. But the piano was still there. An odd new lamp with a curved goose neck funneled a pool of light on the keys and the nimbly racing fingers.

"Boyd!" Lew said, in the doorway.

Quiet. Not a sound.

"Lew Marsh?" he said, smiling shyly as he came across the room. "I wasn't sure I'd remember."

He wore a frayed white polo shirt with "Chicago Riding Club" embroidered on the pocket. His sneakers had once been rained on, and the clean blue jeans had a small rip along one knee. He needed a haircut. But looked intact. All put together, walked with a spring in his step. Great little old mechanism, the human body. In your youth, you could punish it to the breaking point and always bounce back.

"How's Maria?" Lew asked.

"Sounded hysterical when I talked to her."

"That's good. Glad to hear it."

Lew closed the door and draped his coat over the piano. He saw neat stacks of music manuscript under paperweights. Pens. India ink. Ink on Boyd's fingers, too. A working man.

Cannel coal on the hearth split in an oily crack and a sliver of flame licked greedily over it. Then he saw the wall: Dolly was gone. A blank space stared down above the mantel; the original paint had been a lighter blue. A tall bare spot outlined Dolly's absence. Where was Dolly? She surely would cry when she made the return trip on the *Ile de France: Boydie where's my portrait? You've taken down my portrait, Boydie. Why? Why? Why?* There'd be a honey of a scene. Are you man enough for a scene, son? Hysteria, the hot dry flash—ready for that?

What did you do, son—put your toe through it?

Boyd leaned back easily, one arm on the piano, and said, "My first impulse was to turn Maria down. I don't want any more of this than I have to have. But then I realized her call might mean something to Ike." He had an afterthought. "And you."

"Let's go back. When did she call?"

193

"At seven."

"Where is she?"

"She wouldn't tell me, but I've got her phone number." He toyed with a paperweight, still not looking up. "There are some bad gaps in my memory, but I'd know Maria." He imitated her too-cute accent, smiling slightly. "She said I had a *so* generous nature so she thought of me in her trouble."

"Say what her trouble was?"

"Just that she was scared."

"Of Lenni?"

"She didn't say."

"Did you set a time to call her back?"

"No, I didn't. I said when people cleared out of here, I'd call her. She's probably sitting by the telephone."

Lew lit a cigarette, offered the pack.

"No, thanks," Boyd said. He grinned sheepishly. "I even quit smoking, to see if I could. I can. I'm pretty pure."

Laying it on, wasn't he? The monastic life. Used to box at Princeton, you know. Probably worked out in sweatshirt and spiked shoes on the bridle path in the rosy dawn. He had that look; handball, the daily swim, the training table. Drunks never did things halfway. Into the gutter or under a halo. A basket case—or a discus thrower. In his younger days he'd been like that himself.

"How're you making it?" Lew asked.

Boyd put the paperweight down and raised his eyes in a long, cool look.

"Okay, now," he said.

"You seem all right," Lew said.

And heard a sigh.

"For good, is it?"

Boyd let out his breath again. Very faintly. Only an expert would hear it. But he'd sighed. Regret, that was. You knew a deep, pervading, heart-chilling regret when you'd actually retired.

"This time it is," Boyd said. "I gave up. Couldn't seem to win."

"Tell you what I wish you'd do," Lew said, briskly. "Get Maria on the phone, arrange to meet her somewhere—at once. She'll want to stall it, maybe. Tell her you'll see her now—or not at all, you're busy. Then bring her back here. Get her to talk, if you can. I'll listen. She might talk to you, Boyd."

"What do you want to know?"

"Where Lenni is."

"Okay," Boyd said, and went to the phone.

"Then I'll take over," Lew said. "But quiet her down first, get her chatting if you can."

"Maria?" Boyd said into the phone a moment later. *"El clima es muy bueno en May-he-co, no es verdad? El invierno es seco, con mucho sol."* He winked at Lew, and listened. Then he said, *"Vendré por usted inmediatamente."* More Spanish. She was protesting, apparently. Wanted to make it later. But then he was saying, "Where? Where, Maria?" He cupped the mouthpiece and turned to Lew, "She keeps whispering something." He asked, "Where?" And then, with a flourish, *"No puedo esperar volver a verla!"* He hung up. "I learned my Spanish when I was plastered," he said. "I must have a remarkable mind."

"Where?" Lew said.

"1000 Schiller."

"Not far."

"Just around the corner."

Boyd got his coat from the closet. No hat. Looked like Princeton. In the pink, on the balls of his feet, sure of himself. *He's made it,* Lew thought, *the little bastard's made it.* What had it been like up here in this half-furnished apartment, coming back alone from Passavant with his wife in Reno and fresh out of friends? How had he got through the nights, alone, with the terrors still padding in his mind and the jug promising its eraser? Alone, the hard way; he'd done it. You had to hand it to him.

"I hear Paula's back," he was saying. "How is she, Lew?"

"Working hard."

"Happy, I hope."

"Work hard enough and it doesn't matter," Lew said, bluntly. "Step on it, will you? If there's something in this I could catch the midnight edition."

"Let me ask you," Boyd paused, one hand on the doorknob, "What's going to happen to her?"

"To whom?"

"Maria. Does this put her in jail? I feel a little like Judas."

"Judas had a different problem. You're dealing with a tart, Boyd. Lenni Garr's whore, that's what we've got here." He added, "As a matter of fact, if she'll talk, I can protect her. Don't waste any time."

He heard the elevator rising in the shaft and the opening and closing of the sliding doors—and then, in the barren rooms, a pulsing silence. His mind raced over the chances he was taking, the mistakes he had made. He hadn't told Boyd what to say, or how to handle her. Mistake number one. Even his trained reporters were given a full briefing before they started out on an assignment: he guided reporters into every move.

. . . Would Boyd cruise the street first? Walk past 1000 Schiller? Sound his horn and scare Maria out into the alley. Park, wait sensibly, or mess it up? Imagination took over. He began to sweat it out. . . .

What in hell was I thinking of to send him alone?

Not thinking. That's my trouble. A lousy executive, that's me. I have afterthoughts. A good executive thinks of these things beforehand. That's the difference. . . .

Restlessly, he wandered the apartment. No servants. But all very orderly. A clean sink. Cellophane-wrapped odds and ends in the refrigerator. A roast, medium rare. You took an interest in food when you'd stopped drinking. He saw a shelf of new cookbooks with shiny dust jackets. New copper-bottomed pots and pans. Paula had taken the kitchen utensils, maybe. Fair division—I'll take the pots and pans, you keep the freezer.

Lew moved down the hall. The furniture in Paula's bedroom—gone. A denuded room. Bed, drawers, rug, pictures—all gone. His step echoed on the hardwood floor.

But in Boyd's room, on the bureau, there was a silver-framed studio portrait of Paula. He tilted it to the light to read the inscription. "To Boyd, forever, Paula."

The picture had been taken in Santa Barbara, years ago, and seemed a touch old-fashioned, somehow. Hard to know just where: perhaps what dated it was Paula's starry-eyed look of happiness. She'd stepped out of the tumble and tension of the local room into the greener fields— and they must have looked green, indeed. The photographer had caught twinkling amusement in her eyes; amusement—and tenderness; love . . .

Sheets of music manuscript were scattered through the rooms as though composition, attacked in a frenzy, was never quite completed, even now. Sheets as dog-eared as the one-time script of his half-finished novel were on the bureau, the window seat, the dining-room table; there was even part of something marked "Concerto" in the bathroom. In a closed and musty guest room another studio portrait of Paula, a huge silver-framed affair, looked off laughingly from the dresser. "To Dad Copeland, with love, Paula," was the inscription. But he had not seen anything until he stepped into the bar. Snapshots were propped against each bottle on the shelves; there was even one against an ice tray in the refrigerator. Paula beside a dwarf cypress on a wind-swept point at Monterey, Paula in shorts and halter bra and a baseball cap clinging to a mast on a slim racing sloop with Diamond Head in the background. Paula in Santa Barbara, Florida, New Orleans and at the top of the Eiffel Tower. All propped against bottles. In the bracket on the juke box where the song titles had been, another picture looked out lightheartedly—Paula as a little girl, in a white beribboned dress squinting against the sun at the entrance to Ravinia Park.

What's all this?

Little reminders, were they? If things got bad in the night and Boyd found himself padding around barefoot looking for a drink, these snapshots would remind him what the jug had cost him. Lew took a photograph which shielded a bottle of Old Overholt, studied it carefully, and turned it over. It was a Santa Barbara picture torn from a scrapbook. Here was the sort of madness you indulged in alone, at night, when you were fighting it out. Cursing yourself for a fool, you padded around an empty room, putting up little hurdles to remind you: the cost, the cost. . . . The glass front of the juke box had been broken and the records were gone. Dropped out the window, no doubt, in some midnight joust with the terrors. Maria out the window. Paula everywhere you turned.

Lew carefully read the label on the rye bottle, opened it, sniffed, and put it back, replacing the picture against it. Let's face into this, he thought, and the winds of apprehension were working up inside him. Loved Paula, did he? Blocked off liquor with his love for Paula?

What kind of immaturity was it, anyway, at forty-two, to go about in a dream of marrying Paula? A son and daughter—Johnny Marsh, Alice Marsh—and some villa in the south of France? You'd better grow up, he thought. You'd better mature. When did a man mature?

Forty-three? Forty-five? Fifty? Ever?

She wanted to *work*, did she? Work and work, day and night, until she had gone past wanting Boyd? And he had propped her pictures against every bottle in the bar! So what was Reno?

"Boyd's made it, Butch," he could say some morning when they were having coffee in the B/G Sandwich Shop downstairs in the Ives Building. "He's got your picture everywhere you turn. And he's sobered up for good."

And she'd be misty with happiness again.

Reno was an incident.

Love, that's what you called this. That poor, mangled, misused word; this was love.

Or was it?

And what do you do about it?

Christ Almighty!

Forty-seven minutes, now. In a dark fold of his mind he saw Maria running from a shabby boarding house into a spitting rain of bullets. He saw the body of the innocent bystander sprawled beside her on the sidewalk, and the morbid crowds; heard the whine of sirens. Maria de Diego, Lenni Garr's girl. A good story. Boyd Copeland, clubman—a better one.

197

GARR GIRL AND CLUBMAN RIDDLED IN AMBUSH. There was a headline for you, and not exclusive, either. The City Press would hurl it through the tubes onto every front page in town. And Julian would say: For God's sake, Lew, weren't you thinking? Why in hell did you send him off alone?

Well, why did I?

He called the office, asked for Ike. A City Press flash would have reached the office by this time . . .

"Yes, Lew?"

"Anything doing?"

"Nothing. How's it with you?"

"Sweating it out. Waiting for Boyd. He's been gone too damned long."

"Oh, well." Ike could be very reassuring in his swivel chair at that distance. "He'll turn up."

"What photographers have you got on hand?"

"Well, there's Jimmie Kessler. He's using the radio car tonight—just came in for more plates."

"Keep him there, Ike. I'll call." Then, he said, "Hold everything."

He heard the rattle of the elevator cables. But the car stopped on a lower floor.

Ike said, "Butch is up here in the office."

"Doing what?"

"Oh, just hanging around—going out on the 11:11 to Ravinia."

Lew asked, sharply, "Did you tell her?"

"I told nobody, mister. She suspects something's up, though." Ike mused. "Maybe she's stalling in hopes we'll need her. Ain't she a fireball since she got back?"

Lew thought of Julian's remark in council the other evening, Julian with his California tan and improved disposition; he had become a philosopher since his vacation. "A problem enlarges when you shrink from it, boys," he'd said. "Walk up to it—and it's bound to diminish. It's like driving over a hill—start the climb and it flattens out."

I'll climb this one right now, Lew thought.

"Ike? Tell Paula to stand by. Send her up here in the radio car when I phone you."

Ike had all the time in the world. Probably lounging back with his feet on the desk. Probably watching that goddam beer sign.

"Y'know," he said, "I was thinking you might need a dame to help out with Maria. But, on the other hand, considering where you are, Butch might not want to come."

"Give her a fill-in and we'll find out," Lew hung up.

She'd come. "I saw Boyd tonight," she could tell Roger Arnold, who had always liked him, "and he looks fine, Dad. He's even quit smoking, and Dolly's picture is down from the wall. And my pictures! Dad, you won't believe it. There's a picture of me in front of every bottle in the bar." Roger Arnold would invite Boyd to Ravinia for dinner. Chamber music. All the old love songs . . .

Cut this out, he told himself, *cut it out.*

He pressed his forehead against the cool glass of the front window and saw Mr. Easter's legs under the canopy. Fifty minutes now—fifty-five. How much of a lifetime did a man spend waiting, how many years, if you added it up? An hour, now. What in hell was Boyd doing?

Mr. Easter's blue-clad legs moved toward headlights easing to the curb. A new sand-colored convertible, a Lincoln, pulled to a stop. The doorman circled it to the street side for a conference with the driver. Boyd, was it? Asking: Any suspicious characters hanging around, Mr. Easter? Possibly so; the car moved on, making a right turn into the alley. Smart enough. Into the alley. Up the service elevator. Using his head.

A key turned quietly in the kitchen door. Lew flattened against the wall in the dark hallway as high heels clicked across the linoleum. He thought, exultantly: *he's got her!* The too-cute accent gave way to hysteria in the living room.

"No, no, I am not safe here or anywhere, Boyd. Drive me far away— and what you say—charter? Charter a plane, like you do. To Mexico. I am so frighten', Boyd. I am so scared!"

Boyd murmured soothingly. A shrill cry interrupted, "Haven't you got monee in your pocket? Please, show Maria the monee!"

"Chartering a plane isn't going to solve anything now, Maria," Boyd said. "The law will find you in Mexico, too. You've got to have protection. If you're lucky, you'll get away from Lenni, maybe—but you'll never get away from the law."

She was sobbing wildly. No histrionics, honest terror.

"I want to go away. I must go. Now, tonight. I thought you would help me. Oh, Boyd—today I must go to a drug store. Kip was there, and Vincente. They did not see me because I run out through the back. They are looking for me. They will keel me! I have no place to turn. I have no frien' but you. I am alone!"

"I've got a pal who can help you, Maria. Remember Lew Marsh?"

There was a brief silence.

"*Sí.* Oh, *sí*, I remember. The newspaper Fourth Estate! *Sí!* He is your frien'? What will he do? Even Lenni is afraid of the newspaper Fourth Estate. How could he help me?"

"He'd get the State's Attorney to protect you if I asked him to."

"What is this State's Attorney?"

"The law, Maria. Lew Marsh is a very powerful man. He lives right here in the building. If he's home I'll call him and ask him up here. . . ."

In cautious sidesteps Lew moved away from the phone. Grudgingly, he thought: *the kid's all right. Hell, he's as good as my reporters.* His own shoes scuffed against the kitchen linoleum; he held his breath, and waited. The murmuring went on. Presently, over the sound of dialing, Maria asked Boyd to explain to Señor Marsh how innocent she was, and how frightened, and how very, very much she wanted to get away—right now, tonight.

"Lew? Boyd Copeland. Are you busy? I've got a friend up here. . . ."

Lew moved quickly through the empty living room, picking up his coat on the way, and into the elevator lobby, gently closing the door behind him. It was 9:45 now. LENNI GARR'S GIRL FOUND IN HIDING. Taper it off, Julian? Hardly. This would throw it wide open again. Hi-ya, Lenni. The crumbling masonry, kid. Hear it crack?

At 9:48 he pressed the elevator button. Rattling movement began below. The creaking cables brought the cage to the thirteenth floor. He waited until the automatic door had opened and closed before he tapped lightly and made a whistling entrance into Boyd's apartment.

"Well," Boyd said, assuming the attitude of a grateful neighbor, "lucky you were home." An actor couldn't have improved on his reading. "You've met Maria de Diego?"

Of the earth, earthy, sure enough. There was a soiled, slept-in, rat's-nest, wrinkled look about the Little Singer of San Juan Capistrano. No beauty shops, lately. No manicure. Tears had blurred mascara; exposure, or the fever of fear, had cracked her lips. Needed fresh lipstick. No bedroom prettiness just now. Not too clean.

". . . so you see," Boyd concluded an elaborate, noble-sounding explanation, "she's in a spot, Lew."

"Why do they want to kill you, Maria?" Lew asked.

She shrugged helplessly.

"You know too much?" he asked.

She measured an inch with thumb and forefinger.

"I know so little, *Señor,*" she cried. "This much."

Señor, she could not be more innocent! No! A poor, bedraggled, pure-hearted night-club singer from old *May-he-co, Señor,* who had stumbled into bad company. From the beginning, in the memory of her dear mother, God rest her soul, Maria de Diego had tried to break away from Lenni Garr. *Sí, Señor,* believe! Now that everyone was having so much trouble, she would be killed for no better reason than Kip's dark suspicion of her. She wanted monee, a chartered plane, and protection.

Wanted it all in a hell of a hurry, too. Mother of God—this terror—she could not sleep. . . .

"Toots," Lew said, "your only hope is to talk to the State's Attorney." He measured two inches, holding his fingers before her nose. "Tell him this much, anyhow. I'll see that he protects you."

She screamed, "I *will* go to jail!"

"You'll go to a hotel with a matron and a couple of cops to guard you. We'll get the law on your side, Maria. It's the only chance you've got." Lew added, brutally, "I've been waiting for somebody to find your body lying in an alley like an old sack of clothes."

Tears of self-pity streaked the mascara. Lew had drawn a vivid picture. She could see her body in an alley. Blood and bullets, and a crumpled sack of clothes. She had enough imagination for that.

Lew asked, "Where's Lenni now?"

"I do not know."

"You were with him. Where did you leave him?"

"In St. Louis."

"When?"

"Three weeks ago."

Three weeks. You could go anywhere this side of Venus in three weeks.

"Why did you leave him?"

"Señor Marsh," she said, earnestly, "in Duluth, Lenni took all my monee away from me or I would have left sooner. So, in St. Louis, I went through his pockets. It was at night. I didn't even bring my clothes."

"Scared of Lenni, were you?"

"He always watches me," she cried, and turned to Boyd for confirmation. "And he was *jealous*." She made a catlike spitting sound. "In the memory of my mother . . ."

"In the memory of your mother," Lew said, "who bombed Boyd's Lincoln?"

The tip of her red tongue explored the cracked lips.

"About this, I know nothing," she said, stoutly.

Boyd reached into his blue jeans, squatted on his haunches, idly bouncing a fat money-clip from palm to palm. She could see large numerals on the crisp green paper if she moved her eyes fast enough.

"Y'know, Lew," Boyd said, as Maria used her lipstick, "a couple of years ago, when I was still drinking, I went down to Taxco, in old Mexico. Ever been there?"

"Never have."

Maria followed the arch of the money clip like a spectator at a tennis match.

"It's a good little town," Boyd chuckled. "I bought a villa down there. I still own it."

Maria was now fascinated.

"It's an adobe *casa*, on a hillside," Boyd went on. "There's a red roof, bougainvillaea, and a six-foot wall around it. I've been thinking of deeding it over to Maria. What would you say?"

"Nice for her. If she lives."

The smoky eyes dreamed of Taxco, and a six-foot wall. She saw mountain sunsets, and a pig in the patio, maybe; saw herself with a jug of *tequila* under a banana tree; saw a happy *mañana*, far away.

"Who bombed my car, Maria?" Boyd asked.

She grew brave.

"It was Kip," she said, venomously. "It was Kip Zunches, Boyd. I *know!*"

Boyd pulled up a chair. The smile was not on his lips but somewhere around him.

"Any more questions, Lew?" he asked, enjoying himself.

You're all right, son, Lew thought. You'll do. He asked, "What did Lenni know about that bomb?"

Maria flashed, with a remnant of loyalty to Lenni, "Nothing. He would not be so stupid."

"Where is he now?"

"Truly," she said, bending forward with her soiled fingers locked in an attitude of prayer, "truly, I don't know."

"Will you tell the State's Attorney, what you *do* know, Maria—if I get him up here?"

"*Now?*" she cried.

Later would be better. It would be painful and, possibly, dangerous. Later, if at all. But she faced the problem in her busy little mind. No money, no friends, no clothes, nowhere to go. She added it up and got disaster.

"*Sí,*" she said, reluctantly. "I will tell him."

Lew said, as he started toward the phone, "Describe that picturesque villa in detail, son. It sounds right purty. Keep her calm."

The State's Attorney was away, Ike said, when Lew got him. Ike had been checking around, to save time. Three assistants were away, too—quail shooting near Pekin, Illinois. But he found another one, Joe Speares, curing a slight cold in the Buttery. Ike had told Joe Speares to stand by.

"Can we trust him?" Lew wondered.

"Looks like we'll have to. I can't find anybody else."

"Get him up here with a crew then—stenographer, muscle boys and a matron. What about Butch?"

"She wants to come."

Wants to come, he thought. And asked, "Is she being a good sport—is that it?"

"Didn't hesitate a second," Ike said, proudly. "Told me sure she'd go if you needed her. She's our gal."

Oh, fine.

"Send her along. Tell Jimmie to step on it."

He hung up, thinking, I can lose Charley, I can throw away my goddam book, but if I lose Paula . . .

The only drink you don't take is the first one. It's not for you, boy, it's not for you.

"Get him?" Boyd asked.

Lew turned blankly. Get who?

Christ almighty, I'm working a story, he remembered.

"Yeah," he said, moving to the window. "Joe Speares, an assistant. He'll be here soon."

He stood at the south bay watching the sweep of the now quiet avenue, listening to Boyd. The colorful reminiscence went on and on: very soothing to Maria; she was sailing over Taxco in old *May-he-co* on a magic carpet. The hillside houses, the clean mountain air, the blessed quiet of a sleepy town. And there was a piano in the villa. A *piano*, too! And a brand-new, never-used American-made stove. And two coffee grinders. Little odds and ends Boyd had bought when he had thought he was going to live in Taxco forever and work on his music. But, Boyd sighed, his ecstatic telegrams to his wife in Chicago had brought one short reply: *Potent Tequila?* So he had boarded up the house and left by plane for Hawaii, where he had ridden surfboards to regain his health. He'd forgotten about the villa; meant to sell it, sometime. But there it was.

"The Mexican agent in Taxco has the deed," he told her. "You're welcome to it, Maria. Auld Lang Syne."

"Señor Marsh!" she cried. Lew ignored her. "Boyd is sweet, no! So generous, no?"

Betcha, he thought. Open-handed, hard as nails, bright as a button. Quite a boy.

Headlights swerved in the gleaming darkness; the radio car made a U-turn in the street, pulling up to the curb with a flourish. Lew found a better view from another window. Feet moved under the canopy. Paula's buckled overshoes. Jimmie's rubbers. Here they were.

He waited until the distant buzzer sounded. "Surprise for you, son," he said to Boyd, as he went to the door.

And there she was. Your heart went out to Paula when she was frightened. She had a way of catching one corner of her lip between her teeth, leaving an indentation. It was indented now. L-Lew, she said, and squared her shoulders. Jimmie Kessler brushed ahead of her.

Boyd stared in smiling disbelief.

"Hello, B-Boyd," she said.

He held out both hands.

"Paula!" he said, huskily. "You're looking wonderful."

She briefly gave him the fingers of her right hand.

"I had a nice vacation," she said, stripping off her gloves. She turned to Maria, and reminded them, politely. "I've never met Miss de Diego."

Miss de Diego had been in Mexico, where she owned a villa, a piano, two coffee grinders, and was safe. The sight of Jimmie's camera brought her thudding back to a davenport in a half-furnished room in Chicago. She came screaming out of her dream. "No picture! No, no, no!"

A bulb flashed.

"Jimmie," Paula reproved sharply. "Look at that hair! Let her fix it before you take a picture."

Miss de Diego wasn't worried about her hair. Lenni would see the picture. Kip, Cully, Blue-Jaw Vincente—they would all see it. For sure, then, she would lie in an alley like an old sack of clothes.

"You have tricked me!" she screamed, clawing at them. "It's all for the papers, you have tricked me!"

She struck out at Boyd, dodged, kicked at the camera, and stumbled away sobbing. Lew found hard fists raining against his chest and fingernails flashing too close to his eyes. She was an armful of gamey violence, of the earth earthy, sure enough. Three nails scraped in a hard downward pull along his cheek.

"Toots," he said grimly, grinding her wrists together, "don't you want to meet Mrs. Copeland?"

The struggling abruptly ended.

"*Who, Señor?*" she asked.

Boyd met her startled eyes.

"Paula," he said, gravely, performing the introductions with a half-humorous downturn of his hand, "Miss de Diego." He bowed slightly. "Maria, Mrs. Copeland." Then he leaned one arm comfortably on the piano to await developments.

Maria smoothed her dress:

"How do you do, *Señora*," she murmured, with manners. "I have heard so much about you!"

Paula said, crisply, "Let's do something about that hair."

"Sí! It's a fright," Maria apologized. "I lost my luggage."

"B-Boyd," said Paula, and he arched one brow in a politely inquiring air. "B-Boyd, did the movers take all the boxes in the storeroom?"

He considered. "They got everything marked 'Take,'" he said.

She flushed. "I forgot to mark things in the storeroom." She slipped an arm companionably about Maria's waist. "I've something that will f-fit you, M-Maria. A hostess gown. It's r-red."

Cannel coal spit loudly on the hearth. An unseen clock went on busily ticking.

"Lew," Boyd said, "you're bleeding profusely."

Lew unfolded a handkerchief.

Boyd watched with clinical interest. "Y'know, I never had you picked for St. Valentine. Was this your idea—or Ike's?"

Lew dabbed again. Three long pencil streaks of blood on the white linen.

"Paula happened to be in the office," he said, brusquely. "We always use a gal for a thing like this."

True enough, but it had a hollow sound.

Boyd rounded his lips in a humorous o.

"Well," he murmured, going around to the piano bench, "it brings together quite a cast of characters."

He produced bright notes from an old song, inquiring with exaggerated concern, "Still bleeding? You'd better splatter it with antiseptic. Maria's nails are probably poisonous as a snake." He ran all the way up the keyboard and down again in a spectacular display of fingering. "You'll find mercurochrome in the bathroom." He mused, dreamily, "There was a time when I often came home somewhat scratched up, myself."

A catchy tune from *Call Me Madam* filled the room when Lew came back. Boyd sang a rousing chorus: *"They Like Ike!"*

Jimmie's glance said: Can he play! Tonight in the darkroom Jimmie would hold forth: Jeez, that Marsh! Know what the guy did? Sent Butch to her ex-husband's apartment to get a story outa the guy's girl friend. Can you beat it? . . . There was always gossip in the darkroom. Tonight Jimmie would take the floor.

It was 11:01 when the buzzer finally sounded again.

"Call Paula, will you, Jimmie?" Lew ordered.

Boyd punctuated a last note.

"No, no, *I* will," he said, and went whistling down the hall.

The room was suddenly crowded.

Joe Speares had worked his way through law school as a room clerk in the Congress Hotel; there was a professional air of bonhomie about him still. He was a round, double-breasted, bald-pated man who so yearned for admiration that he couldn't be trusted. "I'm very fond of the newspaper boys," he often said, willing to be quoted. "I always try to play fair and square with the newspaper boys."

"What happened to your cheek, Lew?" he asked, curiously. Must be bleeding again. Lew's answer was implicit.

"Maria de Diego's in there," he said, jerking his head. "And it's my story, palsy. If there's a leak I'll cut your heart out."

"Why, Lew," Joe protested. "I always play fair and square with you newspaper boys."

Two bulging State's Attorney's cops found places for their wide bottoms. The pale stenographer set up his stenotype machine. "What happened here?" asked the sweet-faced matron. "Where's the furniture?"

Paula called gaily from the hallway, "We're ready, Lew!"

Maria had been scrubbed, gowned and scented. She made a rustling, dramatic entrance, giving them everything but a first chorus.

The red hostess gown outlined her upthrust little breasts and she smoothed her hips happily during Paula's introductions. *Señor,* she nodded, *Señora,* and murmured a politeness to each with a gracious nod of her shining head. A silver ornament glittered in her hair; a bracelet of heavy dangling pesos made a cheerful tinkle from her wrists.

"And Boyd, of course," Paula concluded.

"Ah, yes," Boyd said, "we've met."

He returned to his comfortable, slouched position against the piano. Very interested, very much at ease. Paula studiously ignored him.

"All right, Jimmie," she said.

The bulbs flashed. Maria gave Jimmie her best three-quarters and both knees. And she knew about silhouettes, too, and gave him side views. Apparently, while dressing, she had decided that she was among so-kind people and would actually find herself owning a villa in *May-he-co.* Out of the frying pan into the bougainvillaea. She couldn't have been happier.

"Now, Maria," Lew said.

The too-cute accent revealed how innocent she was, how young, bewildered, and eager-hearted, and how she had sung in choirs.

"Let's get down to it, Maria," Lew said.

"Well . . ." she began.

That rainy night when she'd first met Señor Marsh at the Huarache Club, and her troubles started, she had been forced to accompany Lenni to the Lorraine Arms. That was an apartment hotel on the near North Side which Lenni owned, *Señores.* Many of his men lived there. Kip

Zunches and Blue-Jaw Vincente; Cully Yates used an apartment on the top floor when late business kept him in town overnight. . . . Well, they were playing a so-dull game of gin when Cully burst in with news of the bombing. Lenni was furious, *Señores, but* furious. *Sí!* He sent for Kip and slapped him right and left and paced the floor in a torment of anger. Then he had called his attorney, Señor Losh Damon, and by sunrise, on that miserable, wet morning, they had crossed the state line into Indiana in Lenni's car. Such a scurrying about, *Señores.* Such anger! They had gone to Detroit, Cleveland—to a dozen cities; whenever Lenni phoned Chicago for information from his attorney there was nothing but bad news. His men were being rousted. They were in jail. Or they were out on bail. Or they were in jail again. Or more bail monee was needed. Or a man had skipped town, forfeiting the monee. Then there were terrifying rumors that Lenni's own men would now try to kill him, since he was, as they said, so-hot. Soon he felt unsafe even in the little wayside hotels; they stopped in tourist homes, and signed under false names, and were forever changing the license plates on the car. And then, one evening in Duluth, because she had had such an innocent, gay little momentary conversation with a saxophone player in an all-night restaurant, Lenni had become abusive. He had emptied her purse, stealing her monee. In St. Louis, one evening, he had violently threatened her. *Sí.* He said he would kill her if she ever told anybody about the stuff in the basement of the Huarache Club, and so she went through his pants . . .

Joe Speares interrupted, "What stuff, Maria?"

"The marijuana, *Señor,*" she said, simply.

The stenographer's fingers tapped the silent keys.

Joe masked his excitement.

"You *know* this, do you, Maria?"

"*Sí,*" she said, basking in their smiles. "All the marijuana that comes to Chicago from Mexico and California—it is because Lenni knows how to bring it here. There are safes for the marijuana behind the bricks in the Huarache Club, in the basement. Pedro Cesena, the head waiter, he knows. And the busboys. They are not real busboys. . . ."

When the paper had stopped rolling and the stenographer leaned back in his chair, Joe Speares said, with a sharp snap of his fingers, "That buttons it up, Lew. We've got enough for an indictment."

Lew grabbed his coat. 11:45, now. Too much to do, too little time in which to do it. But Joe stopped him at the door.

"You'll alert every hoodlum in town if you print this now," he complained. "I wish you'd hold up one more day. . . ."

The opposition papers would give Joe hell tomorrow. Reporters would storm his office all day long. The other city editors would threaten him, remind him of their long memories and what would happen to him, later on. But given one more day, the story might leak out somehow—and save his hide.

"I've got to pick up Kip Zunches again," he lamented, following Lew into the hall. "And what about the Huarache? They'll sweep it clean before I can make a raid."

Lew grinned. "But we'll help you, Joey." He added sharply, "Nobody owes your office for this one, palsy. You're to stay here and talk to nobody until 4 A.M. If there's a slip I'll gouge your eyes out—is that clear?"

It was clear. Joe backed away, worrying about tomorrow.

The radio car's tail light drew ahead of them on the avenue. Lew debated, hesitated, released a long breath and decided to say it, "Your ex-husband has made it, Paula. Got it licked."

She stirred uneasily in the seat beside him.

"You sound pretty definite."

"I'm an expert. Haven't you heard?"

"Aren't you ever wrong?"

"Not about drunks."

Her reaction surprised him. No interest. She thrust her hands deeper into her pockets.

"I've seen Boyd sober before."

"Not like this," he said, for the record. "This is it."

She flared up.

"Dolly's coming back," she told him, bitterly. "I had a letter from Dad Copeland—they can't wait till Christmas. I've seen all this for years. Once Boyd went ten months without a drink—right up to the holidays. But then Harvey and Dolly came home from somewhere. It's always the same old thing."

She didn't want to talk about it; she was sick of thinking and talking about Boyd—she had to forget him, and all those wasted years.

The Ives Building loomed ahead; her mind, like his own, centered on the story.

"I made notes," she said, as they got out. "Will you need them?"

"Stick around. We'll see."

When he rolled copy paper into the typewriter the old excitement caught him. He thought: I'm a reporter, this is what I can do, this is what I'm best at. For a few moments he was conscious of voices, Paula's voice, and Ike's; then the obsession caught him, and time blurred. Somebody said, "That it, Lew?" He stared bemused at the copy boy who had snatched the last page and scurried away. Jimmie Kessler hurried from the darkroom to the night managing editor with a handful of dripping prints; and with no memory of having left his desk Lew found himself staring over Jed's shoulder at Maria's knees, her night-club smile, her tight little breasts in silhouette. "Good going," Jed said. Good pictures, a good story; a cold beat.

"Somebody will turn up with Lenni now," he warned. "It had better be us."

The thought nudged into Lew's exultation: a drink now—down the stairs, across the alley, into Abe's and a drink. He frowned out the window. Well, well—winter, for sure. Falling snowflakes brought the green dwarfs nearer, made them seem brighter, busier. Today's well-written weather hadn't predicted snow. A surprise for everybody: the city would be briefly white in the morning, white and clean. NIGHT CLUB SINGER BARES LENNI GARR'S SECRETS—and snow. Big news in the morning.

I sure as hell wish I could drink, he thought.

"The cops picked up young Eddie Yates in that British car tonight," Jed's voice said. "Doing seventy on Roosevelt Road. They threw him in the can."

Eddie Yates, Cully's boy. Great family man, Cully. The second-generation hoodlums were family men. Lew found himself trying to think about Eddie Yates. The information was important. It meant something. He'd have to mull it over, later on.

He watched the wintry streets and thought: I feel *right* at a typewriter, I'm a reporter. . . . Phrases from his story crowded into his mind. Not bad, either. Pretty good, in fact. I can write, he thought. I've got to get off that desk.

What was Jed saying?

"Condaffer and Swain phoned in asking for you. Did you have any reason for telling them to lay off that kid?"

"What kid?"

"Eddie Yates."

Lew tried to remember.

"They were all set to roust him one night, Jed. Didn't seem much point in it at the time."

"We aren't using the story. But from what Swain said I thought maybe you knew something special."

Lew mused, "I figured if we ever want to force Lenni to talk we might get at him through his son. He's got a boy, too . . ."

The red running letters spelled out their glad tidings behind a thickening curtain of white . . . Non-fattening . . . Made . . . with . . . pure . . . spring . . . water . . . it's . . . good . . . for . . . you . . . He was seeing Lenni's tense face at the Huarache Club. The angry words echoed in his mind:

You kept my old man scared all his life. What's in the papers, he'd say, worrying about us kids—about you guys crucifying his whole family so we couldn't get in any decent private schools. I got my boy in St. Matthias. . . .

St. Matthias!

Maybe, Lew thought. Maybe this is it.

Jed was studying him with a curious awareness when he turned around.

"Anything else?" Lew asked, abruptly.

They had got drunk together once, in the old days. They had rented motorcycles for a week-end fishing trip and escaped without a scratch—or a fish. It had been quite a holiday.

"Everything all right, pal?" Jed asked, nervously.

"Fine, fine."

What the hell. When a man was beset with the compulsion did he flash radar signals? Did Jed know?

"Young Copeland's made the grade," Lew told him over his shoulder. "You might teletype the Old Man about it. Tell him I said so. He'll be pleased."

He went out through the local room. Nightside reporters cluttered around the city desk. At quitting time some of the men visited the Athletic Club for a swim in the unlighted, deserted pool before catching their late trains for home. They were telling Ike and Paula about their muscles.

Lew moved unnoticed through the room.

In the library, an ancient hunchback, eating a peanut-butter sandwich, came from the shadows.

"A prep-school registry, Elmer," Lew said.

He sat at a desk overlooking the alley. Even Abe Rouch's back-door sign was brighter in the falling snow. ABE ROUCH'S BAR—FOR MEN ONLY. Three customers came out, blew plumes of breath, and trudged away, making a fresh path; very companionable, feeling first-rate. Warm handshakes, cheery good nights. Not a drop of blood in their veins—nothing but alcohol and the milk of human kindness.

A red-covered book had been placed in front of him long ago. Lew stared at it. In a dim nearby corner the hunchback sipped milk through a straw.

"Heavy snowstorm," Elmer said, and made a sucking sound.

Snowing, Lew. Early winter, Lew. An inch, Lew, two inches, Lew. Tomorrow the snow-greetings would be skimmed off the top of the mind. Hi-ya, Lew. Snowing.

He studied pictures of St. Matthias. Sheep grazed on a wide, green campus; ivy-grown brick buildings, very old, quaint. St. Matthias, on the shores of a winding river in Wisconsin. Founded 1887, college preparatory, 400 students, Dr. Lee Brill Prescott, headmaster. *Students admitted on recommendation only.*

On recommendation only? But that would offer no problem to Lenni. Lenni Garr could manage high-class recommendations. Lenni knew V.I.P.'s—knew 'em intimately.

"Thanks, Elmer," Lew said, and heard the straw strike bottom in the bottle.

Ike sat alone with his feet on the desk, half asleep.

"Where's Butch?" Lew asked, surprised.

Ike roused. "Butch?" he yawned. "She missed her train. I got her a room at the Bismarck. We thought you'd gone."

He decided to walk. The snow scratched at his face; he gulped down the biting air and increased his pace. Desire for a drink was like a cry from the nerves just under the skin: I want a drink, a drink, I need a drink. . . . Charley would have said: Time to have some of your friends in for an evening, Mr. Lew, it's a big help when the folks get a little bit plastered. They act foolish and take their hair down and that's a big help . . . True, too. Nothing strengthened your own resolve like other people's slackening faces, their thickening tongues, the neurotic nonsense that issued from them, the minor idiocies; a savage pride in your own sobriety re-enforced your abstinence when loose-lipped good fellows launched into "Old MacDonald Had a Farm." Charley's sensitivity had been a help.

I miss you, boy, he thought.

He said into the house phone in the Bismarck lobby when Paula answered, "I've stumbled into something, Butch. Will you please come down?"

The lobby clock shocked him: 3:12. What in hell had he been doing all this time? Dreaming?

She'd been sound asleep. But she splashed cold water on her face, woke herself up with lipstick, and here she was, ready for anything. Work—that was what she wanted: any time, day, night, or three o'clock in the morning.

"Something about Lenni?" she asked, bright-eyed and interested.

He found remote chairs.

"I want you to go to St. Matthias right now," he told her. "Young Anton Garr is a student there. I've a hunch Lenni keeps in touch with him—letters, phone calls, telegrams. The school won't want publicity and I doubt if the boy will talk—so it calls for handling. If you're lucky there'll be a slip or a tip—somebody up there knows where Lenni is."

Excitedly, she ran her fingers through her hair.

"You're pretty good, aren't you?" she said.

"We'll try everything."

While she was upstairs getting ready to go he phoned the North-western Station and found a mail train leaving for Madison at 3:46 A.M. There was, he found, a plane at four. But Paula hated flying. He phoned her room.

"Hurry, Butch. Mail train at 3:46. I'll ride over with you."

There were no cabs in sight—and, anyway, she said, she enjoyed walking the deserted winter streets at night, liked the buildings best when they were dark and quiet. She lengthened her stride, or skipped to keep up with him; the prospect of an important, out-of-town assignment had made her gay.

He said, suddenly, "Boyd has snapshots of you in front of every bottle in his bar."

"That sounds like the sort of thing you do when you're drunk," she decided.

"Or when you intend to stay sober."

"I don't want to hear any more about it," she said, angrily. "What are you trying to do?" She caught his arm and stopped him. "Why did you send me to Boyd's apartment? To meet Maria?"

"No," he said. "I thought you ought to see Boyd sober."

"Why?"

"Because," he said, grimly, "when you're over that one, we're going to get married, did you know that?"

A hell of a proposal, this was. He thought: even without the jug, my timing's wrong.

She was staring at him.

"I'll tell you something, Butch," he said, harshly, "I always planned to marry you."

"You did?"

"I was planning to marry you when I met Alice."

She nodded with mock gravity.

"Must have been crazy about me."

"I love you. The jug got in the way once. It won't now."

"Gosh," she said, catching up with him again, "this sounds like a right honorable offer."

"When I leave for London you're going along."

"I am?"

"You are, if you're ready."

She skipped three steps and caught up again.

"Because you love me?"

"That's right."

"And want me to be your wife?"

"That's right."

"This is a proposal?"

"That's right, Paula."

"Well," she said, breathlessly, "it's awful damn sweet of you, Lew."

They had turned in wide doors at the station. They climbed the long steps in silence.

"Well?" Lew asked.

He was surprised to find tears in her eyes.

"I'll have to admit it's not entirely a new idea," Paula said.

A conductor at the coach steps watched them curiously. He looked at his watch, smiled broadly, called, "All aboard!"

Paula broke away.

In the vestibule she put her forehead against the window, saw him, and waved. He walked along beside the moving train. . . .

16 The city had been lulled into inaction by the snow; the local room was warm and listless at eleven o'clock that morning. Don Bell, sitting in for Ike, swung lazily in his chair.

"If this keeps up," Don said, "this town is going to lose its reputation."

Where were the despairing souls who leaped from windows? The boy who didn't know the gun was loaded? The dolt who crashed his headlights into street cars? The young hoodlums with their flick-blade knives? The sex maniac? All snowed in, maybe.

On a dull day, Lew thought, even the telephones have a strangely muted sound.

"Yes?" he said, lifting the receiver.

It was Paula, calling collect from Hunter's Green, Wisconsin.

"Anton Garr isn't registered at St. Matthias," she said wearily. "He never has been. I've studied the lists for four years back."

"Who'd you talk to?" he snapped.

"Dr. Prescott's secretary."

"Covering up, was he?"

"Lew, this is a cloister. It's quaint and Anglican and the kids have names like Fitzhugh, Field, Garrard and Butler. Healthy little bluebloods."

"Did you tell the secretary who you were?"

"I'm not that rusty." It was her turn to speak sharply. "I didn't give my name."

That would take some doing. Good, wasn't she?

Lew's pencil doodled jug-shaped figures with spindly arms and legs. They marched upward across a sheet of copy paper. He made two more.

"Where are you now?"

"At the depot," Paula said. "It's three miles from the school." She added, wistfully, "There's a train to Madison in twenty minutes."

An animated jug lifted thin knees as if running for a train. Lew sketched in a depot sign, hearing, under a shadow of memory, Lenni's voice saying: *I got a son at St. Matthias!* The black-hearted bastard had been genuinely proud. Big-timing it? Hardly.

"Lew—are you still there?"

"I'm here," he said. "Hold on a minute, Butch."

You can scheme, reason, deduce or beat your brains out, he thought, but there's nothing like a flash of inspiration. He drew a bursting balloon and labeled it: *idea!*

"I still think he's there, Paula. Tell you how to find out: go ask the headmaster if there's a boy in school whose parents he doesn't know."

Her voice brightened.

"Oh," she said, contritely. "I never thought of that."

"Call me back."

He hung up and sent to the library for the Lenni Garr folder. Young Anton Garr had been photographed when he appeared in court with his sisters at the time of Lenni's Calumet City divorce. And someone had dug up a snapshot of him dressed as a Pilgrim Father for an eighth-grade Thanksgiving play. He was a dark-skinned, solemn-faced kid staring into the camera under his tall hat. Later, wearing a track suit and a crew haircut, he turned up at a Fourth of July celebration with a silver loving cup in his hand. No mention of St. Matthias. No late photographs of Anton. . . .

The quiet room was suddenly electric. Lil Claussinius tossed her plugs with a livelier interest. A copy boy sprinting in from the hall whispered big news to a girl reporter. Heads lifted, typing stopped. Lil said, around her gum: *The Old Man is in the building!*

Don instantly figured it out.

"He's here to wrestle with the printers over a new contract."

Lew put the Garr pictures back in the folder and pulled up a sheet of copy.

"Heard from Paula?" a voice asked.

Julian, beside the desk, calmly lighted a fresh cigar. No hypertension, these days. No acidosis. Lew brought him up to date on St. Matthias and wondered, what in hell happened to calm him down out there in California.

Julian blew rich smoke upward.

"Mr. Ives will be interested," he said. "He likes to keep posted on Paula."

Still unhurried, he paused at the switchboard to joke with Lillian, visited the teletypes, and moved serenely on to John Ives's private office. Don, too, had noticed.

"Julian's vacation sure did him a hell of a lot of good," he observed. "The boys are saying he got a thirty per cent raise."

"That so?"

"It's what they say."

Pete Villegas, red-nosed from the cold, came in from the beat and lingered at the desk with happy tidings.

"It's not so quiet other places," he reported, grinning. "There's hell to pay at the State's Attorney's office. I hear the *Tribune* is beating Mr. Speares's brains out."

The opposition, again one lap behind, would lop off a few heads in their scramble to catch up. The P.M.'s de Diego stories had had a sheepish, rewritten note about them. There wouldn't be much left for tomorrow's *Tribune* unless they dug up something new.

"We sure whopped 'em," the boy said, proudly.

That, Lew thought, was yesterday.

This was today.

Then, at two o'clock, Paula called.

"Lew," she said, excitedly, "you were right."

He swung around with his back to the local room. "Are you where you can talk?" he asked, cautiously.

"Drug store. But I can hear breathing on the wire."

Lew laughed. "That's me," he said.

Her tone conveyed more than the words, "*Somebody* is coming here soon."

"Sure?"

"There's more than I know how to handle," she said, urgently. "Would you send Jerry Weintraub right away?"

"Airport in the village?"

"Yes—a little one. A cow pasture with a runway."

"I'll charter a plane and be right up."

"*Yourself?*"

"Rattling my golden chains," he told her.

Hi-ya, Lenni? Nigger killed in a clubman's convertible. How you doing, boy?

"Take over, Don." Lew put on his overcoat. "Tell Julian I'll phone him."

"Yeah?" Don stared at him. "Where'll I say you've gone?"

"Back tonight." The gate swung violently behind him.

The Old Man liked to keep posted on Paula, did he? Well, here was one to make him proud. Julian could roll his cigar between his lips and tell the Old Man all about it—later on.

Lew walked slowly down the stairs, lingered on the sidewalk to chat with a *Tribune* reporter who was on his way to Abe's for a liquid lunch, strolled across the street to the parking lot where, as usual, he matched coins with the attendant for the day's fee. His knees were jumping but nobody could say they'd seen Lew Marsh hightailing it out of the Ives Building because a big one was about to break wide open somewhere. . . .

Winter darkness had settled on the Wisconsin countryside when the chartered Fairchild buzzed the field at Hunter's Green. Paula was waiting near the hangar in a brand-new Plymouth, borrowed from the local dealer. She raced through the drifted snow as he left the plane.

"I've discovered a lot of new stars in the sky, watching for you," she said, taking his arm. She had brought a thermos of coffee, thick white restaurant sandwiches and cigarettes. "Where do you want to go?"

"The school," he said.

"I asked your question and the whole thing opened up," she said, jubilantly, sliding behind the wheel. "You are smart, aren't you?"

Lew, shivering with cold, unscrewed the thermos, splashed hot coffee on his knee, and burned his lip. They turned east on a snowy highway with the windshield wipers flicking away at gently falling flakes.

"What's the name?"

"Tony Gardener. And guess who handles his affairs? Losh Damon, Lenni's lawyer."

"You're pretty good, yourself," Lew said, and took another cautious sip.

"I got kind of panicky, though. When Dr. Prescott told me he expects Mr. Gardener any day now I had a mental picture of Lenni walking in on me—and what could I do?" She gripped the wheel tightly and eased the car over the frozen ruts at the crossroads. "Losh Damon was here two weeks ago. Tony refused to go back to his father. That's all I found out before I ducked for the phone."

"You didn't see the boy?"

"I didn't try to. It was a casual conversation. I couldn't seem too interested."

Lew locked the thermos between his knees and unwrapped a sandwich.

"Who were you supposed to be, Butch?"

"A mother—though I didn't actually say so." She smiled across at him. "I gave off impressions."

217

"You'll have goddam beautiful kids," he told her, taking a big bite. "Even I can see that."

"Lew," she said, gravely, "I fell in love with Dr. Prescott. He's sweet and kindly—a sort of saint."

He detected a note of warning.

"I won't hurt him."

"But you swear a lot."

"Do?"

"More than you realize. You goddam it all the time."

"Getting a little bossy, aren't you?" he asked, pleased.

"Wait 'til you see that sanctuary," she said. "I kept wondering all the time I was with that nice old man, well—if Christianity is true, what are we all *doing?*"

"Riding to hell on a guided missile," Lew suggested. "Were you converted, Butch?"

"No. But I think I met a Christian."

"That'd be goddam interesting. I've always wanted to see one—a real one."

She couldn't be wrong about Dr. Prescott, she said. He had spent a lifetime in schools for boys; and now, seventy or more, he was a dedicated man, as unworldly as anyone she had ever met. They had talked about broken homes, and the effect of divorce on adolescent youngsters; his devotion to his work had been in every word he said. She had managed to get into his office without so much as giving her name; he had assumed, because of something she had said about Reno, and the women she had met there, that she was a divorcee seeking a school for an unhappy young son. She had said, "I suppose you have boys here whose parents you never see?" He had answered: "Only one," and had told her about his deep concern for Tony Gardener, a sophomore, a good boy, well-liked.

"What are you going to say when we see him?" Paula asked, nervously.

"Well, if he's as honest as you say he is, I'll lay it on the line."

Paula was silent for the long, last mile.

"Look," she said, "it's a kind of Shangri-La."

Across the snowy fields ahead he saw a chapel spire against the wintry evening sky. The white road curved between white rolling hills leading gently downward and over a narrow concrete bridge. On a wide place in the frozen river dozens of youngsters in stocking caps and mittens were skating in the light of a roaring bonfire. A boy in a red mackinaw waved a greeting and spun into an expert figure eight, showing off. They went up a steep grade past a picture-postcard dairy farm, on past a lonely field with an abandoned barn, then turned left at wide stone gates and entered an avenue of tall pines. A sweep of lawn was marked by recent ski tracks and wood smoke was in the air. Sanctuary was the word, sure enough. When the motor stopped the trees whispered, and there were no other sounds. The school looked out across two hundred acres of fields and fences, clean and hushed under the winter sky.

"Peace, it's wonderful," Lew said.

He remembered sitting in the old Morris chair on the sun porch of his grandfather's house reading the prep-school ads in the magazines. He had wanted to join Stover at Lawrenceville and go on with him to Yale. . . .

A gnomelike clerk in a boy's green letterman sweater appeared in the lighted doorway of the administration building.

"I'm back!" Paula said, brightly. "May I see Dr. Prescott again?"

"Oh, yes," the little man said, peering at her. "I think he will be very glad to see you."

He took them into a book-lined study where a log crackled on the hearth. Someone had had tea here, not long ago. The curtains were drawn, and the room was comfortable.

"Let's see," the little man said to Paula, hesitating in the doorway, "your name again?"

Paula smiled sweetly.

"He'll know," she said. "Dr. Prescott will remember me."

Lew was thinking, as he looked over the titles on the polished shelves: here was a haven, here were the books he had always hoped to find time to read. *War and Peace*—yes, indeed. And Albert Schweitzer: *In Quest of the Historical Jesus*. That, too. Gray's *Anatomy* and Blackstone's *Commentaries, Don Quixote*—and Toynbee. Be great, wouldn't it, to ease off for a while and read such books? Between assignments, in London, there would be time. In a snug flat somewhere, with Paula in a big chair on the other side of the fireplace. He turned to find her squaring her shoulders.

"What's the matter?"

Soft-soled shoes brushed along the hall.

"The only thing I don't like about this job is the lying I have to do," she whispered.

He glanced up to see a serene, leathery face and a shock of white hair. Dr. Lee Brill Prescott wore a tweed jacket with suede patches on the elbows, a wool scarf, and fleece-lined moccasins. Lew thought: he's Mr. Groton, Mr. Andover, Mr. Lawrenceville, Mr. St. Matthias—and old Mr. Chips, himself.

"Do you know," Dr. Prescott said, taking both of Paula's hands, "I was such a chatterbox this afternoon I neglected to get your name?" He chuckled in self-rebuke. "And you never did tell me why you came to see me! I was so garrulous I must have driven your mission right out of your head." He added, twinkling, "I must say I've been quite puzzled about you."

"I can clear it up." Lew moved from the bookshelves. "This girl is a reporter. I'm her city editor."

Paula hastily performed the introductions.

"And *your* name, miss?" The headmaster was shocked.

She told him, looked for a chair in the shadows, found one and sat down.

"You're from the Madison *Journal?*" the old gentleman asked.

"Chicago," Lew said.

"Indeed?" With a gracious, old-world gesture, he indicated the red leather chair, and said, with a trace of humor, "No wonder I was so talkative. I fell into the hands of an expert." He stopped as he lowered himself into his chair at the desk. "You *do* have a son, Mrs. Copeland?"

"No, sir," Paula said, faintly.

"Didn't you *tell* me you had a son?"

"No, sir."

He sank down and rocked gently.

"You haven't been to Reno, either?"

"That part was true."

"Well, well, it was a fascinating conversation. I'm glad some of it was true." He examined Lew with sharp blue eyes under bristling brows. "I presume, Mr. Marsh, there is a—professional reason for your visit?"

"I'm afraid so. Are you familiar with the name Lenni Garr?"

Dr. Prescott bridged his fingers, pursed his lips and considered.

"No. Should I be?"

"He's a Chicago racketeer."

"Perhaps I'm not quite up to date," Dr. Prescott smiled. "We subscribe to the Hunter's Green *Pilot-Review* and *Newsweek*—but I'm often too busy to read them. The outside world gets so exercised about so many things! This is a Latin school, you know—stressing what we consider to be the fundamentals." He added, comfortably, "It's better for the boys this way."

"You have a student named Tony Gardener?"

He stopped rocking.

"Yes—and a fine boy, Mr. Marsh. Your visit doesn't concern Tony, I trust?"

"Not if 'Tony Gardener' is the lad's right name. I don't think it is."

He bristled. "*I beg your pardon!* Why, of course, it's his name. Tony Gardener came to us most highly recommended."

"Dr. Prescott," Lew said, quietly, "we suspect Tony's real name is Anton Garr. His father is the most wanted criminal in the country at this moment."

The lips moved, repeating the words. "That's a rather alarming statement, sir."

"Losh Damon handles Tony's affairs, I understand. Damon is Lenni Garr's attorney. And Garr, in a loose moment, once told me he had a son at St. Matthias. We've been adding things up."

"You'll forgive me, sir," he lifted both hands to adjust his glasses, "I find this very difficult to credit."

"Who recommended this boy to you?"

"Eh? Most *highly* recommended," Dr. Prescott said. But he was worried enough to scuff his moccasins to the filing cabinet where he read three letters from beginning to end. "A superior court judge," he said, stoutly, coming back to the desk, "a park commissioner and a minister—the Rev. Horace DeWitt of River Forest."

"That just ties it tighter," Lew said. "Lenni Garr has an estate near River Forest."

Dr. Prescott smacked his palm on the blotter as if calling an unruly class to order.

"I can't imagine why Tony would deceive me—if he has—but I do know this, Mr. Marsh: Tony is a good Christian boy, a boy of character. I know about such things. I have dealt with boys all my life long. I fail to see how anyone can benefit if you print this matter in your newspaper." He waved Lew to silence, sternly addressing Paula. "You took an unfair advantage, Mrs. Copeland. I wouldn't have told you a word about Tony had I known who you were."

Paula left her shelter.

"Dr. Prescott," she said, earnestly. "We won't print anything about Tony. His father is a racketeer, a murderer, a dope peddler—and he's in hiding. The police are trying to find him. I came here hoping to get a line on a criminal—a man you'd want in jail."

Dr. Prescott sat down again.

"Tell me, please," Lew said, patiently. "When did Losh Damon come here to get Tony?"

"Two weeks ago."

"He had a good story, I suppose. What was it?"

"He said Mr. Gardener had moved permanently to Mexico and wanted the boy to join him."

"What happened?"

"Tony refused to go."

"Why?"

"He was distraught, Mr. Marsh—he sobbed in my arms, sir. He . . ." Dr. Prescott thoughtfully bumped a thumbnail against his teeth. "He said it would ruin his life if he were forced to live with his father. It's a very distressing situation. I had assumed the problem was one more broken home . . ."

"What did you tell Damon?"

The blue eyes sparkled.

"Sir, I have no legal obligation to turn the boy over to anyone—except the father. I made this perfectly clear to Mr. Damon. I had hoped I might prevail on Mr. Gardener to allow Tony to stay."

"You've heard from Damon recently?"

"I have."

" 'Mr. Gardener' is coming here?"

"So I am told."

"When?"

"No time was mentioned."

"May I see Damon's letter?"

"I think not. He merely informed me that the boy's father felt he could clear things up when he arrived here. Mr. Gardener is due back in the States very shortly. As a matter of fact, I have been expecting him for some days."

"Does Tony know all this?"

"I am forthright with my boys. One must learn to face one's difficulties, isn't it so? Tony begged me to persuade his father to allow him to stay. He is happy at St. Matthias. I shall do what I can."

"His tuition is paid?"

"For this year, yes."

"You still want him here—if what we suspect is true?"

"Certainly, sir," he said, emphatically. "He'll need my help more than ever."

Lew asked, gently, "Do you have scholarships, doctor?"

"We have many wealthy patrons . . ." he began, and broke off. "These are rather prying questions, Mr. Marsh."

"I am asking them because I think we can help you."

Dr. Prescott was skeptical.

"It would seem that we might need help," he said. "Yours would come from an unexpected quarter."

Lew said, carefully, "If you'll let us handle this—if no other paper learns about it—we'll keep Tony's name, and the school, out of the story."

Dr. Prescott nodded, sagely.

"This is what is called a scoop?"

"From your point of view," Lew observed, "it will have certain virtues.

222

We'll pick up Lenni Garr ten miles from here. There'll be no mention of St. Matthias—or the boy."

"But you see," Dr. Prescott said, "I have no way of knowing when the man is coming—nor from what direction."

Lew avoided Paula's eyes.

"Will you leave it to me, sir?" he asked. "We have ways of handling such things."

"After this experience," the old gentleman said, fixing a sad look on Paula, "I not only will refrain from speaking to newspaper reporters, I shall henceforth be wary of attractive young women. However, I'm by no means convinced that Tony has deceived me."

Lew asked, "May I see the boy?"

"I'm sorry. I shouldn't like to upset him again."

"Not to talk to him, doctor," Lew said, restraining his impatience. "If he's Anton Garr, I'll recognize him.".

Dr. Prescott hesitated, saw a plea in Paula's eyes and rose reluctantly. "Very well. We'll find the youngsters at the rink this evening." He excused himself. "Let me bundle up," he said. "It's snowing again."

Ten minutes later, looking like an intellectual Daniel Boone, he joined them on the porch wearing a beaver cap and a bulky sheepskin jacket.

"I will remember this day for a long, long time," he said, offering Paula his arm. "I doubt if I shall ever again encounter such consummate artistry." He called over his shoulder. "Is this young lady highly paid, Mr. Marsh?"

"Not nearly what she's worth," Lew smiled.

"It has taught me a lesson," the doctor said, with a humorous breath that was not quite a chuckle. "I'm getting to be an old windbag. But I'll learn. One is never too old."

They followed a narrow path to the bonfire. Dr. Prescott had put on overshoes, not bothering to buckle them, and they clicked cheerfully as he walked ahead. Boys on the rink called out to him, "Hi, Dr. Prescott!"

He waved, nodding his head in approbation. Skaters cut the corners faster, now that he was there to watch; there were spectacular figure eights, and pirouettes. On the outer edge Lew saw a dark-skinned, solemn, gangling boy who was skating backwards in easy, graceful strides. He had seen the same grave face under a tall Pilgrim hat. When the boy had skimmed into the firelight, Lew said, "Say hello to Anton Garr, Dr. Prescott."

"Good evening, Tony!" Dr. Prescott called.

The boy waved shyly and skated on.

Dr. Prescott turned on his heel and they followed his sturdy figure up the path to the car.

"I have prayed about that boy," he said. "You know, at first blush, you people bear no resemblance to an answer to prayer." He patted Paula's hand. "But I've found in my long life that answers often come wearing disguises." He shook a reproving finger at her. "You dissembled outrageously, but I forgive you. Tony, you see, has had a fiercer struggle than I knew. I understand him better now."

Lew thought: damned if I haven't finally met a Christian. He felt the clear blue eyes looking straight at him in the darkness.

"Ten miles from the school—and nothing in print about Tony. That is the agreement, Mr. Marsh?"

"That's it, doctor."

"It's baffling to me how you do these things," he said, inviting confidences.

Lew busied himself with the ignition key. The windshield wipers flicked the wet falling snow. "How will I know when the arrest has taken place?" Dr. Prescott asked.

"Mrs. Copeland will notify you," Lew told him solemnly.

"Oh." The gentle voice sounded quite relieved. "Thank you. That will be most thoughtful." He doffed his beaver hat. "God bless you both."

Lew drove painstakingly down the trackless road, conscious of caustic looks from Paula.

"And just how do we arrange a stake-out ten miles from here, Mr. Marsh?" she asked, as they reached the highway. "Or were you 'dissembling'?"

"Not dissembling, Butch, dear," Lew said drily. "I had to tell a goddam lie. We'll trap Lenni at the school gates—where else?"

"In broad daylight?"

"Lenni won't operate in daylight."

His crew, he thought, could hide out in the abandoned barn just opposite the gates. He'd send for Weintraub and Jimmie Kessler, and have them drive up at once in the radio car. They'd need cops from the State's Attorney's force, and an assistant. Joe Speares again, maybe. Joe would be glad to get out of town.

A car passed them, eastbound, driving very fast. The snow swirled in a cloud against the windshield.

Lenni? That would be a hell of a break, now, wouldn't it—if Lenni turned up tonight?

"Butch," he said, "we'll have to pick up a local cop and sit it out—until the crew gets up here."

She watched the receding tail lights in the rear window.

"What if he comes now?" she said, anxiously. "What if *that* was Lenni?"

224

Lenni's sentimental meeting with his son would take a while, he thought, and there would be car tracks in the fresh snow, if he had come.

"We'll have to take a chance," Lew said.

They found a fat State cop having dinner in the only cafe on Main Street. Forty minutes later when they drove back with him to St. Matthias there were no fresh tracks on the driveway between the pines. All was well. The skaters had left the rink. The fire was out.

Lew drove across the frozen meadow into the abandoned barn. A chicken, wings flapping, sent up a wild cackling and skidded into the darkness. And then, lights out, they waited.

He sat in the front seat with Paula. The excitement faded away and he thought of Julian's sharp comment on the telephone: "Why in hell didn't you *send* somebody?" It seemed to be a reasonable question now.

The wind rose noticeably at ten o'clock. The cop said there had been predictions of a blizzard. He stood, picking his teeth, in the doorway.

"Your Chicago folks driving up?" he asked. "Hope they make it."

Cops, Lew thought. I'll never learn to care for cops.

"You two going back after they git here?"

"That's right."

The officer worked his toothpick, made loud sucking sounds and inspected the sky.

"Hope you ain't held up," he said.

Paula asked, sleepily, "Just what did Julian say when you phoned him?"

"He was more like his old self," Lew said, grimly.

Angrily, Julian had shouted, "You going to sit there in a cold barn all night waiting for the radio car? Lew, have you lost your mind?" Julian had foreseen the possibility of considerable overtime—Weintraub and a photographer, squatting in Wisconsin for God knew how long. "It's a mighty damn remote possibility, it seems to me." He had hung up abruptly with the words, "I'll expect you in the morning."

Snow dusted in through the open doorway. Lew found a rug in the cop's car and tucked it about Paula's knees. She thanked him sleepily and he stretched his arm along the seat-back to make a pillow for her head. It was a butterfly touch again as she lay back. But almost at once she stirred and said, "I phoned my Dad from here this noon."

"How is he?"

She didn't answer for a moment.

"Boyd was there," she said.

A flat voice said, "What for?"

225

"It seems he's been coming out to the house quite often. Dad's helping him with an orchestration."

"That's nice." Lew asked, harshly, "How's the concerto coming?"

"It's done," Paula said, faintly. "Dad says it's brilliant."

A paper sack rustled in the darkness.

"Mr. Marsh," the cop whispered, "I brung along a little package. Want a nip against the cold?"

The bottle made a tantalizing gurgle.

"Ah!" The cop smacked his lips. "Good for what ails ya!"

Lew left the car.

"Let me have a belt of that, palsy."

"Why, shore."

Lew lifted the bottle against the faint light of the snowy sky. There were four fingers, two good solid drinks. He uncapped it, sniffed deeply, and let the whisky gurgle out into a spreading puddle at the cop's booted feet.

"What in hell are you doing?"

Lew threw the empty bottle in a high arc and heard it land on the snowy road. The cop's face was a belligerent inch from his own.

Lew pushed him back.

"You'll get yourself slugged up," he said, savagely, "and then, for sure, this'll be the night he'll come."

An unarmed man, a woman and a drunken cop—this would be the night.

He went back to the car. Paula opened her eyes and asked, drowsily, "What's the matter?"

"The jug," he growled, tucking the blanket more snugly about her. "If that jerk gets drunk Lenni will turn up tonight as sure as God made little ice cubes."

Paula fell asleep against his shoulder. Once she stirred and said, "Be sure and wake me if he comes."

A newspaperwoman—even in her sleep, he thought.

But Lenni didn't come that night. Nor the next. Nor the next. Nor on Tuesday. And Julian began to complain about the overtime. "It's a long shot, Lew," he'd say, drawing Lew aside after council. Or: "Remember, those are high-priced men you've got stuck away in that barn." And Jerry Weintraub, stiff-lipped with cold, phoning in from the radio car in the abandoned barn, would say, "All we got so far is frostbite." Or "Colder'n the hinges of hell and no sign of Lenni." There were four, then five, then six days and nights of fruitless waiting. But that wasn't the worst of it. At breakfast with Paula in the sandwich shop one morning he sensed an uneasiness.

"All right, Butch," he said, bluntly. "How's Boyd? How's his music?"

She put down her coffee cup and squared her shoulders. But words didn't come right away. Afraid of stuttering, maybe.

"Tell me about it," he said. "Purty, is it? When did you see him?"

He tried to say it lightly. But he hadn't.

"B-Boyd was there last night when I got home. He was working with Dad." She tried twice and managed a smile. "Are you a mind reader?"

With forced gentleness, he said, "Tell me all about it, Butch."

A queer pressure in his head blocked off her words: but presently, in his mind's eye, he saw her walking home under the bare trees from the Ravinia station, to find a sand-colored convertible parked near the cottage. Music floated in the icy air—a wild burst of music. Boyd and her father sat side by side at the piano. She had watched them through the window. She knew the theme and the melody, and the places where it had bogged down before; and it was thrilling—no denying it—it was thrilling to find that he had finally got it done. She had joined them while the last chord still echoed. She'd told Boyd how pleased she was, and that was that. She'd gone upstairs to work on her new story. She'd had a tray.

"Well?" Lew said.

She met his eyes.

"He wants me back," she said. "He came upstairs and told me. That is, asked me. He—he proposed to me—too."

It was there in his throat, but he was able to swallow it. Tasted like rye, damned if it didn't.

"And you said . . ."

"And I said no."

He had been prepared to take it, to keep his voice level and his face straight. But now his heart thumped hard and he felt light-headed.

"You've made other arrangements, Paula," he said, inwardly soaring. "Did you tell him that?"

"N-No," she said.

"Why not?"

"Well, I'm not going to marry him, but I didn't want to be a party to setting him off this time."

"What do you mean—this time?"

"The Copelands are in New York. Dolly's going to do some shopping —and then they're coming home."

Lew said again, for the record, "He'll make it, Butch."

227

She gave him the sad, scoffing glance which came sometimes from the wives of drunks when you tried to reassure them.

"Tell your Dad about January third?"

"Lew, I'm not sure I want to marry again—not even you—not anybody."

Rushed in, he thought; pressed too hard, too soon.

"Okay, Paula," he said, retreating. "Time enough—later on."

He grabbed their breakfast checks.

"I wish there was a story you could send me on, away somewhere," Paula said, as they crossed the lobby. "I'd just as soon go up and wait in that damn barn."

"Running from what?" he asked, mildly.

"I don't even want to be in town when it happens," she said. "I've seen Boyd go through it so many times. He'll look so well, and so gay, and happy—he'll be writing music, and full of dreams—and then it's all ruined, and he's gone again."

"Umhum. It's flickering."

"Oh, stop it, Lew," she said, and left him at the water cooler to go on through the noisy room to her own desk.

17 On the seventh day of the stake-out, Don Bell sidled up to the desk.

"You're giving the boys a pretty rough time," he said out of the corner of his mouth. "What's eating you, pal?"

Edgy, Charley would have said. Edgier and edgier. What I need is a drink, Lew thought, and went on barking at the reporters. Charley's gentle advice ran through his mind: *You got to be more patient!* But Charley hadn't known the patience required of a city editor when he was sweating out a big one. Lew went home in the evening and sat by the fire, listening for the phone, afraid to leave it. He found himself thinking: I'll drop in at Abe's one night and see the old boy. One of those long talks with good old Abe, that would help—and a drink, of course, would help. Always a good, sound reason for a drink.

A day, two days—and nothing. The telephone: Windy in this barn, Lew. Frostbite, Lew. Two more days of that. Two days of: "How about dinner tonight, Butch?" And the honest answer: "But I've got a new story going so well I hate to leave it. . . . Let me get it finished, first." Two more days of that.

And overtime.

On Saturday morning Julian sent for him.

"About this stake-out," he said. "I hate to let it run over another Sunday. The Old Man's watching overtime, just now. So call it off. It's gone on too long."

Lew heard himself shouting, "I'll be a sonofabitch if I'll call it off. I'll take the responsibility. Who do you want me to talk to?"

Julian stared at him, "Are you all right?"

"Haven't had a drink—yet," Lew told him. "That what you mean?"

"Easy does it," Julian cautioned, frowning.

Too many people knew about the stake-out, that was the trouble. He hadn't told Ike, but Lil knew, and Julian, Jed Brooks, John Ives, and the boys at Hunter's Green. Each passing day increased the danger of a leak. Would the local cop tip off a pal? Perhaps someone, phoning home from Wisconsin to the little woman, would say, "We're squatting in a cold barn waiting for Lenni Garr to turn up at St. Matthias—now don't breathe it to a soul, dear." And the little woman would breathe it only to her best friend, the wife of a *Tribune* editor. It had happened before. It could happen again.

When, on Monday, the long promised blizzard swept in from Canada and the swirling snow obscured the road at St. Matthias, Jerry, phoning in that evening, croaked with larnygitis, "How in hell long do you want us to sit here?"

The local room was snug and warm. You could yell "Boy!" and get a cup of coffee. Feeling guilty, Lew said, "Anybody from the *Tribune* been snooping around?"

"Nobody here but the Eskimos." Jerry's voice was a hoarse whisper. "And the dog teams bound for Nome."

The next day when he phoned he was thick-tongued—drunk.

"For Crissake, stay sober!" Lew begged him.

I'm close, myself, he thought.

Coming in that morning he had heard loud angry voices in John Ives's private office. Bobby Ferrig confided, "I hear the printers won't settle. There's gonna be a strike."

Fine, wasn't it? You sweat out a story, run counter to the bosses—and wind up with no paper on which to print it. That would be the ultimate in frustration, wouldn't it, now? The hot dry flash. . . .

During a morning lull Paula came to his desk, spread a letter on his blotter, and said, in mingled pride and disbelief, "Just read that!"

It was a note from the New York agent saying, among other things, *'All the Dead Were Strangers' is a distinguished short story and we'll be proud to offer it.*

"Don't say anything around here," she whispered when he had read the letter. "But I wanted you to see it."

"In the old days," Lew said, answering his phone, "we would have had a drink on that."

After four o'clock the phones were less urgent. The printers' committee left the Old Man's office. Lil Claussinius passed a rumor around her gum: no settlement yet, she said, wisely—Ives and the printers were in a bare-knuckle fight.

Julian left the office early with Paula. The north shore trains were running late; they didn't want to be stuck on a siding for all hours.

Ike, with his feet on the radiator, voiced a concurrent thought as he watched them go. "Boyd's folks got home last night."

Lew had read through a page of copy before the words reached him. "Come again, Ike? I wasn't listening."

"We were over there for a party," Ike said.

"Over where?"

"1360. Boyd invited Sarah and me. He gave a dinner for his folks. Mr. and Mrs. Ives, too. I was right up among 'em."

Lew doodled a jug-shaped figure.

"Was Butch there?"

Ike looked at him oddly.

"No." He swung back to the desk. "He's still nuts about her, though. You know something? He's got pictures of her . . ."

"In front of every bottle in his bar," Lew pulled up another page of copy and waited for the pressure to ease off. "Did he weather it last night?"

Ike laughed.

"Hell, yes," he said, proudly. "He handled his mother with the flip of his hand."

Handled Dolly with the flip of his hand.

Good, good.

Lew leaned back, lighting a cigarette.

"Start over," he said. "Give me all of it."

The best part, Ike said, was Dolly's entrance. He would never forget it, and neither would Sarah. At six-thirty Dolly had swept into Boyd's barren rooms on Harvey's arm, wearing something dazzling from Paris. Frills, flounces and baby blue. She'd rustled and twinkled for ten or more minutes before she happened to glance up at the fireplace.

"And what d'you know!" Ike grinned. "There's a *new* painting up there."

"Of whom?" Lew asked. "Of Paula?"

"No, no—a winter landscape. It's a big improvement. Dolly wanted to know what'd happened to her portrait and Boyd said"—Ike chuckled happily—"Boyd said, 'Mommie, it got torn.'" Ike threw back his head and laughed.

"How'd she take it?"

"Well, at first, she looked kinda bewildered and then she seemed almost, well—relieved."

"How do you figure that?"

"Sarah figured it. Sarah says Mrs. Copeland won't have to go on

231

competing with herself when she was young and pretty. Oh, she moved in on Boyd several times, in a kind of experimental way. But he sat her down—not hard, with humor. Said behave yourself or he'd warm her pretty bottom. Once he told her he'd grown up while she was away. Great, isn't it?"

"Fine, fine."

"There was another thing we thought was kind of revealing. When he was a kid, Lew, up there in Minocqua, Boyd always got a kind of fixed look of affection on his face whenever he was with his mother. It was as though he felt he *ought* to admire her—and couldn't. A strained, forced smile of tenderness. Well, that's gone. And he's been working. He played some music for us—goddam good, too."

"That's great news," Lew said, bitingly. "That's fine, Ike. That's great. Jesus, yes, that's wonderful."

Ike turned in surprise.

I'm letting 'em get to me today, Lew thought, snatching another sheet of copy. *Take it easy, now, quiet down.* . . .

Five o'clock.

And sure enough, there was Sam, garbed for Little America. The trains were running late, but Sam's wife had sent him early. Dependable, that was Sam. Dependable, prissy, firmly married, bundled up and uninspired.

Lew let the gate rock behind him. A sense of impending disaster hung over him, clouding his eyes. *Give me a double, Abe, I'm tired tonight,* he thought and turned resolutely homeward. He hadn't driven today because of the storm—thank God for the long walk home. Edgy? he thought, edgy as hell, Charley. It was the strain of waiting, that was all, he told himself. Charley would have sensed it. Charley would have clowned through dinner. There would have been a bright fire, a brimming zombie glass and the rich smell of a roast in the oven. Yes, indeed, Charley'd been a big help when nerves were in a raw, crawling tangle, under your skin.

But Charley was dead.

And Boyd handled Dolly with the flip of his hand.

He headed into the wind on Wacker Drive and turned north on Dearborn. Chicago flaunted a liquor establishment for every two-hundred-odd citizens, and here they were: bars, with their strip-tease performers, liquor stores with their flowing neon signs—the shabby, the glittering, the quiet, the homey, the clean, the dirty, the crowded, the empty bars.

Come in, Lew, they invited, come in, boy.

Through the beckoning windows you could see customers at red-checked tables; the lucky souls who could take a drink or two and not yearn to hear the last gurgle in the jug.

He unlocked the door to 721. No fire in the fireplace. No welcoming grin under a tall chef's bonnet. No mouth-watering fragrances. No Charley. . . . Quiet, that was all. Warmth and quiet, and a storm outside.

And inside.

Betcha, outside and inside. The winds of apprehension, blowing a tornado.

At seven-thirty he phoned Paula's house.

"Oh, yes, Mr. Marsh!" Roger Arnold said, with a new cordiality. "I'm sorry, sir. Paula has gone out this evening." He added, serenely, "With Boyd."

Lew turned off the lights at eight o'clock and went to bed. Sleep. . . .

Through the open window he heard a trolley bumping across the intersection, the sound of its wheels muted by the snow. Then it was ten. A car, with a loose skid chain, clattered past the alley and sent an echoing clamor against the brick wall outside. Then it was midnight. 12:01 NOVEMBER 28. The clock had been a Christmas present years ago, a gift from Alice. It told the hour, the minute, the day of the year. Time hurtled along all night in neat block letters. The numerals snatched at time but couldn't hold it. . . .

7:10 NOVEMBER 28.

Here was the dark morning.

I might as well get up.

It's piling up on me, he thought, taut with apprehension. *It's getting to me.*

Bums from West Madison, earning the day's drink, had been pressed into service by the Street Department. They swarmed like Chinese on Rush Street, on Dearborn, all the way along. They were the same bums he had seen in the county hospital in the days of his apprenticeship; the same bums who had shuffled along Clark Street in the early morning when he left for his fresh-air job with Charley; the same bums he had seen in St. Louis and Detroit and Los Angeles when Julian had sent him out of town on stories. Always the same, like peas in a pod; the same stubble, the same red-rimmed watery eyes, the same wet noses, the same hopelessness—the same bums, from generation to generation.

There but for the Grace of God go I.

He peered through a clear space in the frosted window of the B/G Sandwich Shop. Not many customers at this early hour. A printer or two. A nightside reporter. A nightside switchboard operator. A janitor. And Hal Ortman.

Lew went in.

Ortman, in white tie and tails, sat grandly at a narrow table against the sea-green wall. His silk hat thrust out from a hook above his head and an opera cape, draped gracefully beneath it, swung in the breeze from the closing door. The well-known columnist at the end of a long evening. Yes, indeed. The Chicago Woollcott. The task of gathering his deathless material sometimes kept him hard at it into the snowy dawn.

Lew sat across from him.

"Opera last night." Hal managed his lips. "Those wops gave a hell of a party!"

Scrambled eggs for Hal this morning. Buttered toast. A soft breakfast. But he toyed with it. He was still pleasantly plastered; hated to lose the glow.

"And drinks!" he remembered, dreamily. "Don't you ever miss the sauce?"

"You're a comfort to me," Lew said. "You're a basket case."

"Feel wonderful."

He nibbled toast, sipped coffee, delicately wiped his lips and made conversation out of his vast store of remembered things.

"I hear you've got a stake-out," he said smugly.

Lew came wide awake. He blazed, *"Who in hell told you that?"*

"I'm a good friend of Joe's," Hal explained, lowering his voice.

"Joe who?"

"Speares." Hal was on the defensive now. "We're pals. Joe had to break a dinner date with me. Naturally, it's safe to tell me *why!* He's sitting in a barn up in Hunter's Green—and colder'n a brass monkey. He phoned me again yesterday."

"Fine, fine," Lew fumed. "Tell it on a quiz show and see what you win."

They all talk too much, he thought, bitterly. They babble. They can't keep their goddam mouths shut.

He ordered a sweet roll, a carton of coffee, and went to the local room. Snow—that was the day's big story; seven inches of snow, and everybody knew it. Wide open, no exclusive—snow. There would be pictures of the lions in front of the Art Institute; of cars stalled in the drifts on Michigan Avenue; of elevateds jammed above the wind-blown streets. And stories of the crowded hotels, and homeless commuters; stories of broken hips and broken heads, of slipping, skidding and heart attacks. The storm would become a page one story. Everybody's.

Ike said, yawning, "Butch phoned in. No trains at all running from Ravinia. She's decided to drive."

Lew took off his suit coat and rolled up his sleeves.

"Tell her not to bother."

"I did. But she wants to come."

The staff straggled in throughout the morning, plopped down their overshoes, unwound their mufflers. Seven inches, Lew. Twenty-above, Lew. High drifts in Wilmette, Lew. Weather reports, all morning long.

Paula arrived at noon, aglow with excitement. Through the haze of work Lew heard her tell Ike about the stalled motorists she'd picked up along the way. The storm seemed wonderful to Paula; she'd seen everything there was to see in the long ride to town. A very special glow about her. The storm? Or the evening with Boyd?

Lew heard Ike say, "Write it, Butch. Just the way you told it."

Lil Claussinius called across the room, "Lew! Phone! In the booth!"

She had finally reached Joe Speares. Joe was shivering in the radio car in the musty barn.

"Well, Speares," Lew said, savagely, "who have you told besides Ortman?" And then he ate his heart out. "If the opposition gets onto this I'll run you out of town, you chatty bastard. Ask Lenni how you'll like it."

Five profane minutes in the phone booth lowered his pressure. Edgy? Hell, yes. Edgier and edgier. You ought to be here, Charley. . . .

Time blurred away. Muted phones, copy, the slap of overshoes, coffee in waxed containers, the shifting curtain of snow; waiting . . . and waiting.

4:15 and Sam Prisk was on the phone.

"I'll be late tonight!" Sam lamented. He had tried everything but helicopters and was now stalled in a cab in Ravenswood.

"Think nothing of it, Samuel. It's like Christmas Eve around here."

Festive, yes, indeed. At 4:01, after the deadline, red-faced caterers had suddenly appeared in the halls. Society editors, unable to go home, decided on gaiety. Whey-faced busboys pushed steaming carts along the corridors. Housemen from the Bismarck brought in long banquet tables. A girlish voice called over the glass partition, "We're having a snowed-in party for *everybody!*" For all the world like Christmas Eve. . . .

Nightside reporters, struggling in from the suburbs, reported hotels jammed to the doors, bars crowded, theaters sold out. Dayside men, finding their nightly avenues of escape blocked by stalled traffic, started a poker game in the morgue; and the furtive drinking began in the darkroom.

It's going to be festive as all hell, Lew thought.

At 4:30 John Ives and the printers' committee bustled side by side downstairs to the composing room and the rumors spread: contract settled! Contract not settled! Strike! No strike!

Ike rocked restlessly in his chair.

"Good day for a drink," he mused.

"Take one and clean out your desk."

Ike regarded him stonily.

"I might welcome that," he said, coldly. "Some night I'm going to get the bends. I'd rather sell suits at Field's. Don did, and enjoyed it."

Lew posted a bulletin. You had to ask 'em nicely; put up a flat order and they'd all get fried to the eyes.

KINDLY REFRAIN FROM DRINKING IN THE LOCAL ROOM.

Don Bell, strolling back from the Society Department, snapped a raw carrot between his teeth.

"The Old Man's paying for it," he deduced. "There's health bread, yogurt and raw vegetables. You can see his touch."

A dayside reporter, who had got halfway home, came back and lugubriously phoned his wife. Strangers wandered in off the streets. Insurance men, trapped in the building, peeked in like small, lonely boys wandering from dull homes to a livelier neighborhood. The corridors were thronged. Coffee fragrances drifted through the room. All very gay.

A late rumor went the rounds—direct from Miss Lila: no strike! The contract is settled.

Throw your hats in the air, printers. No strike, boys. Cheer up.

A phone on Lew's desk shrilled. He heard a loud buzzing on the wire and an unfamiliar, husky voice from far away.

"*Lew!* He walked right into our arms. Do you hear me, Lew? You there? *We got him!*"

He cupped his hands at the mouthpiece. It was Weintraub! "Christ, I didn't recognize you, Jerry." He swung around in his chair, his heart hammering. "Have we got it alone?" he asked.

It was a forced and gravelly whisper from Wisconsin.

"Who the hell else would spend his boyhood freezing in a barn?" Jerry demanded, exultantly, straining a vocal chord. "Snagged him at the school gates. Kip Zunches was driving. We got 'em both."

"What about pictures?"

"Clinical. His mouth opened so wide we could have done a tonsillectomy. We got side views of his soft palate."

"Start Jimmie in with 'em."

"I have."

"Where are you now?"

"Barn. And it's warming up."

"Is he there, too?"

"Sure. He had a nice tan, but it's fading. He's working on his prison pallor." Jerry managed an asthmatic chuckle. "So much iron on him he rattles when he breathes."

"Any trouble?"

"Naw. He was too stunned." Another throaty laugh. "When they put the cuffs on him I gave him your regards."

"How'd he take it?"

"In a frenzy. That's when he lost his tan."

Hi-ya, Lenni? Snuggled down in the masonry, are you, kid? Nigger killed in a clubman's convertible, Kip—cause and effect, you aboriginal sonsofbitches!

"Jerry, keep him right there until after midnight. Then book him in a local jail under a phony name. Now, dictate to Don Bell." He called across, "Don! Call for you. Take it in the booth!"

Too many strangers in the halls. As he watched Don hurry off, new worries crowded the triumph from his mind. There were still a million-and-one chances for a leak between now and midnight. How many people had Joe Speares actually told? Was he obligated to the *Tribune*, the *Sun-Times*, the P.M.'s? Or would it be learned, later on, that the big local cop had a sister on the Madison *Journal* and he had told her? *Patience, Mr. Lew. You sweat it out. But we got him. We got him!*

Jerry's husky voice, still on the wire, was starved for love.

"It's a hell of a story, isn't it, Lew?"

"Good going. I'll switch you over now. Don't let anybody leave that barn until after midnight."

"I'll get 'em *drunk!*" Jerry promised happily and Lew switched the call and left for Julian's office.

Thirty minutes later Julian strolled jauntily to the desk.

"Mr. Ives is all set up about it!" he whispered, beaming. "He wants to see you, Lew—when you get time."

"It won't be soon."

Ike was watching curiously, wondering what was up. Julian beckoned Lew to the window.

"I'll have to admit it was worth the overtime!" he said, guardedly, offering a patter of applause. "The Old Man's really pleased. Six exclusives in a row on the same story!"

"Let's not celebrate the victory before the battle," Lew warned him. "A hell of a lot can happen between now and midnight."

"Good going up to now, though," Julian grinned.

Two hours later Sam Prisk's night assistant spanked his frozen rubbers across the local room.

Ike rolled down his sleeves.

"Okay?" he asked, sourly.

"Drag it," Lew said.

237

"If you can't trust *me*," Ike growled, "you can't trust anybody," and stalked away. Childish. You baby 'em, you butter 'em up, or they sulked.

"Mr. Ives wants to see me," Lew told the night assistant, and shrugged into his suit coat.

A spot of color caught his eye, a pastel sweater, and slim, bent shoulders, and a scarf. Paula, at the typewriter near the corner window, was busily typing something of her own. He walked up behind her, saw a curl at the back of her neck and touched it lightly with his fingers.

"Butch?" he said, quietly, and whispered, "We did it."

"Wisconsin?"

He glanced cautiously over his shoulder.

"Don has just written the story—hell of a story. Under your hat, now. I haven't even told Ike."

He was close enough to feel her sigh.

"When shall I phone Dr. Prescott?"

"After midnight," he told her. "This place is crawling with strangers. If there's a leak I'll slit my throat."

He felt his fingers prisoned in her hands.

"Lew," she said, suddenly, "I've got to talk to you."

He stared into the forced uplift of her eyes.

"Well?"

Now she was having trouble tapping out a cigarette. He offered his own.

"I'm going to take care of young Anton Garr, myself—that is, Boyd and I will." And then it came out fast. "We're going to get married again."

I'm smiling, he thought. I'm smiling at her. I'm okay. I'm fine.

"Well, well," he said. "Tell me all about it."

Break it gently, Butch. Now it comes: reach in here. You can find it. Yes, indeed. Take full notes while gentle fingers tear your heart out. Remember it all. You might want to write a book sometime. Some later time.

"I told Boyd about Anton. It's the sort of thing he likes to do—to help kids like that." She smiled, and added, "Even when he's sober."

The lovely eyes were searching gravely into his face—if he had one. He wasn't sure. Maybe his face had shifted away from him, over to the left, for a better view of the beer sign. A gradual disintegration was taking place; perhaps his face had left the room.

"You were right," she said.

"Was I?"

This was not his own voice, either. His own voice had gone. It had had an appointment with Ives. It was in the private office now, saying: Yes, Mr. Ives.

238

"I can tell, too, now," he heard her saying. "Boyd's really done it. It's in the way he talks about his parents. Why, Dolly *amuses* him!"

Dolly amuses Boyd.

"You know what he told me?"

How could I? This is the first I'm hearing it, remember? This is all news to me.

"What?"

"He said you made a wonderful remark. It was something about—well, what was it you said about not drinking yourself to death because one of your parents happened to be a fool?"

"Did I say that?"

He could hear phones ringing, the lazy sound of a distant typewriter, the thumping teletypes. His voice said, "It's like Christmas Eve around here. Did you see the sign I put up on the board? Kindly refrain from drinking in the local room."

"I'd planned to tell you this morning, but you were so busy," she said. "I'm quitting, of course, but I won't leave until you can replace me."

"We can't replace you, Paula," he heard himself say. "We'll get somebody but we can never replace you."

His face must have come back. He could feel the smile on it.

"Oh, Lew, I do love you," she whispered. "I'm sorry. You see, the other night, for a moment or two I thought we could . . ."

He lightly kissed her forehead, said, "Mr. Ives wants me." He walked a few steps and came back. "Does he know about this?"

"We haven't told anybody but my dad."

Well, that was nice. Roger Arnold had always liked Boyd. He'd be pleased. John Ives would be pleased. And Harvey Copeland. There would be a celebration.

Coffee, hot black coffee in the Society Department. He followed the aroma, asked for a cup, and sipped it, slowly. Sure enough: yogurt and health bread and slim carrot sticks on ice. The John Ives touch.

Miss Lila tugged at his sleeve. He looked into her dry, indoor face.

"Mr. Ives is waiting for you," she rebuked him.

He measured the distance and put his cup down.

"How are *you*, Miss Lila?"

"Isn't this *fun!*" she said.

The Old Man was broad and solid behind his desk.

"Sit down!" he invited, heartily, waving at a chair.

From these high windows the beer sign looked brighter, bigger, more colorful, and the stirring message carried more appeal: . . . . . IT'S GOOD FOR YOU. . . .

Betcha . . . There were times when it was good for anybody. . . . It was an eraser, if you took enough of it. . . . What this country needs is a good five-cent eraser.

"Y'know," Ives was saying, "your handling of the Garr story has been one hundred per cent proficient."

Proficient? Not excellent. Not magnificent. Six exclusives in a row, the town beaten to a frazzle, Lenni Garr safely in the can—and the word was proficient.

Lew said it aloud, testing, "Proficient."

Ives ran an envelope across his tongue and sealed it with a hearty slam of his big fist. He was sending out checks again. Lew thought: *this is where I came in.*

"That's what I pay for, Lewis—and almost never get," the Old Man said. "I pay top salaries, hoping for top performance—and, for the most part, get less than my money's worth. Not you, of course. From the day you went on the desk you've earned your way and more."

This was a lovin'. Yes, indeed. Starved for love like everybody else, aren't you? Well, now you're getting it. You are proficient. You earn your way and more.

It's nice to know.

Ives scrawled a signature, blotted, opened another envelope, ran it over his tongue.

"Still leaving us on January third, my boy?"

"At five P.M."

Ives didn't look up.

"Thought you might have changed your mind."

"No, sir. Not me."

He wrote another check.

"This Garr thing could be a real start," he said. "You'll never find another town more wide-open for a cleanup. This city is the sink-hole of the universe. You know that."

Lew waited. You had to go through the motions here. You had to sit and listen.

"You know," Ives said, "there aren't any greener fields, but it takes a man quite a while to find that out." He chuckled. "For instance—it took me fifty years to reach the age of twenty-one."

He lifted his head. That was a good line; he'd use it. He clicked the dictograph key: "Remind me, editorial: fifty years to reach the age of twenty-one."

Lew watched him through a red haze.

"I told Julian not to mention this to you," Ives said, returning to work. "I wanted to tell you myself. I've thought a lot about what you said to

240

me that morning at the Lodge—about the Guild, you know. You were right. We hung onto pennies too long at the top." An envelope spun into the basket. "I see the pension thing coming, too, don't you, Lewis?"

Yes, Mr. Ives.

Lew thought: I can sit here for fifteen or twenty minutes saying Yes, Mr. Ives, and then drop in at Abe's for a little drink. There's no hurry. Everything's easier when you know that soon you'll be back at Abe's after all these years. What'll it be? Abe would say. What'll it be, Lew?

Yes, Mr. Ives.

I will give Mr. John Cowper Ives an alert expression, my respectful attention. There's no hurry now.

"Julian is getting three-quarters salary for life," Ives said. "We worked it out while he was in California."

Julian is *what*?

Ives masked a jolly, guileful look. "He retires January third. You take over as managing editor on January fourth."

Managing editor. You don't go to London, see? You don't set up shop with Johnny Richards. Foreign correspondent? No, no. You stay here, Marsh, see? Chicago. The windy city. You've been outsmarted by an expert. Like it?

Lew leaned forward in the chair. From that position he could see only one corner of the beer sign. One dwarf. One keg.

"I'll give you a freer hand than Julian ever had," Ives told him, "and I'll tell you why—you have a greater potential." He did some banging with his palm. "I wrote an editorial the other day which might interest you. I said—apropos of Lenni Garr—clean up a city and you can clean up a state—clean up a state and you can clean up a nation—the nation, the world." He pointed a big finger. "We're going to face into our responsibilities like grown men in this country or we're going to hell in a hand-basket. The public has swallowed so much eyewash these last twenty years that sometimes I'm afraid it has become a substitute for blood. But we're a great people, Lewis, and this is a great land. We'll do it the hard way—or we won't do it. I'm going to speak up, say what I have to say, these last years of my life. I want you here—running this paper."

Lew thought: he's faithful to his causes. Good-bye, Julian.

"You can write your own ticket, within reason," Ives said. "We'll talk about it tomorrow, eh?"

For the first time, he looked directly into Lew's face.

"Yes, yes," Ives said, "tomorrow morning. You look tired."

I am tired.

Yes, I'm tired.

Ives had followed him into the corridor.

"One thing I wish you'd do for me."

"Yes, Mr. Ives?"

"I've spoken to Mr. Grear, the music critic, asking him to invite a dozen topnotch music people to my apartment while I'm in town. I want Horowitz, Kubelik, Ganz, Bruno Walter—people of that character. Mr. Grear has the list. He looks like a weak sister to me."

Mr. Grear, the music critic, looks like a weak sister to John Cowper Ives. Lew gathered his thoughts; what was the Old Man saying?

"I want you to check on it and see that it's done right—a croup kettle, eh? Yes—well, Boyd Copeland has completed a remarkable piece of music. I want some first-rate musicians to hear it."

A voice said, "A concerto?"

"Perfectly remarkable," Ives said. "He played it for us." A memory delighted him and he laughed robustly. "You should see the way he handles his mother. Keeps her feet on the ground—makes her behave. It's a pretty thing to watch."

I've got bigger news for you than that, Big Boy, Lew thought. Happy, are you? I'll make you hysterical.

He said, "Boyd and Paula are getting married again."

No dancing in the corridor. No bellowed delight. The reaction surprised him.

Ives walked thoughtfully at his side to the local room.

"I remember," the Old Man said, gently, "you hoped to marry Paula. . . ." He searched for words, and concluded, "It's when you've been kicked in the teeth a few times—and take it—that you begin to grow up, eh, Lewis?" He patted Lew's shoulder. "See you tomorrow morning at nine, my boy."

Tomorrow morning at nine.

Tomorrow. . . .

Lew went back to the desk.

At ten o'clock Sam Prisk came in, full of apology. Lew sent him downstairs for dinner. At eleven somebody said that Ike Bashaw and a printer were drunk as owls in the men's room. Lew went in. Don Bell was there, trying to help Ike sober up. The printer, a jolly, red-faced little man, was singing a Welsh love song.

"Don't bother, Don," Lew said. "You're fired, Bashaw. Clean out your desk."

Ike wheeled around.

"All right," he shouted, "all right. I'm fired. To hell with it. That goddam tension, to hell with it."

"*Get out!*"

Ike took his time about it. Lew said to Don, "You're day assistant, starting tomorrow."

Don looked at him levelly. "You were too damn rough on Ike," he said.

The door was slowly closing. Ike and the printer had gone.

You got to be more patient, Mr. Lew. You won't last out the night yourself. You got to be more patient.

Lew caught him at the elevators.

"Ike!"

Ike turned defiantly. "Yes, sir?"

"Go home and sleep it off. Report to rewrite in the morning."

Ike beamed at him, a sudden, sentimental, drunken grin. He jogged the printer with his elbow.

"Old frien' of mine," he said. "Lew Marsh? Heard of him? Nicest guy in the worl'."

Lil Claussinius looked up from the switchboard. Her relief from the nightside had been stranded in a southbound trolley. She'd been wrangling with the Bismarck for a room for Paula, and had got one. She rang Paula's phone.

"You better get over there fast, honey, and peg it down. The hotels are jumping."

Then she studied Lew curiously.

"What's the matter?"

He couldn't remember: there was something he had planned to do. He said it. "Trying to remember something I had to do."

Paula came by, said a gentle good night, and raced for a waiting elevator. Lil's voice had grown confidential.

"You know what?" she said. "Paula told me something—a sorta T.L. for you."

"When?"

"Oh, one day in the ladies' room when she first came back to work."

"What?"

"She said the other time she was here—you remember, when she was just out of high school?"

"What about it?"

"Well, she said every time you came near her desk she nearly swooned, she had such a crush on you. In those days you were practically her dreamboat. She still thinks you're the handsomest newspaperman she's ever seen, and the best."

He remembered what he was going to do.

Abe's.

He was going to go to Abe's.

243

This was the night. There was an elevator waiting, but he went down the stairs. Puddles of water in the indentations. Footprints across the marble. It was still snowing; snowing hard, but the wind had stopped. The lobby clock said 11:58. Midnight was important for some reason; the witching hour, midnight. He couldn't remember what that was, either—something important about midnight.

He took the alley short cut through the midnight snow.

ABE ROUCH'S BAR—FOR MEN ONLY

The alley sign, smaller than the one in front, was a warm free-hand neon welcome through the falling snow. Everyone had always admired Abe's handwriting. Lew, himself, had suggested a sign in script. It had never glowed brighter.

He pulled open the door.

No other bar smelled quite like Abe's; the malt, the sawdust, the roast beef, the coffee, the pipe smoke, the smell of wet tweeds. He gulped it into his lungs.

Here were the same colored tablecloths and the roomy booths where, with Johnny and Don Bell and Sid Cohen he had held forth, in other days. The bar was crowded with a new crop of reporters, most of whom he didn't know. But he saw a *Tribune* editor, and one from the *Herald*, and somebody he vaguely remembered from the *Daily News*. They were old-timers, the competition.

A proud voice, in a nearby booth, said, "There's Lew Marsh, now."

Lew saw Travis Ashbourne III and young Pete Villegas smiling at him respectfully. They were having beer and roast-beef sandwiches. Newspapermen. Betcha.

Two men moved aside to make room for him. A hush fell on the bar. The *Tribune's* editor's grim, measuring glance was a kind of sardonic approbation. Hi, Lew, he said, and his reserve was an accolade, an earned credential. Everybody, Lew thought, moves through his days wearing his earned credentials. If you have edited a paper, or built a building, or flown an ocean, or written a book or achieved integrity in a foxhole, some of the achievement clings to your name and person—an invisible medal.

"Lew, boy, *Lew!*"

He was wringing Abe's soft, white hand. Looking into Abe's barroom bleach, into eyes filled with tears. Abe hadn't changed much. The slickdown hair was thinner, the paunch a little heavier, the sentiment nearer the surface, that was all. The tears were unexpected. There had never been tears in his eyes in the old days.

Lew slouched with his elbows on the bar.

244

This is the night, he thought, *this is the test.*

"How you been, boy?"

"Fine, Abe, fine."

"Quite a storm, huh?"

"Seven inches," Lew said.

Abe wiped the bar with his white apron and asked, warily, "Well, boy, what'll it be?"

What'll it be?

Well, now—what? Rye? His drink had always been rye.

What'll it be.

Gin was quick. And there was bourbon, Scotch, brandy, vodka and beer. You could start with beer. Beer was a food for some people.

What'll it be?

Who've I got to stay sober for? he wondered. Not Alice, nor Mrs. Pryor. Nor Charley. Nor Paula. Nor Julian. Nor John Ives. Who for?

And then he thought: I'm standing in the socks and shoes of somebody I can stay sober for: I can stay sober for me.

He said, "I just dropped in to say hello."

I'll always fight it, he thought, *but I'll always lick it. The only drink you don't take is the first one—it's not for you, boy, it's not for you.*

"Coke?" Abe asked.

"Not a thing."

In a corner booth five *Daily News* men tossed back their heads in a sudden roar of laughter. That's what he missed nowadays—the laughs. You didn't hear sober people laughing.

Wind whistled through the room. Someone shouted, "Shut it!"

A shivering newsboy carefully closed the door with his knee and came silently into the room with his papers.

Perry Qualters, an elderly *Tribune* reporter, well in his cups, focused on Lew, approached obliquely and threw a drunken arm around his neck. Ol' pal, he said, good ol' Lew. The ol' days, remember, Lew? What fun in the good ol' days, Lew-boy.

"Too bad you can't drink, Lew," Perry lamented.

Abe spun a paper across the bar and shoved seven pennies to the newsboy.

"Too bad you can, Perry," Abe grinned.

The newsboy moved on.

The headline said, LENNI GARR JAILED!

The sudden stunned silence in the room was more rewarding than a burst of bravos. The scramble for hats and overcoats, the race for phones, the opening and closing of the door; all most rewarding. There would be, for these reporters and editors, ire to face, and work to do; the fumbling, hurried, profane effort to catch up.

Lew slid a bill across the bar.

"Abe, when they come back, set 'em up for everybody," he said. "They'll need it."